AWAKENED BY A BILLIONAIRE

LOVECHILDE SAGA BOOK 1

J. J. SOREL

FOURTH EDITION MAY 2023

Line Edit Tiffany Shand

Proof Red Adept

AUTHOR'S NOTE: This is a steamy romance with descriptive sex scenes. There is also some violence and a sexual abuse scene, while not wildly graphic, may still offend.

jjsorel.com

CHAPTER 1

Declan

I HEARD A WOMAN scream, and for a moment, I thought I was back in Afghanistan. Snapping out of that nightmare, I followed the shrieks and saw two men in a dark alley, dragging a woman to a door.

"Hey," I yelled as I ran towards them. "Put her down."

Dressed in a corset, the woman thrashed about in the heavyset man's arms, crying out.

I charged in, punched one of them in the face while elbowing the other at the same time. At least that technique for dealing with multiple assailants, which I'd picked up in combat training, had suddenly served a purpose.

Noticing one thug reaching into his pocket, I yelled, "Run!"

But she looked dazed and could barely stand, staring at me as though facing headlights.

With one eye on her and the pair of meatheads clambering to their feet, I noticed one man brandishing a gun. He fired it, barely missing me, just as I kicked it out of his hand. I then slammed into him, laying him flat.

The other guy stepped in, and before I knew it, two men were on top of me.

The girl screamed as another heavy arrived, trying to drag her off again.

As I took him down, the other pair pounced on me.

Blow after blow, I eventually fought them off.

One thug scrambled off the ground and came towards us, clutching a gun. I grabbed the girl by the waist, who was so drugged her legs had gone all floppy.

With her panting breath on my face, I sprinted, nearly knocking over people crowding the main strip. At least, the intricate network of tiny backstreets and alleys helped us lose the men in black.

Here I was, back home and still running from the enemy. The city proved as dangerous as some hidden village in Afghanistan.

The girl's long dark hair whipped my face as she wiggled in my arms to break free. Her bag dragged along the ground. "Just hold on, will you." For someone drugged, she was a tiger.

I ran into the back of a restaurant and slipped into a kitchen, where a chef and his assistant looked up at us and reached for their phones when I held up both my palms.

"It's a long story. I just saved her from some nasty pricks."

I put her down and, despite her being light, her doped state had made her heavy. Drugged to the eyeballs, she wobbled on her unsupportive legs and was about to crash to the floor when I gently helped her into a seated position, leaning her against the wall.

I removed four fifty-pound notes, the only cash I had on me, from my wallet and popped them on the counter. "Here, for your trouble. Just let us wait here for a few minutes."

Staring wide-eyed at the cash, the pair nodded in unison.

I would have called the cops, but I didn't know this girl's story.

I helped her into a chair, having to hold her up, because she would have gone down like a sack of potatoes. With arms covered in bruises, she had dark streaks down her cheeks where her makeup had run.

"She looks like she's had a big night," the chef said with a raised eyebrow.

I threw him a dirty look. "Get on with your work."

I removed my jacket and wrapped it around her. Her bag fell off her shoulder, and I noticed an envelope with cash in it. As I zipped the bag, I wondered if someone had paid for her services and if she was doing a runner. With that corset revealing a good part of her voluptuous figure, you didn't need to be a genius to guess her line of work.

But I wasn't there to judge. I was there to help her get away, and that's exactly what I'd done.

So why was I standing there trying to figure out what to do next?

Helping her up, I said, "We should be safe to leave now."

As I helped her up, I noticed for the first time her torn stockings and bare feet. "You don't have any shoes?"

Shaking her head, she crossed her arms over her chest, which drew my attention to a ballooning cleavage that usually would have made my pulse race.

But this wasn't the time for arousal. My dick had other ideas, and despite that regrettable primal response, sex was the last thing on my mind.

The pair, although busy working, kept watching on. I suppose we looked a sight: me with a bruised face, holding onto a beautiful, drugged woman like I'd picked her up off the street for my own dirty needs.

"Here." I placed my hand around her waist, and we left the kitchen. After taking a few tentative steps into the dark alley and hiding behind a skip that smelt of rotting fish, I established that we'd lost the thug.

With my arm around her waist, holding her up, I stopped walking. "Where do you live?"

"Nowhere," she slurred.

I turned to face her, while still holding onto her. "What drugs are you on?"

"I don't know."

I frowned. "You took something without knowing what it was?"

She closed her eyes, as though trying to remember something. Her face was in such a desperate need of a clean, I held on to her with one hand and, reaching into my pocket, I grabbed a handkerchief.

"Don't touch me." She pushed me away and stumbled, falling onto her bottom and ending up on the ground, gripping at her arms. She looked up at me with fear before closing her eyes again.

I bent down to help her up. "I wasn't about to hurt you. I wanted to wipe your face. It's a fucking mess."

She blinked repeatedly, as though doing so to clear something from her eyes. "I thought you were one of them."

"One of whom?" I asked.

"It's a long story." She sighed, slumping again, so I had to hold her up. "I just want to sleep."

Unsure of what to do with her as she leaned against me, I couldn't just leave her there alone. Not in that state. "Okay. I'll book you a hotel."

"Can I stay at yours?" she slurred. "On the couch."

My head jerked back. "A minute ago, you were worried I would hit on you, and now you want to crash with me?"

"I'm..." Her head fell on my shoulder, and she closed her eyes.

Resigned to the role of protector for the night, I carried her limp body, which was like carrying a rag doll, to my car.

With my arm around her waist and her head and body leaning tightly against mine, we walked along the main drag to where I'd parked. Some people made snide comments, while others pointed and laughed. By this stage, I didn't give a fuck what they thought.

When we pulled up at my house, she was sound asleep.

As she lay in the back seat, it was as though I was looking at an erotic version of Sleeping Beauty, her long raven hair covering her elfin features and her lips apart.

Hugging my jacket, she was finally peaceful.

Although I hesitated at the thought of waking her, leaving her in the car wasn't an option either.

I opened the car door and, taking her into my arms, lifted her.

She breathed into my ear. "Where am I? What's happening?"

"I'm just taking you up the stairs to the door. Can you walk?" I asked.

Her legs were so shaky that I had to carry her in my arms.

With her head flopped on my shoulder, this was the closest I'd been to a woman in months, and feeling her warm, soft skin on my neck did strange things to me. I tried to think of anything but how she'd looked in that back seat with those sensual curves that would normally keep me up all night.

But as she snoozed in my arms, these guilty sensations kept at me, making my blood heat, a bodily response difficult to shake off, despite all my best intentions.

We finally arrived at the entrance to my family's Mayfair home, where my father stayed mostly, but knowing I needed the space, he'd vacated for my return, which I appreciated. I wasn't quite ready to hang out with the family.

That would happen tomorrow.

For now, I had this drugged sex worker to deal with.

I helped her into the living room onto the couch, where she flopped down.

I glanced at my watch. It was midnight.

When I returned with a bottle of water, I found her sound asleep, so I grabbed a blanket and laid it over her.

She would need clothes, I suddenly realized, so I headed into the room my sister normally used and, going through the cupboards, found leggings, a pullover, socks, and trainers. It felt weird rummaging through her underwear, mostly made up of lacy bras and thongs. I settled for some cotton panties and a tank top. This girl was way too busty to fit into my sister's bras.

I had a shower and studied my bruises on my face, arms, and shoulders.

At least receiving blows was one thing I'd had trained into me.

What the forces hadn't trained into us, however, was how to deal with the aftermath of gore, death, and witnessing physically powerful men dropping to the floor crying like babies.

I WOKE AT SEVEN, and although my body ached, I sprung out of bed, wondering whether I'd dreamt up the damsel in distress I'd saved. Going on my raging hard-on, I could only assume it was some twisted wet dream. Twisted because I could have done without the fucking violence.

When I entered the living room, a corset, silky panties, and torn fishnets on the ground confirmed that the woman who'd somehow taken over my thoughts was real.

I went into the bathroom, and on the mirror she'd written "Thanks!" in lipstick.

Disappointed to see her gone, I wanted to know her story, why she was there with those dangerous men, and why I'd nearly died for her.

CHAPTER 2

Thea

24 HOURS EARLIER...

THE first thing I saw in that shadowy alleyway was a pulsating purple puddle on the wet, cobbled ground.

As I gazed up, the flashing purple sign reading Club Purr made my muscles tense. "Is this some kind of sleaze hole? I only agreed to a waitress-in-costume gig. Where the hell have you brought me?"

Scratching himself as he always did, Travis inclined his head for me to enter through the metal door.

A rotting meat stench that started from the moment we entered that backstreet of Soho made me want to throw up.

I didn't know what kind of costume I'd be expected to wear, but I sensed for the three hundred pounds promised it would be something skimpy. Vague on detail and drugged out as usual, Travis wouldn't elaborate. But beggars can't be choosers, because I was on the street, broke, and in debt to his sister, my now-former flatmate.

"Just go in." He pushed me through the door. "We had a deal."

Sucking back a breath, I rolled my eyes and followed him in.

The foyer smelt of disinfectant and cheap perfume, and photos of lingerie-clad women with come-to-bed eyes lined the purple walls.

"This better not be a strip club." My blood froze. I'd never been in a place this sleazy before.

"Just keep moving." He twitched like ants were crawling over him. His eyes in the dim light resembled empty, dark sockets.

Travis led me into an office, where I met an overweight man with a ruddy complexion who looked in his fifties.

"This is Jack," Travis said.

The seated man, who I imagined owned the club, ran his creepy eyes up and down my body, sending a shiver through me.

He lifted his chin at Travis. "Okay, you can go now."

Travis lingered for a moment, scratching himself some more. He shot the boss a crooked grin. "Are we good?"

Jack ran his eyes over me again before returning his attention to the drug addict. "Go and see Vlad. He's got what you want."

Travis shuffled off, leaving me alone with this sleazy-looking man whose gaze made me want to squeeze into a tight ball.

Stale smoke clung to the air, while photos of racing cars, boxers, and half-naked women dotted the walls.

A woman, who looked to be in her thirties, entered. Her face was heavily made-up with thick eyelashes that curled to her brows. Tied back in a ponytail, her waist-length blond hair, without a strand out of place, resembled a sheet of satin. Dressed in a pink corset, garters, and skyscraper stilettos, she towered over me.

"Get her ready," he said, leaning back with his hands crossed over his fat stomach. "Bring her back so I can see her."

In silence, we moved along a dimly lit hallway to the back of the venue.

The woman opened the door, and I stepped into a dressing room that smelled like a department store perfume counter. My attention went to the rack of lingerie and a lit-up mirror with makeup scattered on the bench.

"I'm Tania." She sounded Russian.

"Hi. I'm Thea." My voice trembled.

Her red-painted lips turned up slightly in one corner. "Relax. They won't eat you." Her blue eyes shone with a hint of cheek. "But then, you might want them to."

I shook my head repeatedly. "Am I to dress like this?" I pointed at her corset.

"This is a gentlemen's club. They didn't tell you?"

"I was told it was a waitressing gig in costume. That's all I know."

A hint of a smile warmed her face. "That's pretty much it." She tugged at my shirt. "Come on. Off with everything. It's nice and warm in here."

She produced a black lace corset with red satin ribbon trim. "This should fit." She studied me as I crossed my arms over my chest. "With those tits, you'll be very popular."

I hated my body. And now I had to use it to survive. I'd barely managed on waiting tables and cleaning jobs. And despite working two jobs, I was still in debt because of high London rents.

I wasn't about to beg my cold, indifferent mother. I couldn't stand the sight of her after how she'd treated me.

Tania handed me fishnet stockings. "What size feet?"

"Six."

She dropped a pair of stilettos in front of me, and I sucked back a breath. How the hell would I manage in those?

"Okay. That should do." She paused at the door. "I'll be back in a minute to help with your hair and makeup. Let me get you a drink. That will help."

In response to her welcomed hint of warmth, I nodded with a vague smile. "A G and T, thanks."

I gave myself a pep talk. Three hundred pounds would pay my debt and find me a room for a night or two. It was only skin, after all.

But will they touch me?

My stomach was tied in knots as I carefully placed my foot in the stocking, trying to avoid ripping it. Travis had reassured me I would only have to wait tables in costume. But he was a junkie, and considering he raided his sister's wallet more than once, he couldn't be trusted.

Battling with the zip, I lifted the lace bodice as high as I could. The corset squashed my D-cup breasts. I could barely breathe.

I rummaged through the costume box and found a pair of lace panties with the most fabric, despite my arse poking out, which was inevitable, given my big bum.

As I clipped on the stockings, Tania returned with two glasses. She handed me one and, as she sipped on hers, nodded. "Mm... you're going to be popular." She pointed to the black spiky, red-soled shoes that could have doubled as weapons. "Put those on. And then stand up. Let me see you."

Wobbly-legged, I rose and held onto the bench for balance.

She chuckled. "You're not used to them, I see. Try walking in them."

I moved around the small room cluttered with stacked boxes, staring down at my feet to avoid tripping. After a minute, I managed.

"Let's do some makeup." Her softened tone helped me relax.

I closed my eyes while she dabbed a sponge on my face.

"You've never worked in a man's club before?"

"No. I work in cafes and restaurants mainly."

"You won't get this type of money working in cafes."

"Is it just serving drinks?" I asked as she brushed rouge on my cheeks.

She stared at me in the mirror. At first, I wondered if it was to look at my makeup, but there was something else in her gaze. As though she was trying to read me.

What is she not telling me?

"You've got pretty eyes. Look up for me." She drew a line under my eye and then pulled my lid to draw a line above. "No boyfriend?"

"No." I looked at myself in the mirror. The shadow she'd applied on my eyelids defined my almond-shaped eyes. "You're good at makeup. I always make a mess of it."

"I trained as a beautician."

"Oh. And you work here now?"

She selected a lip pencil from a box. "I've been here for eight years. I came from Bosnia and started working here. The conditions are good. The money's excellent. Especially if a client likes you."

I frowned. "What do you mean by that?"

She shrugged. "You'll see." Looking into the mirror at my freshly painted red lips, she nodded. "Good. You're very pretty. And with this figure, you can become a very rich woman."

I rose sharply as if something had bitten me on the bottom. "I refuse to whore myself."

She smiled like a mother might at a child threatening to starve themselves rather than eat veggies. "Relax. You won't need to do that. It will be fine. Take a drink. When you're counting your money at the end of the night, you'll be thrilled." Tania removed my hair tie. "Mm... lovely long hair, too. Let's leave it out. Yes?"

I shrugged. "Sure. Maybe clip it back because it falls in my face when I'm serving."

"Mm... no. Loose, I think."

I finished my drink in almost two gulps as Tania brushed my hair, and for a moment, it lulled me back to a state of calm.

She put down the brush. "Okay. All done. Stand up and practice walking again."

I stood up, and she tugged at my corset. "Let's show a little more of these. My god, I wish I had your tits. I'd be a millionaire." She said that under her breath.

I stared at her tall, svelte frame. "You're stunning. You could be a runway model with those legs."

"Maybe if life had been different." She shrugged. "They smuggled me into London and forced me to work."

My jaw dropped. Despite the brutal nature of her experience, she made it sound like she'd arrived in London, like many tourists, by coach. "Oh, really? Like that? I mean, they prostituted you?"

She nodded slowly. Her blue eyes were distant. "But Jack has been good to me."

"Jack's your boyfriend?"

"No. He's more like a father to me. Tough but fair. I'll take you to him now. Okay?" She opened the door for me to pass.

My chest tightened, and my pulse raced. What was going to happen? The drink had made me light-headed. More so than usual after only one drink, but it wasn't enough to numb fear.

CHAPTER 3

Declan

"YOU JUST NEED TO get laid." Carson's hazel eyes sparkled with mischief.

"You would say that. You've got pussy on the mind." I grinned.

I leaned against the wooden bar and sipped my stout.

Memorabilia, worn hardbacks, dusty antique bottles, and mugs sat on glass shelves behind the bar. Being a Saturday night, the rowdy Irish pub bustled with drinkers. I would have preferred somewhere low-key, but my army mate was in the mood for a crowd.

"Well, man, after the shit we've just witnessed, I prefer to focus on the nicer things in life." He rubbed his dark buzz cut.

I couldn't disagree with that. A pretty woman with soft, sexy curves beat dealing with suicide bombers any day.

"Do you think they'll be given a home here?" I asked, thinking about the family we'd helped evacuate from a village in Afghanistan.

He puffed. "Not sure. There's too many of them."

I shook my head in frustration. I'd joined the SAS to help those less fortunate than me, but in the end, it was up to a politician to decide who deserved protecting.

"Hey, Dec, try not to think about it."

"Easier said than done after what we've seen."

"We've only been back a few days. Let's just get laid." His attention settled on a pair of giggling girls across the bar.

Their eyes landed on us, checking us out, and then the women sashayed over.

"Bingo. Here we go." Carson plastered a welcoming smile.

"You can have them both."

"Oh, mate, you're a bore." His grin faded. "It's going to take time."

"Yep. But I still can't get that image of Jackson swinging on that fucking rope."

"You couldn't have helped him. You can't keep wearing it."

I sighed, overcome by guilt for not saving our army mate from himself. "I know that. We all should have been there for him. He was cracking up right under our noses. We all fucking failed."

"He was already lost when he joined the forces. You know that."

One girl stood so close, her piercingly sweet perfume traveled straight up my nose. "Hey." She smiled. "Having a pleasant night?"

Carson gave me a subtle wink. "Can I buy you girls a drink?"

"I think they've had enough," I said, stepping away from one girl whose bare shoulder rubbed against mine.

I wasn't in the mood for girls. Or for much else. The only reason I'd met Carson for a drink was because he'd virtually begged me.

"I'm Nina and this is Wendy." The tall, pretty blonde swayed a little as she spoke.

Carson was already undressing her, going by that twinkle in his eyes.

"So, what do you both do?" Wendy asked. Her eyes slid from me to Carson and back. Shorter and curvier than her friend and wearing a tight top that revealed balloon-like tits, she was hot in that manicured way. Despite her pretty, dark features, I wasn't keen on a random hook-up.

"We've just finished our last tour in Afghanistan."

Her brown eyes lit up. "That's why you're both so big and muscly." She touched Carson's arm.

"Is it like on TV? Jumping out of airplanes and crawling in jungles filled with dangerous creatures?" her friend asked.

Carson gave me a side glance and smiled. "It wasn't exactly the Amazon jungle, but we encountered dangerous creatures."

"Mainly of the human kind," I muttered.

The girls laughed as Carson passed them drinks. He looked at my empty glass. "Another?"

I shook my head. "I'm off. I'm tired."

"That will leave only me." Carson looked like I was about to throw him into a cage of tigers. He was normally fearless. Six foot four, muscle on muscle, he was that guy you wanted backing you.

"I'm sure you can handle yourself."

It wasn't the first time he would've found himself in a harem situation. Whether a pair of girls qualified for that title, my tired brain couldn't say.

I was a one-on-one man myself. But Carson liked his little adventures.

Nina cozied up close. "That's sooo sad that you're leaving."

"Dec's a heartbreaker. Underneath those movie-star looks, he's a bore."

I tipped my head and smirked. "Reading hardly makes me a bore."

"That's him all over. While we're out and about looking for fun, he likes to curl up with a book."

I sniffed. "Nothing like a bit of education."

"I would've thought your expensive education would have supplied that."

Wearing a wide smile, Nina said, "You're not only tall, with gorgeous blue eyes, but rich too?"

"He's from one of the richest families in the UK. An eligible billionaire."

I rolled my eyes and shook my head. "I'm off."

"Oh, don't go. I've never met a hot billionaire before."

I leaned into Carson and whispered, "Thanks, mate."

He shrugged. "Embrace it, Dec. You're a catch."

I waved. "See you soon."

Just as I was leaving, Carson cracked one of his dirty jokes, and the girls giggled some more.

My phone vibrated and, seeing that it was my brother, I took the call. "Ethan." I stepped into a side street away from the bustling crowds streaming along that busy strip.

"Hey, bro, what are you up to?"

"I'm in London. I just caught up with a friend." I rubbed my beard, reminding myself I needed a shave.

"Of the female variety?"

"Nope. Just a friend from the army."

"I would have thought you'd be shagging half of London by now. That would be me if I'd been staying in some craggy, remote region starved of pussy for three months." He laughed.

"You're bragging." I sniffed. "Carson mentioned something along those lines. But no, I'm just catching up on sleep. I'm not really in the mood to fuck around."

He hissed. "How you've changed."

"My days of screwing around ended years ago, Ethan."

"Pity for you. Women love a man in a uniform. Maybe I can borrow yours sometime."

"Not going to happen." I scoffed. The stains of war were somehow incongruous for a playboy. "Why is it every time we chat, the subject of women comes up straight away?"

"They're nice to talk about and look at and to undress. You haven't turned, have you?"

"Nope. Hot-blooded pussy man. I'm just not chasing."

"Since when have you chased women? They generally throw their panties at you."

I laughed at that ridiculously exaggerated version of my former days of hooking up with whomever, wherever.

"There's a dinner here next week. Cleo keeps asking after you. In fact, half of the chicks I run into ask about you. You're one popular dude."

"As are you," I said.

Reminded of the luxury that awaited me now that I'd left the army, I should have been upbeat, but I felt flat. "I'm back in Bridesmere to-morrow."

"Can't wait to see you," he said. Unlike some brothers, we weren't competitive. If anything, we were close. "So much has been happening here. I might bring in the cameras. I'm thinking of signing the family up for a reality show."

He liked to play on the fact I guarded my privacy. "Don't you fucking dare."

He laughed. "I knew that would rev you up."

"How's Dad?" I'd only just caught up on sleep and had needed that week to acclimatize to being the son of a wealthy dynasty and not dealing with crazy situations involving jaded soldiers, distressed civilians, and negotiating with men who may or may not have wanted to blow me up.

"Dad's hardly at Merivale these days."

"Still?" It was no secret that our mother and father didn't get on. There were whispers of a divorce, but with so much money at stake, they fought instead.

"You were on the news, you know? We have a hero in the family."

My brother was one of those dry-delivery types. I couldn't tell if he was ribbing me or patting me on the back.

"I was only doing my job." My shoulders tightened.

"You saved a fucking school from being blown up, Dec. You earned the accolade."

I remained quiet.

"It's good to know you're back for good. I missed not having you to spar with." He chuckled.

I released a breath, grateful for the change of subject. Crazy family shenanigans I could do.

"How's Savvie?"

"She's in Paris."

"What's there? Apart from shopping, of course." My twenty-seven-year-old sister was your typical rich heiress who flitted through life in designer clothes and changed boyfriends as often as her hairstyles.

"Probably some *garçon*," he said. "Speaking of younger men, Will's hanging around a lot."

"He's Dad's business partner. There's nothing strange about that, is there?"

"That's the thing. Dad's rarely home these days. He's in London most of the time. But Will's always here. I think he's sleeping with Mother."

"You said that last year." Back to the drama that was my family.

"You'll see it for yourself. They're not even hiding it anymore. Are you staying at Merivale?"

"Maybe for a few nights, but I plan to move into the village," I said.

"Into your converted church?"

"Yep. It's ready to go. The architect sent me the photos. I love it." A feeling of excitement hit me thinking of the eighteenth-century Georgian church I'd had converted into my new home.

"I'll see you tomorrow, then."

"For sure. Bye, then."

I closed the call and headed out onto the crowded streets. It was nice being back home, but the city wasn't my favorite place. I needed to exorcise some of the mental crap that had followed me back from Afghanistan. And the best place to find myself again was the seaside village where I grew up.

CHAPTER 4

Thea

JACK CIRCLED HIS FINGER. "Turn around."

Holding my breath, I whipped around while crossing my arms. His eagle-eyed gaping made my veins ice.

He turned to Tania. "Show her the ropes."

With legs like concrete, I followed her to the back of the venue. We entered through black curtains that led to a stage.

"Do they have performances here?"

"Yes. You could say that."

Too wound up to probe further, I ignored the questions banking up in my head and moved along.

Get a grip. It's only skin. Think of the three hundred pounds.

Droplets of sweat trickled down my arms as I sucked back nerves and stepped into a dimly lit, surprisingly stylish room filled with men.

Girls in skimpy gear carried trays around the decorative room, which reminded me of the Playboy palace with its rich dark velvets and paintings of nudes.

Smoke and an indefinable seedy stench thickened the air. I imagined that's what lust might have smelt like—musky and sickeningly sweaty.

I pointed at booths with red velvet curtains. "What happens in there?"

"Private lap dances," Tania said in a cool tone.

"Private as in sex?"

"It's up to the girl. There are guards everywhere, so the girls are protected, and they make a lot of money that way."

"I'm not doing that." I crossed my arms.

"Just get used to the floor and carrying trays. Sometimes they may ask you to join them at their table. You get a kickback for that."

"On top of my three hundred pounds?"

Her eyes narrowed slightly. "Was that what you were promised?"

"That's what Travis told me I'd get."

She nodded slowly, as though she had to think about it. "Then, sure, that's what you'll earn as a retainer, but there's more to make if you play your cards right."

My brow pinched. "What does that mean?"

Tania puffed out a breath like I was being a pain. "As I just said, share a drink with the customers and you'll get tips."

"I was told it was just serving." My voice went up a register.

Trying not to lose it, I felt angry and trapped. I didn't want to mix with a bunch of creeps, the thought of which made me want to gag. But then I had to remind myself I had little choice. I was totally broke.

"Let me get you another drink. That will help you relax."

For someone who didn't normally drink much, I was already on my second drink. I couldn't resist. Anything to dilute this sudden build-up of anxiety.

She returned with two shots, and handing me one glass, she gulped hers down, and I followed suit, coughing and clearing my throat.

Feeling extra light-headed, I said, "Let's do this" like someone about to dive into an icy lake in the middle of winter.

Tania led me onto the floor filled with tables of men. They all turned and stared at me like I was some novelty act. Some even whistled, while others smiled at me.

I kept my arms crossed.

The other staff looked even younger than me and came in all shapes and nationalities. It amazed me how many pretty girls worked at such a dive. I guess it showed how tough it was in that outrageously expensive city, where working a forty-hour week barely paid rent.

At least the club was busy, so I could get lost in the crowd.

Tania crooked her finger, and I followed her to the bar, where she introduced me to the bar staff. "This is Jan and Liz."

I nodded a greeting.

"Get her another shot," Tania said to Liz.

She passed me a vodka, and I took it without question. "At this stage, I might drop the tray." I swallowed the shot in one face-scrunching gulp.

"I don't think you'll have too many complaints." Tania returned a wry smile and handed me a tray. "Just walk around and collect glasses for now. And take orders as they come, okay?"

"Won't I need a pad and pen?" My words sounded slurry, which should have worried me, since I wasn't much of a drinker, but I needed to find a way through, and at least the booze helped ease my nerves.

"I'm sure you can manage. Most customers either drink beer or have straight spirits. They're not too complicated."

I collected a few glasses, and the men seemed well-behaved, which made it easier, and after a while, I went with the flow. Until I came to one table where an old man asked me to join him for a drink. His droopy eyes were all over my breasts, and I shook my head and scurried off.

After an hour of collecting glasses, delivering drinks, and being ogled, I took a break and went to the bathroom behind the stage, where two girls sat smoking.

"Hey there," one girl said. "How are you finding it?"

"It's okay. I mean, this corset's seriously scratchy. I can't wait to get back into my clothes."

"Yeah, I know how you feel. So, are you going to auction?"

"Hmm?" My brows gathered.

"You didn't sign up for the auction?" She looked surprised.

"What do you mean?"

"We're all selling ourselves tonight."

"Selling your body?"

Silly question. What else would they be selling?

The pair nodded. "We're selling our virginity to the highest bidder."

Although the girl, who looked around eighteen, sounded as if she was discussing selling something mundane like a car, I noticed a slight tremble in her voice.

What?

My mouth dropped open, but words failed me as I grappled with what I'd just heard. "Holy shit. Really?" was the best I could offer, because I felt like chucking up.

One girl chewed on a nail. "It's great money."

"It would have to be," I said almost to myself, disguising my actual horror at hearing their story. The thought they'd agreed to such a radical and appalling arrangement made me shudder.

"A friend did it last week, and she got one hundred thousand pounds. It's set her up for her twenties. I'm not seeing anyone. We're a rare species, apparently." She chuckled. Like her friend, she was only wearing a bra and panties.

"So, you go on stage like that?" I asked.

They nodded. "There's about eight of us so far. The other girls are in there. Some of them are shitting themselves." Her eyes settled on my body. "You'd do well. You're probably not a virgin." She wore an apologetic smile. "Sorry, I know that's personal."

"I *am* a virgin."

Just as I spoke, Tania came by and said, "Can I have a word?"

I followed her into another dressing room, where girls, who I figured were also selling their innocence, were applying makeup.

Tania smiled at the six girls. "Can you give us a little space? We'll start soon. I've arranged for some champagne."

I felt their fear mingled with anticipation.

"You're like everyone's mum," I said.

She smiled sadly. "I like to look after the girls. I also work on the floor. That's why I dress like this."

Despite being older than the others, I imagined Tania being popular.

"So, what exactly were you told about tonight?" Tania asked.

"That for three hundred pounds, I'd *only* be required to wait tables in costume."

She held my gaze for a moment. "You knocked back a client. He wasn't too happy."

"You made out earlier that it was *my* choice whether I drank with them." I was so shaken by the whole virgin-selling shitshow that all niceties were off the table. I'd put a pause on that demure, lost-girl act years ago.

"Then you heard me wrong." She dropped the soft act and gave me a stony stare. "I heard you talking to the girls. You realize you could make a fortune tonight. It's an opportunity I wish I'd had."

"You mean me fucking someone?"

"I mean, you auctioning yourself to the highest bidder."

"No fucking way. That's not me." I crossed my arms in defiance.

She tipped her head. "Two men have already asked if you have a reserve."

"A reserve?" My face scrunched in horror, like I'd been asked to sacrifice an arm. "I'm not a commodity. I'm a fucking human being."

"Yes. Someone who's broke, has nowhere to live, and is still a virgin."

I frowned so intensely my head ached. "How do you know that?"

"Your friend told us."

"He's no fucking friend of mine." I puffed.

I recalled how three hundred pounds sounded a lot for a waiting job, but was too desperate to say no. I should have known Travis would lead me into some kind of slimy rabbit hole.

"But Travis wouldn't've known I was a virgin." I wanted to scream out of sheer frustration.

"He did." She wore a crooked smile.

His sister must have blabbed about me.

"I won't do it." Staring her square in the face, I became that wilful teenager telling my mother to go fuck herself after blowing me up for wearing tight jeans. All because her sleazy new husband couldn't stop perving at my arse.

"There's this handsome client who's in his late forties, early fifties at the most. Filthy rich." She nodded as though that was something rare to be celebrated.

My slimy stepfather was around that age when he tried to rape me. *No fucking way.*

Wearing a sympathetic smile, Tania must have noticed my shaking hands. "I accept it's not a simple decision. But he's offered a hundred and fifty thousand pounds. You won't even have to parade like the others."

My jaw dropped at that suggestion of me prancing around like in a cattle call, and as I went to protest, she raised a finger for me to wait.

I was about to tell her to stick it and make a run for it when she returned with a glass of champagne. "Here. The girls are all enjoying one."

Staring down at the bubbly, I took a steadying breath. I had one hour to go and then the money would be mine. The sudden shock of seeing those girls ready to sell themselves had almost sobered me up. At least the alcohol would make me numb enough to finish my shift.

Just as I was about to take the glass, I asked, "Does that mean you got me here on false pretenses and that I won't get paid?"

"No. The money's yours. Just collect glasses and sit with the clients. But you can also choose to walk out of here and become an independent woman."

"I'll pass. I'll just finish the hour for that three hundred I'm owed."

I took the champagne and gulped it down like someone about to face a trial.

Just as I was about to leave, she grabbed my arm. "You'll have to lose your virginity sometime, and this way you'll be rich enough to make your own way in life."

"Is that what you did?" I had to ask.

Her eyes stared at me without blinking. "I would have, had it not been robbed from me. I had a shitty home life."

"Someone in your family?" My spine stiffened, sensing where this was going.

"Stepfather. I was thirteen. He ripped it out of me for free." She wore a haunted expression that one didn't fake.

"Shit. I'm sorry." I touched her arm.

Deflecting my sympathy, her face hardened again.

She didn't do pity. Nobody understood that better than me. After drowning in self-pity throughout my teens, I'd spent the last six years buried in denial. Because if I allowed myself to dwell on what had happened back home, I would have descended into a bottomless pit of depression.

"I'm strong." She squared her shoulders. "My life's good now. I'm only telling you this because the whole man-woman thing is complicated. Men want young, pretty things, and for virgins, they're willing to pay big. These are very rich men. This is an invitation-only club."

"I'll go back out and keep working." I mirrored her cool tone and walked off.

Inside, however, emotion tangled me in knots as my disturbing, unwelcomed past filled my thoughts.

My mother might as well have pushed me out the door herself. But she'd never been a good mother, so her not giving a shit about me came as no surprise.

Only I hadn't been ready for the wide world. I'd had plans. Plans to finish my studies. All that crumbled along with my sanity.

And now here I was again, having to maintain a level of dignity, surviving in a jungle of men hungry for sex with someone young enough to be their granddaughter.

Doing my best to fight back nausea, I went back to serving. Between the odd pinch on the bum, I delivered trays of drinks without spilling them. And after a while, I got used to being leered at. I even had a drink with a couple of men, which came with a fifty-pound tip, which I stuffed down my top.

When the parade of virgins started in a lit-up corner on a raised platform, a waitress in tiger print, about my age, stood close and offered me a drink from her tray.

At least alcohol had helped get me through what had been both a surreal and rather eye-opening, if not alarming, night. With only fifteen minutes left before my shift ended, I took the drink.

The girls came out one by one. In bra and thongs. They were mostly slim and very young.

I leaned into the girl and said, "Do you think she's even eighteen?"

"No idea. I don't question what goes on in here. I just do my job. Occasionally, I fuck the odd client when he's paying well."

My eyebrows shot up. She made it sound so normal, like she was agreeing to the occasional chat.

Maybe I needed a counselor. No. I definitely needed a counselor. Just couldn't afford one. Men freaked me out.

I liked the look of some boys, and hot actors were nice to ogle, but older men with that hungry look in their eyes turned me to ice.

One girl bent over and opened her legs, and the bidding started. It went to fifty thousand pounds, and she was sold to a fat old man.

Ick.

"He'll be a quickie." My co-worker giggled.

The room swirled around suddenly, and my legs started to wobble. "I think I've been drugged."

"You have." She pulled a wicked smile.

"You did it..." I could barely talk, let along call her a fucking bitch.

Next thing, someone was practically carrying me to the back of the stage, where a man in a suit, smelling of strong cologne, held open a checkbook.

"This is—"

I interrupted Tania and spat out, "Satan. That's who you are. You drugged me."

"Obviously not enough, it seems."

"What did you give me?" My raised voice slurred.

"He'll look after you. He's a reliable regular." Her honied voice made me want to slap her, but my arms felt like rubber. "Who knows? You might even like it." From nice in that kindly aunt way to being a scheming, betraying bitch, Tania's face had turned hard and ugly.

I stepped out of my heels so I could stand up without swaying.

"I need to get my bag." I left before they could say anything, even though my jelly legs made it tricky to move.

Tania followed me into the dressing room.

Cursing my stupidity for taking those drinks, I struggled as the room spun.

Tania held out an envelope with cash, but when she saw me leaning against the bench, propping myself up, she slipped the cash into my bag.

I was about to speak when the arsehole with a checkbook joined us. His shoes creaked as he walked, and then his tie dangled onto my skin as he leaned close.

I flinched as his wrinkled finger grazed my shoulder, and his face went all blurry.

Clutching my bag, I had to stay alert and look for a way out, despite heavy eyelids begging me to curl up into a ball and sleep. But the stench of danger kept my blood pumping, as a predacious, suffocating mix of cologne and depravity thickened the air.

Strangling fear squeezed my vocal cords because, for a minute, I thought I was back in my childhood bedroom.

I picked up one of my shoes to use as a weapon, and when he turned to speak to Tania, I rushed out of the room and, holding onto the wall, scrambled towards the flickering exit sign.

CHAPTER 5

Thea

THREE MONTHS LATER...

THE ROOM looked like there'd been a drunken out-of-control party. Smashed and empty bottles. Dirty plates and glasses. Smeared cream cake and lipstick on the floor and walls. The bed looked like people had been wrestling on it. Furniture destroyed.

Why did I always end up with the penthouse suites? I stepped out into the hallway to wheel in my cleaning trolley. Up ahead, Lucy pushed hers out of an adjoining room.

"Hey, any princes?" I chuckled.

That was our little joke. She had this continuing fantasy often shared after work while sipping on a well-earned drink about her having her own Jennifer Lopez moment with a Ralph Fiennes lookalike billionaire.

For hard-working girls like us that's what kept us sane: silly little fantasies and laughs at the expense of the filthy rich clients we cleaned after.

"Nuh. Just lots of mess. And..." Her hazel eyes shone with amusement. "A bin full of used condoms."

I twisted my mouth. "Gross." I pointed. "You should see what fucking awaits me in there. I mean, what do these people get up to?"

"Ah, the weirdo habits of the super-rich. Here, I'll help. That way we can get lunch together."

"You're a star," I said as she followed me into the room.

Lucy's brown bob swished around as she shook her head. "Holy crap. You weren't kidding. This is crazy. And look at the walls. Lipstick drawings of a dick and balls. Have you called Alan?"

"I'll have to. This is crazy-shit messy. We're going to need paint stripper to get that off."

I puffed out a tired breath. I'd been working at Lovechilde's, a five-star hotel, for three months, and while the conditions were fair and the pay higher than most cleaning jobs, the work exhausted me, mainly because I often worked double shifts for the extra money.

After an hour of solid cleaning, with me continuously thanking Lucy, we headed down to our lockers.

A notice on the board read: Live-in housemaids wanted for Merivale House. Bridesmere by the sea.

I asked, "Where's Bridesmere?"

"I went there once for summer. It's a little over an hour's drive from the city. It's a gorgeous fishing village, like something out of a TV show, with lots of brightly colored shops."

I nodded with interest. I had nothing holding me in that super-expensive city, and although Annabel, my flatmate, was nice enough, I wouldn't miss the emotional rollercoaster that was her life.

"What? Are you thinking of applying?" Lucy stepped out of her uniform, picked up a pair of jeans and yanked them up her long, skinny legs.

"I am. And it's live-in, which means I can save on rent."

"Mm... I guess. But wouldn't you miss the buzz of the city? Those villages can get a bit stuffy, where everyone knows everyone's business and all the goss."

"My life's not that interesting to fire up gossip." I fidgeted with my skirt's zip. Unlike my skinny friend, I'd stacked on weight. "I need to save. I want to go back to college. You know that."

Yep. She knew all about my aspirations which weren't that unrealistic. I just wanted to finish my music degree and teach children piano. That's where I was heading when my repulsive stepfather from fucking hell interrupted my life.

"Then why not apply? I'll miss you though." Her mouth turned down.

I touched her arm and smiled.

Her face sparked up. "Hey, that's where the very sexy and eligible Lovechilde billionaire sons live. The same Lovechildes who own this hotel."

"Oh? How do you know about them?"

"I read all about them in *Hello*. The eldest of the two was a soldier, I believe."

"Really? Why would he do that?"

She shrugged. "Who knows? Prince William and Harry joined the armed forces. I guess it's what sons of wealth do."

"Unlike you, I'm not looking to hook up with a filthy-rich guy. I don't even want a boyfriend."

She scrunched her longish face. "You're weird. And you're not even a lessie. I mean, look at you: you're fucking gorgeous. If anyone can attract a prince, it's you."

I laughed. "Luce, you live in a dream world."

"That's all we've got." She smiled sadly and my throat lumped up. Lucy had had a tough life. She lost her mother to cancer and had never known her father.

I put my arm around her shoulder. "You'll meet a lovely guy. I'm sure. You've got the biggest heart, and you'll make the greatest mother."

She smiled wistfully. "Hope so. But not from fucking Tinder, right?"

"Right. Promise me not to do that again."

My flatmate had brought home enough of those dates for me to know that one didn't find their Mr. Future from the swipe of a phone screen.

IT WAS MY SECOND visit to Merivale House. The first time was a day trip for the interview, and the following day, Janet, head-of-staff, called to inform me I'd gotten the job and asked me if I could move in by the weekend.

Within a day, lugging all my possessions stuffed in a suitcase and a backpack that tugged heavily at my shoulders, I caught a bus.

I landed in the village like a dazzled child at a theme park. The shimmering ocean, tinkling sailboats, and a bustling pier of fishermen and tourists captured my imagination, and suddenly the anticipation of possibilities swept me away.

A nice, if not strange sensation, because I'd never aspired to anything much before. Just to survive without being hit on and to get my music teaching degree, but with the wind in my hair and salty air brushing my face, a force of hope made me smile.

It felt right being there. I almost kissed the air. Maybe it was knowing that I'd left behind ugly memories and that this was a fresh start.

Merivale, I'd discovered was a mile from the village, and so I caught an Uber, despite what would have been a pleasant walk through a forest to get there.

The grounds as we drove to the house were covered in hedges, and the lawn looked like lush green velvet.

I'd been instructed to enter through the servants' quarters, and there I met Janet.

She took me on a tour of the main house, and my jaw dropped and remained that way. Crystal chandeliers glistened in the sunlight. Golden-framed art highlighted by a dark bluish-green wall. A serpentine staircase. Etched windows and stained glass. Marble statues.

At the back of the opulent three-story mansion lived the servants' quarters.

My room had an en suite and a window that looked out to green rolling meadows. The cozy room came with a television and had all I needed. But more significantly, I had a room of my own. No more messy flatmates playing their crappy music and keeping me awake with their screechy sex.

As she opened the door to the en suite bathroom, a scent of lavender hit me, as shiny clean surfaces smiled back at me. I thought of the bathroom I'd shared in London with its mold stains and toilet that didn't always flush. I wanted to hug Janet. Who would have thought a clean, pleasant-smelling bathroom could bring so much joy?

"Let me show you around the kitchen." She moved so quickly, I had to take wide strides to keep up.

We entered the large space fitted with marble and stainless-steel surfaces. Pots and pans dangled in the center over the large, commercial-sized kitchen, and an appetizing baking smell sent my stomach rumbling.

"This is where we keep the fresh linen." Janet opened a cupboard with stacked white napkins and tablecloths. "Normally, you'll be required to clean the bedrooms. That starts tomorrow, and I'll be on hand to show you where things go. You're prepared to work Sunday, I take it? You read your contract?"

I nodded. "Mondays and Tuesdays are my days off. Although I'm happy to work seven days if you need."

She shook her head decisively. "No. We can't have staff burning out. This is a big house as you can see. There's silver to polish. There are windows and mirrors to wipe down. Most cleaners disappear after a year."

"Really?" My eyebrows rose.

A smile twitched on her lips. "As I said, the work's intense. Normally, the caterers bring their own staff. But after the last event, things went missing, so the family has asked for the full-time maids to help the butlers."

"Of course, that's all good. I've done waitressing."

"Good. There's a lot that needs doing." Janet rubbed her hands as though she loved being busy. "It's Caroline Lovechilde's birthday. There will be forty guests dining."

"That's the mother?"

"Yes. For the staff, it's Mrs. Lovechilde."

I nodded. "Have you been here long?" I asked as we scuttled down the hallway and into a room with a huge dining table.

"I've been here for ten years. They're a good family. I helped raise the children, who now as adults are a little on the spoiled side. To be expected, considering how indulged they were." She smiled tightly. "Other than the eldest, Declan, that is. He's a true gentleman."

Just as astoundingly opulent as the rest of the house, the dining room boasted crimson walls covered in more gilded art, and bay windows that looked out to the columned marble entrance and beyond onto the vast grounds.

Janet took a cloth out of her apron and wiped a silver candelabra on the dining table. "As you can see, we start preparing early."

"What time do the guests arrive?"

"At six. As is customary, the guests gather in the front room for cocktails, and then at seven they come here for a seven-course meal." She wiped dust off a vase. "Jennifer, the girl before you, missed things. She was always flirting with Ethan."

"Ethan?"

"That's the son. Come, let me show you around, and then we'll discuss the evening's procedures. Don't want to overload you."

"I'm good." I smiled. I liked her. Although she was jumpy, I sensed a considerate, hard-working woman in Janet.

We walked along the hallway into the front room with a wall of windows that offered a view of the manicured grounds with a hint of the sea beyond. The dark teal walls astounded with their white scrolled edges and a painting of naked nymphs on the ceiling.

Awestruck by its beauty, I stared up at the sky scene. "It's fabulous."

"Yes." She smiled. "Once a month, the house is opened to visitors. There are some major artworks, and the building was designed by a celebrated Victorian architect, which attracts scholars. The house has its own page in history due to its unique design."

"I do like the columned entrance," I said.

"Right." She snapped out of her chat mode. "This is where the guests will hang out for the first hour. Your role is to help with the drinks."

She moved to the front door, and we stepped outside.

"I'll show you the path you must use to get to your quarters. You must never come through the front entrance."

I followed her along the cobbled path fringed with flowerpots to a courtyard that led into the servants' quarter. My heart expanded and I wanted to hug Janet but refrained. That would have been a bit too weird.

CHAPTER 6

Declan

My bedroom was just as I'd left it ten years ago. I opened the glass doors and stepped onto the balcony. Sea air smacked me in the face, and I breathed it in deeply for an awakening hit.

We were about to celebrate my mother's fiftieth birthday, and at a loss for gift ideas, I'd bought her favorite perfume so that the handwoven scarf from Afghanistan wouldn't seem too paltry a gift.

The red cashmere scarf flooded me with memories of a remote village located in rocky, hard-to-get-to mountain terrain. Against a backdrop of gun blasts, I entered a cave where a pair of frightened eyes framed in a slit of black fabric pleaded for mercy.

Her eyes switched from fear to joy as soon as I emptied my pockets of all the afghanis I possessed—a much higher sum than her asking price for the exquisite scarves she and her daughters wove.

I answered a knock at the door and found Ethan holding a couple of bottles of Guinness. He waltzed in casually, like a man without a care in the world.

"I thought you might be thirsty."

I took a bottle from his hands. "I am. Good timing."

He stared down at my bed, at the scarf and bottle of perfume. "Mother's presents?"

"Yep." I sipped on the cool bitter liquid. "I need to wrap them. I didn't get her a card."

"Neither did I." He sauntered about picking up the odd knickknack. "I bought her a painting."

"That's a little more substantial than this, I guess." After being reminded of my mother's birthday yesterday, I remembered the scarves as I unpacked my case. An earthy scent coming off the cloth swamped me with memories of that harsh terrain. From above in an aircraft, that jagged land resembled a giant's broken teeth.

It was a place I'd never forget. Not like a warm, fuzzy memory that a visit to Venice or Prague produced, but in a haunting, life-changing way.

"What do you give someone who has everything?" Ethan chuckled.

My brother was the counter opposite of me. While I was the serious one in the family, he was the clown. But it worked for us. Two years apart, we grew up playing, fighting, and then talking about girls.

At least we weren't competitive, like some brothers, which pissed my mother off, who viewed competition as healthy.

From a shelf filled with odd bits and pieces, Ethan took a cricket ball, a souvenir from my college days when I bowled for the winning side. He tossed it from hand to hand. "Cleo's coming, I take it?"

"I guess so." I flicked back a wave of hair. My hair had grown back quickly, and while I'd instructed the barber to cut my sides to number two, I asked him to keep my dark-brown locks longer on top. After eight years of wearing a buzz cut, I welcomed the change, but now the unruly strand kept falling on my face.

"So, are you back on? Now that you're back for good?"

I shook my head. "We caught up the other night."

He sat on my bed and bounced on it. "You don't sound like a man in love."

"When have I ever sounded like that?" I sipped on stout and stared out the window, soaking in the view that seemed endless thanks to the inky ocean.

He studied me for a moment. His eyes twinkled with amusement. "You're not batting for the other side, are you?"

"Fuck, Ethan. What's wrong with everyone? Just because I'm not in love means I'm gay?"

"Blame the overzealous rumor mill dying to catch us with our dicks out." He chuckled. "That said, I wish you'd start fucking around again, so they lay off me for a while. I mean it's kinda weird that you're not fucking around, considering how women throw themselves at you."

"They throw themselves at you too." I flicked through my shirts from when I was younger. I'd filled out since then. All that intense army training had broadened my shoulders.

"Fucking is fun. You must admit."

"Not before dinner."

He laughed. "You're such a bore."

"You've got your buddies to talk pussies with, haven't you?" I asked, buttoning up a green shirt that was way too tight. It was time I shopped.

"I do. Other than sport, what else is there?"

"Philosophy. Books. Politics. Anyway, enough about my sex life."

He took a slug from his bottle. "Nothing wrong with fucking around. It's good for the ticker. An orgasm a day keeps the blues away."

I laughed. "Who says that?"

"Me."

"Sounds like you need a life, Ethan."

"I'm good." He took another sip. "So, *have* you fucked Cleo since returning?"

I puffed out a slow breath. I could see my brother wasn't going to leave this alone. "I've seen her a few times."

A quick tap at the door and Savanah, our sister, swanned in. "Here you both are." She eyed the Guinness and, lunging for it, took a sip.

Ethan pulled a face. "Hell, Savvie, you just put fucking lipstick on the rim."

She poked her tongue at him before turning to me. "Are you crashing for the weekend?"

"I only live—what? Two miles from here? But I know it will make Mother happy to have us all here together, so I thought I might," I said, my energy drained at the thought of socializing.

Always the same questions: When are you going to settle down? Are you going to do some real work now that you've left the army? As though training with the SAS and flying planes was some boyish frivolity.

"So have you got a hot date lined up?" Savanah asked, picking up a framed picture of Johnny, my beloved, childhood Border collie.

"Nope."

"Cleo's coming," chimed in Ethan, wagging his eyebrows.

"Mm... you're still seeing her then?" she asked.

"We've caught up a few times." I had no idea what I was doing with Cleo. We'd kicked around a bit before I went off on my last tour, and a few weeks after I returned, I ran into her. After a few drinks, she drew me into a dark room and sucked me off.

As much as I loved having my cock sucked, Cleo didn't make my blood heat up.

Savanah looked at Ethan for clues, and he returned a shrug. "He's not been himself since coming back from war."

"It wasn't exactly a full-blown war." I puffed out a breath. I hated talking about that messy and ugly campaign. "I'm fucking fine. Don't start."

"Ew." Savanah pulled a face. Acting like children poking fun at each other was how we related even as adults.

"You don't sound fine," she said. "So what do you think Dad will give Mummy?"

"A divorce." Ethan's droll remark reminded me of my parents' fractious relationship.

"Dad's virtually living full-time in London now. He's got a penthouse there, you know. I've seen it."

Ethan looked impressed. "I think he's got a mistress."

"How fucking predictable." Moving her head from side to side, she smoothed down her green fitted dress in the mirror, turning to look at her backside. I noticed she'd lost weight again. She was super-thin as I'd already remarked. That earned me a hug.

I hadn't meant it as a compliment, but then I found women's obsession with being skinny baffling.

"Well Mother's not exactly easy to be around," Ethan appealed. He joined my sister in front of the mirror, combing his hair, which he wore in a similar style to mine.

He had my mother's dark eyes, while I'd inherited my father's blue eyes. But apart from that, we were both the same height, and our hair was the same dark brown.

He cared more for his appearance than I did.

Savanah was the veritable princess of the family. Designer everything. Her long, normally brown, hair was blonde for now, and her eyes were like mine.

"Okay, you two. I need to shower and get ready before the guests arrive."

"What are you giving Mummy?" Savanah asked.

I pointed to the scarf. "And a bottle of Chanel No. 5."

She lifted the woven piece. "Mm... it's pretty. Soft." She ran her fingers over the cloth.

"It's cashmere. I got you one too," I said.

Her face lit up in surprise. "Really. Super. I can wear it in Switzerland. It looks warm."

"Handwoven." I thought of the cowering seamstress and how her world was so different from ours.

As was tradition at these Merivale dinner parties, cocktails were served as guests arrived.

Cleo stood close and whispered, "You're staying here, I'm told. So am I."

I took a sip of beer and looked at her for a moment. She was a beautiful girl for sure. With those big blue eyes and tall svelte body, Cleo was any man's dream. Only I liked my women earthy and not caked in makeup. Maybe a little shorter. Maybe a little darker. I don't know what it was, but my dick barely moved around her. I should have wanted her. I was hot-blooded like any thirty-two-year-old man.

"I'm still getting used to being back. I might be a bit tired." That was me skirting around the edges rather than diving in and just telling her my heart wasn't into anything serious.

"You've been back for a few months. And you weren't tired two weeks ago when we..." Her brow arched. "Fucked."

One of the older guests turned to stare at us.

I whispered, "Hey, keep it down."

She laughed. "Don't worry about Kenneth. He's into all kinds of kinky shit."

"Aren't they all," I said almost to myself.

"What's wrong, Dec? You don't seem yourself." She pouted like a little girl.

"I'm good. I still haven't seen my mother. Excuse me a moment."

I walked off and although I felt bad leaving her like that, I noticed Charlie had pounced on Cleo. Good. He was a rich, good-looking boy and, going on Cleo's brightening smile, proved a good replacement for me, which suited me. I had no desire to be anyone's date.

Then I saw *her*, and my heart raced like mad, only this wasn't from fright.

CHAPTER 7

Thea

I NEARLY DROPPED THE tray of drinks. Lucy's description of the Lovechilde men as being drop-dead gorgeous was a massive understatement. Especially Declan Lovechilde.

He also kept staring at me. The way his eyes trapped mine for what seemed longer than a casual glance, made it hard to think straight. His ocean-blue eyes followed me along, making the tray tremble under my hands.

Why was he staring? There were so many stunning women present and being just the maid, I was meant to blend in with the furniture in my non-descript uniform of white shirt and black knee-length skirt.

He said something to Janet, and then he followed her over to me. My heart nearly leaped out of my chest. I looked behind me to see if they were looking at someone else.

The next minute, Janet stood by my side and gestured. "Mr. Lovechilde, this is Theadora, our new maid."

He returned his attention straight back to me. Like he might have missed something by looking away. My face burned as he stood so close, I could smell him.

His cologne rushed through me like a divine drug. The scent triggered all kinds of emotions. Like those intoxicating smells that flush us with comforting nostalgia. Only it was generally mowed grass or roses: nature's smells, not a tall, sexy billionaire's cologne.

My mouth trembled into an uneven smile. "Just call me, Thea. I prefer that."

I had to force myself to stop staring at the most handsome face I'd ever seen.

He held out his hand, and I took it. His big hand swallowed my much smaller one. As his warm and cushiony palm touched mine, a bolt of electricity sizzled through me.

I swear I felt my head wobble. His questioning, hypnotic gaze made me feel like it was just us. Everyone had faded into the background.

Going on Janet's confused frown, she'd noticed something happening too. I prayed this cataclysmic introduction wouldn't affect my job there. I'm sure women's faces burned all the time around this insanely hot man.

What might have been one second seemed like ages, and the tingling sensation from where his skin touched mine remained after he removed his hand.

"Welcome to Merivale, Theadora." He spoke in an arousing deep voice.

I caught myself nodding stupidly, unable to stop gaping at his gorgeous face. Forcing myself to turn away, I couldn't risk falling into those blue eyes again.

Dizzy as though I'd downed shots of his cologne, not booze, I crept away.

What the fuck was that?

As I went about my tasks around the dining guests, I sensed his gaze burning into my skin. Keeping my eyes down, I cleared empty glasses and topped up drinks. If it hadn't been for Declan Lovechilde, I would have actually enjoyed myself. There was something quite elevating about being surrounded by beauty. And by that, I didn't just mean Mr Lovechilde. Although, my god, how did he get that body? And that face. Those eyes were so blue one could easily drown in them.

Stop it! You're not meant to be getting hot and bothered over the boss.

I entered the kitchen and met Janet, who was instructing the casual staff.

"How are you going?" she asked.

Apart from the threat of fainting thanks to that gorgeous Declan Lovechilde, I'm okay.

"Um... good, thanks."

"I need you to help with the serving of first course. Rick, one of the butlers, isn't well."

"Sure." I hoped that Declan Lovechilde wouldn't look at me, because I was likely to drop soup in someone's lap. "I'll just go back and clear a few more glasses from the front room."

A very pretty girl who reminded me of Emily Blunt entered the kitchen and sashayed over to us.

"Janet, can you be a sweetheart and help me with something." She glanced over at me.

"This is Thea, our new maid." Janet turned to me. "This is Savanah Lovechilde."

I held out my hand. "Pleased to meet you." I smiled. "You look lovely."

Her face brightened. "Why, thank you." She studied me for a moment. "I hope you like it here. I'll try not to be too demanding." She looked at Janet and smirked.

Watching them walk off, I felt a tinge of envy. I gathered Savanah didn't lack anything. With a click of the finger and presto: beautiful clothes, cool friends, and an easy life. I did like her style. She wore a purple-and-blue knee-length dress, with an asymmetrical neckline and midriff cut-outs, that draped elegantly over her slim body.

I exited the kitchen and walked among a group of young men. One turned and smiled. "You're new. I haven't seen you before."

I nodded as he placed his empty bottle on my tray. "Can I bring you another?"

He shook his head. "I'm Ethan, the son." His mouth turned up at one end.

Another stunner, but very different from Declan. Unlike his intense brother, Ethan struck me as light and playful.

"And your name?" Ethan asked.

"Thea."

"Well, Thea, I hope you enjoy your time here."

"Thanks, that's kind of you." I smiled and carried the tray away carefully with two slightly trembly hands.

After the guests settled at the large dining table, I was placed on drinks duty and instructed to ensure that everyone's wine was topped up.

Easy enough, one would have thought, only with Declan Lovechilde at the table interrupting his conversation to stare at me, I found myself having to take deep breaths and was close to hyperventilating. Talk about nerve-wracking.

A beautiful, bubbly woman sat by his side and while she seemed to be chatty, gesturing expressively with her hands, Declan Lovechilde responded with the occasional nod. His face was neutral, if not somewhat uninterested.

Caroline Lovechilde, the mother and, judging from how she commanded the discussion, the head of the house, sat regally at one end of the table, while Mr. Lovechilde, who I met earlier on, insisting I call him Harry, sat at the other end. He laughed a lot, and since I kept topping up his glass, I gathered he liked to drink.

Unsurprisingly, Savanah had many admirers. Young guys hanging on her every word, while Ethan sat between a pair of beautiful women, chatting and laughing loudly.

With the main course served, I was given a break and decided to go outside for some air. Dying to sit down, I headed for the courtyard area by the servant's quarters. There I found a girl and a man lost in conversation. When they noticed me, they waved for me to join them.

"You're new around here. I'm Jason, the cook."

"I'm Thea." I smiled.

"And I'm Amy," the girl said. "I normally do what you do, but I was in the kitchen tonight. We're down on staff."

I virtually flopped onto the chair. "You don't mind me sitting here?"

"Not all. We can fill you in on all the goss." She giggled.

Jason looked at me and rolled his eyes. "Don't get her started."

Amy slapped his arm. "You love it. You just pretend not to be interested."

"You make it sound like a soap opera." I chuckled.

"Oh, it can be that," Jason said.

"You've been here for a while?" I asked.

Amy nodded. "We both started four years ago. So have you met the family?"

"I have. They seem nice," I said. "Not that I've had a chance to chat to them. Just a few words with the younger members."

"Declan's only been back for a few months. He doesn't live here, though. He's in the village. Lives in a converted church."

"Oh? That's different," I said.

"He is different," Jason said.

"In a good way," Amy added. "He's a bit serious. But he's respectful. Keeps to himself. He went to Afghanistan, you know. Story has it, he's changed a lot. We've noticed it, haven't we?" She looked at Jason who responded with a nod.

"He's not married?" I asked.

"None of them are. Savanah has a different boy a month. Ethan's a playboy, and Declan sees Cleo on and off, we think," Amy said. "She's here tonight. All over him. She's a photographic model."

That figures.

I glanced down at my watch. "I guess I should go in and help with clearing the table."

"I'll be there in a minute to help," Amy said.

Just as I was stepping into the hallway, I nearly bumped into Declan and only just managed to avoid a collision.

"I'm so sorry." An apologetic smile quivered on my lips.

Once again, his penetrating gaze paralyzed me. He frowned as though trying to solve a puzzle.

My face burned and a dizzy sensation swept through me. No male had ever affected me like this. I'd never allowed myself to be charmed or become tongue-tied like my gushing girlfriends. That wasn't me. At all. I don't even think I blinked. I must have looked like a stunned rabbit in car lights.

Just as those sculptured, luscious lips parted to say something, his mother joined him.

"There you are. I need you to have a word with your father." She glanced briefly at me.

Does she think I'm flirting with her billionaire son?

"One minute," he said in a deep, resonant voice that made him seem even more powerful.

I wanted that job more than anything, so I scuttled away before falling into those aquamarine eyes again.

What was he about to say to me?

I entered the dining room where the conversation had grown a lot louder, and pushing a trolley along, I collected plates, looking down to avoid Declan, who at that moment was helping his very drunk father off his chair.

I loaded dishes with half-eaten lobster and all kinds of delicious untouched food that, had it been London, I would have taken home. That's how I saved on grocery bills, by filling my bag with uneaten scraps.

But I'd already eaten what to me was a banquet of roast beef and veggies and a delicious apple pie dessert. Thanks to this new job's generous conditions, my meals were provided for during my five-day-working hours.

And with that comforting thought warming my belly, I pushed aside nagging questions about the owner of those soul-piercing eyes and continued clearing the table.

As I leaned over to collect a dirty plate, one of the older guests groped my bottom. Jumping back, I gasped, and my teeth cut into my lip, close to drawing blood.

For some reason, I glanced over at Declan, who'd seen what had happened.

Before my next breath, which took a while to arrive, he pounced on the man, and pulled the seat out, forcing Mr. Sleazebag to stagger to his feet.

The drunken guest lifted his arms in protest. "I didn't mean it. It was a slip of the hand." He chuckled dismissively.

Having removed his blazer, Declan was all muscle, going on the rippling mounds clinging to his tailored shirt. I thought his muscular arms would burst through the fabric as he went into battle mode.

Sweat poured down my armpits.

What the fuck's happening?

Even though I wanted to knock the prick's teeth out myself, I had to play it cool.

"Apologise and then fuck off." Declan's face darkened.

The drunk grinned as though this was a joke. "Hey, Declan, it was just a bit of fun."

The last thing I needed was a scene of my own making. Well, not really my own making. But I'd become the center of attention.

"Fucking apologise, Derek," Declan demanded, standing intimidatingly close to the creepy drunk.

A woman next to Derek, and the whole table, for that matter, stopped what they were doing and watched on as though riveted by a gripping drama. I just wished I wasn't in the starring role.

I wanted to shrivel into a ball and become invisible.

"Look, it's okay," I whispered to Declan, barely able to breathe. My eyes welled up, and my throat constricted as I fought off a panic attack.

"No, it's not okay," he snapped, glaring at the staggering drunk.

Within a flash, Caroline Lovechilde joined the fray and tugged on her son's bulging arm.

"He can't go around touching up the maid and somehow it's all fine."

"Darling, come with me." She looked up at her guests and raised her eyebrows with a forced smile as though to say "boys will be boys."

She widened her eyes at Derek, who licking his wounds, wore a fabricated apologetic smile.

He turned to me. "Sorry, love, it was just a slip of the hand."

Love? Really? Arsehole.

I couldn't resist a sarcastic smirk before hurrying away with the trolley.

Tears burned at the back of my eyes. I couldn't tell if it was his fondling, or Declan defending me, but I needed a good howl.

Janet approached me. "Are you okay?"

My mouth trembled. It took all my inner strength to avoid an emotional eruption. "I'm fine."

Her eyes shone with sympathy as though she'd also experienced being touched up by a drunken guest or two in the past. "Take a few minutes off."

"Thanks." I hesitated. "Um... I hope I'm not going to lose my job over this."

She wore a sad smile. "You'll be all right, love. Just take a breather. It will all calm down. These dinners are famous for outbursts. I've seen punch-ups. Arguments. You name it."

Now that took me by surprise. "Really? In this scene?"

"Oh, you wouldn't believe the stuff that goes on in this family."

As fascinating as that comment was, I was glad to find myself alone in the bathroom, where I plonked myself down on the toilet, buried my face in my hands, and cried.

It was more than Derek's groping. My tears came from all the attention. The fuss and plain old confusion. I also sometimes just cried. There was something releasing about those warm tears, although triggered by pain, I always felt calmer afterward.

After fixing my face in the mirror, I went into the kitchen for a glass of Coke. I needed some pepping up and just as I emptied my glass, Declan entered.

His eyes landed on mine and held me captive again.

Chapter 8

Declan

Normally at these family dinner parties, it was either one of Ethan's casual girls threatening to rip out the fake eyelashes of some other flirty girl or Savanah telling someone to "get fucked." But never me threatening to whack someone. I was the sensible one who didn't get drunk, try to hit on someone's wife or ramble on about some incendiary political minority group about to ruin the world with their idealistic views.

My mother pleaded with me. Derek was a big investor in one of her latest ventures.

I stood my ground. "He crossed a line. Staff are off-limits. All women are."

She shook her head. "What universe have you landed on? Staff have been touched up since the time of the Danes and probably before that."

My mother and her English history. Despite being the most educated in our family, with a master's degree, she hadn't quite caught up with women's rights. Ironic for someone who wore the pants in the family.

"In those times, the English lived in their own shit," I argued. "We've come a long way since then. Thanks to the Romans, we have excellent sewerage, and thanks to progressive thinking, women are treated with the respect we all deserve."

I was no longer that son that would do her bidding. I passed that baton over to Ethan years ago after I left home for the army. One of the few reasons I joined the SAS was to escape my mother's ruthless ambition for us to be the richest family in the UK.

"Your father's acting like a first-class idiot again. Why does he have to make a fool of the family like that?"

"Maybe it's got something to do with how close you and Will have become," I said.

"That's my business. Anyway, your father's got his lovers in London."

My parent's loose morals when it came to who they slept with made my skin crawl. "There's such a thing as divorce, you know."

She twisted her mouth. "It's very complicated. We own all of this together. And I have big plans for this place. Your father's portion is essential. We stand to make a fortune. If only he'd sign on that dotted line."

"I'm glad he hasn't stooped that low. What are you going to do about the farmers? Land that they've been leasing from the family since your beloved Henry the Eighth."

She pulled a face. "He's one of my least favorite kings. However, I admire him for breaking away from the corrupt clutches of the papal state."

I leaned in and kissed her on the cheek. "I hope you liked your present."

"It's very pretty." She half-smiled.

"If I see Derek, I'll knock out those wine-stained teeth of his," I warned.

"The army's changed you." She walked off.

I entered the kitchen and found Theadora sitting on a chair, resting her legs.

She flinched as though I was the last person she wanted to see. "I appreciate your stepping in earlier." She looked down at her hands. "But I don't wish to cause problems. I don't want to blow this job."

"I've got enough say in this family to decide who comes and goes." I remained there, holding her hesitant gaze. "You don't remember?"

"Remember what exactly?" She opened her hands, and those dark, searching eyes held me captive.

Janet entered the kitchen. "Oh, there you are," she said to Theadora. When she noticed me, Janet looked from me to our new maid. "Oh, Mr. Lovechilde, do you need something?"

Yep. This girl's story.

"I came here for a glass of water," I lied. "I'm good, thanks."

Janet said to Theadora, "They're about to serve dessert."

When the older woman left, Theadora jumped up off her seat to get back to work.

"Wait," I said. "When do you finish?"

Her lips parted and it took her a moment to answer. "In about an hour. After I've cleared the table."

"Meet me out the front by the labyrinth."

Her face twisted into a confused frown, bordering on baffled. I sensed a question shining in her wide eyes, but she simply nodded slowly and then hurried off.

Was this her? She didn't seem to recognize me.

TAKING A DEEP BREATH, I soaked up the dewy salt air and walked to the hedged labyrinth where we played as children. The center proved a perfect spot for secret meetings. It was also there that, as a fifteen-year-old, I lost my virginity to an older, more experienced, girl.

Theadora sat on a filigree iron seat. She'd undone her plait, and her long dark hair blew around her face in the gentle breeze. She was so beautiful she made my pulse race.

I sat next to her. "Theadora."

"Please call me Thea."

I smiled at how her face contorted with aversion. "I love your name. It suits you."

She looked down at her feet, something she did a lot. "Mm...if I had the time and money, I'd change it."

"That would be a shame." I couldn't take my eyes off her. Most of the women around me, including my sister, had this unhealthy obsession with wearing lots of makeup. Whereas Theadora didn't wear anything but her natural beauty.

Recalling her mascara-streaked face the night I rescued her, I kept asking myself: Was this the same girl that did drugs and was potentially selling herself?

"So, you wanted to speak to me about something?" she asked, fidgeting with her fingers.

"You don't remember?"

"Remember what?" She looked up at me with wide questioning eyes.

"I saved you from those pimps." I took a breath.

"Pimps?" Her brows knitted.

"You were drugged to the eyeballs," I said. "So, I'm not surprised you've forgotten."

"Oh... shit." Her face lit up with shock. "That was you?" A line formed between her brows. "They weren't pimps. Or mine..." She cupped her mouth with her hand. "You think I was selling myself?"

I took a moment to choose my words carefully. "Well, seeing you half-naked in a corset and drugged... I naturally assumed..."

"You thought I was a drugged-out prostitute?" Her face filled with horror. So much so, that guilt slithered through me for jumping to conclusions.

She bit into her lower swollen lip that I'd already been eyeing off all night.

"Thank you." She shook her head as though trying to make sense of something shocking. "God knows what they would have done to me."

I rubbed my jaw. "You weren't selling yourself, then? What about the drugs? I mean, you fell asleep as soon as you got into the car. I carried you inside."

"Oh, my god, that was you," she said, as though it had only just dawned on her. She looked away into the distance. "I was working in costume as a waitress. I only agreed to dress like that because I needed the money." She glanced at me briefly as though seeking my forgiveness. "Girls wearing very little paraded on stage in front of a room of men. Greasy, sleazy men."

The hatred in her voice was visceral, and disgust coated her eyes. "It was an auction. They were selling their virginity."

"Right? So they tried to auction you?" I asked.

Was this stunning woman still a virgin? Impossible.

She bit into her lip again and for some reason, that one action drew my attention away from the gravity of her story to her lips again. I hated myself for feeling this overwhelming urge to ogle her. To touch her. To take her into my arms.

An obsession that started three months ago. I hadn't stopped thinking about her. My dick hadn't forgotten either. She'd had a starring role in all my fantasies.

Assaulted by guilt, I was no better than the reprobates she described at that trashy bar. But I couldn't deny the rush of blood down south. I desired Theadora as I would something rare and supremely sensual.

With those larger-than-usual tits spilling out of her corset, and curvy arse, her image had remained etched in my erotic memory.

I'd even searched the internet to see if she was selling herself. I'd never bought sex before.

In a way, I almost would have preferred knowing she'd worked as a prostitute rather than being a virgin.

What would I do? Undo those popping buttons and rub those full breasts against me? Or taste her until she screamed out my name?

But a virgin?

"They drugged me," she continued. "And lucky for me, I managed to escape in time. That's when you found me trying to fight them off, but then the drug must have kicked in because the next thing I remember was waking up on your couch. Thanks for leaving me the clothes. I've still got them." Her lips curled into a shy smile, and my world lit up.

"Keep them. They're Savanah's. I figured you'd need something a little more comfortable to wear." I raised an eyebrow. "I didn't want to undress you."

I would have loved to have undressed her, but only with her consent. She didn't need to know that. She didn't need to know how my dick had ached for days after seeing her looking like an erotic version of Sleeping Beauty on my sofa.

A photo I would have paid a fortune for.

Even now, I would have gone on a diet of stale bread and water to have Theadora on my couch in that corset.

Get a fucking grip. This girl has been abused and mistreated by an ugly portion of society—men that deserve to have their balls chopped off.

"That explains why you've been staring at me all night," she said with a hint of a smile. "At least now, I know." She shook her head in wonder. "Who would have thought? What a small world." Her face filled with youthful wonder, which made my mouth water for a taste of those rosebud lips.

"Are you comfortable here?"

She nodded. "I love it here. It's amazing. The first time since leaving home, I've got my own space."

"How old are you?" I studied her closely.

"Twenty-four," she responded, playing with her fingers again.

And you're still a virgin?

"You left home early?"

"Yes." Her face turned dark again. I sensed from that change of mood that something or someone had chased her out.

I changed the subject. "I can show you around sometime if you like."

My curiosity about Theadora surged. I wanted to get to know her. To dig deeper.

CHAPTER 9

Thea

I HADN'T SLEPT A wink, thinking about Declan Lovechilde, and how he was that mystery hero. I'd wondered whose couch I'd slept on. I'd even considered visiting his house in Mayfair to thank him, but couldn't bring myself to face anyone related to that frightening night. Even my rescuer.

I'd even developed a crush on him. My first ever.

Here I was thinking that I couldn't feel anything. That I was made of stone. An empty vessel. That arousal was some hormone-ravaged teenager hangover for girls living in a fantasy world like Lucy.

My heart raced, thinking of how his beautiful eyes seared through me, electrifying my body by sending a sizzling bolt through me. He'd woken me up sexually. What else could this sudden all-consuming swelling heat be?

Men had always scared me. But with Declan, it was this alien gush of desire that terrified me. Perhaps I was crushing on him because he saved me.

Yes, that was it.

Get a fucking grip.

What would he want with a girl like me, who had nothing to show but a head full of hang-ups? I was like twenty-four going on fifty some days.

In any case, Declan Lovechilde was way out of my league.

Sick of sitting on the bed daydreaming about Declan, I sprung up, got dressed, and headed out. It was my day off, and I planned to make the most of it.

I borrowed a bike I'd seen lying about and asked Janet if I could use it. She told me that someone had left it behind and to feel free.

I was about to ride to the village, when Ethan approached me, wearing torn, faded jeans and a green polo shirt.

"Hey, there you are," he said.

My eyebrows gathered. Why would he be looking for me? "Do you need something?"

He chuckled. "It's a figure of speech, you know. Like how are you? That kind of thing."

I gripped the bike handles. "Oh. Right. Okay."

"So are you off taking in the sights?"

"I thought I might ride down to the village."

"Justine's Café makes great coffee and freshly baked scones."

Just as I was about to respond, Declan strode towards us. Wearing jeans that clung tightly to those muscular legs, he was even hotter in broad daylight. I gulped. In that blue fitted polo, it looked like his arms would burst a seam.

My heart skipped a beat, and the threat of a dizzy spell had me leaning on my bike for support.

Declan switched his focus from me to his brother. "What's happening?"

Ethan grinned. "I'm about to invite our new maid to breakfast."

"Her name's Theadora," Declan said with authority. I could tell he was the one that pulled his younger brother into line.

"So it is. Thea..." Ethan looked at me. "Can I call you that?"

"Yes. I prefer that." My eyes darted back and forth between the brothers. Sweat started to treacle between my shoulder blades.

"I thought you'd be with Cleo. Didn't she stay the night?" Ethan asked.

Declan's eyes switched from his brother's to mine. "She did."

"Then why aren't you breakfasting with your girl?" Ethan asked, half winking at me.

By this stage, I wanted to sneak off.

"She's *not* my girl. She knows that and so should you. She stayed in the guest room."

Declan's tanned features seemed flushed. I sensed that he wanted to talk to me, which bamboozled me.

And while he was so handsome my body was doing things I'd never experienced before—butterflies, heart racing, and all kinds of weird, visceral gurgling—I was also terrified. After everything I'd been through, men frightened me.

I needed some space, if only just to breathe again.

"My apologies," I said. "I've just realized, I need to call a friend urgently."

Before they could say anything, I jumped on the bike and after an embarrassing wobbly start, off I went down that long driveway past the labyrinth, with the sea air smacking my face and my hair flying in the wind.

I'd looked forward to going to the village, but I didn't want to complicate things by hanging out with playboy Ethan, who would have probably unclasped my bra before lunch in his racy sportscar. The thought of which made my legs stiffen.

Whereas the thought of Declan fondling my breasts made my vagina ache.

Regardless of how he'd awakened desire in me, I wasn't that deluded to lose my head over a man that could make women swoon with just a gaze from those ocean-colored eyes.

Inner chatter rattled along with me as I rode out of the lace iron gates.

To think Declan thought I was a working girl. That bothered me.

What a relief I cleared that up, but it still made me nauseous to think he carried that idea of me all night. No wonder he kept staring at me. He was probably wondering what a former prostitute was doing working as a maid.

Grr... What a hideously appalling thought.

As it turned out, the ride down to the village cleared my head. I loved soaking in the avenues of wispy trees, and the trickling brook with ducks splashing about brought a smile. It was like I'd woken in a parallel universe where only fertile nature existed. After the polluted city, the air was like a baby's breath.

Pedaling slowly, I drifted along, letting go of everything. I hummed *Clair de Lune,* a tune I used to play on piano, as I rode past thatch-roofed cottages with brightly painted doors and flowers of every color crowding their entrance.

As I rode into the shopping area, the chilled, postcard-like village reminded me of something from the travel shows I occasionally watched while scoffing down crisps, imagining myself being a cheery, carefree tourist.

No one seemed in a hurry. Friendly smiles everywhere. Not like the city, where everyone looked stressed. The air was thick with salt and rotting fish. Pleasant though. Anything beat the heavy smog of London.

I found a nice spot with a view of the pier, from where I watched fishermen bringing in their catch and tourists taking photos. Allowing myself to indulge in a heap of calories, after having ridden there, I ordered chocolate cake with my coffee.

AFTER SOAKING IN THE village atmosphere, I rode back, and being a warm, sunny day, I decided on a visit to the bay, which was only a short walk from the house, or the hall, as everyone called it.

I tossed on a pair of shorts and a T-shirt and replaced my trainers with flip-flops and off I went. That earlier interaction with the brothers entered my thoughts, and as I walked along, I called Lucy.

"Hey," she said. "How's living in the lap of luxury?"

"It's nice. I mean my room's pretty basic, but I'm there alone. I have a TV and everything I need. They feed me. It's the job from heaven, and the work's not as back-breaking as the hotel."

"That sounds amazing. So why do I sense something in your voice?"

I smiled. Lucy could read me well. Even over the phone.

I recounted what happened with the brothers and that Declan was the mystery man who'd rescued me.

"Shit. Really? How the hell did you not remember *him*?"

"Good fucking question." I sighed. "His cologne registered though. Soon as I smelt it, all kinds of strange feelings took over. You know, like when you smell something that brings on nostalgia."

"Oh yeah. Every time I catch a whiff of Homme, my panties melt."

I chuckled. "Let me guess, Jaxon's cologne of choice?"

"Yep."

Jaxon broke Lucy's heart.

"And to think you ran away," she said, switching back to my story. "If you'd stayed, he might have bought you breakfast."

"Maybe," I said.

"And now you've got both of those hotties chatting you up. Go girl."

"Let's not jump to conclusions here, Luce. Declan was just curious about me." I grit my teeth. "And to think he thought I was a zonked-out prossie all those months. That spins me out."

"At least, now he knows. And Ethan Lovechilde. He's fucking hotalicious."

I giggled. "Declan's hotter."

"A double date?"

"I'm not aiming that high."

"Why not? You're stunning. You could make a fortune on Onlyfans."

"That's not me. You know that," I said. "I'm happy being a maid until I get my degree." I descended rocky steps onto a pebbly foreshore. "I'm just stepping onto the beach. I'm going to work on a tan. I haven't seen the sea since my mother took me to Brighton when I was little. That's when she couldn't find someone to mind me."

"You'll show her. Things are moving up for you, girl."

I had no plan to contact my mother, ever.

"Have you got a bikini?"

I scrunched my face. "No way. Can you imagine me in a bikini?"

"You'd look amazing. And maybe soon, you might even find out what it feels like to have a man."

"I'm scared. You know that. And I've never really felt like sex before."

"Yeah. Yeah. Yeah. So you keep saying. But wait until you meet someone you like. And you never know, from what you've told me so far, it sounds like you might have a billionaire or two chasing you. Woo-hoo..."

"I think they'd run if they knew I was a virgin. Declan probably knows. I told him I was being auctioned off that night."

"That probably gave him a hard-on."

"Don't be silly." My face scorched. I did notice his eyes smolder a little after I'd mentioned the "V" word.

"If I was going to lose my cherry, I'd want it to be with a hot, older billionaire."

"That's a fairy tale," I said.

"When should I visit?"

"Whenever. Although you'll have to stay in a B&B in the village. I'll pay." I missed my one and only best friend.

"Let's do that soon. Love you."

"Love you back." I closed the call.

I WIGGLED MY VERY white toes in the water and looking up, I saw him walking towards me in nothing but a pair of shorts and a loose white shirt flapping in the gentle breeze.

Declan stood before me. The sun-drenched shimmering water accented his hypnotizing turquoise eyes.

I crossed my arms, as my hardened nipples throbbed. The cool water had nothing to do with that bodily response.

"Theadora." His deep husk made my name sound artistic and not like the name of a bonnet-wearing wench in those bodice-ripping novels my grandma favored.

"Mr. Lovechilde," I returned with a thin voice.

"Call me Declan, please." He smiled and trapped me with those sparkling eyes. "It's a nice day for a swim." I noticed him clutching a towel.

Lost for a response, I just nodded.

His masculine beauty rendered me incoherent.

I don't even think I blinked.

He stared at my T-shirt. "Did you bring your swimsuit?"

"I'm not a swimmer." I shrugged. "I'm scared of the water."

He frowned. "Oh, really? You can't swim?"

I shook my head.

"Your parents never taught you?" The surprised note in his voice reminded me what a stunted childhood I'd had.

"I didn't exactly have a typical family life. After my mother married my stepfather, she forgot I existed."

"That sounds terrible," he said.

"It's okay. I'm good now."

Scared of a man touching me, but good.

"Now that I come to think of it, I taught myself to swim. My parents weren't exactly invested either." His mouth curved slightly. "I went to boarding school. Most of us there had parents keener to drive a profit than drive us to school or sport on weekends."

"I also went to boarding school," I said.

"We share that in common." He ran his tongue over his lips, and I had to look away like I'd stumbled on something pornographic.

I couldn't stop thinking of how it would feel to have those lips on mine.

Lucy had spoken, almost ad nauseum, about the joys of orgasms, but I hadn't even as much as touched myself. I'd never felt this intense burning sensation. Ever.

From the moment my breasts developed, my stepfather's creepy eyes were all over me, and my body just shut down.

"Well then, I might jump in," he said, his eyes lingering and my heart racing like mad.

Was that crackling between us? Or was I hallucinating?

And why did I get this feeling he wanted to say more?

"Enjoy." I smiled back.

He lowered his shorts and stripped down to Speedos.

Arse-gripping, bulge-divulging Speedos.

I couldn't look. Even though I wanted to ogle him. Who wouldn't? My lord. This man. That body.

He had a dusting of hair on a mounded chest that led to abs that rippled down to a V-shape. His long, muscular legs were all sinewy like footballers. His thighs were chunky like a rugby player's. And those strong arms that had carried me that night.

I took a mental snapshot, and as I made my way back to the hall, all I could think of was his big bulge in those tight Speedos.

What was happening to me?

I had to call Lucy.

"Hey, it's me again."

"I'm on the Tube," she said.

"I just saw him in his Speedos, and I'm kind of losing the plot." I giggled.

"Did you take a picture?"

My head lurched back. "That's crazy."

But wouldn't I love a photo.

"So did he have a nice, packed lunch?"

My face scorched. "I think so."

"Ooh... nice. I think he likes you," she sang.

"How can he like me? He's a hot billionaire."

"He saw you in a corset and not much more. He's probably had a hard-on since."

I laughed. "You're bad."

"You need to learn to be a little bad yourself. I've got to go love. Here's my stop."

"Love ya."

I put my phone away.

As I walked up the hill to the grand old hall, all I could think of was touching myself. The burning ache, making it painful to walk, insisted I do something.

CHAPTER 10

Declan

LOVECHILDE HOLDINGS OCCUPIED THE top floor of a glass-and-steel asymmetrical tower owned by the family company. Surrounded by a wall of windows, the large office, where we met for our board meetings, offered dizzying panoramic views of the city and beyond.

Ethan strolled in late as always.

I planned to insist he stop flirting with Theadora.

Am I chasing her?

We normally had different tastes in women. While I went for curvy women, he had a thing for long-legged, lean models who spent most of their time staring into mirrors. That's why his sudden interest in our new maid surprised me. But then she was only the most beautiful girl I'd ever seen.

That posed a dilemma since a long-term relationship wasn't on my to-do list. I wasn't even interested in marriage. Never had been.

Theadora didn't strike me as the casual sort of girl. If anything, she struck me as fragile, reminding me of a delicate bud that required careful handling in order to bloom. Since seeing her in that corset, despite my guilt for ogling her in that exploited state, I'd been on fucking fire.

My father lounged back and chatted comfortably with his former partner, Will, and despite Will's obvious relationship with my mother, their friendship continued. My father didn't carry grudges. For a multibillionaire, he was quite chilled, which is why I related to him more than I did my formidable mother.

"Ethan." My mother pointed to a chair. "You're late."

"Sorry, the traffic was woeful."

She rolled her eyes.

As her sons, we were both a disappointment.

She hated me joining the SAS. Even a Medal of Valour couldn't raise a smile or earn me a hug. Ethan seemed to spend most of his time drifting, and although he always voted on her side, I sensed he hadn't quite decided what he believed in, other than pretty women in bikinis.

"Okay, let's start," she said. "Will and I have been looking into carving up the acreage adjoining Merivale Hall. Our sights are on a luxury resort for international travelers seeking a five-star experience by the coast. This project would deliver in our conservative estimation around two billion pounds a year."

"What about the farmland? Our farmers have been here longer than we have. Who's going to feed the region?" I asked.

"They'll be paid out of their leases a generous amount. Some can stay on and apply for one of the many jobs on offer."

"We're talking about a lot of land. Does a resort need so much?" I asked.

"There'll be stables for horse riding, tennis courts, and a golf course. Space for people to enjoy."

"As you know, I own an acre, one mile north of the hall next to Chatting Wood. I've got my own plans to develop."

"And that is?" she asked.

"A boot camp." I looked around me, and eyebrows flung up everywhere, while my mother remained stony-faced.

I continued, "Also an organic farm."

Ethan smirked. "For bored executives seeking a thrilling weekend of being bossed around?"

I smiled weakly. "Troubled youth."

My mother looked like we were about to be attacked by enemy forces. "No. Absolutely not. We're not inviting anyone like that into the region. Can you imagine? There'll be all kinds of crime."

"There'll be security," I said. "And the teenagers will have a curfew imposed."

"Are we talking about kids that have committed crimes?" Will asked.

I nodded. "Petty crime. Drugs, break-ins, car infringements, that kind of thing."

"You cannot be serious." My mother's eyes lit up with alarm.

"I'm very serious. I've mapped it out. My partner was in my squadron."

"Are you doing this for free?" Ethan asked.

"I'll give my time for free, yes. I've been in discussion with certain government agencies. They're keen to get on board with healthy grants. It's going to save them in the long run. Fewer career criminals. Get them while they're young. Give unfocused youth something to do. If I can help even ten percent make a better life, this project will be a success."

Ethan turned and tossed me a nod and a 'good on you' smile. Whether that was irony or not, I couldn't tell with my brother. He seemed to have a foot in both camps. Underneath it all decent, despite his tendency to vacillate.

"Let's put it to the vote," my mother said.

"It's my land. The project doesn't need to be voted on. It's going to happen." I stared her squarely in the face.

"Mm... we'll see." She turned her attention to the group. "For now, I want a show of hands for the resort."

Everyone, bar me and my father, raised their hands. Ethan only halfway.

I leaned in. "Do what's right? Remember when we were kids, we'd play on those farms? Remember the animals, the fresh butter, and yogurt?"

He looked over at our father and lowered his hand.

It was a weak withdrawal given that my father had the power of veto. And he wasn't, much to my delight, buying it.

"Harry," my mother implored.

"Nope. I hate it. It's not happening. I'm with Declan. And I like his ideas. An organic farm is a great place to start. As for rehabilitating troubled youth, he could do worse things with his money."

I looked over at my father and nodded with a smile.

Just as my mother was about to protest, Savanah came rushing in. Removing her coat and panting, she asked, "What have I missed?"

"Only that our plan is being stymied by your father," my mother replied.

"Oh, really? But Daddy, it's a sound project. I had my heart set on it."

"What happened to the design degree?" he asked.

She looked at the other board members, who reminded me of cut-outs. Family friends and lawyers, whom I called the Noddies due to their agreeing on everything.

"I'm still there. But this is a really cool project," she said.

"I'm not signing off on it. That's my final word."

Savanah turned to my mother and rolled her eyes. They were thick. My mother had always favored her only daughter. I just shrugged it off. It took some pressure off me and Ethan. Until now. My mother hated to lose.

I waited until everyone filed off, muttering away to each other, and my mother, shaking her head, cast one of her cold stares at my father, who responded with an air kiss, just to piss her off.

My father was the joker. I enjoyed his company and felt blessed that he was there for us when we were growing up. Teaching us how to ride horses and toss a cricket ball or grip a tennis racquet. It touched me that he attended the ceremony for my Medal of Valour. He was the only family member there, and his presence meant the world to me.

"Dad, can I have a word?" I asked.

"Of course, Declan."

Savanah stormed over. "What's got into you, Daddy?"

My father gave me a 'let's humor her' grin before turning to her. "What's upsetting you? Your monthly allowance, which would feed an African village for a year, has run out again?"

"No. But why hold out on this project? I had ideas. I was looking forward to working on the interior design."

"Not while I'm alive, darling. The farmlands employ lots of families in the region. We're filthy rich."

"But the resort will employ a ton of people. Isn't that supporting families?"

"Food, sweetheart. The farms produce quality produce." My father looked at me, and I nodded.

"He's right," I said. "We don't want to start importing all of our food."

"Hmm…" Savanah rolled her eyes and charged off to join my mother who was in deep conversation with Will.

"What's with Mum and Will?" Ethan asked my father as he poured three shots of whisky and passed us each a glass.

Our father was a quiet achiever. Someone I'd modeled myself around. I preferred that to my mother's approach, which was about scheming, coercion, and speeches fit for a podium.

She could have run for office. For her, position in society was all that mattered.

"The truth is they're together," my father said, his eyes moving from Ethan to mine.

"Are you sure?" I asked, gulping down my drink.

He smiled tightly. "I've known about them for a long time. She admitted that a while back."

Ethan's eyes darted from my father to me. His frown deepened, and his body seemed to grow tense. His shock mirrored mine. This unsettling confirmation about our mother's affair shook me to the core.

"Like sleeping together, you mean?" he asked. "And you were going to tell us when?"

"It's up to your mother." My father strolled over to the cabinet and lifted the bottle of scotch. I passed, but Ethan took another.

While the news of our mother's infidelity had rocked us deeply, my father treated the affair as if discussing her replacing an older model car.

"Does this mean you're separating?" I asked.

"We already are. I live here now and she's at Merivale."

"Are you happy with that arrangement?" We stood by the window and my father, like me, stared downward at the sprawling metropolis of rectangles, domes, and spires, with its continual flow of bustling humanity.

"I prefer the city. I like the throng. The energy."

"Does this mean a divorce?" Ethan asked.

My father shook his head. "I'm not willing to carve up the estate. I'm discussing having a heritage layer over Merivale and the adjoining lands."

My mother stormed over. "You do that, and I'll sue the pants off you."

My father smiled. "What, for being a bad husband?"

"That's a start and for not telling me you liked men." She had her hands on her hips.

I side-glanced Ethan, whose jaw had dropped.

"Like, gay, you mean?" Ethan asked.

"Who's gay?" Savanah asked striding in with a coffee.

"Dad, apparently," I said, rubbing my neck.

"Oh, really?" Savanah smiled. "How cool."

Ethan's grimace deepened. "We're not at some showy party, you know. This is our dad."

Savanah turned to our father. "Are we your children?"

Good question.

"Of course, he's your father." My mother puffed. "We *were* once in love."

My father's face softened, and I released the tight sensation in my chest. It warmed me at least to know that we were the product of love. As soppy as that seemed. Being given life should have sufficed, but the romantic in me believed that children produced by love grew up happier.

Were we happier? I regarded my sister as she bit into a fingernail, and my brother, who looked like he'd been in a tornado by how often he'd fingered his hair.

Me? Well, I was happy. Happy to know that I'd saved an Afghani school from being blown up by a suicide bomber, and that I'd saved Theadora from having her virginity auctioned off to some dirty fucking pig.

"How long, Dad?" Ethan asked. My normally unflappable brother had never looked so serious.

"A while now." He gave me an apologetic smile.

"Like did you just wake up one day and decide you liked men?" Savanah asked.

"Mm… well."

"Yep, he was cheating on me," my mother said. "And that's emotional abuse, in answer to your earlier question about my suing you." She pointed at my father's flinching face.

"It's not, darling because you've been sleeping with Will for just as long."

The three of us collapsed onto chairs. Talk about airing a family's dirty secrets.

"Come in, Will," my mother called out.

He walked in sheepishly. Ten years younger than my mother, William had been my father's partner for twenty years. A mathematical whizz with an astrophysics degree, he set up a hedge fund management business with my father when Will was in his mid-twenties.

Will sat down and held my mother's hand. She looked at him, and her intensity softened into a subtle but warm smile.

"So, Dad's gay, and Mum's a cougar," Savanah said, smiling as though the family just received some kind of societal accolade. "Cool."

"Oh, come off it, Savvie. This isn't some fucking Netflix remake of *Dynasty*." Ethan shook his head. He turned to me. "What do you think?"

"I suspected Mum with Will. They've been close for a long time. Always sitting next to each other at dinners. Walks on the grounds. I mean, it was pretty damn obvious. And Dad… well…" I looked over at my father, sensing how difficult this discussion was for him.

"Well, what?" Ethan pressed.

"I don't know. Maybe." I knitted my fingers. I'd seen my father walking out of a well-known gay club one night just before I left for my last tour. Something I didn't feel the need to share, even with all the intimate details of our parent's relationships being shared.

"Does that mean you're going to go all Elton John and start wearing outlandish jackets at our family functions?" Savanah asked our father.

He smiled at her. "I think I'll stick to my tweeds for now."

"This will become a marriage of convenience then?" I asked.

My mother looked at Will and then my father. "Not sure. Now that it's all out, I would like a divorce. But your father's being obstinate about developing."

"That land has been in my family for hundreds of years. I'm not about to turn it into a millionaires' playground."

"Mm... we'll see," my mother said, looking at Will, who gave her his signature understated but supportive smile.

I walked out of the room knowing we hadn't heard the end of it.

CHAPTER 11

Thea

THINGS WERE LOOKING UP. A career I'd desired for a long time was now within my grasp. I'd passed the entrance exam with flying colors, and now I was enrolled in a music teaching degree. Only a bike ride away, the college was just outside of Bridesmere.

To celebrate, I went to my favorite café in the village, ordered a cupcake and coffee, and called Lucy.

"Hey, girlfriend." I giggled.

"Hey, sweetie. How's life in billionaire heaven?"

"It's my day off. But guess what?" My voice bubbled over with joy. "I got into a course."

"That's great. You mean a teaching degree?"

"Yep. I sat for the music exam, and I knew all the pieces from boarding school. My written exam went well too."

"You went to boarding school?" she asked.

"Yep."

"Your mother must be loaded," she said.

"Yep. Rich and snobby. Not a nice person." Despite knowing Lucy now for three years, I'd never discussed my mother with her.

"At least you've got one."

"I'm sorry about your mother." A note of sympathy touched my words.

"That's okay, love. So how long's the course?"

"It's three years part-time. Mainly online but there's class time and piano lessons, and the college is close enough for me to ride my bike."

"You've got a bike?"

I laughed at her surprise. I wasn't exactly consistent when it came to exercise. "It belongs to the hall."

"The hall?"

"Merivale Hall, the house where I work. Everyone calls it the hall. Anyway, it's like a community bike. When I asked if I could borrow it, the caretaker virtually gave it to me. It's a buzz riding along the leafy paths."

"That's awesome, sweetie. So tell me, how's your hot billionaire?"

"He's not my anything." I fiddled with my cup. "I haven't seen him for a couple of days, which is good in a way, because I find it hard to concentrate when he's around."

She chuckled. "When are you coming to town?"

"Mm... not for a long time if I can help it."

"Your mother's not asking after you?"

"No." I plucked at the pilling on my cardigan. "I don't care."

To avoid falling into a rabbit hole of depression, I tried not to think about my mother's lack of interest. I went out of my way to avoid those movies about families that hugged excessively and screamed with joy over the silliest things. Their only drama being curtain choice or something equally trivial that had them speed-dialing their therapists.

Seated outside where I could get a view of the pier, I stretched out my legs onto a bench, when I saw Declan walking my way.

His eyes landed on mine, and I nearly dropped my phone.

Get a fucking grip. He's only a man. Mm... but what a man. And does he have to look like that?

"Hey, Luce, I have to go. I'll call you soon."

I closed the call quickly and wiped my mouth just in case I'd dribbled chocolate icing on my chin. Or was that drool? My bodily responses to this man were insane.

What happened to Ms. Cool, Calm, and Collected around hot men? I'd always been the one to hold up Lucy when she was about to collapse from some hot guy giving us the eye.

Great-looking guys didn't do that to me.

Until now.

"Theadora," he said, with that resonant husk that reverberated through me, tugging at my nipples.

Catching a whiff of his cologne, I felt a throb between my legs again.

Although I hadn't shared this with Lucy yet, in a way I felt shy about it, I'd finally had my first orgasm. All it took was imagining Declan groping my tits while his hard, naked dick rubbed against me, and I came so hard I virtually chewed through the pillow to avoid screaming.

What next, a vibrator?

If Declan Lovechilde continued to look at me with those lingering gazes that registered straight to my core, I would have to resort to something drastic, like getting a boyfriend.

"Mr... I mean... Declan," I stammered. It felt strange calling him by his first name, but he'd insisted, and we had a history, stashed away in my subconscious, going on how my body responded to his male scent.

"Enjoying the sights?" he asked, pointing at the pier and boats that swayed in the breeze.

"I love it here," I said.

He looked down at my cupcake. "Mind if I join you? I could use a coffee."

"Oh... of course."

I hoped he hadn't caught the waver in my voice. And oh shit, my cheeks scorched again. What was it about this man? My brain seemed to scatter into pieces around him.

Okay, yes, he was built like a beast. A very sexy, just-enough-hair-on-the-chest version. His eyes robbed me of speech, including those fleshy lips that he often thumbed over. And his voice. Oh my god, that voice. And don't get me started on his strong thighs and butt in those Speedos. Phew. And when did I start talking to a make-believe person?

"Can I get you another?"

"Um... sure, why not." My mouth trembled into a smile.

As I watched him stride like a man who owned the world into the café, I took deep, calming breaths so that he wouldn't think me completely stupid, because that's what I became around him.

He returned and sat down. His long legs stretched out in front of him. His blue eyes twinkled like the sea before me. I seemed to interest him. But why? He could have had any woman he liked.

"I'm glad I've seen you. I'm looking for a maid."

"Oh? In London?" I asked, unsure if that's what he meant.

"Just five minutes from here. I live in a converted church."

"Oh." I nodded to stop my wobbling head. That's how it felt while his eyes seared into me. Even a normal conversation with him did strange things to my heartbeat, resembling an avant-garde rhythm section.

He studied me with a crooked smile. "You look surprised."

"I imagined some slick penthouse in London."

"My only home in London you've stayed in." He raised an eyebrow.

"Oh, of course. Mayfair." I smiled weakly. "That was an odd morning. I had to ask someone walking a dog where I was. They looked at me as though I'd landed from another planet."

He lowered his cup and wiped his mouth with a serviette. Even that gesture made me feel a throb between my legs.

"You should have waited. I wish you had." There was a penetrating need in his eyes that shook me.

"Why?" I frowned.

"Well for one, I would've learned more about your situation. I could've helped. And had I known what had taken place, I would've reported it to the cops. You were drugged. That's a crime. As is trying to sell a woman without her consent."

His reminder of that night felt like cold fingers creeping up my spine.

"I'm sorry for being quick to judge." His eyes softened, and I nearly dropped my cup. "I shouldn't have jumped to conclusions based on how you were dressed."

"We all do it." I shrugged. "Anyway, I couldn't have gone back there. Even now, just talking about that place gives me the chills."

"I bet it does. What a nightmare for you." He brushed his sharp jaw. "I did wonder about you."

His gaze hijacked my senses again, making my face burn. I wish I'd worn some makeup.

"Did you?" I looked down at my hands to avoid those eyes that were making me dizzy. "I hate thinking that you thought I was a working girl all those months."

"I don't judge women who work professionally." His brow raised.

"That's important. Women have a right to do what they want with their bodies as long as they're not forced by creeps."

His eyes darkened. "I hope that's never happened to you, other than that night, of course."

I looked away and shook my head ever so slightly. I wasn't about to tell him about my sleazy stepfather.

Sucking in some air, I needed to steer this conversation away from the intimate, if only to start breathing properly again.

"I'm not sure I've got time to work anywhere else at the moment."

With those big shoulders in that blue polo that emphasized his muscles, he reminded me of Superman about to burst forth and conquer the world. Only Declan Lovechilde had managed to conquer my sanity.

I added, "What with the hall and college..."

Who needs sleep when a handsome billionaire is inviting you into his home, you dork?

"College?" His perfect brow furrowed.

"I've just enrolled at Hildersten College."

"That's just up the road," he said. "Nice and close."

He sounded relieved, which took me aback in a nice way.

I played with my cup. "I've been wanting to study for a long time. And now, thanks to my job here, I'm earning enough to cover the fees.."

"What are you studying?" He sipped his coffee and then ran his tongue over his lips, and I had to remind myself to concentrate on our conversation and not his mouth.

"Music education. I plan to teach music."

His face lit up with wonder as though I'd admitted to being at the forefront of scientific exploration into immortality.

"You play music?"

I nodded. "Piano. I learned at boarding school."

"Then you obviously went to a good one."

I sighed. "I did."

His brow creased. "You sound sad."

I'd taken a sip of my cappuccino and licked the froth from my lips. His eyes seemed to home in on that action, and I noticed them hood.

Mm.

"I don't like to think of those years."

"Boarding schools can be sad, lonely places." He nodded pensively. "I hated my experience there."

Our eyes held longer than normal for a pair having a casual conversation.

Were we being casual? For me it felt like he was unraveling the straitjacket I'd been wearing for years, making me oversensitive to everything.

"What age group do you plan to teach?"

"Maybe little ones. It might be easier. Not too many hormones to deal with." I chuckled.

He grimaced. "Wild teenagers. Not nice. They treat the arts as an excuse to mess around."

A few minutes of silence followed as we drank our coffees, giving me time to consider his offer. I could use the extra cash, and who needed two days of rest?

"When were you needing someone to clean?"

"Whenever possible. I just need a few hours, here and there." He sounded hesitant.

"Are things okay?" My brows knitted.

As he held my eyes again, he seemed a little lost. I saw a new face. Still striking, but like someone who'd struggled. The more I got to know him, the deeper he struck me. Considering he was a former soldier, I imagined he'd seen his share of battles.

"I'm kinda scattered at the moment." His mouth curled at one end. "Since returning from my tour, I'm having trouble focusing."

"It must have been horrible constantly having to look over your shoulder."

He knitted his fingers. "Somewhat. Hypervigilance challenges one's sanity. That's for sure. You go without sleep and food sometimes. You find yourself in the roughest terrain, scaling mountains. One wrong move or decision and it's over."

"I can't imagine what that's like," I said, noticing his face drawn and distant as though reliving something dreadful. I wondered whether he suffered from PTSD.

"I'll be fine. Once I get my projects up and running." A faint smile warmed his face again.

"I guess I could come over today or tomorrow and do some cleaning if you like." That spontaneous response had forgotten to consult my rational brain. *Me in his personal space?*

He studied me closely. "Only if you have the time. I'll pay double what you're getting at Merivale. And to be honest, I'd prefer to employ someone I know and trust. I don't like strangers in my space."

"I get that. I'm a very private person myself." Those tiny places I'd shared with virtual strangers came to mind. "To be honest, this is the first time I've had my own living space. It's given me a new lease on life."

He looked at me with a hint of sympathy. "I'm so pleased you saw fit to apply for the job. You were working at the family hotel, I believe."

"Yes. I loved it there. The tips were amazing. But it's nicer here."

Another long pause followed. Our eyes met again.

"I'd like to clear out the space for an office. I've got a project to launch."

"When would you like me?"

Oops.

"I meant..." I pulled a tight smile.

"I got you the first time." He grinned. "Whenever you can fit me in."

"I can come over now if you like." I pointed at my bike.

"Oh, you're riding. I like to ride too. There are some nice riding paths around here." His smile lit his face, and he had a boyish, sweet shine about him. A new look. One of many. Declan Lovechilde had a few layers to him. If only my body would stop burning up around him, I'd like to get to know him more as a person. He struck me as a good man. Not that typical bossy billionaire who snaps fingers and expects everyone to drop to their feet. Having never met one in the flesh, perhaps I'd read one billionaire romance too many.

"I've discovered a few nice paths already. And the ride from Merivale's fantastic."

He pointed at a cobbled laneway surrounded by cottages with thatched roofs and sleepy willows. "You can follow me if you like. It's only a five-minute walk from here."

He stood by as I lowered to unchain my bike.

"That's probably unnecessary round here. Most people know each other," he said.

My damp fingers fumbled about with the metal wheel for the right sequence. Normally an effortless procedure, but with Declan there my clammy fingers became uncoordinated.

After I managed to unlock it, Declan took the bike. "Here, let me wheel it for you." He grinned. "Unless you want to jump on the handlebars while I ride."

I giggled. "That sounds dangerous."

He raised his eyebrows, and our eyes held again.

What did he think I meant by dangerous?

CHAPTER 12

Declan

I WHEELED THE BIKE into my front yard and leaned it against a tree.

"My god, you live here." Theadora stared up at the blue-stone gothic building which I now called home.

I nodded. "When it came up for auction, I snapped it up. I had an architect repurpose it."

Her beautiful brown eyes filled with wonder, and my heart beating faster than usual had little to do with the uphill ride.

I hadn't even known I wanted a maid until I saw her sitting at the café looking gorgeous with that thick, raven hair in a messy bun. Theadora licking the top of her cupcake aroused all kinds of dirty thoughts, like having that little pink tongue sliding over my dick.

"Come on in." I opened the front door and stepped out of the way.

We entered the open-plan space with beamed ceilings and stained glass windows that splashed beams of color over the freshly painted white walls.

"Incredible." She turned on the spot, taking in the rectangular room, big enough to host a large crowd.

I crossed my arms. "I like being here."

She pointed at the windows showing scenes of angels and other heavenly bodies. "It's very religious."

I smiled. "It was a church."

"Are you a believer?"

I shrugged. "I'm open. I like to think there's a god. I've done some praying in my life."

She nodded thoughtfully, her eyes soft and filled with questions. "Me too."

"What? Praying or hoping there's a god?" I had to ask.

"Both." Her eyes met mine, and I held her there. I had to get to know this girl. If only to understand why she had such a hold on me.

Her curves and pretty face, certainly. My bodily desires had the edge there. But there was more to this attraction than lust.

Her eyes seemed so deep and filled with all kinds of stories. Not shallow and seeking the next bit of fun, like Cleo or some of the girls I'd dated.

I moved to what was once an altar and now my kitchen. "Can I offer you a drink? A juice?"

"Just water would be nice." She turned around again, staring up at the vaulted ceiling.

The view of her jeans hugging her curvy arse made me forget what I was doing.

How am I meant to concentrate with her around?

A bad idea. I should have called the agency and employed someone who didn't look like Theadora, especially in that tight blouse and those jeans.

I handed her a glass of water. "I'll show you the rest of the space if you like."

We stepped into the back of the church to an adjoining room with a view of the garden, which I used as a study.

"I'm sorry it's a bit of a mess."

"Well, that's why I'm here," she said, rolling up her shirt sleeves and sounding assertive. Her pretty eyes lighting up put a smile on my face too.

I liked her spark, despite her fragile moments. I'd noticed her remote downward glances like something haunted her. My soul understood that expression well.

Her body called out to me too. I wanted to savor her. Ravage her.

As she bent over to pick up a box, I caught a glimpse of her cleavage, and my cock just grew an extra inch.

THE ARCHITECT WALKED AROUND the land and pointed to where a forty-bed dorm would go.

Curious as always, Ethan joined me as I discussed the design of the boot camp with the designer.

"You're really doing this?" he asked, nodding a greeting to Hamish.

"You bet," I said.

"Boot camps are popular, I suppose." Ethan's face sparked up. "Hey, why not open it up to the public? You know, like a kind of mini *Survivor* training ground." He waited for my response and then added, "I know, troubled youth transformed into upstanding community do-gooders within a month. A kind of *Biggest Loser* meets *Survivor*. Without the pounds to shed, of course." He laughed, pleased with himself.

"What did you sprinkle on your Muesli this morning?" I asked.

"I don't do Muesli." He pulled a face. "Can't stomach all that squishy cereal muck."

I chuckled. Ethan and his bouncy outlook on life at least made for some entertainment.

We spent the next hour being shown the dimensions and where the gym and various partitions would be placed.

I shook Hamish's hand. "That looks great. When can they start?"

"I'll speak to the builders today and get back to you."

After Hamish left, I turned to Ethan. "This is a serious venture, you realize."

"I know that. But will it turn a profit?" He followed me along as we walked back to the hall.

"The government grants are a done deal. They'll cover the running costs. I've got my finger in a few pies. And there's the farming element of this project."

We entered the hall, where, in the distance, Theadora dusted shelves filled with valuable antiques passed down from generations of Lovechildes.

Ethan paused and cocked his head towards her. "Now that's a pretty sight. She fits that shirt well. I'm about to ask her to polish the silver in my room."

I grabbed him by the arm and dragged him into another room.

"Listen, Ethan, she's out of fucking bounds. You got that?" I stared him square in the face, and he returned the same cocky grin he wore when as boys we'd fight over who was going to bowl first in family cricket games, or him cheating at tennis.

"Have you fucked her?" he asked.

"No."

"But you'd like to, wouldn't you?"

"She's not that type of girl," I said. "She's inexperienced." I didn't hide my frustration, because had Theadora not been a virgin, I would have asked her out by now.

Although I wasn't looking for a girlfriend, seeing Theadora bending over had me in a state of constant arousal.

"How do you know?" he asked.

I told him about the incident in the laneway.

He whistled. "She must have looked fucking nice in a corset."

You're telling me... more than fucking nice. Like a lifetime of wet dreams and more.

"She was drugged. She can't remember a thing."

"How heroic of you," he said. "I don't stand a chance then. If she owes someone a fuck, it's you."

I grabbed his arm roughly. "Don't talk about her like that."

"Hey, you're acting all alpha." He pulled away. "She's a virgin. I've never had one of those." He grimaced. "Tight."

"You go near her..." I pointed a finger into his face.

He held up his palms. "I like them a bit older and more experienced myself. But she's got nice tits."

"I mean it. No games, Ethan."

He jumped back. "Hey. Cool it. I'm playing with you. I can get my own girls." He adjusted his shirt.

"Anyway, it's not all about tits, you know." I took a deep breath. This wasn't an easy argument because I'd jerked off more often than normal with Theadora's buttons undone and her tits bouncing up and down in my face. A fantasy that just kept following me into the dark of night and the shower.

"You better ask her out then. I've noticed some of the male staff checking her out."

I puffed out in frustration. So had I. How could anyone not look at Theadora like that?

Just as I was about to move off, I heard my father and mother in the front sitting room that adjoined the main entrance.

I looked at my brother, and he lowered his brow. We walked towards the door when my mother said loudly, "You can't do this to the family. I will sue the pants off you."

Our father laughed. "Do your best. While I'm alive that land remains with the farmers."

"I can cite emotional abuse. That you were always gay and only married me for show."

"And you were screwing my business partner behind my back. You've been with Will for how long exactly?"

"We're going to develop."

"Over my dead body, you are." He stormed out and nearly bumped into us.

He ran his hands through his hair and gave an apologetic smile. "I guess you both heard that?"

Just as I nodded, Amy, one of the maids known for wagging her tongue, stepped out from the shadows and, seeing us there, smiled meekly before slipping away.

I turned to my father. "This is turning into a bloody soap opera."

He smiled sadly. "Come for a walk both of you. I want to explain."

We stepped outside onto the lush grounds.

"Let's head this way." He pointed at the green meadows that reached over to the sea. "I've always loved this aspect of Merivale."

"Me too," I said.

He stopped walking. "I'm sorry you had to learn about me this way."

"It has come as a bit of a shock," Ethan responded.

My father turned to me, and I added, "Look, each to their own. But I did wonder if we had another father."

"You're my children. I loved your mother." He'd aged a lot. Those deep blue eyes, the same as mine and Savanah's, confirming we were his offspring, looked tired, suggesting he was living life to its fullest.

He pointed at the fields with grazing livestock. "When I was a boy, I loved roaming around the land, and all the animals. I was particularly fond of the horses. I loved watching the trainers breaking them in. Powerful stallions up on their hind legs." He smiled. "Saw one of them knock out a rider once. Not a pretty sight." He paused. "Your grandfather made me work on the farms when I was a teenager, during my summer holidays. He believed that hard work made a person. And although I would have preferred to knock around with my friends, I enjoyed it."

His eyes filled with tears, and Ethan looked at me and grimaced.

"Anyway, I hope you can still see me as your father. A man who loves his family."

"Dad, you will always have my respect. And to be honest, I'm relieved you're not signing off on Mum's proposal."

My father hugged me and then turned to Ethan. "And what about you?"

Ethan shrugged. "Look, it's all come as a shock, of course. I'm not sure where I stand. I need time for it all to sink in. Not you being gay. I mean the land and Mother's plan."

My father reflected on this for a moment. "That's your prerogative."

"I'm relieved that you're not signing off on it," I admitted. "Otherwise, we'd be looking at trucks and cranes and not a flock of grazing sheep."

"But you're about to bring in developers," Ethan said.

"There are no farms there."

My father smiled. "It's a grand idea. The army has served you well." He turned to Ethan. "I want a hotel in New York. I've got some agents scouting around for the right building. Heritage, of course. We need to stick to our brand of old-world luxury."

"I'll scout around if you like," Ethan said in his customary upbeat manner. "I love New York."

"Let's talk about that later." My father looked out into the distance. "I'd like you both to meet Luke. He's a lawyer. We've been together for two years now. If I set up a dinner, would you like to come and meet him? Savanah's keen on it."

Ethan and I nodded at the same time.

My father smiled. "Great, I'll make a booking."

After giving each of us a hug, he walked back to the hall.

Ethan turned to me. "That was intense."

"You're not kidding."

"How's this going to work?" He opened out his hands. "Can you imagine Christmas? It will be like a dog's breakfast."

"At least it's out in the open, I suppose. Mother being with Will came as no surprise."

"Our mother with a boy toy. Ick." He winced. "Something tells me Mother's not going to give up. She's got her heart set on that resort."

I puffed out a breath. "Mm... she doesn't do 'no'."

"I can't get over the fact that Dad's gay," he said as we ambled back towards the hall.

"I saw him outside a gay club one night in London a few years back," I said.

Ethan stopped walking. "And you were going to tell me when?"

"I wasn't sure what to make of it. I thought he could have been there with a client."

"It feels weird to me," Ethan admitted.

"It does. But these are modern times. Sexuality's a fluid thing now."

"Is it for you?" Ethan smirked.

I shook my head decisively. "I like pussy."

We just stepped into the door and discovered Theadora.

"Speaking of," Ethan whispered.

I tossed him a dirty look to which he returned a chuckle before flitting off.

CHAPTER 13

Thea

I WAS STRIPPING BACK Declan's bed when he entered. "You've been at it all morning. How about a cup of tea?" His eyes seemed to sparkle in the morning light streaming through the windows. "I just picked up some cinnamon buns, freshly baked from the local bakery."

It took me a moment to respond. He was so fucking handsome my brain fogged. "That sounds delicious. I guess I could use a break." I placed the sheets in a laundry basket. "Let me make the tea."

"No. You deserve a break. Let me." He smiled sweetly and off he strode with those powerful long legs. Bulging thigh muscles flexed, while his jeans hugged his butt. I tried not to stare, but my eyes had a mind of their own.

I joined him in the kitchen and sat up at the wooden bench, where he passed me a cup of tea and a bun on a plate.

I lifted the willow-patterned cup and sipped. "That's perfect. Thanks."

"It's a sunny day. Why don't we sit outside in the courtyard?" he said.

I followed him outside the glass doors onto a cobbled area with a glass table, wrought-iron chairs, roses in ceramic pots, and a winged angel sculpture.

"It's lovely out here," I said, as sunshine caressed my face.

He pulled out a chair for me. "I like it."

For a minute or two, we sipped our tea in silence.

I took a bite of the soft bun that melted in my mouth, setting off a delightful explosion of spice on my tongue. "Mm... this is delicious."

He smiled. "I'm a sucker for Milly's buns." His equally delicious mouth curved at one end. "I meant..."

I laughed. "I got you the first time. They are scrumptious. I better watch it; I tend to put on weight."

"You've got nothing to worry about there."

His gaze trapped mine, and my cheeks fired up again.

"I hope you didn't hear me and my brother talking yesterday."

The part about you liking pussy?

"No," I lied.

His expression softened like he'd been pardoned for some kind of crime. "Good. Ethan can get a bit below the belt sometimes."

"I'm used to men like Ethan," I said. He raised an eyebrow, and I elaborated, "When I worked at the hotel, I noticed how lots of wealthy guys hadn't quite made it to adulthood."

He chuckled. "Yep. I've met a few like that myself. Ethan is in that privileged, yet-to-mature cohort, but he's a good sort, underneath that frisky exterior."

I nodded. "I can see that. He seems like he skips through life. I guess if I was filthy rich, I might just do that too."

"How are your studies going?"

"My assignment's going well. I have my first practical today. I'm looking forward to playing the piano again."

"There's a piano at the hall," he said.

"I've noticed."

"Feel free to use it."

"Your mother won't mind?" Mrs. Lovechilde intimidated me.

"Why would she?"

"She seems rather strict."

"Is she speaking down to you? I know she can be tough on the staff." His eyes shone with concern.

"It's nothing I can't handle. But I've seen her running her finger along shelves, checking for dust. I do my best to be thorough."

He smiled sympathetically. "Although she's difficult at times, having played piano herself, she's got a soft spot for music."

"You weren't musical?" I asked.

"I dabbled in guitar." He took a bite of his bun and again I had to look away. Even watching him eat was like an erotic act. He swallowed and wiped his lips. "I played bass in a few bands when I was younger, much to my mother's chagrin. I'm more into the outdoors these days, and I like reading. When I can get the time."

"You read?"

He grinned at my stunned response. "Don't sound so surprised."

I returned an apologetic half-smile.

"It started with Enid Blyton books when I was in third grade," he added. "And after that, I never stopped. I'm sure it was the Biggles books that got me obsessed with flying." He sniffed. "Books gave me an escape. Boarding school wasn't the greatest experience." His lips curved into a tepid smile.

A pang touched my heart. I got the feeling he understood the pain of being alone.

I smiled sadly. "We share that."

"Your parents ran a business?" His deep searching stare almost blinded me. Those eyes so many shades of blue, I found it hard to speak.

"Not as such. It was just my mother and"—I hesitated for a moment. Even mentioning that man twisted a nerve—"stepfather."

"Was he bad?"

My brows knitted. "Did I show something then?"

He nodded. "I got a vibe that he was unpleasant."

"He was more than unpleasant."

A line appeared between his eyebrows. "Was he mean to you?"

"You could say that." I fidgeted with my cup. "Let's just say that my mother did me a favor by sending me away to boarding school."

"Did he touch you?" His eyes darkened with anger like he was about to hurt someone.

I bit my lip.

How did this become so damn personal?

A tear slid onto my cheek, and I quickly wiped it away.

He took my hand.

"You can tell me. I'll pay for any legal fees."

My mouth dropped open, and I remained speechless. He might as well have offered to kill my stepfather. "No. Not that. I couldn't stand it." An embarrassing shrill affected my speech. Taking a deep breath, I calmed myself. "He didn't go all the way."

"How old were you?" His voice strained.

I took a deep breath. "He moved in when I was thirteen." I dug into my palms. "He'd look at me in a creepy way. My mother noticed and instead of throwing him out she sent me away."

His eyebrows knitted as he shook his head. "You're fucking kidding me."

"When he drank, he'd come into my room, and after I screamed for him to leave, my mother would have words with him. He always blamed alcohol. I was seventeen when he tried to rape me, so I ran away and haven't spoken to or seen my mother since."

That cool, abridged outline didn't even scratch the surface of what really happened. I couldn't articulate the vile nature of what he did to me, and how shame and disgust took possession of my young heart, turning me into a penniless orphan.

I couldn't tell him how I woke with my stepfather's sweaty hands all over my tits. His sozzled breath on my neck, while clawing at me. His finger entered me roughly, while he grunted and breathed heavily. "Fuck... you feel nice."

I screamed. Pushed him away and had to fight him off as his hands stuck to me like tentacles.

My knuckles throbbed with sharp pain after I punched him in the face then scrambled for my dressing gown and ran into the night. At the time, my insomniac mother, having taken sleeping tablets, was dead to the world. Accusing me of being a flirt, she didn't believe me when I called her the next day from a friend's house, where I'd stayed after she'd offered me a couch to crash on.

"What's his name?" Declan asked with an icy tone that made my spine stiffen.

I rose, agitated, wringing my hands. "I don't want you getting involved. I shouldn't have told you." Shaking my head, I felt tears threatening to erupt. "I don't know why I did."

He came and wrapped his arms around me. Instincts told me to break away, but I was too fragile to fight it. Instead, I collapsed against him and drew in his warmth like someone who'd been dunked in ice.

Without warning, a wall holding back a river of emotion burst, and I found myself weeping and shuddering in his arms.

It was as though pent-up emotion poured from me all at once. The more his arms tightened around me the more I sobbed.

Only Lucy knew about what had happened to me, and even with her I didn't cry. I'd learned to bottle things up. If only for my sanity, because I knew that if I allowed myself to dwell on things, I'd lose the plot.

However, here I was bawling my eyes out and spilling my emotions all over a man I hardly knew.

As I calmed myself down, my cheek remained on his hard chest while his strong arms continued to hold me. I felt safe. Like he would protect me. It was strange. I could have stayed there and fallen asleep.

I'm not sure how long it lasted, but I eventually took a deep breath and unraveled myself from his arms.

A strand of my hair had come loose, and he tucked it behind my ear, while his eyes penetrated mine deeply.

Brushing my damp cheeks with my arm, I snapped out of my trance. "I'm sorry."

He towered over me. His eyes were soft and filled with sympathy. "No. Thank you for sharing that. I needed to understand why you wear fear on your face."

I had to step away from him to gather my senses. His scent was drugging me again.

"What do you mean?" I couldn't let that comment pass.

"Just that I saw it when Ethan was hitting on you. I'm sorry about my brother, by the way."

"No. It's okay. I'm used to it."

He smiled gently. "I'm sure you are."

"I meant not like that." I took a breath. "I didn't realize I gave off that damsel-in-distress vibe."

"I don't see you like that. There's a strong woman in there, for sure. But you're right not to trust certain men."

There we remained in silence while I searched for my voice. "I guess I should get back to cleaning." My tongue was in a tangle. I couldn't believe we'd entered such a personal space.

Had I really told him about my stepfather?

What the hell had possessed me?

I couldn't resist this man, but I had to. I needed my job more than I needed to fall into the arms of a beautiful man.

And he was beautiful. In more ways than just physical.

I cleaned the bathroom, which was always pretty clean anyway. Was there anything about this Declan man that wasn't perfect?

I wish there was because I was seriously falling hard for my boss.

DECLAN WAS IN HIS study at his desk writing when I knocked at the door. "I'm off now."

He rose and walked me to the door. "Can I drive you to school?"

"No. I've got the bike. I'm good." He kept staring at me again, and all of a sudden I felt naked. "Thanks for everything. And I'm sorry if I got a bit emotional earlier on."

His gaze radiated warmth and empathy. "Thanks for sharing. I can see you've been through a lot. If there's anything I can do, please reach out. Even if you want to talk. Anything."

I swallowed back another lump. "I can't believe how kind you are. The work. The generous wage. That's all helping."

He nodded. "Take care on that bike."

I smiled and waved.

CHAPTER 14

Declan

As THEADORA RODE OFF, I sat there watching her from my study window which looked out onto Winchelsea Lane. Her movements were smooth with her body pitched forward, and my body was on fire, as always, after spending time with her. However, this time, it was the hideousness of her upbringing that disturbed me. I struggled to focus. All I could see was her innocence threatened by this monster parading as her stepfather.

I called the hotel and asked to speak to HR. "This is Declan Lovechilde."

"Mr. Lovechilde, how can we help?"

"I'd like the file of a former employee, Theadora Hart."

"I will get onto that now."

"Thanks." I closed the call.

Paedophilia sickened me. And while Thea might have been seventeen when he tried to rape her, just hearing about how he'd tried to touch her when she was younger confirmed that the guy had to be taken down.

He'd only do it again.

My MOTHER WAVED HER finger at Amy, who then scurried off.

"I hope you're not giving the staff a hard time again." I kissed her cool cheek.

"She's been slacking again. I asked her to clean my room, and it's still not done."

"Just be patient." I followed her into the front drawing room. "On that note, Theadora, the new girl."

Her eyes narrowed slightly. My mother and her suspicious mind. "What about her? And yes, I know she's very pretty. So if you're thinking of bedding her, do so in your own time and space. But don't bring it here."

I shook my head. "Why do you always expect the worst from people?"

"You're single. You're handsome. You're a billionaire." She sat on the floral sofa facing a bay window that looked out to the sea. "When are you going to marry?"

I took a deep breath. "I've only just returned."

"You've been back three months. If you marry a nice, wealthy girl, preferably from a peerage, she might pull you into line. I sure as hell can't."

I shook my head. "Why are you like this?"

"I'm your mother. I want what's best for you."

"You want what's best for you, I think. In any case, I'm not interested in marrying anyone. Why don't you pick on Ethan or Savvie?"

"You're the stable one." She picked up a magazine.

My eyes landed on a portrait of a horse against a stunning landscape, one of many original pieces that hung on the yellow walls of that room.

"I was going to say that Theadora's studying to become a piano teacher. I suggested she use the piano here."

She studied me with that scrutinizing stare of hers. She could read my attraction to Theadora. Or was that me guilting over how obsessed I'd become?

"Mm... only when she's not working." She pointed. "And not too early or late."

"I can have the instrument moved to the back."

"You'll need to have the piano retuned if you move it. I can't stand an out-of-tune piano."

I had to smile at my mother's fastidiousness. "Why didn't you continue with your music?"

Gifted on the piano, my mother had studied from an early age. Or so the story goes. My mother rarely spoke of her life growing up. Unlike my dad, who loved sharing his experiences as a boy growing up on that large estate.

"Lovechilde Holdings is a full-time job, Declan. If you and your brother got more proactive, especially now that your father has turned his back on us, I would have time for the piano."

"He hasn't turned his back on us. He just wants to uphold certain traditions."

"You're an idealist like him. That's your problem." She flicked through a magazine specializing in the latest resorts.

"The farms make more than enough money. Why don't you just sit back and enjoy your life? Travel. Play the piano."

She drew her head back and looked stunned like I'd suggested she get a tattoo. "I'm not one for such frivolities. And I plan to make the Lovechilde name synonymous with power and one of the wealthiest families in the world."

I had to laugh at that inflated ambition. "Hello, Elon Musk. Bezos. And goodness knows how many other tech billionaires out there who are always going to be hard to catch up with."

"You don't know what I plan to do. And the last thing I'll do is flit our wealth on rocket launches." She wore an ironic smirk. "I certainly didn't plan for a boot camp at the back of Merivale. What can I do to stop this madness?" She looked over my shoulder, and her face softened.

I turned and acknowledged Will with a nod.

"I see the builders haven't wasted their time," he said in that placid manner of his, which made Will hard to read.

My father's former partner had been with us for as long as I could remember, and now that his relationship with my mother was out in the open, he'd moved into the hall. I'd always liked Will, so despite this latest development, I treated him as I'd always done.

My mother sighed. "See if you can convince him."

I looked at Will. "It's happening. The wood cuts in the middle. There's no access from the camp to the hall."

He just shrugged and handed my mother a file.

"I'll leave you to it then," I said.

"Savanah tells me you're to meet your father's new boyfriend. He listens to you, Declan. See if you can convince him."

I wondered about the urgency in her tone. Why did my mother need this development so badly?

"I'm on his side, Mother." I leaned in and kissed her on the cheek. "I've got to go."

CHAPTER 15

Thea

DECISIVENESS WAS NEVER MY strong suit. I'd knocked twice and still no answer. The key that Declan had given me to his home left an imprint on my clammy palm as I debated whether to let myself in.

I pictured him handing me the key. His stare was deep and penetrating as though that key symbolized something more significant. Something intimate. Everything seemed intimate between us. Even him showing me where the cleaning products were stored.

And then there was that emotional scene in the courtyard yesterday when he'd cradled me in his arms. Even now, as I shifted from leg to leg at his door, butterflies entered my stomach and my heart pounded thinking about it.

Taking a deep, calming breath, I let myself in and scanned the room just as a burglar might. Why did it feel like I was encroaching on his space?

"Hello," I called out repeatedly, as I stepped into that open-space room awash with speckled colors pouring through the arched windows.

A leather sofa rested against the wall, accompanied by shelves of knickknacks. The large TV screen mounted on the wall seemed incongruous amongst the spiritual motifs on the stained glass windows, which, along with the vaulted ceiling, was the only remnant of a church.

I called out again and headed to the laundry where the cleaning products were stored and decided to start with the bathroom.

When I entered, steam hit me in the face. I turned to the mirror and saw Declan with his back to me.

I could see all of him, including a sculpted butt that could have been carved by da Vinci himself. I gulped. And then he turned to the side, unaware of my presence.

He placed one hand on the glass wall and with his other hand on his dick, he bit his lip. His eyes squeezed shut, and his large hand moved up and down his enormous penis. The thick veins popping out against the folds of his skin.

Stunned by this erotic vision of him pleasuring himself, I remained frozen on the spot. Fixated by him biting his lip. His eyes squeezed shut as he pulled on his swollen, veiny shaft.

Snapping out of my trance, I snuck off and shut the door as quietly as I could.

Holy fuck.

Leaning against the wall for support, I was breathing hard. My body was on fire as his large hand wrapped around that engorged penis echoed in my imagination.

I hurried off and made a start on the shelves instead.

My breathing had only just steadied when Declan entered the living room with a towel wrapped around his waist.

Now if I wasn't already a wreck after witnessing him jerking off, I'd become a drooling mess thanks to him parading half-naked as naturally as one would in tracksuit bottoms.

He reminded me of a hunky Hollywood actor with that strong chest, glistening with watery droplets, and bulging muscles.

"Oh. I'm sorry." I almost stumbled back when he finally noticed me there.

He smiled, looking completely unfazed. "Hey. I'm glad you let yourself in."

"I knocked and called out." My cheeks scorched. "If you like I can come back."

"No. Of course not." He strolled into the kitchen. "Can I offer you anything?"

Yes, please put some clothes on before I melt on the spot.

I shook my head, hoping he wouldn't think me a prude for blushing like a virgin at an orgy.

He held my eyes for a moment and then continued to make himself a juice.

To avoid hyperventilating, I left him and started on the bathroom.

It felt intimate being there all of a sudden, but I was there to clean. And that envelope of cash he'd handed me for four hours of work after my last shift incentivized me to accept the work with a big smile.

I'd even managed to save a little. Now that my credit card debts were paid off, my life plan had taken shape. But how could I manage to remain sane around this man and his suggestive gaze? Was that it? Did he want me? Or was I just imagining it?

I had to remain focused. There was my degree and my new life to consider. Independent and self-reliant, I would live a clean life. Okay maybe not so clean where a certain male was involved. Dirty thoughts and fantasies were allowed.

Now I had a brand-new scene to add to my latest fantasy: a damsel-in-distress act that ends in my rescuing hunk fucking me senseless.

I shooshed a strand of hair away from my face. Talk about fucking steamy. And by that, I didn't mean the bathroom mirror I was wiping.

THAT NIGHT AS I lay in bed, my fantasy degenerated into a shower scene from a seedy porno involving a well-hung man fondling and fisting his dick. Declan naturally played the lead.

Thanks to seeing him on the beach that day in those tiny swimming trunks and now him naked, wanking off, I had a persistent throbbing ache between my legs. I'd turned into a seriously horny virgin, who suddenly wanted desperately to have sex.

Close to drawing blood on my lip to quell a shriek, I imagined his big dick pounding me, and an orgasm sizzled down to my toes. For a virgin that was a stretch.

Mm... a big stretch.

Gathering my senses after being showered with a heart-pounding golden release, I felt a sense of relief mixed with frustration.

All it took was a hot, buff male and I'd gone from being frigid all my teen years, to sex starved in the span of two weeks.

But the fact that Declan had awakened my libido made for a sticky situation.

In more ways than one.

He's my boss. One does not fuck their boss. Do they?

I needed to talk to Lucy. Hers would be the voice of reason. Or would it? She didn't exactly think rationally where hot men and sex were involved.

Declan was my savior. My hero. He'd risked his life for me. The simple "thanks" that plopped out of my mouth seemed pretty inadequate.

Maybe a gift? But what?

Your body, stupid. Noooo...

CHAPTER 16

Declan

I PARKED MY CAR in Grosvenor Square and walked up the steps to the three-story Edwardian home overlooking the park, where, as a boy, I kicked a ball around with Ethan.

As I entered the kitchen that overlooked the backyard, I found Ethan by the espresso machine.

"Are you here alone?" I asked.

"Yep." He rubbed his head.

"A big night?"

"You could say that." He pressed a button and black liquid spluttered out. "Do you want one?" He lifted a demitasse.

I shook my head and opened the fridge for a bottle of water.

"So why are you here?" he asked.

"I'm meeting Carson, an army mate." I stared down at my watch. "I just dropped in to get a book I left behind."

"You're going ahead with it then?" He placed the little cup to his mouth.

"Yep. The builders have started."

"Mummy's not happy." Ethan leaned against the wooden cupboards of that large kitchen big enough to cater to five hundred guests.

"It's hard to make Mother happy, save us marrying royalty," I said.

"That's not happening with me. I've got a thing for the unwashed."

I looked at my brother and shook my head. "That can get a bit smelly."

"Yeah. Nice."

I chuckled and rolled my eyes. "You're sick."

He shrugged. "It beats inbreeding."

"So you're looking at siring a child soon?" I headed for the living room.

He followed me, sipping his coffee. "Are you kidding? I'm too young to become a father."

"You're thirty. Dad was twenty when he married." I grabbed my book on organic agribusiness from the coffee table.

"What about you? You're thirty-two," he returned.

"Haven't met the right girl." My eyes rested on the sofa that Theadora had fallen asleep on that night.

Ethan inclined his head. "You seem to have a fondness for busty housemaids the last time I looked."

"Theadora's her name," I said. "Don't refer to her as an object."

"Ooh... it's like that, is it?" His smirk faded into a look of curiosity. "Have you fucked her yet?"

"Although it's none of your business, I haven't."

"But you want to. I can tell." He raised a brow.

"I *am* a man."

What Ethan didn't know and would never know, since I liked to keep my dirty thoughts private, is that I'd been fondling my dick more than usual since meeting Theadora.

"What about Dad?" Ethan shook his head. "Who would've thought? He's arranged that dinner next week for us to meet his partner."

I exhaled. "Each to their own."

"But he's our dad," Ethan pressed.

"So? Homosexuality's everywhere."

He nodded pensively. "Not my thing. I mean they tried me at school." He chuckled. "Public aah... a pederast's feast."

"That's kinda cliché, isn't it?"

"Clichés represent the common paradigm," Ethan said, putting to use his degree in sociology.

"Whatever, but I didn't get hit on at boarding school," I said.

"That's because you were known to punch kids when they played up."

A smile grew on my face. Yep. That was me. Fighting with anyone that got in my face.

"I'm not surprised you joined the army," he said.

"Hey, I'm no longer that guy."

A poor argument given the punch-up with those brutes while saving Theadora. I would have done that a million times over. I shuddered to think what would have happened had I not arrived when I did.

"Are you coming to the dinner?" He roused me out of the rerun of me carrying Theadora's heavy drugged body away from danger.

"Sure. It would be good to meet whoever it is that's making our father happy."

"It's certainly not Mother," Ethan said, returning to the kitchen. "Divorce is in the air," he sang instead of "Love is in the Air."

I chuckled. Ethan was a bit of a clown when he wanted to be. One of his finer points.

"Mm... don't know if it's going to be that simple." I stared down at my watch. "I've got to go."

He saluted me.

One hour later, I walked into a pub off Leicester Square where I found Carson at the bar waiting for me.

It was midday, and a bit early for a drink, but knowing Carson, who had the liver of an Irishman, time didn't matter.

Sipping a stout, he waved for me to join him. "Hey, mate. Good to see you."

I patted his broad shoulder. "You, too."

"What are you drinking?"

"A beer, I guess."

The bar attendant, a woman who looked as old as the pub, ambled over, and Carson ordered drinks and a bowl of chips.

I nodded at the barmaid and then picked up the cool glass. "Can we sit at a table?"

He nodded and followed me to a spot by the window.

Carson was stronger than most, and fearless. One had to be in our squadron. He was the one that came back from our messy tour of Afghanistan and helped pick up the pieces for many of the guys in our unit.

SAS training made us strong physically and mentally, but emotionally that was a whole different story.

Carson still had his demons. He just didn't talk about them.

With what we'd seen and experienced, it was best we kept it between ourselves. When I felt like the ground was crumbling beneath me it was Carson or Travis or one of my other army pals that I reached out to. Not a shrink. Only soldiers understood what we'd been through.

"So, you've got a proposition, I believe?" He sat back and sipped on his dark ale.

The barmaid shuffled over and laid down a plate of hot chips and a tiny bowl of tomato sauce.

He looked up at her and nodded.

He pointed at the bowl. "Help yourself."

I shook my head. "I had a big breakfast."

He smothered a chip in sauce and popped it in his mouth. "Tell me about this new role."

"You'd have to move to Bridesmere. Would that be an issue?"

"Nup." He wiped his mouth with a paper napkin. "Are there plenty of pretty girls?"

I smiled. "I suppose there are, going on Ethan and his endless pursuits."

"Your rich brother goes for commoners?" His dry, gravelly delivery made me chuckle.

"He goes for whoever's pretty and willing. But sure, he doesn't mind getting down and dirty with a farmer's daughter or two."

He sniffed. "I like the sound of your brother."

"You'll meet him soon enough. Ethan's a bit of an airhead, but he's a good guy deep down."

"That's all that counts." He munched on a chip. "So, a boot camp for troubled youth. Mm... I could've used one of those."

Carson had been locked up for stealing cars and minor infringements when he was a teen. Brought up by a single mother, who he preferred not to talk about, he'd grown up on the wrong side of town and learned to make his breakfast by the time he could say "Mama."

"That's why you'd be perfect. You've been there," I said.

Lost in thought, he wore an abstracted expression. "You do realize we're not miracle workers, don't you?"

I smiled faintly. "Look, if we can help three out of forty, then we're still potentially saving a life or two in the future."

"You've got your sights set on low. I reckon we can at least save five." His eyes gleamed back at me, and a smirk grew on his face.

"I know what you're getting at. It's as unknown as a campaign in Afghanistan. But that's the point." The fire of ambition flowed through me. "If we don't do this, no one else will."

"They have similar programs in youth prisons. But hey, count me in."

"Thanks, mate. That means a lot."

"So when do we start?" he asked. "And are you recruiting a few others?"

"Maybe Travis. I'll contract some counselors and maybe a hip-hop and piano teacher."

The piano idea just popped out spontaneously. I was just as surprised as Carson, whose puzzled frown amused me.

"Hip-hop. Sure. I get that. But fucking piano?"

"Well, maybe not that. Music of some sort."

He nodded pensively. "Some of the guys liked to muck around with rap lyrics, so that could work. It's big among street kids."

"As is street dance. I think this could work. I'm also thinking of getting them to grow things."

His brow creased. "Like gardening?"

I smiled at his surprised tone. "Mm... organic veggies."

He nodded slowly. "That might work. Beats teaching them how to fire rifles and play video games."

I sniffed. "That would be counterproductive."

Savanah strutted by the window. Noticing me, she waved, and the next minute, my glammed-up sister entered the pub.

Looking incongruous, in that rundown pub, Savanah wore a short dress that looked painted on. As her older brother, I didn't approve of my sister's femme fatale ways, but she was twenty-seven, despite always being that little sister to me.

Carson's eyes landed on my sister as she swanned over, gliding along effortlessly on shoes that made her stand close to six feet tall.

"Starting a bit early, aren't we?" She pointed at my barely touched beer.

She was right. I wasn't much of a drinker. But I had the odd one socially.

"This is Carson, a mate from the army."

"Oh, you're in the SAS?" She looked impressed, which was mysterious given her dismissive attitude to my involvement in that elite squadron.

"Was," he replied in that deep voice that reminded me of aged whisky and cigarettes.

"This is Savanah, my younger sister."

Carson extended his big hand and took my sister's pale, manicured hand. Her smooth, white skin looked out of place against his large calloused hand.

She checked him out longer than she should have. My sister had a thing for brawny guys. Normally creeps that I had, on occasions, saved her from.

"Can I offer you a drink?" Carson stood up with his empty glass. That was him, a considerate giant. Even little details like taking his glass back to the bar.

That's why he was an important friend. Apart from sharing in the horrors of back-to-back campaigns, he was always there for everyone. Never too tired to help. A team player.

She looked at me as though seeking my approval. "Um... I'd love to, but I've got an appointment."

He lumbered off, and Savanah turned her attention to me.

"He's cute."

"Cute's not how I'd describe Carson. But sure, he's popular with the girls."

"Whatever. I don't date them unless they have at least seven zeroes in their bank accounts."

I shrugged. "And that's landed you well, so far."

"Stop being all protective big brother. I can look after myself," she said, as her eyes followed my friend standing at the bar.

"Look, Savvie, believe it or not, Carson's deep. So no fucking around with his head."

"Hey, chill. One can look, can't they?" She kept her eyes on Carson as he strode back. "Is he part of this boot camp that's got Mummy frothing at the mouth?"

"Would you be more approving if he was?"

She shrugged. "I've always had a weak spot for rugged alpha males. But don't worry, I won't try and jump his bones." She giggled.

I rolled my eyes. "Carson is going to run the whole show for me. I plan to hang in the background."

"You realize this is going to create no end of shit for you? I mean, imagine if things get stolen. The cars. The art." She giggled as though the thought of that entertained her.

"Mother asked me to talk some sense into you."

Carson sat down and with a wry grin commented, "Your big brother's pretty set in his ways."

Savanah pulled a crooked smile. "Tell me about it. He's stubborn, all right."

"He's got a heart of gold. That's all that matters."

I returned a smile.

"I best be off, I suppose. I guess I'll see you around," she said to Carson.

He nodded. "Looking forward to moving close to the sea."

"The village is sweet. A little inbred. But sweet," she said, revealing her snobby attitude.

"Maybe my presence will add to the gene pool," Carson said with his dry wit.

I laughed. "We'll have to warn the girls."

"Mm..." Savanah lifted her chin. "Oh, well, ta-ta." She fluttered her hand and off she went.

Carson watched her leave. "She's something else."

I sensed mutual attraction and although that worried me, knowing Savanah and her man-eating ways, Carson was a grown man who'd had his fair share of adventure. As long as it didn't impact our business arrangement, I'd keep well away.

CHAPTER 17

Thea

DECLAN HAD ASKED IF I could sort out his files, and being my day off from the hall, I agreed.

As always, I rode my bike from the hall, which was around two miles from his home, when a storm came over followed by a huge downpour.

Drenched from head to foot, I let myself into his home. I started to shiver, and since I was alone, removed my clothes and tossed them into the dryer.

I had a quick hot shower, and with nothing to wear, grabbed one of Declan's T-shirts, hoping he wouldn't mind.

The heating was on, making it comfortable walking around barefooted on the luxuriantly warm wooden floorboards.

I grabbed the box of files and popped them into their appropriate bundle—accounts in one bundle and architectural designs for the boot camp in another pile. I lingered over the drawings, impressed by Declan's vision.

Helping damaged teenagers seemed like the farthest thing I would have imagined a billionaire doing.

I thought about my troubled youth when I spent most of my time worrying instead of hanging out with kids my age. I would hide in my room when my mother and stepfather were home, and when he was there alone, I'd jump on my bike and ride for hours.

As a teenager, would boot camp have helped me? I'd spent so many gloomy hours alone, thinking of ending my life.

I took a deep breath, tossed those dark thoughts aside, and continued to place the paperwork in its respective file.

After I finished filing, I headed into the kitchen for a cup of tea and to clear away the dishes.

I opened the dishwasher and bent over to remove the cleaned dishes when "Theadora" sounded over my shoulder.

I turned and nearly dropped a plate.

My mouth dropped and my eyes virtually popped out of my head. I must have looked idiotic.

Who else was I expecting?

Having gone commando, I'd flashed my bum when bending over.

He's seen more than your arse, you idiot.

I gulped back a lump. "Oh, I..."

He rubbed his neck. His face had turned red. Probably not as red as mine. But it was his eyes. Oh, my god, they had changed to a darker blue. How the hell did he do that?

Running his tongue over those lips that had launched a thousand fantasies, he cleared his throat.

"I see you've taken to wearing my clothes."

"Um... aah..." Having turned brainless, I stammered. "I got caught in a storm, riding over here. I had to have a shower, and my clothes, which should be dried now, are in the dryer."

His mouth twitched into the makings of a smile like he found my awkwardness amusing. Or that could have been me misreading him. I wasn't exactly thinking straight after the humiliation of him seeing my naked bum.

"Sure. I don't mind. It suits you. Stay like that if you like."

A nervous giggle scraped my throat. "I'll go and see. They should be dry by now."

I scampered off before he could respond.

Having changed back into my dampish clothes, I entered the living area and found Declan on the sofa reading through documents.

"I finished the filing."

He looked up and his gaze lingered. "Good. Thanks for that. It wasn't too messy, I hope?"

"It was easy. And look, um... about your T-shirt. I got it from the basket of washed clothes. I didn't go through your drawers."

"It's all good. I'm not worried. It suited you." His eyes held mine and my legs went to jelly.

"Um, I best be off then." I went to get my backpack.

"How's your course going?"

"Good, thanks. I'm managing to get things done."

That wasn't quite true. Due to my hours at the hall and now working for Declan, I'd fallen behind. The fact I'd become addled since catching him in the shower hadn't helped.

And now, he'd caught me. He'd seen my big arse.

How fucking embarrassing.

"You're finding the time, I hope?" His eyes drilled into mine as though he could read my thoughts.

"I just need to organize my time a little better, I guess."

He reached into his leather satchel and handed me an envelope heavy with cash.

I stared down with disbelief at all the notes. "This seems too much."

He waved it off. "Don't worry. We're helping each other."

"But hey, look, I'm fully waged now. I'm not expecting charity." My voice cracked.

"It's *not* charity. I *can* afford it. Your help is of real value to me. I'm a very private person. Trust is worth paying for."

"That's understandable. I don't trust people easily either." I shifted from one spot to another.

"Do you want a coffee?" he asked. "Or do you have to run off?"

I glanced down at my watch. "I'd love that, but I'm running late."

"Let me drive you." He put down the file and rose.

I shook my head. "No. It's fine. It's a quick bike ride."

"It's wet outside. Please, let me." He tilted his head, and with that half-smile of his, I would have agreed to anything.

I followed him outside, and he opened the SUV door for me.

"Thanks," I said, climbing in. "This is so kind of you."

"The pleasure's all mine." He smiled sweetly.

As we drove down that leafy laneway, which glowed an iridescent green, I asked, "Do you know the way?"

"Sure do." He took the roundabout up the hill that I often struggled with when riding my bike.

"Are you just learning scales?" he asked.

"I'm meant to practice those on my own. I'm learning a Beethoven piece."

"I spoke to my mother about your using the piano in the west wing sitting room."

"That would be amazing. I thought I might need to buy a portable electric."

"No need," he said. "Use it when you like."

I released a breath, which he must have heard because he glanced at me.

"Is there something the matter?"

Yes. I can't stop playing with my clit when I should be playing the piano.

"No. It's all good. And thanks for your generosity, by the way. All of this wouldn't be possible without it." I choked up.

Regardless of how he'd fired up my libido, Declan was such a kind man. I just wish he didn't look like he'd just stepped off a Hollywood set.

He pulled out in front of the college and turned to look at me. His hand landed on the top of my hand, unleashing an electrical storm through my body. And that was just from his hand resting gently as any good soul's might.

Get a fucking grip.

"I'm not going to rest until those deviants are charged for what they did to you, including your stepfather."

My head turned so sharply I felt a twinge of pain in my neck. "I don't want that."

He gazed into my eyes, and they softened into that swoony turquoise. I almost forgot that we were discussing the monsters of my past.

"Declan, please, I beg you to forget everything I told you." I couldn't breathe all of a sudden. It was like I'd been winded. I could feel a panic attack building as colliding thoughts spun out of control.

I removed my hand abruptly and started to wring my hands, looking anywhere but his handsome face. "I shouldn't have said anything. I'm good now. I've moved on." Although I squeezed muscles to conceal an involuntary spasm from head to toe, I managed a quivery smile as I faced him.

His hand came to rest on mine again, calming my agitation. My heart warmed at how his gaze resonated with sympathy. I think he understood my pain, by the way his eyes reflected tenderness towards me. "Your stepfather needs to be reported." His voice was soft and cajoling in sharp contradiction to this vile subject matter. "And one day soon, I will convince you to do that. He's a fucking worm."

He's more than a worm.

The thought of sitting in a courtroom dredging up those creepy bedroom scenes turned me to ice.

Lost to these disturbing thoughts, I hadn't noticed Declan opening the door and offering me his hand to help me down. That chivalrous gesture helped me snap back to the here and now as I took his large hand.

Declan wouldn't meddle in my past. I'd see to that.

With that in mind, I let go of everything and breathed him in instead.

One didn't need drugs around this man. A whiff of his unique scent wafted through me, and I tripped off to a warm, sensuous oasis away from ugly experiences.

"Thank you. I could have done that myself." My speech center had finally woken up. That cologne was killing me. It should be made illegal for tampering with my motor skills.

"I'll see you at the hall. There's a dinner tomorrow." He smiled sweetly.

Good. All that dark shit forgotten.

"That's right. I have to work."

Despite work eating into my study, I couldn't wait to see him.

I was besotted. Infatuated. Just like the legion of women who encountered Declan Lovechilde, no doubt.

But did he look at them as tenderly as he did me?

CHAPTER 18

Declan

I OPENED MY LAPTOP and scrolled on an image of a woman wearing a corset, bending over without panties. While searching the net, I found a girl in a corset with long dark hair. I'd saved that sexy image and now, tugging at my cock, I imagined that was Theadora, who had a starring role in my wet dreams.

The woman on the screen had her back to me. Her long dark hair undulated down the curve of her spine.

She bent over so I could see her slit. Pumping away, I couldn't get that image of Theadora bending over out of my mind. No panties.

No fucking panties.

What was a man meant to do? Helpless to do anything but perv.

It wasn't just her curvy body that made my pulse race, but also those deep, beautiful eyes. I itched to keep talking to her.

After dropping her off, I returned home, and feeling tense, I opened my laptop seeking relief.

It didn't take long. I nearly burst a vein, I came so hard, groaning like a man fucking for the first time, and this was just my hand. My maid had triggered an insatiable hunger that I needed to do something about. Like soon.

My mother loved hosting dinner parties. Any excuse and she'd have Merivale filled with chatter and laughter. Both my parents were social animals, but my father was unsurprisingly absent.

The only reason why I was even there was because of Theadora, who'd steadily become an obsession.

By now, had she not been a virgin, I would have propositioned her.

The pain in her eyes, when she opened up about her ugly past, had twisted a knot in my heart. If ever I wanted to fucking hurt someone it was after hearing about her stepfather. I wanted his head on a platter.

Pushing that violent thought aside, I focused instead on offering her friendship and support.

How the hell could I try to take her to bed? Wouldn't it seem I was taking advantage of her, given that she worked for me?

Theadora gracing my presence was far more satisfying than ordinary sex, which pretty much described all the sex I normally had.

I sensed that my heart needed to be involved for stars to explode.

Like with all family functions, the guests mingled in the red room, situated at the front of the hall, housing the modern European art collection that my father had spent his life procuring.

The regular guests included: politicians, dignitaries, eminent businessmen, society folk, and their entitled children.

Taking a drink from a tray, I joined my brother, who was chatting to a couple who'd just set up a hobby farm.

Ethan turned to acknowledge me. "Ah. We were just talking about you."

"Nothing too nasty, I hope," I said, nodding at Allen Olsen, an old family friend, and Kelvin, his partner.

"We're fascinated by your latest venture. You might recall that Kelvin worked in law enforcement for years before becoming the lord of the manor." Allen chuckled.

"Mm... More like the slave of the manor," Kelvin quipped, rolling his eyes.

Allen nodded. "That land will kill us. We're trying to clean it up so that we can get organic status to grow produce, but hell, it's got all kinds of nasty chemicals. They might as well have drenched the grounds with DDT."

"I'm expecting to find a whole lot of rotting corpses next," Kelvin added.

Allen giggled. "You wish." He turned to me. "He's a *CSI* tragic. Anything to do with remains and he goes all Sherlock on me. We found a goat's remains. What looked like leg bones and he was agog. All night on the net, studying for clues."

Kelvin smiled sadly. "I was devastated to learn it was only a goat's remains."

Ethan and I shared a grin. Allen and Kelvin were the earthier, if not more eccentric, of those who visited Merivale.

"We like the idea of the boot camp, though. If there's anything we can do, we'd love to volunteer," Kelvin said.

"I'm hoping to set up a garden," I said.

"What a marvelous idea. Get troubled youth working with nature. Veggies or flowers?"

"Maybe both," I said. "I've had the land assessed, and I can obtain an organic farming license, apparently."

Allen glanced at Kelvin. "We're jealous. But please do involve us in any way."

"Are you part of it?" Allen asked my brother.

"I haven't been asked."

I turned to him. "You're always invited to help. You know that."

"Will there be any pretty girls?" he asked.

I rolled my eyes. "He's beyond rehabilitation."

Kelvin and Allen laughed.

"But seriously," Kelvin added. "You might want to organize a charity event or two. You know, to raise some funds for the initiative."

"That thought has crossed my mind." I rubbed my neck.

"I know," Ethan said. "A masked ball. I'll arrange it."

Savanah joined us. "Did I hear 'masked ball'?" She turned to Kelvin and Allen and waved a greeting.

"I was just suggesting we host a charity event here at Merivale," Ethan said.

"Oh, that would be fun," Savanah said. "We've never hosted a masked ball before."

"We're talking about raising funds for the boot camp," I said.

Her mouth turned down. "Mummy will hate that idea." She thought about it for a moment. "But we don't have to tell her."

"I think we do. She lives here most of the time."

"She's off to Antibes next month. She always goes for a two-week holiday in June."

Ethan nodded. "Let's arrange it then. Leave it to me."

I shrugged. "Sure. It's a great idea." I turned to Kelvin. "Thanks for suggesting it."

"We'll help in any way. Just call out. And we do expect an invite," Allen said.

"Of course. You'll be the first on the list," I said.

"Will you invite Carson?" Savanah asked.

"Maybe. He's not really into this scene though."

"No. He's kind of feral." She pulled a face as though she'd touched something dirty.

"Who's this?" Ethan asked.

"He's a former army mate in charge of running the boot camp."

"How nice. Butch soldiers." Allen giggled.

Savanah turned to Allen and smiled. "Shirtless, I imagine."

I rolled my eyes but couldn't exactly protest. Men had been objectifying women forever, so now it was our turn.

The head butler, Gavin, announced dinner.

I hadn't seen Theadora and wondered if she would be serving. I certainly hoped so.

What was I planning here?

The thought of Theadora fucking someone else turned me to ice.

I wanted her, but I also wasn't ready for marriage. To anyone. Rich, poor, or whatever. I didn't see myself as the marrying kind.

When I entered the dining area, Theadora was the first person I saw.

I allowed my eyes to follow as she moved with that subtle sway of her hips. Graceful and sensual at the same time. Her hair was up in a bun, revealing that long swan neck. Her white shirt hugged her plump chest, and with her black, knee-length skirt clinging to her curves, my dick had joined the party.

She noticed me staring and returned a faltering smile, and her cheeks fired up again. I was embarrassing her by ogling. But her effortless sensuality, made sexier by lack of artifice, proved too irresistible.

While the guests sat at the long table, my mother, accompanied by Will, walked in with her close friend, Reynard Crisp. Lost in conversation, she was probably planning some takeover.

Reynard owned gold mines in Africa and was one of the UK's richest men. Tall, with ginger hair and piercing blue eyes, he wore a permanent smug expression.

I kept my conversation with him to a minimum after he puffed on a cigar at one of our family events one night and insisted that climate change was invented by extremists determined to bring the industrialized world to its knees.

In his early fifties, he'd never married. I'd never seen him with anyone at these functions. My mother always hung close, though, which made me question whether they were having a fling, but with Will doting on her, that theory was soon dashed.

I even wondered if Reynard Crisp was gay, having never seen him with a woman at any of the functions, but then Thea entered with a tray, and his eyes zeroed in on her. And there they stayed glued on her, for the whole time she worked.

My attention flitted from him to her, and the skin around my knuckles tightened.

When she bent over the table, his eyes landed on her arse, and my head filled with all kinds of violent thoughts.

I was so preoccupied with wiping that arrogant grin off his face that when Cleo, who, like all our other dinners, made sure she sat close, tapped my arm.

"Hey, you didn't hear a word I said," she whined.

"I'm sorry, what was that?" I kept watching Theadora instead of looking at Cleo.

"That you've got everyone's tongues wagging about your boot camp."

"Oh, that. Yeah." I was tired of hearing about it.

Theadora came over and offered to fill my glass. She smiled shyly and I nodded back.

I looked over at Reynard, and his eyes were still plastered all over her, undressing her. She'd become his obsession.

Theadora is my obsession.

No one else's.

Only mine.

She left the room, and his eyes followed her out.

"That maid has got Reynard all hot and bothered," Cleo said.

Cleo's comment made me realize I wasn't imagining it. Reynard was eye-fucking Theadora.

"So when are we going to, you know?" Cleo smiled flirtatiously.

"Cleo..." I was about to speak when Theadora entered the room again.

"That maid's got you all hot and bothered too, I see." Cleo's eyes narrowed like she'd seen through me.

Was I being that transparent?

I turned to face her. "What were you saying?"

She ran her finger up my arm. "Would you like to catch up later?"

"I'm sorry if I gave you the wrong impression. I was drunk and back from tour..."

"You seemed hot for it." She ran her tongue over her mouth.

Yes, she gave good head, all right. But my mind was filled with that dark-haired voluptuous beauty that was bending over at the cabinet and had Reynard looking like he was about to pounce.

"I'm not going there, Cleo. Why not Sebastian? He keeps checking you out."

"Mm..." She drained her wine and clicked her fingers at Theadora, which annoyed me.

Theadora came over and stood between me and Cleo.

"Can you top me up?" Cleo asked.

"Of course, one moment."

When the dinner was over, I got up and, needing some space, stepped out. As I walked down the hallway, I saw that Reynard had cornered Theadora.

Stepping between them, I faced Reynard. "I need to speak to Theadora."

"You're on a first-name basis with your staff?" His eyes shone with so much innuendo, it was as though he'd asked if I'd already fucked her.

I wish.

I turned to Theadora. "Can I have a word?"

She nodded and followed me outside. My passing glance at Reynard had "lay off" written all over it.

His mouth lifted at one end before stalking off.

When we stepped outside, the fresh air was a welcome change after the steamy tension gripping me.

"Thanks. You kinda saved me," she said.

"Was he hitting on you?" I studied her wide brown eyes which seemed frightened to me.

"He just wanted to know all about me. Asking lots of questions. He kind of creeped me out, to be honest."

"He's got that way about him." I stretched out my arm. "Come on. Let's walk.

"I'm still meant to be working." Her eyebrows gathered. She looked anxious.

"I'm sure they won't miss you. The dinner's over. And if my mother makes a fuss, I'll tell her that I needed you to do something for me. Yes?"

She nodded slowly. As she peered up at me, a depraved question invaded my thoughts: How would those virgin lips wrapped around my cock feel?

Stop it.

She's not like that.

She's never even touched a dick, let alone sucked one, you horny fool.

CHAPTER 19

Thea

With those cold, undressing eyes that felt like greasy fingers, Reynard Crisp seemed to have taken a shine to me. He cornered me by asking questions about where I was from and so on. Thank goodness Declan rescued me from him.

At least Declan's eyes didn't creep all over my body as though he'd pounce on me any moment. Even though in my fantasies that's exactly what I wanted him to do: rip my clothes off and grope me.

"I think I should go back and help with the dishes," I said.

Declan stared down at his watch. "When are you meant to finish?"

"In an hour."

Looking lost in thought, he nodded.

"Thanks for intervening. He seemed to want to know me, and by the looks of it, he's close to your mother."

"Don't worry about Reynard Crisp. I can handle that," he said as we walked up the steps through the columns. He stopped and turned to face me again. His face in the moonlight looked older yet even more handsome than ever. I couldn't believe this man showed so much interest in me. "Can we talk? After you finish?"

"I don't finish until ten o'clock."

A sweet smile touched his lips. "That's not too late, is it?"

I shook my head, ignoring that assignment I'd planned to finish.

"I'll meet you in the rose garden." He pointed in the direction of the pond. "Have you seen it?"

I nodded. "I love smelling the roses."

"It is fragrant, especially on a warm night."

His gaze trapped mine again and then we separated: me back to work, and him back into a party of husband-hungry, designer-clad society girls.

I couldn't blame them going all ga-ga over him, looking the way he did in that pale-blue jacket that accented his eyes, a fitted white shirt, and slacks that showed hints of his muscular thighs.

I worked in the kitchen, which gave me a chance to breathe properly, despite the butterflies in my stomach.

What does Declan want to say to me?

After I finished my shift, I changed into a pair of jeans, along with a long-sleeved cotton top, and replaced my pumps with sneakers.

I unraveled my bun and let my hair fall down my back, running my fingers through it and massaging my head. I tied a little bun at the back so that my hair didn't fall over my face.

Leaning into the mirror, I dabbed some lip gloss on my lips and a spray of perfume, hoping all that earlier tension hadn't produced smelly armpits.

I headed out into the night, clutching my arms. Despite a bite in the air, the salty breeze had an awakening effect.

From a distance, and with the light of the moon, I could see a tall figure standing inside the filigree iron rotunda with clinging roses.

A pleasant perfume intensified the closer I got, making me feel slightly lightheaded. Or was that me bathing in Declan Lovechilde's heart-pumping masculinity?

I stepped inside and found him there waiting for me.

After losing myself in his eyes, I finally found my voice. "It's so stunning here,"

"It's special." His mouth curved. "Made even more so by you being here. It's a painting I'd pay a fortune to own. You under the moonlight amongst the roses."

How romantic.

I smiled. My eyes warmed with emotion. He kept gazing at me. His big blue eyes had this shine about them, as though there was something he needed to say.

"You look beautiful with your hair out," he said, standing so close I could smell his cologne threatening to turn me into a puddle.

"You're a stunning woman, Theadora." He looked indecisive as he rubbed his jaw.

"You can call me Thea," I said, despite loving how he made my name sound.

His gaze burned on my face, heating my blood. My cheeks fired up, and my nipples stiffened.

Before my next breath, I felt his warm, soft mouth on mine.

His firm, strong body pressed against mine, as his tongue ran gently along my parted lips.

Despite my head telling me to run away, my pounding heart kept me there.

His lips explored mine, moving slowly. Warm and moist and sensually soft. Our exploring tongues twisted together.

My body was on fire. I felt his huge bulge settle on my stomach.

Fear snapped me out of this hot, sensual haze, and I managed to pull away from those addictive lips.

"I'm seriously attracted to you." His voice was quiet and a hint of vulnerability came from his hooded gaze.

I fell into his firm chest, and again he pressed his lips to mine. It was like a dream. His strong arms held me firmly against his beating heart. I surrendered myself completely. I can't say how long we kissed, but it seemed like forever.

Despite the surge of blood-pumping arousal, I broke loose again. Reluctantly. My heart moaning for me to return to his embrace.

"I haven't stopped thinking about you. From the moment you laid on my couch," he said softly. His breath on my neck sent warm ripples through me.

That comment took a moment to reach my brain.

My brow creased. "From *that* first night?"

He stepped away from me, which was a relief of sorts. I couldn't think with him so close I could smell his desire.

"I didn't touch you. If that's what you're asking. But I *am* a man." His eyebrow lifted. "I thought about you. I was worried too." He exhaled an audible breath, as though it had been torturous for him.

Overwhelmed by a burning sensation, I ached for him to touch me. My panties were sticky.

But I needed a job more than I needed to fuck this insanely sexy man.

Speechless, I looked away for a moment, if only to stop myself from falling into his arms again. New sensations swept through me. Surprising given how, before meeting Declan, the thought of a man touching me turned me to ice.

He opened his large hands that I'd fantasized smothering my breasts. "I'm not trying to take advantage of you. I just want you to know I'm seriously attracted to you. I can't stop thinking about you. And when Reynard came hunting you down, I realized then and there that I don't want anyone to have you."

"Have me?" I chuckled nervously. "I'm not a commodity."

His mouth curved up at one end. "No. Of course not. I didn't mean it like that."

"I have nothing but this job, and I haven't enough saved to move. I must finish my degree. I am determined to make something of myself so that I no longer have to clean bathrooms."

He smiled sadly. "I'll make sure you're protected. And you *will* do good. I know that. I promise that."

I shook my head in disbelief. "But why? Why are you offering something like that? That's a huge promise to make."

He shrugged. "Because apart from wanting you more than my next fucking breath, I also feel the need to protect you."

"But you hardly know me, Mr. Lovechilde."

"Declan, please." His eyes softened in the moonlight, and in I fell again. My god, this man was killing me. How could he be so fucking beautiful?

He ran his tongue along his bottom lip, and the memory of his mouth on mine had taken up camp in my soul.

Using all my inner strength, I looked elsewhere, if only to get a grip on reality. "I have to work for you, and this could become sticky."

In more ways than one.

My eyes returned to his. "I would like to. I'm just frightened you'll hurt me. And then I would have lost a job and everything too."

He took my hand and looked into my eyes. "Will you have dinner with me tomorrow night?"

I responded with a slow, hypnotic nod. "That would be nice."

"Good. Let's do that. I'd like to get to know you more."

I was about to respond when we heard laughter.

Declan lifted his hand. "I'll leave first if you like. And you can wait a few moments. It's Ethan at play." He raised a brow.

I smiled and appreciated how sensitive Declan was about my situation there. Despite my inexperience with men, so far all I'd experienced were selfish losers who were only interested in my bra-cup size.

When I returned to my room, I was way too scattered to focus on my music assignment, so I called Lucy instead.

"Hey, babe. How's working for the sexiest billionaire on the planet going?"

I laughed. "Have you seen all the billionaires to compare?"

"Nope. But hey, the Lovechilde boys are gorgeous."

"Men, more like it." I sighed.

Ethan was more a man-child, not so attractive, but Declan, with that deep voice and thoughtful intelligence, was a man. A hot-blooded man.

The makings of an orgasm fluttered through me just from rocking gently over a pillow.

"He kissed me." I walked over to the window and stared at the sky when a white streak flashed before me. "Oh my god, I just saw a shooting star."

"Make a wish now."

I took a breath and saw Declan's handsome face and that look of arousal burning into his gaze.

"He kissed you?" Lucy sounded starstruck like she'd experienced the kiss herself.

"Yep. Declan kissed me."

"I bet it was dreamy."

"Oh, it was more than that. I'm on fire."

"You're going to have to let him fuck you."

"I want him to. But what if I get too attached? And then there's this job. I'm also cleaning for him."

"That part's easy. Make sure you wear a short skirt and no panties, and do a lot of bending over in front of him."

I laughed. "You're fucking sick." My clit throbbed thinking of that little fantasy.

"Look, just go with it. And hey, if it doesn't work, do what most women have been doing forever," she said.

"And what's that?"

"Just let him fuck you and remain in your job until your degree. Don't let fear stop your fun. Enjoy life. Enjoy his penis."

"My god, Luce, you make it sound so easy." I giggled at her pragmatic take on fucking my boss. She did make sense, though.

But would it be just fun? If only a kiss drowned me in this much emotion, what would I be like going all the way?

Declan had a certain intensity about him. That's why I liked him. He struck me as deep, if not mysterious at times. Mainly that preoccupied, distant gaze. I recognized it well enough. Anxiety was my middle name.

"It's all in your head, love. He's obviously into you. And he's thirty-two. Make him continue to want you."

"What's age got to do with it?"

"Well, he must be ready to settle down," she said.

"I don't want to marry anyone. I'm determined to stay single."

"You're nuts. Marriages aren't all fucked up."

"Whatever. I didn't even like men until I met Declan."

"That's sexist."

"I thought sexism was more men hating women."

"Mainly. But it's also unfair to hate men," she said. "I've met and known lots of decent men in my life. I hope to marry one. Well, maybe not so nice. I don't mind a bit of a bad boy." She giggled.

"Not on my watch, baby girl. Bad boys grow up to be wife beaters. Remember that."

"It's not so black and white, Thea. In any case, that's our role to tame them. You know, like *Beauty and the Beast*."

"But that's a fairy tale."

Did Declan have the beast in him? That thought brought back the relentless throb in my panties.

"Whatever. I can look after myself," she added. "And you need a little more resilience. This oversensitivity of yours is a fun thief."

I sighed. "You're right. As always. I love you, Luce."

"I love you too. When are you coming to town?"

"Like real soon. I need to do some shopping for new clothes."

"Yay. A shopping spree. Love that idea. I need your sharp eye. You're great at second-hand."

I laughed at her referring to our shopping at charity shops together. "I can buy new now."

"Woo-hoo, look at you. All cashed up. And about to bonk a billionaire."

A smile cracked my face. "I'm not that cashed up. But my credit cards are sad from a lack of a workout. I'm debt-free for the first time ever." My heart sang at that admission. "And I'm not sure about fucking Declan."

"I'll drum some sense into that virgin brain of yours. And then you'll see how nice penises are."

I thought of Declan holding his big dick.

I already know that.

"I'm lucky to have you, Luce."

"Always here for you, babe. And remember sex is fun. It's good for you."

"I've got to finish an assignment. Speak soon. Luv ya."

"Luv ya back."

CHAPTER 20

Declan

To avoid gossip, I'd booked dinner at an out-of-the-way village. Although I couldn't care less if people thought my dating the maid was something worth gossiping about, I understood Theadora's need for discretion.

The restaurant looked out to the ocean and being dusk, the sea rippled in shimmering dark greens, while streaked in fiery orange and purple, the sky was a work of art.

Theadora, also a work of art, made heads turn in a sexy, fitted red dress.

"Red's your color," I said.

She blotted her lips with a napkin and smiled.

Unlike some of the women I'd dated, Theadora, I'd discovered, was an unfussy eater. She didn't see food as an enemy.

We talked about music and her aspirations. She showed interest in the boot camp, and the conversation moved freely between us. I found her to be intelligent and enjoyed her company.

We stepped out into the night.

"That was lovely." Theadora clutched her arms.

"Are you cold?"

"A little." She gazed up at me with wide, searching eyes.

I brushed a stray strand away from her face. Her lips glistened after her tongue brushed over them.

An action that made my dick twitch.

I took her into my arms and held her. "Here. I'll warm you up."

We stayed like that for a moment. Her short delicate frame in my arms—soft and a perfect fit.

"Do you feel like a walk?" I asked.

She nodded.

We walked in silence to the water's edge, where a moonbeam rippled a silvery pathway along the sea.

I placed my jacket over her shoulders. "Are you warm enough?"

"I am. But what about you?"

"I'm fine."

I studied her. Her big eyes filled with questions.

"Are you okay?"

She turned to face me. "I'm terrified."

"I'm not here to hurt you."

"I know that. But..." She took a deep breath. "I've never experienced anything like this before. You're very passionate."

"I am about you." I paused for a response, but she looked away as though I'd challenged her again. "I can't imagine any hot-blooded male not being seriously aroused by you. And you strike me as a little passionate yourself." I inclined my head.

What could I offer her? A relationship?

The thought of that terrified me.

But as I fell into that beautiful face, I wanted this girl. And I wanted to be her first.

Although I had no right to lay claim on her, my body was calling the shots. But it was more than my dick dominating: there was something about Theadora that made me want to protect her.

"Have you ever dated? Or kissed a boy?"

Am I really asking a twenty-four-year-old that?

"I went out with a few boys, but..." Her mouth drew a tight line. "Men scare me." She looked away as though ashamed of something.

"That's understandable. You've had a rough time. This stepfather of yours sounds like the fucking devil. You really should consider pressing charges."

She shook her head. "I don't want to dredge up the past."

I took her soft little hand and caressed her palm. "I can't stop thinking about you."

"You've seen more of me than most men," she said drily.

I studied her face and noticed a smile grow, which put me at ease. "Both times by sheer accident."

Her brow lowered. "Both times?"

"In my T-shirt." How could I admit that her bending over in front of me had turned me into a walking hard-on?

"Oh. Yes, of course." Her brow creased. "How horrible."

I shook my head. "It was anything but horrible. You're a very desirable woman. You're not a woman a man easily forgets."

She held my gaze and then looked away as though I'd challenged her again. Unlike most women I'd met, Theadora didn't milk sexy compliments. If anything, they confused her.

We stepped up onto the pier. "I love the smell of the sea," she said.

"Me too. I don't think I could live anywhere else."

"Not even London?"

"I go there often for business or to meet up with friends, but I'm more a seaside village type of man."

"You haven't traveled?"

"Other than my army tours, I've traveled through Europe and the US."

"Have you ever been married?"

"No." I stopped walking and took her hand while searching for the right words again. "Would you consider us spending some time together?"

This was difficult. Normally sex just happened. No negotiating or spelling out terms. However, with Theadora, the last thing I wanted to do was frighten her by tearing away at that pretty dress.

How I would love to do that.

"By that you mean, sleep with you?"

"Yes." I turned to stare at her in the face.

We kept walking in silence.

"I would however like to keep this between us."

"Like me be your private lover?" Her wide, searching stare penetrated deeply like she was trying to find my soul.

I hadn't planned on suggesting that, but seeing her under the moonlight had swept me away. All I could think of was taking her home and making love to her slowly. To hear her breathy moans while I ravaged her.

"Yes."

"Why?"

Now it was my turn to hesitate. "Because there's a lot of pressure on me. Paparazzi are on my back in London after an article about my returning home. It seems everyone wants to know who's in my bed. And by that, I don't mean a teddy bear."

Her head drew back and she giggled. "You sleep with a teddy bear?"

I shook my head and chuckled. "Not since I was five."

I leaned against the rail of the pier and stared down at an undulating, moored boat.

I massaged my neck. "I can't stand all that attention. And it wouldn't be fair on you."

"Would I be one of many? I mean will you also have a girlfriend? Or do you have someone?"

I shook my head. "I wouldn't want you with other men while we're together."

"Me with someone else?" She sniffed. "There's not much likelihood of that."

"Seeing Reynard Crisp making a move on you the other night got to me. He can have anyone he likes."

"I'm not interested in him." She looked down at her feet. "He gave me the creeps."

"You're a good judge of character. I'm not a fan either." I smiled sympathetically. "I'm just not ready for a serious relationship."

Her brow puckered as she searched my eyes for deeper understanding. "Yet you want exclusivity?"

I exhaled a breath. "It's mainly to protect you. I'd like to get to know you in our own private way."

She looked up at me and nodded slowly. "What about my work?"

"You can continue at Merivale if that's what you want. I'd prefer you didn't."

"Why?" She inclined her beautiful face.

"I don't want men hitting on you. And there are lots of Reynard Crisps around."

"Don't I know it." She spoke under her breath. "It's not just the job, but I also live there."

"I'd help find you somewhere. A place of your own. Close to college. Close to me."

"Close to you? And what happens when you're no longer interested in me?"

I shook my head. "I can't think like that. All I know is that I want you. And I don't want anyone else to touch you. I want to be your first."

"Is that what this is? Some strange fixation with bedding a virgin?"

"No. It's not what draws me to you." I took her hand. "Come, let's go back."

We walked back to the car in silence.

I turned towards her. "I would make sure you finish your degree and support you."

"Even if you tire of me?"

I released her hand and stopped walking. "To be honest, I've never really wanted a woman as much as I want you. But I have things I need to do. And the thought of marriage and children doesn't fit in with my plans."

"You plan to run boot camps, and that's it?" The note of surprise in her voice made me smile.

"No, of course not. I have other ideas. I want to help all the adjoining farms transition to organic. I plan to support as many carbon-neutral ventures as I can find."

"So you want to save the planet?" Her tone was neutral, despite that huge mission statement justifying sarcasm.

"Well, I don't know if I can achieve that single-handed, but sure, I'd like to focus on projects that are devoted to nurturing and not destruction."

Her mouth curled slowly. "I respect that. It's an admirable ambition."

I opened the door for her, and Thea's dress rode up a little as she wiggled in the seat to adjust it, and my temperature rose.

CHAPTER 21

Thea

As we drove in silence, my head filled with all kinds of questions. Sleeping with him. Yes. I wanted that badly. But the thought of leaving my job and being a kept woman played havoc with my independent nature.

What if he broke my heart?

He turned to look at me as he pulled up at his home.

What now?

I'd walked to his place after insisting we meet in private.

Even just going to dinner with him seemed difficult enough.

How was I to do this?

Sweat dripped between my shoulder blades.

"Come in and have a drink or a cup of tea," he said.

I held his gaze with a battalion of thoughts firing away.

"Don't worry. I won't do anything. Unless you want me to," he said. A slow curve of his lips made my mouth salivate. I wanted to be kissed again.

Hell, I wanted him to touch me. Everywhere.

But become a kept woman? Was that what he'd suggested? He hadn't exactly spelled it out.

I had to call Lucy, badly.

As he held the door open for me, his eyes glowed with a hint of uncertainty.

I reminded myself Declan wasn't like those men who would hurt me given the chance. He'd had his opportunity. That night on his sofa, he could have taken advantage of me.

I followed him in. Enjoying how his blue blazer sat on those big shoulders.

"Can you excuse me a minute? I need the bathroom," I said.

"Of course. Can I offer you a drink?"

"What are you having?"

"I thought I might open some champagne." When he smiled, his eyes sparkled like the sea under the afternoon sun.

"I'd like some too." Our eyes held again.

Champagne only meant one thing. I was going to ask for tea, but my pounding heart seemed to be making all the decisions.

Tea would have meant I remained that clueless girl who would continue to deny herself the feeling of a penis. Champagne, well, that was another path. A path to becoming a woman. A path to feeling a man. This time, on my terms.

As I sat on the toilet, I called Lucy.

"Hey there, babe." She yawned.

"Did I wake you?"

"No, I was just watching television."

"I'm at his house. He's asked me to become his mistress."

"Mistress? But he's not married."

"I mean for me to be a kept woman. You know, he fucks me and in return, he sets me up somewhere in the village so that I can finish my degree."

"Wow. That's without even trying first."

I grimaced. "You mean he may not like me once he's had sex with me?"

She giggled. "It's more than chemistry. You know how people smell, how they are in the bed."

"Well, I'll be shit in bed because I haven't got a fucking clue." I squeezed my phone.

"He'll take control. Let him. That's where all the fun is. Especially if he's experienced. He's hot. Lucky girl."

"What about if he hates how I feel? Or I'm too inexperienced?"

"That's silly," she said.

"What would you do?"

"I'd let him fuck me for sure. By now I would have his big dick blowing at the back of my throat."

"Ew. Do I have to swallow his cum?" I pulled a face.

She giggled. "You don't have to do anything, sweetie. You're stunning. You've got the body of a siren. You won't have to do anything but dance over his naked dick."

I puffed out a shivery breath.

"Just go with it, babes. And if he wants to get you a place and support you while you're both screwing, why not?"

"I can't be a kept woman. How can I learn to become self-sufficient?"

"Hello. Isn't that what you've been doing since leaving home?"

I couldn't argue with that. "I better go. Thanks. You're the best. I love you."

"I love you too. Don't worry. I'll hold your hand through this. Become a woman."

"My sexual awakening, I guess." I sighed. She was right.

My body wanted this.

My heart wanted him.

But will I come out in one piece?

And whether it was intentional or not, in a moment of extravagance, I'd bought myself a thong and a tiny lace bra.

A pulsating swell overcame me again. I felt sexy wearing them.

Declan had removed his jacket and had undone the first two buttons of his shirt. His mounded chest revealed itself against the fitted shirt, and all I wanted to do was run my hands up and down it.

He passed me a glass of bubbly. "Here you go." He smiled. "All good?"

"Um... sure." I studied his face. "Why ask?"

"I heard you talking."

"That was to Lucy. I wasn't talking to myself. I'm not that crazy."

He sniffed. "Hey, I've been known to mutter to myself on the odd occasion. It's not a sign of madness. It helps me get my head together."

I held my hand up. "Yep. Me too. It's a habit that started as a child. I guess being an only child I only had me and my dolls. And I'd chat to them."

He sat close to me on the sofa and stroked my cheek. His eyes glistened with affection, which warmed my spirit. That gaze wasn't like his hooded sexual gaze but one of friendship.

Apart from Lucy, I hadn't seen that in a person before. Least of all my cold mother.

Sipping on champagne, a crisp, complex flavor that tasted of wealth, I loved how the bubbles bounced on my tongue.

Declan went to his turntable. "What would you like to listen to?"

I shrugged. "I don't mind really."

"Classical?"'

"No. Not that."

He smiled. "Really?"

"I've been listening to Beethoven all week. I'm learning a piece."

Jazz filled the air. "How's that?" He tilted his head and smiled. His brown hair was in a tousled wave and his face tanned and healthy, highlighting those eyes that had taken up residence in my soul.

"I like it."

He returned to my side and faced me. "It's nice having you here as my guest for a change."

"It feels odd that I'm not cleaning."

"I want that to stop."

I swallowed. "Okay. Sure."

I would miss the money. But at least I'd paid off my debts.

"I can still set up an account for you," he said.

My face contorted. "I am not going to prostitute myself."

He shook his head repeatedly. "I didn't mean it like that."

"This isn't a good idea." I shot up off the couch and dashed outside before he could stop me.

CHAPTER 22

Declan

I FOLLOWED HER OUT. "I'm sorry if you misunderstood me."

Her dark eyes fired up. "I understood it well enough. You want to pay me to sleep with you. Doesn't that make me a prostitute?"

I ran my hands down my face. "That's not what I meant. Sure, I want you." I exhaled a tense breath. "I'm just trying to help you get ahead."

"Why are you following me?" Her sudden feistiness took me by surprise. I couldn't find the right words.

"I'll walk you home," I said.

"You don't have to. I'll be fine."

"I'll walk you home," I repeated. "It's dark. You don't have to talk to me."

She stopped walking and turned to face me. She ran her tongue over her lips, and her gaze held mine. Pleading. Asking for something. But for what?

Theadora had woven a spell on me. I no longer recognized myself. I had to tread carefully, that much I knew. I had to respect her and not claw at her body like a man possessed.

Possessed was how I felt. Possessed by her beauty, her softness, her fire.

"I'm sorry. Why don't you finish your drink? I promise not to touch you." I held my hands up.

"You don't want to?" She frowned.

Now that threw me. Talk about confusing. "Well, of course, I want to touch you. You know that. But I'd prefer to have you around than not. Chatting, sharing a drink's nice."

"We've chatted all night," she said.

I took her hand. "We can also remain silent if that suits you. Just come back inside."

She followed me in, much to my relief.

Just as we stepped into the living area, I turned, and she looked up at me. Her tongue rolled over her lips, and before my next breath, my mouth took to her lips as though starved of that kiss for too long.

Our lips melded into each other's moist softness. Her mouth was made for mine. I'd never enjoyed kissing someone as I enjoyed kissing Theadora's warm, plump lips.

I ran my fingers up her waist and smothered her tits with my hands. They were bigger than I'd imagined. My dick turned hard as steel. Her breathy moans encouraged me, and her nipples stretched the fabric of her dress.

Although she'd unleashed a force of primal need, I had to tame the beast. I couldn't frighten her off.

We had to take this slowly and carefully. I needed this girl naked. To feel her and devour her.

I ran my hands over her firm and shapely arse.

My heart nearly leaped from my chest. Blood engorged my dick.

I had to release my zip. My insistent dick pushed against my briefs.

I pressed against her on the wall. My mouth on hers. My hands exploring her curves.

"Come with me," I said.

She followed me into the bedroom.

I removed my jeans and remained in my briefs. I held her again and she seemed soft and pliable in my arms as I slid down her zip.

She stepped out of her dress, and I had to take a step back so that I could see her.

Crossing her arms, she shivered in her thong and tiny black bra.

"Are you cold or frightened?"

"Frightened," she said.

"We don't have to do this." I was virtually coming in my briefs. Her tits hung over so much. She was a very big girl.

And her thighs were curvier than most of the women I'd been with. I liked that.

Very much.

Theadora had me salivating. She was a spectacularly sexy woman. A natural. Inherently sensual. The way her body responded to my touch and her hips gyrated when I pressed against her.

She dropped her arms, and my breath hitched. Her tits spilled out of that bra which barely held them. I wanted them in my mouth or to rub against me naked.

"You're the most beautiful woman I've ever met."

She pointed at my briefs. "Take them off."

That took me aback. I liked it though. "With pleasure." I removed them, and my dick was so red raw I knew I wasn't going to last.

"Play with it," she said.

I liked this sudden shift in power. "Excuse me. You want me to wank?"

She nodded with a coy smile which was just as arousing as seeing her in skimpy underwear.

"I'll come if I touch my dick."

She bit her lip. A smile grew. She was enjoying this new position of power.

I would have done anything to taste her, but just her in that thong was enough to make my pulse race.

"Lie on the bed then," I said.

She did that and opened her shapely legs just enough for me to notice her slit through the lace of her thong.

Talk about explosive. Blood drained my brain and flushed me with so much arousal, I couldn't remember my name.

I lifted my foot onto a seat and pulled my dick for her.

"Do you want me to touch myself?" Her voice had gone all soft and breathy.

"You don't know how fucking much. Do you like touching yourself?"

She nodded and she hooked into her thong.

"Wider. Let me see," I said, pulling at my dick. Blood pumping through me. I knew I wasn't going to last.

She wiggled out of her thong and opened her legs wide and there she was touching her creamy cunt and I was wanking and an almighty release threatened.

"Touch your tits." I struggled to talk.

She unclasped her bra, and as they tumbled out, I exploded.

I sank to the edge of the bed. "See how hot you are?" I wiped myself with tissues and sat by her side, pressing my lips into her fragrant, silky hair. "Did you enjoy that?"

Nodding, she bit her lip.

"Do you mind if I lick your pussy?"

Her eyes settled on mine. "Only if you want to."

Drunk with lust from gazing at her naked curves, I nodded repeatedly as though I'd been offered a rare, delicious treat.

I trailed kisses over her neck and to her nipples.

She let out a groan.

"Am I hurting you?"

"No. I like the way you're touching me," she said.

"Good." I sucked on her nipples until they were erect.

I held her hips with her writhing in my hands.

Anticipation gushed through me again. No woman had ever made my heart race like this.

I needed to devour every inch of her. I wanted to taste her. To show her what real pleasure felt like.

CHAPTER 23

Thea

HIS LIPS SEEMED TO radiate electric currents. Sparks alighted wherever he placed them on my skin, sending delicious sensations deep into my core.

As his head settled between my thighs, I stiffened. But then all it took was his tongue lapping over my swollen bud for me to fall under a blissful spell. It felt like a flower that just kept growing and showering me with warmth.

His tongue twirled and fluttered like he was feasting on a treat. My legs trembled, and a hot wave surged through me, for that was a million times more intense than my finger.

Arching my back, I climbed to a rosy peak and exploded. If I thought that was it, I was in for a big surprise, because just after I'd taken off, another sensation even greater arrived until I couldn't take it anymore.

The intensity of the orgasm that blasted through made me scream. All the while he fondled my tits.

I just wanted him to do anything and everything to me.

And then he placed his finger at the entrance of my slit.

My body felt loose like on a hot summer's day.

As his finger slid in, a mixture of subtle pain and pleasure pulsed through me. Everything felt so tender.

"You're so tight." He touched his dick, and my mouth watered.

He removed himself and gazed at me with hooded eyes. His dick had gone purple and rock-hard, with swollen and throbbing veins.

My heart raced. I could hear it pounding in my ears.

Was that fear or arousal?

Both.

Only one man had placed his finger inside of me and that had turned my teen years into a nightmare. Nightmares that I still experienced whenever men looked at me.

Every male except Declan. That's why this burning need sweeping through my body confused me.

I squirmed and he stopped, pulling out his finger. His brow creased, but his eyes still smoldered.

"Am I hurting you?"

Biting my lip, I felt a lump in my throat.

Oh no, not fucking tears.

I don't cry.

When do I cry?

I rose. "I just need the bathroom." I scurried off on the warm wooden floor.

One could walk barefoot in a billionaire's home and not feel the icy sting of poverty. Abstract thoughts like that pumped through me, clashing with deeper questioning voices.

Am I really about to go all the way?

The tightening in my veins. The doubts in my head. All added up to one very fucking confused girl.

Woman not girl, I reminded myself.

I am a woman who is about to fuck her boss.

I sat on the toilet and cried. I can't say whether the orgasm had opened me up or his finger entering me had brought up memories of my monster stepfather. It all just flooded out of me.

Five minutes later, I stepped out. Naked and clutching my arms. Declan was in bed, sitting up looking concerned.

"Are you okay? I heard crying." He tapped the bed. "Sit for a moment. We don't have to do anything." The affection shining in his eyes stole my breath.

How could he be so compassionate at a time like this? I would have thought fucking me was his only concern.

He rose, grabbed a robe from the armchair, and placed it over me. "You look cold."

I gave him a tight smile. "Thanks. That's so understanding of you. I'm so sorry to do that. In the middle of that moment..."

Wearing a sympathetic smile, he shook his head. "I get it. This is a big thing for you. I only hope I didn't hurt you."

"No. You didn't. It was amazing. I mean, I've never experienced anything like that." I smiled coyly. "With your tongue. I came more than once."

His lips tugged at one end. "You're very responsive and tasted divine."

I had to look away from his soul-piercing eyes.

"Why don't you just stay? We can cuddle. I'd like that." He smiled so sweetly, and his tone was gentle and understanding.

I couldn't believe that anyone could be so selfless. From what I'd read and seen—and yes, I'd watched the odd porno—men needed to get their dicks in any which way.

Declan was not one of those men. Or was he just great at putting it on?

"Nooo...." screamed my intuition.

I slipped back into bed and removed his robe which smelt of his bath soap. A scent that could have doubled as an opiate.

His strong arms welcomed my tight body, and within a second of breathing him in and my cheek on his firm chest, my inner demons faded away.

He stroked my hair and I wanted to cry again.

Swallowing back lumps in my throat, I tried to summon that strong, tough woman I'd always prided myself on being. Where was she?

I never cried when my mother didn't call me for my birthday. I didn't even cry when she refused to believe that her husband had tried to fuck me, nor at her suggesting that I'd somehow seduced him. Led him on.

No tears. Just festering anger corroding into cancerous hate.

But here I was with a man I barely knew, despite my heart feeling all cozy, and cathartic tears poured out of me. Shattering that crusty layer to pieces.

What would I find? A frightened child, an angry girl, or an aroused woman?

Could I survive in this world exposed and raw?

As all this crazy shit went around my overactive brain, I pulled an apologetic smile.

"I'm sorry," I muttered.

"Please don't be. You don't have to do anything you don't want."

"But that's the thing. I want to."

Once again, his eyes trapped mine, and I forgot what I was even saying.

How the fuck does he do that?

Declan could have been a hypnotist.

His hair was messed up from where I'd massaged, okay, maybe pulled on it, while he devoured my pussy. And those perfect lips shone in readiness to take me under his sexy spell again.

His lips parted slightly, and the next minute, as though pulled in by a magnetic force, my body rubbed against his.

Our tongues met and my entire body came alive as I wrapped my arms tightly around him.

Unleashing a torrent of arousal, the feverish kiss sent scorching tingles down to my toes. Desire had set me on fire. My skin flushed and my sizzling core ached for him to go *all the way*.

I ran my fingers over his stomach, and he looked at me without blinking. Holding me captive by his arousal.

My gaze remained on his cock, while my heart convinced my jaded brain that I could do this.

I wanted that huge dick inside of me. To feel something. Pain. Pleasure. To rip into me and awaken me so that I could finally become a woman in touch with her feelings.

Having never seen a naked dick, let alone touched one, before stroking Declan's, I wrapped my hand around his thick, long shaft.

Distended veins throbbed against my jittery palm which surrounded his velvety, steel-hard dick.

"If you keep doing that, I'll come," he said. "I'm very sensitive." His hands ran over my breasts, and a breathy moan left my mouth.

I fell on my back and opened my legs.

This time I placed my finger inside of me.

His eyes darkened. His face flushed with heat.

I was on fire.

I wanted to send him crazy with desire.

My body burned to feel all of him.

The harder, the more painful, the better.

To remove the numbness that had been my life.

"Oh, Thea...." He breathed, watching me finger myself. His finger entered me again, and then another finger.

He groaned like he was in agony. "You feel hot."

I stroked his hard dick. "I want you to fuck me. To be my first."

His eyes bore into mine again, intoxicating me with the passion radiating from him.

My belly tightened with longing. I wanted his skin to slide on me and in me.

He leaned over to a drawer and brought out a condom.

"I'm on the pill," I said.

He turned and wore a frown. I giggled at how surprised he looked.

"Oh. Right. Okay. Um." He rubbed his head, and my eyes settled on those huge muscular arms that I longed to have around me again.

"I've had a recent blood test. I can show you if you like," he said.

I shook my head. "I believe you."

"I can make love without a condom?" His brow furrowed.

"Why are you looking at me like that?"

"I'm wondering why you're on the pill?"

"To regulate my cycles. And I figured I'd fuck one day." I smiled.

His lips curled and dimpled his cheeks, and I wanted to devour him.

I touched his dick again, and he hissed.

"Am I hurting you?"

"Nope. You're making me want to come."

"You're pretty sensitive," I said.

"Only around you. I'm not normally this aroused..." He shrugged.

He held me and kissed my neck. His tongue entered my ear, and I was a goner.

Who would have thought a tongue could give so much pleasure?

I loved the way he touched me and his grunts and groans. Especially now as he nibbled at my nipples.

His deep guttural sounds, like he was eating the most delicious meal, vibrated all over my prickling skin.

Parting my legs wide, he took his weight on his arms, which seemed to make the veins on his biceps pop.

He tickled my clit, and within a few strokes, I came again. The fire of anticipation had settled in my sex so that the slightest touch made my nerve endings sizzle.

I could feel his heart pounding against my chest.

"I am going to enter you slowly. Tell me to stop if it gets too much, okay."

"Uh-huh."

The head of his dick entered, and the stretch was so intense I bit into my lip.

The pain of ripping through my wall sent a sharp, acute twinge through me.

I'd read about this. I expected pain. I expected blood. But I didn't expect addiction.

Addiction was what I felt as soon as we overcame that barrier. I fell in love with his dick pounding into me.

My vaginal walls clung on tight. With each entry, the heat intensified. Even the sound of wet friction turned me on.

With my hands on his firm, well-toned arse, I pushed him in deep. Pain and pleasure met. Like the merging of day and night which always made my heart sing.

He rocked his hips, and his dick slid inside and out, discovering me. All of me.

My mouth remained apart. But unlike my pussy, it was dry from all my sighs and moans.

It was pure erotic pleasure.

"Oh my fucking god, Theadora. You're going to make me lose my mind."

"Is that a bad thing?" My breath mingled with my words as he split me in half with that slow, grinding dick.

My nose on his dampened large shoulder sucking back his maleness.

"You are beautiful. I've never felt a woman like I feel you right now." His voice trembled with emotion.

Oh my god. Not tears. Not from him too.

CHAPTER 24

Declan

WHAT A WOMAN. THE way she felt. Her body fitting perfectly with mine. Her tightness and heat. My eyes watered from the sheer pleasure. The type of pleasure I'd read about but had never experienced before.

How was I ever going to be the same again?

Skin on skin. Her muscles gripped my cock like she'd fucked hundreds of men. Only she hadn't.

I was her fucking first.

That was enough to bring tears to my eyes.

I rode her slowly. Her pussy taking possession of my cock.

Her pussy had also taken possession of my senses.

As had Theadora.

I entered slowly. Her walls gripped my shaft like a thousand fingers squeezing the life out of it each time.

With each thrust, the sensation intensified, until I felt like I would lose my mind from ecstasy.

She rocked her hips as I grasped her ass, allowing me to sink deep inside of her.

Her pussy spasmed around my pounding dick and she cried out, taking me with her.

The rush was so intense, I think I might have blacked out because I went somewhere I'd never been before. I didn't even know I had so much fucking sperm. It just kept flowing out of me, like I'd burst a vein.

The volcanic-like eruption sent me flying. I landed on a soft, warm cloud with Theadora in my arms as stars sprinkled over us.

Holy fucking hell.

What was that?

It took some time for me to return to normal.

Talk about a brain meltdown. Profound and indescribable pleasure.

My eyes watered. Not just from euphoria but from the emotion of experiencing Theadora.

With that voluptuous body, those sultry dark eyes, and rosy lips, she had me completely under her spell.

I was never going to be the same again.

WE ALL MET UP at my father's favorite Italian restaurant in London.

"So, Papa, are you going to invite us to your new penthouse apartment?" Savanah's face lit up. "I know. A cocktail party."

My sister seemed to spend her life looking for the next party.

Sipping wine, my father smiled. He looked happy if not a little tired, which concerned me. He was no longer that young man that could party hard, not like his boyfriend, who I sensed enjoyed a party or two.

"You're a lawyer, I hear," Ethan said, turning to Luke.

He nodded. "I've just started a practice. Thanks to this generous cutie." He touched my father's arm affectionately, and they shared a lingering gaze.

They were in love. Or at least my dad was. In Luke's case, I didn't know him that well. He struck me as nervy by the way his eyes darted about.

"What do you specialize in?" I asked.

"Entertainment. That's my interest. I studied piano as part of my degree."

Theadora entered my thoughts. I didn't need much to think of her since she'd become my obsession.

I hadn't been able to reach her all day. It was the day after our first steamy night together. I even went looking for her at Merivale, only to find that she'd gone to London.

Had I frightened her off?

I'd promised myself I'd achieve my goals in the coming year. Unhinged from the last tour, I had to keep focusing or else I'd lose myself. Instead, I'd now lost myself to lust.

If I thought fucking Theadora might have doused the spark that started from the moment I saw her in that corset, I was wrong. She had ignited a fucking blaze.

"So you look after bands?" Savanah asked Luke.

He nodded while draining his glass. "All kinds of artists and performers. I organize their contracts."

"There must be lots of parties," she said, sounding impressed.

I rolled my eyes. "Do you think of anything but?"

She poked her tongue. "Just because you're the do-gooder, doesn't mean we all have to be."

Ethan chuckled.

And so it went on and on. I was only half there as small talk drifted from Savanah to Luke and Ethan.

"I like your idea of a boot camp," my father said.

"Thanks. Mother seems to think I'll be running Satanic rituals."

Ethan laughed. "Now that would be fun."

My father explained my project to Luke.

"Mm... nice. I'm rather fond of the butch, sweaty soldiers on that reality show."

"Me too. Now we'll have that live. It's kinda going to be fun," Savanah said.

"I'm not planning a circus here. And we are talking about teenagers and not soldiers," I reminded her.

She shrugged. "Mm... whatever. We can have fun imagining it, though, can't we?"

I had no argument there. A bit of playfulness never hurt.

Savanah dominated the rest of the dinner, chatting about music, clothes, and parties. With my head elsewhere, I didn't get much of a look into Luke's character.

He struck me as shallow. But my father was happy and that was all that mattered.

After dinner, I shook Luke's hand and headed out into the night. Ethan and Savanah tagged along.

We stood at the end of the lane. "What do you think?" Ethan asked.

"Luke appears a little jumpy to me," I said.

"He's coked out," Savanah said.

"How do you know?" I asked.

"Hello. Did you see his dilated pupils? And he kept sniffing and touching his nose. Classic."

"And you would know?" I asked.

"Everyone does a little sniff," she said, looking at Ethan.

He nodded sheepishly. "Yeah. Sure. At parties it can be fun. Or in the bedroom."

"I thought you'd kicked it?" I asked him.

"I'm not doing it as much. I'm with Savvie. Luke was definitely coked out. He hardly touched his meal."

"Do you think they're in love?" I asked.

"Mm... Dad seems besotted. He's a good-looking dude, I guess," Ethan said.

"But he didn't seem as into Dad," I maintained.

Savanah frowned. "Do you think he's after Daddy's money?"

"I'm not sure. Dad's set him up in a practice. He can afford it. It's his money after all," I said.

"Mother would hate him," Savanah said, chuckling. "But then she's got Will." She shook her head. "Who saw that coming?"

"I did," I said. "They've always been close."

Savanah's phone beeped. She peered down at it. "I've got to go and meet some friends."

She pecked me on the cheek and then Ethan and headed off.

"What are you up to now?" Ethan asked.

"I'm going back to the village."

"What, tonight? Now? Why not stick around? We can do some of the bars?"

"No. I want to get back. I've got an early start."

He looked disappointed. "You're not much fun."

I hugged him and headed to my car which I'd parked a few blocks away.

For some reason, I peered through the window of a pub and froze on the spot. Theadora was seated in a booth with a girl and two men. One of the men sat close to her. Too close. He seemed very interested.

Why wouldn't he be?

Jealousy froze my veins. We'd only been together yesterday and now she was out with a man?

Stepping away from the window, I leaned against the wall and took a deep breath.

How was it she was dating a guy?

Was that why she'd turned off her phone?

I tried calling her. Still no answer. I sent a text instead.

No response.

I'd entered villages where people were strapped with bombs, and yet I couldn't walk into a pub and claim what was mine.

Mine?

Taking a deep breath, I squared my shoulders and entered the Irish pub.

CHAPTER 25

Thea

MY EMOTIONS WERE ALL over the place. I had to get away from Merivale. Weird as it seemed, I couldn't face Declan in my work environment. How would I act? Would everyone notice my face flaming? Even before we'd slept together I blushed whenever he was around.

How could I remain blank and unaffected around him?

The morning after, he'd been so tender. This is after hardly sleeping. My lips ached from kissing. His beautiful, fleshy, devouring mouth was all over mine as he entered me and made me fly. Nerve endings sparked a blaze that smoldered one day later.

It was nice being in London with a credit card ready for some action. A novel experience for someone who rarely walked into department stores for anything other than essentials.

The only annoying part was my phone breaking down and me having to buy a new one.

We'd been shopping all day, and when Lucy suggested a drink, I jumped at the opportunity to put my feet up.

As it was, she'd extracted more joy from shopping than me. I ended up with two pairs of jeans, two shirts, a skirt, pumps, and heels. The heels were a spur-of-the-moment choice. As someone who generally favored comfort, I don't know where that came from. Perhaps those Merivale functions and seeing women draped in designer clothes and skyscraper shoes were rubbing off on me.

Lucy plopped our drinks down on the table and sat across from me. "You haven't told me what it was like," she said, pushing the bowl of chips into the center of the table. "And don't fan your face again. I get it. He's hot."

I giggled. "I keep heating up just thinking about it."

"I bet you do. So did you enjoy it? Having a snake slither all the way in." A serpentine hand movement followed, which made me laugh. "Well. Did you... come?" she persisted.

I bit my lip and nodded. Despite our close friendship, discussing the sensations I'd experienced felt very personal.

But I also wanted to talk about it. My head had it on loop. Declan holding me while he thrust deeply into me and the look in his eyes when he climaxed. How he called out my name and then wouldn't let me go all night.

"It hurt, yeah? My first time was horrible," she said.

"It was very painful, but he was also very gentle with me, and after that, he just knew how to position himself inside of me."

"He found your G spot." Her voice boomed from excitement. I might as well have admitted to finding a million dollars.

"See, I told you it exists," said a woman to her boyfriend. She leaned over to us and said, "He thinks it's a myth like the Loch Ness monster."

I chuckled, despite my embarrassment.

Leaning into Lucy, I whispered, "Stop telling everyone about my sex life."

She laughed.

"How often did you do it?"

"I lost count, to be honest." I smiled into my drink as I took a sip.

"Holy shit. He's either ridiculously virile or popped a little blue pill."

"He didn't pop anything. He hardly left my arms."

"You've got him under your spell, then. Nice. So what now?" She dipped a chip into some sauce before popping it in her mouth.

I puffed a breath. "Great question. I don't know. I have to work for his mother and live there at the estate." I played with my glass. "He made it clear he wasn't after a relationship. But he also doesn't want to share me. That confused me."

She nodded, mulling over my words. "That's definitely a contradiction. So has he called you since?"

I shook my head. "Although my phone's broken."

"But you called me this morning and it worked."

"It stopped working after then." I sighed. "I don't know how to face him. What to say or do."

"Just go with the flow, babes." She opened her hands. "Why are you worried?"

"Because I can barely string an intelligent line around him. That was before we'd gotten together. And now just talking about him revs up my heart palpitations." I looked her in the face. "What if he just used me?"

She munched on a chip. "Did he keep kissing you?"

My lips curved slowly. "He sure did. My mouth still hurts."

"There. That's always a sign he's into you."

A couple of attractive men in their early to mid-twenties swaggered over.

Lucy watched them heading our way, "Mm... they're kinda cute. I like the dark one."

"Oh, please, Luce. Don't encourage them. I'm not in the mood."

"Hey, just because you got to fuck a hot billionaire with a big dick doesn't mean I can't have a little fun."

"True. But what about if the other one tries to hit on me? I really don't need this."

"I'll tell them you're gay."

Before I could respond to that ridiculous idea, the pair were standing at our booth. "Mind if we join you?"

Talk about confident.

"Why not. Only don't hit on her. She's into girls." Lucy said, making me want to scream at her for being so blunt.

The man with red hair settled next to me. "Hi. I'm Jamie. We share that in common." He spoke with a strong Irish accent.

It wasn't the first time I'd been described as gay. I'd used that as an excuse to stop men hitting on me at pubs. It didn't always work. They were often intrigued and would ask questions like: What did it feel like to be fucked by rubber instead of a hot-blooded dick?

Jamie was attractive and funny in that amiable Irish manner, making it seem like we'd known each other for ages.

Had I not been so crazy about my boss, I might have even enjoyed flirting.

Flirting me? Since when?

"So did you hear the one about the Irish, Italian, and French man who walked into a bar one day?"

I rolled my eyes. "No. You're going to tell me though, aren't you?"

He started to tell his joke when my attention went to the door and in strode Declan.

I kicked Lucy, who'd given her undivided attention to Jamie and his long-winded joke, which was amusing due to how his face animated.

I cocked my head towards Declan, who was heading for our table, and she finally cottoned on just as Jamie finished the punchline and Jeremy his buddy chuckled along, only they'd lost us.

Both Lucy and I were more interested in the man who'd stolen my heart and mind.

I could barely speak, just an embarrassing "Uh" tumbled out of my lips, like I was staring at an alien.

"You're here," he said at last.

I nodded slowly.

"Oh my god. You're Declan Lovechilde. You're a fucking legend in my house," Jamie said.

I turned towards the Irishman with shock all over my face. "You know each other?"

Jamie shook his head. "No. But my father's in the army. We saw the story on the television. How you saved a school from being bombed. You're a fucking hero."

He sprung up and shook Declan's hand. "A selfie for my dad?" he asked, acting all cute, and Declan, who was just as speechless as me, nodded hesitantly.

Lucy jumped up. "Here, I'll take it."

What the fuck?

Declan stood next to his new fan and smiled. Dressed in black jeans, a pale-blue fitted shirt, and a honey-colored blazer, he belonged more on the cover of *Man Beautiful* than in an Irish pub filled with ordinary people like me.

It dawned on me. What would he do with someone like me? I was more that pub than posh.

After Jamie stopped gushing, Declan turned to me. "I was just walking past when I noticed you."

I remained flummoxed. All that stuff about him being a hero and the fuss had left me speechless.

Come on speak. Remember A, B, C?

At this point, I wanted everyone gone. Instead, Declan's ridiculously deep blue eyes impaled me, because it seemed as though he was fucking me. Or was that just a memory of the morning when he looked at me that same way while his dick burned into me?

Time stood still. And what's worse, everyone seemed to be staring at us.

"I went shopping. Um... this is Lucy, a good friend of mine."

Lucy lifted her hand. "Hey there. Lovely to meet you."

"This is Declan, my boss." I felt obligated to introduce him to the men at our table. "Of course you know because you've seen him on television..." I babbled away.

Put me out of my misery now.

"I best leave you to it, then," Declan said, his eyes moving from me to Jamie.

He thinks I'm with Jamie. Fuck.

CHAPTER 26

Declan

IT TOOK ALL MY inner strength not to return to that pub and insist, yes, insist, Theadora come with me.

She was with another man.

So fucking soon?

My sheets were still warm from her beautiful body. Her rose perfume filled my space. And she was out with a guy?

Maybe they'd known each other for a while. He had his arm around the booth, looking very familiar, and they were all laughing when I walked in.

Fuck.

I tried texting her but no answer. Uncertainty kept me there on that main drag. If I went back in, it would seem as though I was being a control freak. If I didn't, she'd end up sleeping with that guy.

Fuck.

I heard "Declan" and turned to see Theadora running up to me.

Her lips parted as she hurried towards me, reminding me of how she looked bouncing on my dick, and my jeans tightened.

"I wanted to invite you to join us, but then you left."

"I didn't want to bust in on your party," I said.

"It wasn't that. Those guys just joined us. Lucy's like that."

"Like what?" I had to know if this friend of hers was a bad influence.

"Well, she's friendly." She pulled a coy smile. "I didn't invite them to sit with us. But they're nice people, I suppose."

"I've been trying to call you all day." I hated how desperate I sounded. I was fucking desperate. I wanted this girl. Now. Naked. In my arms.

Maybe a week away together. Perhaps after that, I could get her out of my system.

I couldn't concentrate. Everything revolved around Theodora. Especially now that I'd had a taste.

A taste? A fucking banquet.

Her eyebrows knitted. "Oh. Did you need me to do something? Like organize your files or cleaning?"

My heart swelled with affection at how innocent she seemed. Her face resembled that of a girl's all of a sudden. Endearingly so. I wanted to smother her with cuddles and buy her everything her heart desired. If only just to bask in her pure soul.

Wearing a questioning, wide-eyed stare, Theodora made me smile sadly. "No, Theodora. I just wanted to see you."

"Oh." Her brows puckered as though my wanting to see her was some abstract concept.

"I don't want you to work for me anymore." I took her hand and stared into her eyes. "I'd prefer it if you allowed me to set you up in your own place."

She removed her hand abruptly as if my palm was made of broken glass. "To be a kept woman?"

I hated how that sounded too. I shook my head. "No. I just want to give you everything. Help you."

"I don't need your or anyone's help. That goes against my nature." Under the streetlight, her eyes shone with intense emotion. "I'm seriously independent. I've had to be." Her voice cracked.

I took her hand. "I respect you for that. I didn't mean it to sound sordid." I took a deep breath to consider my words. "I just want to help you earn that degree without you having to worry about money. I've got plenty of it."

"I get that." She looked down again and drew a circle with her toe. "But it wouldn't seem right to me. I'm not good at taking gifts at the best of times. And now... with us..." She exhaled and that faltering smile of hers pushed away her earlier fire.

She stepped out of the way of a couple of staggering men.

"What are you doing now? Or are you going to hang out with those guys?"

She shook her head decisively. "God no."

I had to smile at the way her expressive face twisted into a grimace.

"I'm sure they're crestfallen," I said.

Her head drew back sharply in that self-deprecating way of hers. Theadora didn't see herself as the male magnet she truly was. "I doubt it. Anyway, Lucy told them I was gay."

My eyebrows flung up, and I laughed. "Well, I'm glad you're not." I retraced that comment. "I meant nothing against gay women."

She laughed, which unclamped my shoulders.

"Can we perhaps go somewhere and talk?" I slanted my head.

"Did you have something in mind?"

"I've got plenty of ideas that involve just you and me." I raised a brow. "We can stay here for the night."

Her eyes met mine. "In Mayfair, you mean?"

I thought of Ethan, and what I wanted to do to Theadora involved lots of hot, noisy sex. I wanted to hear her moan and for me to groan loudly, like I did when we climaxed together.

That was a first for me.

Everything about Theadora was a first.

"Why didn't you answer my calls?" I asked.

Her eyes searched mine. "My phone broke down. I just bought a new one and haven't set it up yet." She kept staring at me as though I was an enigma. "Um... can you wait while I say goodbye to Lucy?"

"Of course."

As she moved away, I watched her swaying bottom in those tight jeans. My heart picked up pace. The anticipation of touching her soft curves and her writhing, voluptuous body rubbing against mine made my blood thicken. I also just wanted to listen to her voice. To hear her talking about anything and everything.

She warmed the air around me.

A few minutes later, she walked gracefully towards me. As a contagious smile grew on her lips, our eyes locked, and the street crowd turned into a blur.

"Have you eaten?" I asked.

"Not really."

"Let's go to Lovechildes. It's not far. I've got a penthouse suite there."

"Oh, you're staying there?" She frowned. "I used to work there."

I twisted a strand of her hair. "I know."

"I might have even cleaned that room. How weird is that?"

I sniffed. "Yep. It's a coincidence all right. A beautiful coincidence."

She looked up at me, and I kissed her on the lips. Her soft mouth was cold from the night air.

"Ethan's at Mayfair. We have a private suite that's ours. My father used to stay there, but he's since moved into a new penthouse with his boyfriend."

She stopped walking. "Wow. Your dad's gay?"

I nodded. My father could have turned into a weed-smoking Rastafarian for all I cared. With her soft, petite hand in mine, life felt nice. Really nice.

THEADORA EVEN MADE EATING erotic. Or was it the way her little tongue kept sweeping over her plump lips?

"That's so delicious," she said, pushing her plate aside. "I've cleaned this room, but I've never been a guest here."

"It's so strange how things work out," I said. "Your working here, I mean."

She sipped on her wine. "I don't think I can be a kept woman, Declan."

That sudden shift in subject jarred, despite our arrangement needing to be addressed. Silly of me to think I could just get down and dirty with this girl and leave tomorrow for tomorrow.

I walked over to the window and stared at the crescent moon sitting perfectly over Big Ben as though digitally enhanced.

"I admire that in you. Most people would have their hands out." I turned to face her. "Giving is something I enjoy."

She joined me at the window and shook her head. "Are you really this nice?"

I shrugged. "I have my moments."

"Are you really a war hero?" Her eyes met mine, and I smiled tightly.

I didn't like talking about my time as a soldier. "I was just doing my job."

"But you saved a school, Jamie said."

"I just talked a teenager out of blowing himself up."

"My god." Her eyes widened with shock.

Yes, it was shocking. That pimply teenager resembled any boy who played war games on PlayBox, not in real life.

"He was about to pull the string. Luckily, I managed to talk him out of it."

She shook her head in disbelief. "That's insane."

I nodded.

"You look sad." She tipped her head.

"I'm okay. I just don't like talking about it."

"Are you suffering from PTSD?"

I took a deep breath. How did we get to this topic?

"Not really. But there are times when I catch up with the lads. My army mates. Just to get things off my chest."

"You can talk to me if you like. I'm a good listener." Her gentle tone sent shivery warmth to my soul.

I opened my arms. "Come here for a moment."

I wrapped my arms around her and held her. "This is healing enough for me. Having you here." Her head reached my chest. "You're a lot shorter than I thought."

"I'm short. I bought some heels today. I would have worn them, but my feet were sore from shopping."

She giggled and my universe turned technicolor. All that talk about grey, craggy terrains, and impossible wars faded into a field of flowers.

"You're beautiful any which way, Theadora. Remember that. And I've always had a weak spot for petite girls."

"Cleo isn't petite," she said, stepping out of my arms.

"Cleo meant nothing to me."

She sat down on the winged chair and placed her feet up on the side. I loved seeing her so casual and at home around me. "I get it. You're a very eligible, hot billionaire."

I shrugged. "I don't see myself that way."

"I want to keep working at the hall. Do you mind?"

That pesky issue of her working for my mother brought me crashing down again.

"That's your right. It's just that my mother's a difficult woman, and I want to keep seeing you."

She undid her bun, and her hair came tumbling down. She rubbed her head. "Aah, that's better."

"I agree." I pointed at her shirt. "How about undoing a couple of buttons? Or better still take it off."

The corners of her lips twitched as she unbuttoned her shirt, revealing a cleavage bursting out from a skimpy red bra.

"You're so beautiful." My voice went hoarse from desire.

She smiled and her cheeks flushed.

"I can ride over to your place whenever you like," she said.

"That will work, I guess." I went to the bar and poured some Scotch into a glass. She shook her head at my offering her a glass.

"I can keep this a secret," she said.

"You'd be comfortable with that?" I gulped down some spirit. All this talk about how we were going to be together stressed me.

I wanted Theadora close to make sure she was safe and not being propositioned by sleazebags like Reynard Crisp, who hung around Merivale like a bad smell.

She shrugged a shoulder. "Sure. I mean, you're just fucking me."

"It's more than that, I think." I rubbed my jaw. It wasn't easy talking with her on that chair with her tits half hanging out. "I want you. That's all I can say. I've desired you from the moment..."

Oops. I couldn't admit to that, could I?

She removed her shirt and my brain started to go into meltdown.

"Let's go into the bedroom, shall we?" I asked.

"Did you want to fuck me when I slept on your sofa in Mayfair?"

I took a deep breath. "Look, you were beautiful to me then, yes. But I would never have done anything. You were drugged, for fuck sake."

She ran her tongue over her lips, and her eyes softened.

I lifted her off the chair and carried her to the bedroom.

She giggled as I planted kisses on her neck and cheek.

"I'm probably really heavy after all that food."

"You're seriously light."

Placing her on the bed, I helped pull off her jeans, and my breath hitched seeing her in those tiny red panties.

"When can I start taking photos?" I pulled a half-smile. I didn't normally film or photograph girls I fucked, but Theadora in that skimpy bra and panties made for libido juice.

"Only when you let me photograph you." She cast me a teasing smile.

"I'm hardly a painting. Not like you."

I stripped down to my briefs, and my dick bounced out, relieved at being freed.

She stared at my dick as I held it in my hand. "I like seeing your big dick." Biting her lip, she looked like she'd admitted to something taboo like sucking my cock, which wasn't that taboo, but enough to make her guilty smile make my dick stretch to my navel.

"I've been hard all day thinking of you," I said. "No, that's a lie."

Her eyebrows gathered.

"I've been hard from the moment you left yesterday."

"That sounds painful." She giggled, opening her legs enough for her slit to show through the lacy fabric of her panties.

Pre-cum soaked my hand.

"You're really fucking sexy for someone who hasn't had any experience."

"That's because of how you're looking at me. And I've seen porn."

"Have you just?" I grinned. "Any favorites?"

She opened her legs wider. Her tongue ran around her lips.

I met her on the bed and rubbed my dick against the crotch of her panties. She was soaking wet.

"I like watching men fucking girls from behind."

"Like up the bottom?" I asked, my brows lowering.

"Nope. Like we did in the shower, with your hands all over my tits."

I hissed behind my teeth. Pre-cum soaked my stomach. What a nice memory that was. Balls buried deep against that peachy arse. Her pussy tight and hungry for my dick.

"Do you want to feel my hard dick inside of you?" I asked, blood charging through me.

Her cheeks turned red and she nodded.

I hooked inside her panties and ripped them off. Held by a fine thread that was easy to do and an apt gesture for how desperately I needed a taste.

"Hey, they almost cost me a day's salary." She laughed.

"I'll set up an account for you in a lingerie shop. With pleasure," I said.

I parted her thighs nice and wide and placed my head between them. Her female scent made my dick rock-hard.

I lapped and licked her swollen clit until she came all over my tongue, and those whispery moans grew into extended groans as I swallowed everything she had.

I sat her on top of me and unclasped her bra. Taking her tits into my hands, I sucked on her nipples, which reminded me of ripe raspberries. My favorite fruit.

"Sit on my cock."

She slowly lowered onto it, and I grunted from excruciating pleasure.

"You're so tight." I clutched her bum and she bounced over my dick.

I loved watching her face and how she bit her lip as she rocked and gyrated on top of me. Around her, I was constantly arousal.

I buried my face in her tits, licking and nibbling at her nipples, sending a rush of blood down to my dick.

"You need to come, like now." I barely got that out as I sucked back whatever control I had.

Her movements increased. Her head fell back. Her pussy walls clung to my dick for life.

As she screamed, pleasure shuddered through me, and I burst into her. Stars spewed out from behind my closed eyes, just like my flooding sperm.

She fell into my arms, and we lay together. Panting and sighing.

I kissed her warm, soft lips and floated away to paradise.

CHAPTER 27

Thea

THE PIANO SITUATED AT the back of the house meant I could practice to my heart's content. As someone who preferred privacy when playing, this suited me well. It was this reluctance for an audience that had stood in the way of my becoming a performer. That was apart from my disruptive upbringing. My mother hated me playing because I drew attention to myself.

Looking out over the forest, the room offered a relaxing ambiance when practicing repetitious scales. Nothing but trees and sky to look at. I'd landed in heaven.

That's how my life suddenly felt. Helped by the sexy, handsome man who couldn't take his hands off me.

As I lifted the lid, the smell of wax polish flooded me with memories of practicing at my grandmother's. I loved visiting her cottage in the Cotswolds, which gave me a break from the tension at home. I could almost be myself there. I didn't lie in bed stressing every time I heard footsteps or look over my shoulders while in the bathroom. The day she died was the day I fell apart.

Running up the black and white keys, I couldn't believe how perfectly tuned the piano sounded. Declan had mentioned that small detail. His eyes shone bright as though knowing I'd be excited. I hugged him. He'd done so much for me, and now this—a perfectly tuned piano away in a secluded part of the hall.

I kept questioning where we were heading. My head was filled with him.

On one hand, he didn't want to call me his girlfriend, while on the other, he asked whether there were men in my class.

I reassured him that they were younger than me.

And why would I want a boy when I had a man? I kept that question to myself.

Declan wouldn't be easy to replace. The things he did to my body. He had a sixth sense when it came to pleasure points, which seemed to be all over my body. He was insatiable. But then, so was I.

It felt odd, our secret little affair. Since that London stay at the hotel, we hadn't stayed apart one night.

I'd cycle over to Declan's. He even hated me doing that. He'd offered to buy me a car, but I rejected his offer, making him promise not to.

After he'd driven me to school, students spotted him dropping me off, and that got them curious. I shrugged it off, and now I had girls wanting to be my friend so they could learn all about the happenings at Merivale.

I just told them he was heading in that direction. It was getting a little tricky keeping us a secret.

Declan kept asking me to take his offer of an apartment close to school, and for me to leave Merivale. After everything that had happened in my life, I'd made myself a promise to remain independent.

What if something happened to this arrangement with Declan? The thought of which made my heart shrivel into a pea.

After warming up, I practiced Debussy's "Claire de Lune," which I was to be marked on.

Most students had chosen songs from musicals and even pop, but I loved playing classical. Tradition had always been important to me.

Maybe my mother's rich tastes had rubbed off on me subconsciously, seeing how she held the upper-class establishment in high regard to the point of elitism.

She would have loved the fact I worked for the Lovechildes. I could imagine her asking questions about décor and clothes and all those things that mattered little to me.

Lost in the moment, I closed my eyes, and when I opened them, I was startled to find Mrs. Lovechilde standing at the doorway.

"Oh, I'm sorry. Am I being disruptive?" I asked.

Dressed in a jacket and fitted skirt with her hair in a chignon, she reminded me of every other wealthy woman I'd ever seen. It was like a uniform spelling wealth.

"Continue. I'm rather fond of Debussy," she said, coolly. "I didn't realize you were so accomplished."

"I'm having to be marked on this piece as part of my college degree. I appreciate your letting me use this fine instrument."

She lifted her chin and studied me.

"Declan… I mean Mr. Lovechilde, mentioned you used to play," I said, making small talk since she lingered.

Her eyes plowed into mine.

Did she read a connection between me and her son?

"I played that piece. Not as good as you." She turned and was met by a tall man. "Oh, Reynard, nice to see you. I was just talking to the maid. She knows her way around Debussy, it seems."

The tall, red-haired man, who'd propositioned me at the dinner party, approached the piano and signaled for me to continue.

I wasn't used to an audience, and with those cool, undressing eyes all over me, my fingers trembled.

I stopped. "Sorry, you're making me nervous."

"You're not just a pretty face, I see," he said, staring down at my thighs. Being a warm day and not expecting people, I'd dressed in shorts and a tank top.

The tank top unfortunately gaped at the neckline, and I could feel his eyes all over my breasts.

"Let's have some afternoon tea," Mrs. Lovechilde said.

He turned away and walked out of the room. I took a deep breath, got up and closed the door, and then continued to work on my piece.

Justin, a student about my age, came up to me just as I stepped onto the college grounds.

He'd been running and sounded puffed. "Hey, Thea, we're having a little get-together tomorrow night at the Thirsty Mariner. You know, the pub in the village?"

I nodded slowly. Tomorrow night seemed like a lifetime away. What was I doing? Or more specifically, what did Declan have in mind?

Seven days together. We'd seen each other every night. He always initiated of course. I was still stunned, I think. This whole romantic episode felt like a dream.

I'd promised myself to get a life. And mingling with fellow students seemed like a good start.

"Sure, that sounds like fun," I said.

"Great. It will be nice to have a drink and a chat. You're killing the practical. You're a great musician."

I smiled. "Thank you. I've only just started playing again. There's a piano where I work."

"You work at the Lovechildes' estate, I hear." His dark eyes shone with interest.

"I do. I live in the servants' quarters. It works out well for me. And I love Bridesmere. The coast is amazing."

"Isn't it? I'd like to move to London though. Once I get my certificate, that's where I'm heading."

A familiar SUV drove by. Dark windows, but I knew the car well enough. Although I'd ridden to school, sometimes Declan came by to offer me a lift.

My phone pinged. "Excuse me."

The message read: "Lift?"

I looked over at the car. He'd parked down the street behind a tree. Nice and discreet.

"Um... I best be going. Tomorrow then, at the pub."

"Yep. Seven o'clock at the Mariner." His eyes held mine for a moment, and I sensed attraction.

I smiled and left him, then collected my bike.

Having parked in front of a large peppercorn tree, Declan jumped out and opened the back for my bike. He lifted it like it was a toy, those muscles rippling through his fitted T-shirt, and the swelling between my legs started again.

It was as though I was in a constant state of arousal, even when he wasn't around. He hadn't taken his hands off me all week. Every night. He'd send me a text, and I'd ride over like a woman possessed.

I'm not sure whether he'd take a "No." There was a determination in his eyes.

Maybe to do with being filthy rich and how they were used to getting what they desired. Declan didn't strike me as that quintessential arrogant rich man. Not like Reynard Crisp. I wouldn't have been attracted otherwise.

He opened the door for me and even lifted me up. I giggled. "I can do it myself."

"You don't like me fondling you?"

Those sparkling blue eyes always left me brainless.

He pinched my bottom and I laughed. "I do. I'm just not used to this special treatment. I could have just as easily ridden my bike over."

"I hadn't heard from you. I wasn't sure if you were popping in," he said.

Was that a glint of insecurity in his eyes?

"I like to know where you are," he added.

He ran his tongue over his mouth, and like magnets our lips crushed.

I drew away from his steamy kiss. Mainly because any minute we'd have sex in the car. Especially with those wandering hands of his.

"Mm... you feel fucking hot," he said. "I'm walking around with a permanent hard-on."

I rubbed his thick length through his denim. "I've noticed."

"Who was the guy?" he asked.

CHAPTER 28

Declan

SHE WAS SO BEAUTIFUL that it hurt to stare at her. Her full lips parted like an invitation. Her chest heaved as she took short breaths. Theadora didn't know the effect she had on men, which only added to her attraction.

I'd never been jealous before but seeing that man standing close while chatting with her made my veins tighten.

All this emotion confused me.

I wouldn't have been so raw had it not been for an earlier encounter with that pompous prick, Reynard Crisp.

Wearing his signature arrogant smirk, he'd commented, "You should ask your staff to wear more clothes."

"They're not my staff. That's my mother's jurisdiction."

"You're a Lovechilde, and one day this will all be yours. I'm sure you carry some clout around here."

"Why are you here again?" I hated this man.

"I've got some business to discuss with Caroline. I was talking about your maid: the pretty, curvy one. I saw her playing the piano earlier. She wasn't wearing much. Not even a bra, from where I stood." His eyebrow rose. "Quite a show. I've seen her before, by the way."

My mind was too scattered to question him further. Instead, I drew on my army training by remaining hard-faced toward the enemy.

"You're interested in her yourself, are you?" His smirk made him uglier.

"None of your fucking business." I shoved my shoulder into him as I walked away with my hands in a fist.

Theadora had to remain my dirty secret. Even if that was becoming increasingly frustrating.

I wanted us to walk on the pier, hand in hand. Or dine together in the village. Or to keep her warm by holding her for that walk along the cliffs.

I just wanted us to be together. And that was after just one week?

I kept telling myself it was nothing but lust.

Intense, addictive lust.

I couldn't just jump in feet first until my dick went down. Until that happened, I was not in a fit state to make any commitment.

As we drove off, Theadora said, "That was Justin. He's taking the same course as me."

"Did he ask you out?"

She turned sharply and stared at me.

"What's that look?" I asked.

"Does it matter if he did?"

I drove up the hill and round the corner to Winchelsea Lane and pulled up at my home.

The answer remained stuck at the back of my throat.

I remained silent while we walked to the door.

Of course, it fucking matters.

No one was to touch her. No one.

Even the thought of Reynard Crisp seeing her braless disturbed me beyond words.

I opened the door and let her in.

"The answer is yes. It does disturb me. He wants to fuck you."

Stunned, she stopped at the entrance. Her mouth parted, as though I'd admitted to some wicked crime.

"How can you say that? You were miles away."

"Because I can read body language." I headed to the fridge and, taking a bottle of water, unscrewed the top and offered it to her.

She took it and sipped. "If I was interested, which I am not, what right have you got over me?" Her eyes were wide and fiery.

"I don't share. You know that." I took a slug of water and wiped my lips.

"I'm not interested in him or anyone. Only..." She sipped her water and looked away. "You."

I took the bottle from her hand and held her.

Warm, soft, and tactile, her body melded into mine making my heart sigh.

I not only wanted to make love to her, but I wanted to protect her.

"We've only been together for a week," she said, stepping out of my arms.

Looking overwhelmed, she rubbed her forehead. Like me, she was trying to understand this burning, unable-to-stop-touching passion of ours.

I exhaled a breath. "It's intense for me."

"It's intense for me too. You're the first man ever, and I have no idea how I should treat this." She opened out her hands. "I have a right to talk to men, though."

I nodded slowly. "That you do."

As she wore a tight T-shirt revealing the outline of her hardened nipples, I was reminded of Reynard's comments. "You were spotted not wearing a bra at Merivale."

Her face reddened. Whether that was embarrassment or anger I couldn't say. But as I was getting to know her, I'd noticed her feisty side, which only inflamed my arousal.

"That was my private time. I was practicing. I didn't expect anyone to come into the room."

"So he just waltzed in while you were playing?" I frowned. Why was that fucker even there?

"Your mother came in first."

My eyebrows sprung up. "My mother saw you without a bra?"

She puffed. "I was wearing a fucking bra." Her voice, despite being abrasive, quivered. "I'd unloosened it while I was practicing. And because I had a tank top on, well…" She shook her head and knitted her fingers. "It all happened suddenly. One minute she's in there chatting to me about the piece I was playing and the next minute that creepy guy came in and started staring down my top." Tears coated her large eyes.

She grabbed her backpack.

"Where are you going?" I asked.

"I'm leaving. I can't stand this. You're making me go crazy. I can't concentrate on my work. With the little practice I get, this happens. I didn't ask for this."

She stormed off, leaving me there completely bewildered.

Snapping out of it, I went after her as Theadora charged off up the hill. Her bike was still in the back of my car.

I ran after her. "Come back. I'm sorry."

She turned and her watery eyes met mine.

Watching on, Alice, an older neighbor, happened to be in her garden with her Jack Russell.

I waved at her, and Theadora, noticing my dotty neighbor, gave me a subtle eye-roll.

When we were in my front yard, I said, "Thanks for not making a scene in front of Alice. As it stands, everyone will hear about it tomorrow."

She shook her head. "It's becoming difficult to keep a secret."

I scratched my jaw. "You're right. Small villages have their charms but also setbacks. People love to gossip."

I led her inside. "I've got pizza." I tilted my head. A peace offering of sorts.

"I guess I could eat. I am hungry," she said, with a faint smile.

"That's better." I kissed her cool lips.

She sat at the island in the kitchen, and I opened the pizza carton and got her a plate. "Help yourself."

"Mm… thanks. Yum. Just what I feel like, carbs." She smiled shyly.

Back to that uncertain girl.

I liked every shade of Theadora. Feisty. Shy. Sexy. Nervy. Sad. All of her.

"About earlier." I wiped my mouth with a paper napkin. "I didn't mean to tell you what to wear."

"That's okay. It's understandable. It's not a nice look. Me getting around in tiny shorts and a tank top."

"I'd love to see you in tiny shorts and braless." I smirked.

"That's because you're insatiable." She pulled a face and made me smile. "But hey, I'll stick to wearing loose clothes. Even if it means shopping at a charity shop for vintage grandma clothes."

I laughed. "You'd look great in a sack. But hey, wear what you like. But maybe a bra. You're a big girl."

My dick stretched as my eyes traveled down to her tight blouse. Her nipples hardened, and I wanted to devour her more than my slice of pizza.

"Talking of clothes, well underclothing." I felt myself blushing. Ridiculous really, considering how I generally ripped her underwear off with my teeth. "I bought you something."

I couldn't resist after walking past a lingerie shop. I had this thing for lacy underwear, and Theadora wore it well.

Very well.

"Oh really." Her eyes sparkled with curiosity. "Mm..." She held her chin. "Let me guess. Lacy and skimpy?"

I nodded. "After destroying all of yours, I felt it my duty."

She giggled.

After we ate, we settled on the sofa.

"How's the boot camp going?"

"It should be up and running by the end of the month."

"That's so soon," she said. "Will you be running drills too? Or just overseeing it?"

"I'll just oversee it. Carson will be in charge. He's formidable when it comes to getting results. I'm too much of a softy."

Her head pushed back. "You don't look like a softy." She ran her hand over my biceps. "You're certainly not built like one."

I rose and grabbed the shopping bag from the bedroom. "Here. For you. Or I should say for me." I arched an eyebrow. "You don't mind, do you?"

She shook her head as she held up a white lace crotchless teddy. "Wow, they forgot to sew in a gusset."

"I thought it would be nice." I grinned.

"Especially now I've had that Brazilian." She arched her eyebrows.

"Thank you for doing that. You didn't have to." Boy, my cock loved it though. "I like seeing you. All of you."

"Should I try it on?"

I nodded. Unzipping my jeans to release the ache. Just talking about sex made me hot and bothered.

"Give me a couple of moments. Do you want me in the bedroom?"

"What I want to do to you, yes. It might be more comfortable," I said.

A few minutes later, she called out, "Ready, Mr. Lovechilde."

I laughed at her silly reference to me being her boss and her my dirty maid. I liked the game though.

Anything that placed a wedge between us and reality.

She laid on the bed, propped up against pillows. Barely covering her, I'd bought the tiniest garment I could find.

Her nipples spiked through the lace, making me salivate.

I pointed. "Open your legs for me."

Wearing a coy smile, which only made me hornier, she parted her legs, and I groaned at how pink and juicy her slit looked.

My cock turned to steel, and I removed my jeans to release it.

"Aren't you a sexy, dirty little maid." My voice was hoarse with arousal. "Touch yourself."

She stroked her clit and then entered herself with her finger.

My heart pounded like this was my first time with her.

"Can I have a taste now?" I sat on the edge of the bed and palmed her tits, fondling and squeezing them, getting off on how warm and soft and firm they felt.

I kissed her sweet lips and then trailed kisses down to her nipples. Biting through the lace. I tore at the lace and sucked on her nipples while running my hands over her small waist.

"Sit on my face," I said.

"What?" She laughed. "Are you serious?"

"Yep. Very. Just do it."

"Mm... bossy."

She enjoyed this game as much as I did.

"Nothing like dancing cheek to cheek," I quipped.

"I'll squash you."

I held her by the hips and positioned her curvy bum on my cheeks, and I proceeded to lick, nibble, and lap up her juicy pussy.

She writhed in my hands. "Oh my god. Please stop."

I kept sucking at her clit until she spurted cum all over my face while digging her nails into my shoulders.

Pain had never felt so good.

I helped her off.

"Holy shit. That was crazy." She giggled.

"On all fours," I said.

She turned around and with her arse grinding against my pelvis, I entered in one deep thrust and grunted.

Me grunt? I'd never been vocal when fucking before.

I watched us in the mirror, and as her tits fell onto my palms, I pounded into her like a man drugged on sex.

The image of my red raw cock entering her balls deep, and me gently tugging on her hair so her head fell back made for a wet dream that would never leave me. I was sure of that.

"Can you see how fucking horny you look?"

"Uh-huh," she murmured. Moaning as I pounded into her.

The white lace framing her bottom accentuated its delicious curves.

I pumped and pumped into her. Blood gushed through me. I closed my eyes and released an agonized groan.

Her cunt convulsed uncontrollably as she cried out at the same time as I shot deeply into her.

Falling on my back, I puffed and panted, then taking her into my arms I kissed her tenderly.

I felt her silky, soft hair between my fingers while I drew in her sweet feminine smell as I would a rose. I squeezed her tightly, and she giggled. I gazed into her eyes, and my heart soared like a bird in paradise.

She felt so comfortable in my arms. A perfect sleeping potion. I always had sweet dreams, and in the mornings woke with a smile feeling her warm breath on my chest.

CHAPTER 29

Thea

HIGH-PRESSURE JETS MASSAGED EVERY inch of my body. A euphoric sigh issued from my lips as the cascade of water heated my skin and relaxed my muscles. Talk about pampering of the royal kind.

Declan stepped in, offering to wash my hair.

Muscle on muscle. A strong, powerful body. Long, muscular legs. I wondered if he still worked out. I'd seen gym equipment tucked away at the back. One didn't get that kind of body sitting around.

I'd gotten into the habit of googling him, given that every time we met there was little talking going on, other than him asking me to take my clothes off, or telling me how beautiful and sexy I looked.

There was the odd article relating to his bravery as a soldier. Mostly magazine articles reminding the world of wannabe Cinderellas that he was a hot, eligible billionaire. Images of him looking annoyingly photogenic. He never looked ugly. Even in the mornings with that thick, messy wave of hair, and aquamarine eyes all sleepy and sexy.

Most of the articles were general fluff about women throwing themselves at him, and him talking of an ambition to help troubled youth. No mention of marriage or the desire for a family one day.

They painted him as a playboy, which made me lose sleep.

I had to keep reminding myself this was just hot sex with my boss. Former boss, now that I'd agreed to stop cleaning for him.

He even admitted that he only employed me because he wanted to fuck me. I could have gotten shitty over that, but instead, I fell under his spell and drowned in those soft turquoise eyes.

At least he was honest.

The water jets sprayed us from all angles. As I closed my eyes, his arms embraced me from behind. He kissed my neck and ran his tongue along the ridge of my shoulder.

I leaned back against him, letting him support me as he washed my hair. His firm fingers massaged my scalp, sending ripples of pleasure through me.

Even my mother didn't wash my hair. I had a nanny to do that.

Tears burned at the back of my eyes. I was getting too attached. Fear gatecrashing my state of bliss.

"You're spoiling me," I said, turning around.

He smiled sweetly and then kissed me tenderly. And there was the contradiction or reassurance. Or both.

Declan was always sweet. We shared simple experiences, like playing chess or watching television. We'd have long conversations about everything: countries we'd like to visit, movies and books we loved. He was keenly interested in my ambition to become a teacher.

He always held my hand or draped his arm over me.

It wasn't just hot sex.

The glow of warmth between us made my heart burst from my chest. A kind of euphoric orgasm. But then fear and insecurity would sneak in and spoil the party.

It was like a battle between my head and my heart. My body however seemed to dictate. Just a whiff of him, or seeing him shirtless, or that insistent bulge tenting his briefs, and I was a goner. My heart and head standing by, helpless to meddle, waving their finger, yelling, "Beware."

I washed him with a sponge and a squirt of divine-smelling body wash.

Instead of sponging his dick, I played with it in my hand. My mouth watering at how thick it grew in my clutch.

While the thought of sucking a man's dick would have once made my stomach turn, sucking Declan's dick had become a steamy obsession.

I got down on my knees.

With the warm water cascading over me, I looked up at him and put his dick in my mouth.

"Angel, you don't have to do this."

I melted.

Angel?

His dick grew even harder stretching my mouth. Where the hell was all that dick going to go? I even gagged.

"You really don't have to …. oh god, that feels nice." Biting his lip, Declan's eyes hooded. "Where did you learn to do that?"

I removed it from my mouth and said, "I've been practicing."

His beautiful face contorted. "What?"

I laughed and placed his dick in my mouth, moving up and down.

He stopped me. "What do you mean you've been practicing?"

Declan had a possessive streak, which made my heart smile and my free spirit frown.

"With a banana. Lucy showed me."

"Really?" His brows lifted. "Then she's a good teacher."

His dick was so big my mouth hurt, but I continued to move up and down while sucking, as the head dripped pre-cum onto my tongue.

"I need to be inside you," he said as though struggling for air.

We'd fucked for half the night. Like every night for that past week or so. Was it seven days? I couldn't recall.

Hormones and endless orgasms had fogged my brain. At times, I couldn't even remember my name.

It was incomprehensible but I'd become just as insatiable.

He turned me around and sucked on my neck, sending delicious sparks to my cleft.

He rubbed his dick and balls against my bum.

"I don't want to do anal," I said.

"I don't go for that. I'm addicted to your tight, little creamy pussy."

His dick entered, and he pounded into me until I saw stars and flew into another universe. Our groans echoed loudly against the tiled walls.

He blew so hard I could feel his sperm gushing inside of me and the veins of his shaft pulsating against my walls.

"You're an addiction, Theadora." He breathed against my neck.

"So are you." I turned to face him.

A deep searching expression shone in his eyes. Was that vulnerability peeking through? Or me seeing myself through his eyes?

THE THIRSTY MARINER REMINDED me of a maritime museum. Tankards and jugs with animated faces sat on shelves. The walls held images of fishing boats from the olden days while navigating instruments and all kinds of seafaring objects sat in glass cases.

There was a stage set in the corner with musical instruments, including a piano as old as the pub.

Justin and six others, whose names I couldn't remember, joined me at the bar.

Being my first social outing with fellow students, I wasn't quite sure where to place my attention among the loud, excitable bunch.

After seeing Declan every night, it felt odd not seeing him. But I was becoming too attached. I needed this. To hang out with people, if only to remind myself that there was life outside of Declan's bedroom.

My body wasn't so convinced after that steamy bathroom scene.

Between us, we generated enough steam to keep a house heated.

The red mark on my neck where he'd devoured me meant I had to wear a scarf to the pub.

Luckily, I had the night off.

Just as I was leaving the hall, I noticed a caterer arrive for what looked like another dinner party. Luckily I wasn't asked to work. I couldn't exactly wear a turtleneck under my shirt.

"So, you're more into classical than contemporary?" Justin asked, standing so close his cologne drifted up my nose.

I nodded. He had nice brown eyes and a tall, strong body, and had I not been smitten with Declan I might have even been attracted. But no one compared to my former boss.

"You're very talented," he said.

"Thanks. Are you majoring in piano too?" I asked, realizing that I knew very little about him, other than he was in the same course.

"Guitar's my instrument. We're playing tonight. Just jamming really. Twelve-bar blues. That kind of thing."

"Oh, really?"

He nodded. "Mirabel Storm, who lives in the village, is a great singer. She writes her own songs. Normally, she plays on her own, but lately, we've been joining her for a few tunes. Perhaps you might want to jump on the piano?"

I gulped down my wine at that suggestion. Me? Play in front of a crowd? "I'm not great at improvising."

He frowned. "If you can play Debussy, I think you can improvise around blues chords."

"Is it just rock?" I asked.

"Mirabel is a blues-cum-folk singer. She writes her own songs. Mainly about the environment."

"I look forward to hearing her," I said.

"Why don't we have a round of shots? Maybe that will free you up. It's a lot of fun. It's become a bit of a regular thing for us. And you're the most accomplished musician out of all of us."

I smiled. Who didn't like a compliment?

"We'll see. Maybe after a couple of drinks, I might loosen up."

He smiled brightly. "That's more like it."

After a few drinks, I did get into the swing of things.

Mirabel Storm performed her songs and swept me away. Her voice reminded me of the sea. Wispy at times and filled with anger and bite at others. With long red hair and big green eyes, she was stunningly beautiful in an earthy way.

After finishing her set, she joined us, and we were introduced.

"That was amazing. Great lyrics, and I like your choice of chords," I said.

"Thank you." She smiled.

"Theadora's a great piano player," Justin interjected.

I rolled my eyes. "I'm not that good. I hardly ever practice."

"Perhaps you might want to play along in the next set. I'd love some piano. I write mainly about the sea," Mirabel said.

"I noticed. Your voice sounds like the wind. I love your floaty style and how you vocalize your lyrics."

Mirabel's green eyes sparked up. "That is such a compliment. It's exactly what I aim for. To make pictures with my words and vocals."

"It's very haunting," I said. "At times you remind me of Kate Bush."

Her face lit up. "Oh my god, I love her."

"So do I." I smiled.

"Are you from these parts?" Mirabel asked, accepting a glass of red wine from Justin, who was hovering close. He seemed to enjoy my company for some reason, and he was a big fan of Mirabel's, which was understandable given her talent and down-to-earth vibe.

"I've only recently moved here," I said.

"She works for the Lovechildes," Justin added.

Mirabel nodded slowly and I noticed a slight curve of her lips. "At Merivale Hall?"

I nodded. "You've visited?"

"Like yeah. I grew up there on a farm. My family was in the dairy industry for two centuries."

"So you've lived here all your life?" I asked.

"I have. I mean, I hang out in London when I can, and I've traveled throughout Europe, busking."

"Do you have any recordings?" Relaxed and a little tipsy after a couple of shots, I liked being there, chatting with new people.

"I do. I sell them when I busk. That's how I make a living." She sipped her drink while studying me. "So, you've met the sons and daughter?"

I nodded. "Mainly Declan. I was cleaning for him at his home up to recently."

"He's the nicer of the three. But he's got a nasty skeleton in the cupboard."

My spine stiffened, and a queasy feeling settled in the pit of my gut, turning my cheery mood on its side.

"Oh, really? He doesn't strike me as someone who'd go out of his way to be nasty." I chewed on a nail. The natural pessimist in me always assumed the worst.

"He's not that bad. Only he just broke many girls' hearts. It's hard to dislike him because he's generous and has done a lot for the community. Not like his loudmouth dick of a brother."

Was I the next one he would hurt?

My mouth was so dry from pounding anxiety, I guzzled my drink. After all those years of keeping my emotions bottled up, how did I let myself become so vulnerable?

Justin, who'd been standing close, joined the conversation. "But you had a thing with Ethan when you were sixteen, didn't you?"

Mirabel rolled her eyes. "We had a moment. Just a bit of kissing. Nothing more. I was only sixteen. That's how I know he's a tosser. That was my first song about him."

I nodded absently. I wanted to hear more about Declan and that nasty skeleton and not so much about Ethan.

CHAPTER 30

Declan

I STARED DOWN AT my watch. It was 9 p.m. Another dinner. This time Will's birthday. When the cake arrived, I sighed with relief knowing I could leave after that.

"Where's the new maid?" Ethan asked.

"Her night off, I suppose." I pulled my poker face. My brother and I generally opened up about our women, but this was different.

"Have you fucked her yet?" He grinned.

"None of your fucking business."

He stared me in the eyes. "You have."

I chose silence instead. My brother could read between the lines. By now he knew the answer.

The candles were placed on the cake, and "Happy Birthday" was belted out by the guests.

It was an intimate gathering for a change. Just a dozen people.

As it was Will's birthday, my father was there with Luke.

"Isn't this cozy?" Ethan chuckled. "I think it shows maturity. Mother accepting Father for what he's become and Father accepting her, even after cheating on him all these years."

"Yeah, one big happy family."

"You haven't gotten used to it?" he asked, grinning at my sarcastic tone.

"Nope. There's tension. You can feel it, can't you?"

"It's all about the resort development. Mother's in Dad's ear non-stop about it."

"At least that's something that isn't being trashed. Just their marriage." The butler passed me a slice of cake, and I thanked him with a nod.

"Since when have you been so conservative about marriages? The last time I heard, you were against the whole forever and ever concept," Ethan said, swallowing a spoonful of cake.

I shrugged. "I'm just referring to the cheating that's been going on under this roof. They should have separated first. But yeah, I'm not that keen on commitment."

So why the fuck am I sweating over Theadora going to the pub tonight with that good-looking student?

"Here's to another forty years," my mother toasted.

We rose and drank to Will's health.

Ten minutes later, I left, and as I stepped onto the front grounds, I found Ethan sharing a cigarette with my sister.

"I thought you'd both given up," I said.

"I have. But Savvie hasn't, and I need a hit of nicotine after that charade."

"I don't even know why Mummy insisted on a dinner." Savanah turned to me. "I hear the boot camp's launch is in four weeks. Are we invited?"

"I wouldn't have thought that's your kind of thing," I said.

"Mm... I'm rather fond of alpha males." She puffed out smoke.

"Are you still going out with that coke dealer?" Ethan asked.

My sister scrunched her face. "No. He's so yesterday. I'm single at the moment."

My sister and her bad boys. "Is he still stalking you?" I asked.

"He is. I might need a bodyguard. What's Carson up to?"

"He's going to have his hands full with the boot camp. I've got him in charge of the training program. I can put out the word. Some of my former army mates are now working in security." I grew suspicious. "You don't strike me as worried."

"I can look after myself. But yeah, I might hire someone for when I'm in London."

I peered down at my watch. "I've got to go."

"Hey, can you give me a lift into the village?" Ethan asked.

"Sure." An uncomfortable feeling settled in my stomach. I had no intention of going to that pub earlier, but my need to see Theadora had deepened by the minute.

"Where are you off to?" Savvie asked.

"I thought I might drop into the Mariner for a drink and see what the locals are up to," Ethan said.

"Singing sea shanties, guzzling stout, and stinking of fish." Savvie giggled. "I might tag along though. Anything to get away from the tension in there. I can just hear Mother talking endlessly about the resort and Father sinking back the drinks. Hey, do you think Luke's into him? Or do you think he's just after his money?"

I was too busy trying to figure out how I could shake off my siblings from visiting the local to answer.

"He doesn't strike me as being in love," Ethan said.

They followed me to my car and jumped in.

When we arrived at the pub, Ethan asked, "Are you coming in?"

I regarded them both: my brother in his designer blazer and slacks and my sister in a shimmery dress more suited for a London dance club.

"Maybe for one drink, then," I said.

"Yay. Go, bro." Ethan climbed out of the SUV.

"I'll be there in a minute. I'll just park the car."

I parked and sat there for a moment, lost in contemplation, as I rubbed my face.

Bailing out was not an option. I had to know that Theadora wasn't going to end up with that guy from college. He was dead keen. That was obvious enough.

I buried my head in my hands. What was I doing? After spending every night together, I was already suffering withdrawal symptoms.

Perhaps I had to offer her something.

But what exactly?

I had to get my shit together first and maybe travel a little more. Or was that just me making excuses?

I could stare suicide bombers in the face, but not love.

Love?

How did one distinguish between love and lust?

With all these questions swimming in my head, I walked slowly to the pub.

MIRABEL STORM STRUMMED HER guitar while singing a haunting and mesmerizing song. All eyes were on the stage, modestly lit by one spotlight, where Theadora, looking like a goddess, accompanied on the piano.

With his attention riveted to the stage, Ethan's eyes beamed with appreciation. "They're so accomplished," he whispered.

Smooth and polished, the music struck me as well-rehearsed. I wondered how and when Theadora had gotten with Mirabel to practice.

I ordered a pint and then zeroed in on Theadora again, whose presence was captivating. Regardless of our intimate relationship, I would have still been entranced.

Her fingers ran over the keyboard with confidence and agility. Playing the piano like it was her lover.

"I didn't realize our maid was so talented," Savanah said.

Theadora's eyes widened slightly when seeing me, and I returned a smile.

The song ended and the bar erupted into rapturous applause. As she moved off the platform, Theadora was swept into a huddle of enthusiastic patrons, all offering their appreciative support. She smiled shyly and then her eyes caught mine again.

Just as she made her way towards me, Justin jumped in and hugged her. Jealousy curled deeply in my gut. I longed to go up to her and hug her. To sweep her away from the men that suddenly surrounded her.

Ethan snapped me out of the conflict ringing in my head.

"Say. That was amazing. I think I'll sign them up." He chuckled.

Mirabel joined us at the bar and greeted me before shifting her focus to Ethan, who looked a little uncertain. A rare response from my gregarious brother.

Like Ethan, I'd become jittery. I could either go and claim Theadora or maintain the cool distance of a former boss. But seeing Justin with his arm around her turned that idea on its head. To not claim her was like waiting for a predator to strike.

I ordered a whisky.

"I'll have one of those too," Ethan said. His eyes stuck on Mirabel.

She looked at me and said, "I haven't seen you for years."

"I've been away on tour with the SAS."

"I read about the boot camp. I can't imagine your mother's too pleased." She smirked. It was no secret that Mirabel resented my mother's ambition to develop the farmlands.

"Can I buy you a drink?" I asked. "That was sensational, by the way."

"I'll just have a pint, then."

I ordered her drink and then gulped back a shot.

"Planning on a big night?" she asked.

I shook my head. "Say, that worked well with the piano. Have you met Theadora before?"

"No. Only tonight. It was inspiring for sure. I think I'll see if she's interested in doing some gigs."

I hated the sound of that, and all the men that would descend on her.

"So, Mirabel, you raged up there. That was something else," Ethan said.

She looked from Ethan to me. "You both stand out in your designer suits."

"We had a dinner at Merivale. I heard you were playing. That's why I came," Ethan said.

Her eyes softened, supplanting her mocking grin, and I left them in their little bubble.

My sister, meanwhile, had struck up a conversation with a local character known for dealing weed and coke. When it came to bad boys, she had a nose for them. I silently rolled my eyes and decided to ignore that whole situation. When it came to out-of-control trains, my sister rode the front carriage, singing along to Amy Winehouse.

Squaring my shoulders, I took a deep breath and went to claim what was mine.

Theadora's breasts seemed to burst out of a tiny blouse. Her milky soft midriff and cleavage poked out, and her tight jeans showcased that sexy arse. She was by far the most beautiful woman there.

My bed was the only bed she would be sleeping in tonight. I would see to that.

Justin stuck to her like glue. It was obvious he wanted to fuck her.

"Hello, Mr. Lovechilde," she said as I stood behind Justin.

How was I going to avoid knocking this guy's teeth out? He was all smiles and touchy-feely towards her. My knuckles cracked. An over-whelming urge to tell him to "fuck off" consumed me suddenly.

"That was a great performance. You're a natural," I said, drawing on my Mr. Cool act. When it came to controlling emotion, the army had trained me well.

"Thanks." Her rosy lips curled slowly, making my mouth water. All I could think of was kissing her all night long. I'd never been much for kissing, but with Theadora that's all I could dream of at that moment.

I tried not to devour her with my gaze, but testosterone had the upper hand. I was sure I'd given the game away, going on how her college friends turned to stare.

"Can I buy you a drink?" I asked.

She shook her head. "I'm good, thanks."

She might as well have slapped me because that rejection heated my jaw.

Feeling like half of my legs had been chopped off, I plodded back to the bar and stood next to Savanah, who was ordering a drink.

"Hey, are you fucking the maid?" she asked.

Seething frustration at my inability to navigate this squeamish game of pretense, I muttered, "Don't you fucking dare, Savvie."

"Oh, you are." She poked at me. "She's gorgeous. You could do worse."

"Mm... tell me about it. Don't tell Mother, whatever you do. And it's just a fling."

Is it?

Savanah scrutinized me. Head inclined. "I think it's more than that," she sang with a delighted smile. "Anyway, you better go and rescue her, because that guy's all over her, and he's kinda hot."

My jaw clamped. "Thanks for the advice, sis."

CHAPTER 31

Thea

I COULDN'T HELP BUT swoon, seeing Declan there. Especially after Justin said he'd never seen him at the Mariner before, which meant Declan had come to see me.

At that thought, my inner tart danced shamelessly with glee, while the independent version crossed her arms declaring, "Sexy, hot billionaire or not, no man is going to control me."

Talk about being conflicted. But I couldn't let my heart run away to some fantasy island where a lover with big muscles and sparkling blue eyes welcomed me every day with multiple sheet-clawing orgasms.

We were meant to be a secret. So I was doing him a favor, even if knocking back that drink invite pained me.

Despite this inner turmoil, accompanying Mirabel's stirring song about the sea drowning in plastic proved a highlight of my fledgling musical career.

Justin kept whispering and breathing down my neck.

I wasn't interested.

How could I be?

Of course, I wanted to leave with Declan and go back to his place and try on whatever sexy item of lingerie he'd picked up for me. My body throbbed with desire thinking about him. It felt strange, us being in the same room and not touching.

Two weeks into this affair, I kept wondering why he hated committed relationships, while Mirabel's reference to some scandal involving Declan percolated at the back of my thoughts too.

"Do you want to go out to a club?" Justin asked.

"It's a bit late, isn't it?"

"It's Friday." He moved his hips around. "We can dance into the morning. There's a great club in Trentham. Only twenty minutes away."

I stared over his shoulder. Declan's eyes burned into mine. I could play this game and go. Drive him crazy. Or would it?

I had a right to do whatever I wanted.

Dance music suddenly blared, and the pub erupted into an impromptu club.

"There's no need to go anywhere. There's dancing here," I said.

He led me by the hand. "Come on. Let's have a dance."

Before I could say no, Justin had his hands around my hips and was close to dry-humping me.

Talk about frisky. He'd been drinking.

I stepped away from him but continued to sway my hips with my arms in the air. Others joined us including Savanah, Ethan, and Mirabel, who kept rolling her eyes at Ethan, despite my sensing her attraction.

I closed my eyes and felt a breath on my neck. A familiar scent traveled through my senses, and my nipples tightened.

I turned and was joined by Declan, who, I soon discovered, danced like he fucked, causing my legs to turn to jelly.

His inviting eyes burned into mine.

Oblivious to my new dancing partner, Justin moved in close, and Declan narrowed his eyes.

Ignoring my lover's dark response, Justin grabbed me.

"Take your hands off her," Declan said, his chest virtually bumping into Justin's.

I knew that if I didn't walk away there'd be a fight, so I left them and hurried outside.

A few seconds later, Declan followed.

"What are you doing here?" I asked.

"I came to see you. You didn't respond to my texts about catching up later tonight."

I studied his handsome face, which under the moonlight looked older but sexier. He massaged his jaw. Something he did when emotionally challenged.

"You nearly caused a scene in there," I said.

He looked me in the eyes. "Why didn't you respond to my texts?"

"I turned off my phone." I was about to walk off.

"Hey." He took my arm.

"You don't own me."

His eyes shone with that uncertain fragile expression I caught a glimpse of when he first entered me. That look registered deep in my soul.

I just wanted to fall into his arms and put a pause to this stupid game, despite my tougher side dictating that I make him sweat.

I wanted him to commit to us.

This arrangement confused me. He didn't like to share, nor did I. It would tear me apart to know he was fucking someone else.

"Do you want to fuck him?" he asked.

"That's none of your business. I'm just your fuck buddy," I said. "You don't own me."

"I do own you."

That powerful statement made me freeze on the spot. I turned to face him again.

He took my hand, the warmth of which shot up my arm and to my heart, while his gaze burned into me.

"You've only ever been with me." He tapped his heart. "That makes you a part of me."

I had to tear myself away. His eyes shone with so much depth I was close to falling in again and drowning in emotion.

"But I thought you wanted me as your plaything. I've got a right to meet people and have other relationships. What happens when you are no longer interested?"

A line deepened between his brows. "Do you want to go out with other men?"

"Do you want to go out with other women?"

He trapped my eyes while taking ages to answer. Every second made my heart pound harder—frightened of what he might say.

"I haven't even looked at another woman since falling for you."

Falling for me?

"I was your first. Doesn't that mean something to you?" he asked, sounding even more fragile than ever.

I nodded. Hell yeah. Of course, it meant something. I'd lost more than my virginity to this man. I'd lost my fucking mind.

My heart too.

I bit my lip and looked down at my feet. I couldn't tell him that. It would disempower me.

"You want to go back in there and keep flirting with him?" he asked, looking dejected.

My heart broke. I hated this game I was playing.

"I haven't planned anything. I don't want to fuck him, no. But at the same time, if I did, I'd have a moral right to."

His indigo eyes reflected a hint of torment or, strangely, like when he was about to climax.

Everything about him echoed sex.

I couldn't allow my fucking vagina to control me.

No matter how hot and swollen he made me.

"You're right," he said at last.

He was about to walk away.

Shit.

"Where are you going?" I asked.

"I'm going home. I'm tired. I don't like games, Theadora." He paused and again looked deep into my eyes. "I think I'm in love with you."

He walked away and left me standing there. My jaw was wide open and my heart raced.

In love? With me?

I paced about in the dark. The salt air sobered me up after what had been a boozy night.

Declan Lovechilde was in love with me?

Or was he only really in lust with me?

And me. What did I feel?

I didn't even know how to love when all I'd done was hate for most of my life.

My brain went into meltdown. I couldn't go back into the pub. Not after that.

I was embarrassed by what had happened inside. If anything, Declan had shown everyone that he'd come to claim me.

Everyone watched. Dressed as though he'd been at a dinner party, which he had been, he'd stood out. He'd stand out in charity shop clothes. Beautiful people always did.

My phone beeped.

His message read, "I meant it."

Tears streamed down my cheeks.

I called Lucy.

"Hey, sweetie," she said. "How's your gorgeous billionaire going?"

"Oh, Lucy." I poured my heart out, relaying what had happened, while sobbing through my words. "What should I do?"

"He told you he loved you. Fuck, Thea, isn't that enough?"

"I don't know. It's probably lust."

"Well, yeah. Can't have love without lust. Unless it's family love, of course."

I gulped. "Do you think I should go to him?"

"God yeah. I mean, he's hot, rich, and into you. What more can you want?"

"I just freaked at how possessive he's become. He nearly punched Justin in the face. I'm scared he'll stop me from doing what I want to do."

"Look, sweetie, you can have your career and him if you like. Why aren't you chasing after him? And he makes you come. He loves eating pussy. Shit. You've won the fucking lottery."

I laughed and cried and my heart felt like it was going to explode.

"I best go."

"What are you going to do?" she asked.

"I'm going to go to him and get down on my knees and suck his dick."

"Aah... that's my girl. That's more like it."

DECLAN ANSWERED THE DOOR and found me shivering with my arms crossed. That visceral reaction had more to do with a deluge of emotion rather than the crisp air.

"Are you cold?" he asked, letting me in.

I nodded. "I must look a fright."

He wiped my cheek. His brow lowered. "Have you been crying?"

I nodded slowly and bit my lip.

"Come on. I'll make you a nice cup of tea."

I followed him from behind, perving on his firm butt in fitted black jeans, and all I could think of was gyrating over him in skimpy lingerie.

I also just wanted to hold him. To feel his warmth all over me.

I went to the bathroom, and my mascara had run all over my face. I looked a fright.

After I'd wiped my face, I joined him in the kitchen and watched him pour hot water into a teapot.

We stared at each other and without saying another word, our mouths collided in a crush of passion.

He lifted me and carried me into the bedroom, sat me on the bed, and we held each other. No ripping at clothes or passionate little bites and gropes, but a deep embrace.

Smooth and moist, his lips, tasting of whisky and a hint of salt touched my lips, and I lost myself. Warmth spread through me as our kiss deepened. He pulled me in tight as he cradled my head in his arms.

I floated away to our own private world as our tongues entwined like tendrils of a vine.

I felt love on his lips. I felt love in his arms.

My heart opened wide and welcomed him in.

CHAPTER 32

Declan

"YOU HAVEN'T WASTED TIME," Carson said, exiting the gym.

"I've had them working around the clock. I want this to happen sooner than later."

"What's the hurry?"

I shrugged. "I like to stay busy."

"How are you sleeping?" he asked as we stepped onto the field where training equipment had been laid out.

"I haven't had a nightmare since being with Theadora. It's been a month now. We haven't spent one night apart." I raised an eyebrow at that startling admission. I thought my need for her might have abated, but if anything, my desire for Theadora had only strengthened.

It wasn't just the sex, however. She'd become a part of my life. Our sweet moments together, like making pancakes for breakfast or cooking an evening meal together, really mattered to me. I loved her laugh and the way she danced when she was happy and how she cracked up at my silly comments.

"That sounds like she might be the one." He pulled on a swinging rope to test its strength.

I nodded slowly.

After the pub incident, and with me opening up to Theadora about feelings that I was only starting to understand, we'd decided to make it official. I now thought of her as my girlfriend. It was a natural progression, and one I accepted with open arms.

No more sneaking around.

"You look well. Happier than I've ever seen you, I think," he said.

"That shouldn't come as a surprise. We weren't exactly bubbling over with joy in Afghanistan."

He pulled a tight smile. "Do you miss flying?"

"I do. A lot. I mean, I put myself through all of that just to fly."

"You could have just gotten a pilot's license, you know." He smirked.

"I know. But I needed discipline. I needed to get away." I rubbed my neck.

"Me too. It was either the army or joining a criminal gang." He dribbled a ball on the ground. "But hey, we're alive. Life's great. Pussy on tap. Who can complain?"

I laughed. Pussy on tap. All right. Beautiful Theadora. That put a smile on my face.

"In any case, I've got a Gulfstream on order." A smile beamed through me. The thought of my owning a plane excited me.

His brows hit his hairline. "Holy crap. I forgot how rich you are."

Yep. I was loaded. Thanks to my grandfather's generosity.

"You'll fly it, I imagine?"

I pulled a face. He might as well have asked if I wanted food after fasting for a week. "I reckon. I mean would you buy a Ferrari for your chauffeur to drive?"

He laughed. "For starters, I don't have a chauffeur. But sure, I get your point."

"Does your mother know about the plane?" he asked.

I shook my head. "She hates me flying." Cold water just doused my warm glow. I imagined my mother demanding I take it back, like when she admonished my grandfather for gifting me a hunting rifle for my eighteenth birthday.

"So where did you meet this girl? I thought you have sworn off relationships," he said, jumping up on the parallel bars and swinging effortlessly.

"Theadora works for my mother as a maid. She lives here on the estate."

"Hanging with us lower classes, hey?" He chuckled.

Although he was playing with me, and I could take a joke like anyone, it still felt like a kick in the ribs. More as a reminder of my mother's bigotry.

"In my book, it takes more than money to make a person."

He narrowed his eyes. "You seem pretty smitten. Are you going to marry her?"

I shrugged. "Marriage has never been on my to-do list."

He nodded thoughtfully. "We're on the same page there, for sure. A fucked-up institution."

"I'm not that cynical about marriage. It's just that if I tie that knot, it will be a bowline."

He laughed at my reference to our army training. "Secure. Easy to do, and dependable."

I chuckled at his paraphrasing our military master.

He tossed me a ball, and I reached up with one hand to catch it. "Since being with Theadora I'm no longer the same."

"You say that as though it's painful." He bounced the ball.

"It's confusing, not painful. A couple of weeks back I saw her with a guy who was trying to get into her pants. A guy she goes to college with, and I wanted to fucking kill him. Now that was a pretty fucked up reaction, wouldn't you say?"

He studied me for a moment. "You're protecting what's yours, I suppose. Jealousy and love are inseparable."

"Yeah, too right. I've never been this way about a girl. Ever. I was her first, you know." I kicked the ball back to him.

He looked surprised. "Really? Wow. Like the olden days. When couples had sex for the first time on their wedding night. Imagine that."

I caught the ball. "There's something really powerful about knowing that she's only ever been with you though."

"I get that. But it's also chemistry. It's all about the connection. In and out of bed. The fit, man." He chuckled. "You can't exactly annul a marriage because your new wife is shit in the sack."

"But it's a two-way thing. She can learn. It's up to us to pleasure her."

"That's if she lets us. I met a girl last week who hated me going down on her." His grimace at how preposterous that was made me chuckle.

I nodded. "Love tonguing pussy."

He laughed. "Yep. One of the finer pleasures in life."

I thought of Theadora and how she loved me devouring her pussy. She was an absolute natural in that department, and she seemed to love having my dick in her mouth too.

But it was the fit. How she felt when I was inside her. I'd never experienced such explosive orgasms before.

There was much more than that though. We talked about everything. I enjoyed her company. I wanted to share my day with her.

I kicked the ball. "If she's not around I think about her. All the time."

He nodded slowly. "You're in love."

I scanned his face. "But is it love? Or just lust? From the moment I saw her. Even though she was drugged-out and asleep on my couch and even with me thinking she was a working girl, I became almost instantly obsessed."

His eyebrows sprung up. "You thought she was a working girl?"

I'd told him how I'd saved Theadora.

He shook his head. "What a way to meet. And then she gets a gig working here. Shit. What are the chances?"

That thought had crossed my mind on a few occasions.

"You look happy, man." He slapped me on the back. "And hey"—he stretched out his arms—"this circuit's a ballbreaker. Can't wait to get to work. Do we get to try it first?"

"That's what the publicist wants so that she can bring in a film crew and have us former soldiers going through the motions."

"Let me guess. Shirtless?"

I rolled my eyes and nodded. "Uh-huh. I've even had a producer approach with an idea for a reality show involving troubled youth and how we help them find a cleaner path."

"That will take longer than eight weeks, won't it?"

"I'm not expecting miracles here."

"Have you sourced the first forty kids?"

"Yep. Recently released. Repeat offenders convicted of minor misdemeanors. We're staying away from the violent ones though."

"What age group?"

"Thirteen to seventeen," I said.

"Out-of-control hormones. Ugly. Remember us?"

"Sure. But instead of breaking into cars, I was looking for where I could park my dick." I pointed at Chatting Wood. "I fucked my brains out in there."

He laughed. "I bet you did. A girl from every farm?"

I went serious for a moment. "That's why I joined the army."

"Oh, shit, you got a girl in trouble?"

"Sort of." I rubbed my jaw. "Come on. Let's go into the hall. I'll get you a drink."

As we made our way back to Merivale, Theadora's question about Jasmine entered my thoughts. Mirabel Storm had shared more than just music with Theadora. I left it vague. I had to because I didn't want to bring up that ugly chapter in my life.

The army might have temporarily bludgeoned my past out of me, but now that I was back, it was still staring me in the face.

I WALKED INTO MY mother's office, which also doubled as a library, and found her peering at the sweeping vista of endless green fields through the window.

Noticing me at last, she pointed at a chair.

"The media for the boot camp has been instructed to stay away from Merivale."

She exhaled an audible breath. "That's not why I asked you here."

Immaculately presented, my mother didn't wear jeans or activewear or slouch around in comfortable clothes like most people might in their own homes. I can't even recall seeing her without makeup. On those rare occasions she kissed me on the cheek, she'd always leave a lipstick stain behind.

I loved that Theadora didn't wear makeup most days. Her skin tasted better, and devouring her exquisite, chemical-free lips made me one very lucky man.

"It's come to my attention that you're bedding the maid."

"Theadora," I said, squaring my shoulders. "Her name's Theadora Hart."

"Yes. Well. She's very beautiful. I can see that. I like to have attractive people at Merivale. Particularly at dinner parties. I've always turned a blind eye to the odd guest flirting with the staff." She played with a gold-engraved fountain pen. "I'm liberal-minded like that."

"You have to be."

Her tight brow twitched. "If you're about to judge my relationship with Will, please spare me. This is the twenty-first century. Women and younger men are no different to men your father's age falling for women or men half their age."

I shook my head. "How can you be so cold? You were married for thirty years."

"We've changed. Or I should say, your father's changed. He was once ambitious and dreamt of making the Lovechildes as respected as the royal family. Since he started hanging out with pretty boys, he's lost his drive. This irrational nonsense about leasing the land to farmers ad infinitum proves that."

"If you want me to switch camps and vote on the resort, then forget it. Our leased farms produce a quarter of the food for this region."

"The economies of developing countries have a right to expand. We're helping them transition from poverty to working class." She inclined her head.

"While denying our people jobs?" I raised an eyebrow. "I'm not in the mood to discuss politics."

"Nor am I." She tapped her pen on the desk. "I insist you stop seeing the maid."

"I'll see whoever I like." I sprung up off my chair.

She pointed at my vacated seat. "Sit."

I puffed out a breath and returned to the armchair.

"Lovechildes do not have relationships with the *bourgeois*. If you must bed them, like your playboy brother, then fine, but do it out of the spotlight. You know how people love to gossip."

My jaw clenched as I bit back a tirade.

She sat forward and crossed her hands over the green leather-lined desk. "How do you think she came to be here?"

I frowned. "What do you mean?"

"I mean she didn't just turn up here by normal employment methods."

"Get to the point, Mother."

She flinched at my gruffness. "Reynard Crisp arranged it."

My jaw dropped. "What?"

"She was auctioning her virginity of all things." She shook her head. "How tacky. Only a commoner would behave like a gutter slut."

Nerves churned away in my stomach. My brain burned with a flurry of questions. "Crisp knew about that?"

She nodded slowly, as her lips curled slightly. "Rey bought her. And now you're sleeping with her." Alarm lit her face. "I hope you weren't there. Please tell me you're not frequenting these tawdry establishments. Not a Lovechilde. You can have anyone."

I lifted my palm in the air. "Hey. Stop. I happened to be walking by when Theadora was being attacked."

I was still trying to process Reynard Crisp being the man who'd offered to buy Theadora's virginity. I wanted to chuck up from revulsion.

A roar remained trapped in my chest, in storage for Crisp, because when I'd finished with him, he'd have to get that smug face reshaped.

At least now I understood why that slippery snake was all over Theadora at the dinner party.

Taking a deep breath, I continued, "As I passed the laneway, I saw three men dragging her back into that club. She'd been drugged, and I basically saved her from being raped."

I wanted to slap myself for not reporting the incident to the police.

"That's her side of the story. You don't know for sure. It could have been a performance. A game."

My forehead contracted. "A game? How would she have known I was going to be there?"

She shrugged. "There are pictures, you know."

I sat forward. "What kind of pictures?"

"Lurid images that confirm that she's a tramp. I wouldn't even have her here if it wasn't for Rey."

Why is my mother supporting that piece of shit?

"Have you got those images?" I asked.

"Rey has. He's ruthless, you know? He always gets what he wants. In any case, this thing between you and the maid has gone far enough. It won't be long before the press gets wind of it. If forced, I'll leak the images."

"I couldn't give a shit about how they make me look, but I care for Theadora's sake."

"Then leave her. You could have just had sex with her and kept it private, but you were seen together holding hands for god's sake."

"That's the woman I'm going to marry." That took me by surprise.

Her face crumpled. "What? That common slut?"

My body tensed. "Don't you dare call her that. She was a virgin when I met her."

"Oh, was she really?" She chuckled coldly.

"Maybe I should have kept the bloodied sheet to rub in your face."

"Don't be boorish."

"Why are you involving yourself in Crisp's dirty little games?"

She stared down at her knitted fingers. "He's a good friend. He likes the girl." Her eyes met mine again. "And Rey doesn't do 'no.'"

"That's a euphemism for rape, Mother."

"Just leave her, Declan." She adopted the same gentle tone she'd used on me as a teenager, urging me to eat vegetables, stop hanging out with farmers' daughters, and not fly planes. "Ethan's a lost cause. You're the sensible one. Marry one of our kind. Strengthen the Lovechilde line."

"You know nothing about me, Mother. Until I met Theadora, I had no intention of marrying." I stared out the window, as a storm brewed within.

There was so much going on that her initial hair-raising comment about Theadora's employment at Merivale had almost slipped my mind.

"What were you implying earlier about Crisp and Theadora's work here?"

"He made sure that a notice was placed in her private area, offering an overly generous wage and conditions, and she took the bait."

"But how did she come to work at the hotel?"

"That was a coincidence, I believe. Rey tracked her down, and when he discovered her at the hotel, he took it one step further to bring her here so that he could groom her."

"Groom her? Are you fucking kidding me? And you were privy to this?"

She shrugged. "We help each other. That's what we do."

Who was this woman I called Mother?

CHAPTER 33

Thea

CAROLINE LOVECHILDE REMINDED ME of a cold version of Nigella Lawson. Wearing a green figure-hugging sheath, Declan's mother even dressed like the guru chef. Her dark, shoulder-length hair, without a strand out of place, was like a thick sheet of silk, while an impeccable makeup job highlighted a flawless milky complexion.

Her cold, scrutinizing stare had me on my seat's edge.

She passed me an envelope. "I have to let you go. In there, you'll find a generous amount. It should set you up and help you finish your course. There's a legal document for you to sign, stipulating that you move away from Bridesmere. Legal ramifications apply if you fail to comply."

"You're sacking me?" My forehead scrunched.

She crossed her arms. "I believe you're attending Hildersten. I'm sure you can arrange a transfer to a London equivalent."

It felt like someone squeezed the life out of my shoulders.

Her long, red-painted fingernails pointed down at the envelope. "Open it."

My hands trembled as I tore open the envelope. A check for one hundred thousand pounds fell out.

My eyeballs bulged. "That's a lot of money."

"It's very generous, yes. It's yours to do as you wish. But you must leave Bridesmere for good. And never talk to my son again."

My body froze. *Leave Declan?*

"I'm doing you a favor." She wore a cool smile. "He's not a stayer. After he's had enough of you, he'll toss you away. He's going to be one of England's richest one day. A man like that has no future with a woman like you. Especially with your background."

"My background?" I shrilled. Taking a deep breath, I composed myself before adding, "My mother's very wealthy, I'll have you know. She's not as wealthy as you, of course. Not many are. But I was raised in Kensington. I went to a public school."

"Good. Then you'll have no problems readjusting to life in London or wherever you go. Only not Bridesmere. Not here. Ever."

Ever?

Declan was my lover. My boyfriend. We'd held hands in the village. He'd even kissed me in public.

I looked her in the eyes, refusing to allow this woman to intimidate me. Caroline Lovechilde was no different from my cold, entitled mother. "And if I say 'no'?"

"Then you're being childish. Declan will never marry you. He's broken a lot of hearts."

My body froze. "He's told me everything."

"Oh, really. You know about Jasmine?"

I nodded. I didn't really. When I'd asked Declan about her, he intoxicated me with a deep, hungry tongue kiss. Those hot lips always made my brain melt, and the past, let alone the next day, dissolved into non-existence.

"There's also these." She tossed me a manila envelope.

"Open it. This is what awaits you if you don't do as I say."

I stared at her and she'd turned ugly.

I opened the envelope and a bunch of photos stared back at me.

The first showed a woman with long dark hair in a corset sitting on a man's lap. It got worse. The next image showed the same woman on her knees with a dick in her mouth.

Acid splashed away in my stomach.

They were back shots. And although she had the same hair, it wasn't me. Declan's was the first dick I'd ever put in my mouth. Something I wasn't about to divulge to his mother.

"But these aren't me. You can't prove they are."

"Look at the other one."

The photo showed me sitting in the dressing room wearing the same corset as in the back shots.

"I never did those things. They drugged me. That's when Declan saved me."

"They drugged you, and you probably did do those things. They're plain to see. Disgusting sleaze that will tarnish your reputation for life."

Tears burned at the back of my eyes.

Her mouth curved up at one end. It was the most sympathetic I'd encountered her. "I have nothing against you personally. What you get up to in your private time is your business. But no woman with this kind of tacky past is going to be with a Lovechilde. Take the cheque and go."

"And if I don't?" My heart shattered as a million thoughts barrelled ahead like trains colliding at a terminal.

"Declan will see these images."

I rose. I left the cheque on the table.

"He won't stay with you." She waved the cheque. "Take it. You can set up a new life. Get a good head start. No one will know about any of this. These photos will be destroyed. You're a beautiful, talented girl. Become a concert pianist. Do whatever you like. Only leave my son. You will not marry him under my watch."

I charged out of her office. My heart pounded in my ears as I went back to my room. The room that had given me so much peace and autonomy.

I called Lucy. After bawling in her ear, I blew my nose and sobbed through my soul-crushing news.

"Holy fuck. Are you sure the photos aren't you? You *were* drugged."

"I know. But I remember everything that happened. It was when I was about to be carried into a room that I managed to escape. That's when everything gets a little hazy. I remember fighting off the three men and someone coming to my rescue, who then held me up as we made a run for it."

"What are you going to do?"

"I have to leave. Like now. I can't have him see the photos." I gulped back a sob.

"You should talk to him. From what you've said, he sounds pretty committed."

"It's only been a month. And we've been having lots of sex. It hasn't been discussed."

"From everything you've told me, he's committed. Hell, he told you he loved you," she said.

"But the photos. Hell." I sobbed a little more before blowing my nose. "If I don't show him, his mother will. Fuck. Just when life was smiling at me. This shit happens."

"Are they that bad?"

"Yep. There's one of someone who's meant to be me sucking some guy's dick. I didn't do that. I'm sure."

"Yikes."

"There, you see. Even you admit it's fucked up."

"Oh, it's fucked up, all right." She sighed. "What are you going to do?" *Good fucking question.*

"If I stay, he'll see the photos. If I leave, I'll have nowhere to go."

"You can stay with me, sweets. But are you sure that's the right decision? Maybe you should just show him. He'll understand."

"I don't know. He's seriously jealous."

"Wow. He's into you then."

"More my body, I think." I thought of the tender kisses and how he held me all night in his arms and how he was always holding my hand or doing something sweet. Tears streamed down my face. My heart snapped in two.

"He loves the fact I've only been with him. And now he'll see these photos... yuck. I want to puke, just thinking of it. I have to leave. I can't have him thinking I'm a whore."

"Hello, you were a fucking virgin when he slept with you. You can't fake that."

I exhaled a loud breath. "Yep. The sheet was a mess. And I'm sure that's not me blowing whoever in that fucking shot. I'd never had a dick in my mouth until Declan's."

"Then tell him, for Christ's sake."

"I haven't got much time. She wants me out, like today."

"Oh, sweetie, I would tell him."

"Mm... Thanks for being here for me. I love you."

"I'm here for you, always," she said.

I choked through a "bye" and ended the call.

As I sat on the edge of that comfortable bed with sheets like silk, I held my face and stared glumly at the polished floorboards.

I studied the photos closely. The woman certainly had my body. Was that me? Why could I recall running away, but not that?

Why hadn't I remembered Reynard Crisp's face?

I wanted to scream as all these questions raged through me.

I couldn't let Declan see the photos. It would kill me. That dark cloud of uncertainty hanging over us.

I wanted him to think of me as that pure soul he'd admitted to falling in love with.

Yes, in love. With that pure version of me.

I lumbered back to Mrs. Lovechilde's office and knocked on the door.

On hearing "Enter" I stepped into that room that smelt of my mother's perfume. Not only did they share the same cold hearts, but the same fucking fragrance.

"If I leave, will you promise not to show him? Can I have the photos destroyed?"

She studied me and nodded. "Good, you've come to your senses. I'm glad. It's not easy to survive this kind of thing. I will destroy them." She opened her drawer and removed another envelope. "Here it's all there. Now off you go."

I took the envelope.

"You've forgotten something," she said.

As I stared at the cheque, a replay of me sharing with strangers, which is where all this trouble started, entered my thoughts.

I'd paid off my debts, but I only had enough money for about one month's survival. And what of my degree?

My hand shook as I picked up the cheque.

"That's wise. You can have a good future. Set yourself up for life. And none of this will follow you."

CHAPTER 34

Declan

THEADORA WASN'T TAKING MY calls. I couldn't find her. She moved out yesterday according to Amy. No one else could say more than that, although Amy's eyes pointed toward my mother's office.

I walked straight in. She looked up from the large antique desk that my grandfather, my father's father, had sat behind. I loved visiting that room as a boy. The study radiated a nostalgic smell of old books with its two stories of shelves filled with original editions. All that room's charm however faded as soon as I caught sight of Reynard Crisp loitering about.

My mother peered up and removed her glasses. "Declan. Just give me a moment."

"What did you say to Theadora?" I ignored Crisp entirely.

She winced at my harsh tone. "Can it wait?"

"No, it can't." I flicked my head towards Crisp. "Get rid of him."

She looked at Crisp and rolled her eyes.

"I'll leave you to it." He was about to move off when I stepped in front of him and stood face to face. "If you're behind Theadora's disappearance, I'll do more than wipe that fucking smirk from that mortician's face. You're not to go near her." I grabbed him by the scruff of his tweed jacket and sneered into his flushed face before releasing him.

Remaining deadpan, he straightened his jacket and walked off.

"You're behaving like a brute," my mother said. "The army turned you. You were never like this."

"You don't know me. And I don't need you to tell me who I should be dating, sleeping with, or marrying for that matter."

"Marriage?" Her face scrunched with horror. "You are still talking about marrying this tramp?"

"Stop fucking calling her that." My voice rang loud.

Her attention went to the open door. "Lower your voice."

"What happened? She's not answering my calls. And I'm told she moved out yesterday." I leaned on the desk. "What did you say to her?"

She shrugged. "I offered her a generous sum. The deal was that she leaves Bridesmere and never returns. If you can't find her, then I imagine that's what she's done, which heightens my regard for her. A woman needs money if she's to make her way in this world."

"If anyone should know that it's you." My voice dripped with ice.

Her face contorted with disapproval. "I have done nothing but work hard for this family."

"Father's the one with the pedigree, Mother."

She lowered my face and returned to her paperwork. "Ask Reynard to come back in, will you? And don't threaten him."

No chance of that.

I lingered. "What is it between you?"

She shrugged. "We're good friends and have been for years. I like his company."

"Are you lovers too?" I asked, feeling sick.

"Despite it being none of your business, no, I'm not sleeping with him. Besides, I'm too old for him. He goes for girls of Theadora's age." The glimmer of a smile coated her eyes. A cringing reminder of just how having too much money fucks people up. They think they can buy anything.

I headed to the gym at the back of the house. I needed a punching bag. Crisp wisely made himself scarce. Otherwise, I would have punched his face instead.

CHAPTER 35

Thea

THE SMELL OF ROAST beef hit me as I entered my new flat. Embracing domesticity and relishing in the comforts of a fully equipped kitchen, Lucy sang along to Bruno Mars as she stirred a pot.

I think my rich upbringing must have subconsciously asserted itself when signing the lease for our apartment in an upmarket suburb.

Offering her free rent, I asked Lucy to move in with me. I was so jumpy, after everything that had happened, I feared being alone.

"How was your exam?" she asked.

"Good. I think I'll pass," I said, running my finger along the rim of the pot for a taste of the gravy. "I'm looking forward to a break. Maybe we can go to Spain or something. Interested?"

It was amazing what heartbreak did for one's productivity. I'd buried my head in work to avoid thinking about Declan. Even though he was with me every damn, agonizing minute, especially at night.

It had been a month since I left Bridesmere, and my tears had finally dried.

I think I'd cried myself empty.

"I'd love a trip to Ibiza. Only I can't keep living off you, lovie."

I smiled at her sad face.

"I'm loaded."

"It's expensive here and you aren't working."

"That's about to end. I've just landed a gig teaching music to preschoolers."

"Oh, really?" Her face brightened. "Great."

It hurt to smile. My underworked facial muscles strained each time my mouth curved.

"Have you called him?" she asked while stirring the gravy.

Puffing out a breath, I shook my head.

"He keeps coming into the hotel. And then there's that red-haired man in the limousine. He followed me home today."

The sprinkling of warmth from hearing of Declan's persistence quickly turned to ice. "Reynard Crisp came into the hotel again?"

"It's my day off. But I could swear I saw his car drive past earlier. He knows where we live."

"Fuck."

I thought of the spine-chilling encounter I'd had with Crisp a few days back.

He'd somehow traced my college and was waiting outside.

The door of his chauffeur-driven Bentley swung open, which had fellow students gawking as though a celebrity had arrived.

"How did you find me?" I asked.

"Let's go somewhere away from your audience, shall we?" He wore a menacing grin that turned me to stone.

"I'm not getting in there with you." I just kept walking while looking out for a cab. Normally I rode the Tube, but it was a block away.

The car crawled along, and when we were away from the college, I stopped and gave him a filthy look and the finger.

With that cold smile of his, I got the feeling Crisp got off on my brush-off.

The car stopped and he jumped out.

I turned to him as he came towards me. "Fuck off. I'm not interested in anything you have to say."

Some might have described him as handsome, given his tall, distinguished manner, and sharp appearance, but it was those narrowing blue eyes fringed with orange eyelashes that gave him that dangerous, untrustworthy vibe.

"I just want to talk." He touched his face, and the large sapphire on his finger glistened in the daylight.

Yes, he was filthy rich. Richer than even the Lovechildes, I'd heard. So what? That meant nothing to me. If anything, it made me dislike him more.

In the hope he'd go away if I gave him a minute, I paused.

Even his pine scent made me nauseous. Did my stepfather wear that cologne? Or had my senses memorized something of that night at the club?

"I didn't drug you. You need to know that."

"But you know who did?" I inclined my head.

He didn't even blink. Instead, his eyes traveled over my body again. "You *were* meant for me."

"I'm no longer a fucking virgin. So can't you find someone else to harass?"

His mouth tugged up at one end.

"You're going to run out of money soon. I can give you everything."

"I'm not interested." I kept walking.

He followed me. "You were interested back then. You auctioned your virginity. I bought you."

I stopped and pointed my finger in his face. "I was drugged. I had no fucking intention of selling anything. Now leave me alone. I just want to live a normal life away from sleazebags like you."

He even had an evil chuckle. He seemed to get off on my barbs. "You're not still pining for Declan Lovechilde, are you?"

"I'm not talking about him to you. Can't you stop this? You followed my friend home. That's stalking. I'll report you to the police."

Now a decent person would have by now gotten the message, but not Reynard Crisp. With that patronizing glower, he remained steadfast.

"Have dinner with me."

"I'm not interested. Now leave me alone." I picked up pace.

"Those images will be leaked. Do you want that? It will destroy your teaching future."

I stopped walking. "Mrs. Lovechilde gave me her word that they would never surface."

"How do you think she got them?" That menacing smile returned.

"Why are you doing this?" My voice cracked.

"Because I want you." He went serious. The smirk had faded, and he trapped me with his piercing stare.

"I'm no longer a virgin."

His finger slid along my wrist. "I don't care."

I pulled my arm away as though I'd been nipped by a snake. "Don't come fucking near me."

As I hurried off, a sinking sensation gripped my stomach. I sensed he'd hassle me again.

MY NEW JOB WAS a welcome distraction. The children were so sweet as they banged away on percussion, while some of the little ones, dressed in tutus, danced. I was employed four hours a day. Morning shifts. Which suited me fine. The wage was just enough to cover my rent and the odd bill.

Although I would have liked to have put a deposit down on a flat instead of the exorbitant rent I was paying, I needed a full-time job to get a loan.

All in good time.

I got home and found Lucy on the sofa watching television. She looked at me and said, "I've been trying to call you."

"My phone's flat. What's up?"

"He came in again today."

I rolled my eyes. "Crap. Not him again. Can't he find someone else to harass?"

She shook her head. "It wasn't Reynard Crisp."

"You mean Declan?" A sudden knee tremor pushed me onto the couch.

She nodded. "He asked me if I could give him your number."

I puffed out a deep breath. I'd changed my number. I had to. I couldn't cope with all his messages and calls. It was the only way I could run away properly.

"You should talk to him, Thea. He looked tired and concerned and hot."

I sniffed. Yep. Declan was one of those freaks who looked even more gorgeous when tired and stressed. He was such a deep soul, my heart bled.

"I can't face him, Luce." I sighed. "I took that money. How does that make me look?"

"It makes you look practical. You're poor. You were blackmailed."

"I guess I was in a way. But I didn't have to take it, did I?"

Overwhelmed by guilt, I'd done a deal with the devil when I banked that cheque.

"What else did he say?"

She sucked back a breath. "To convince you to call him. He made me promise. Something tells me he's not going to stop until you do. You should."

"But then I'll have to talk about the photos and the money." I bit into my fingernail already gnawed down to the skin.

"Tell him the truth. Those photos aren't you."

"I'm not sure." I scratched my greasy scalp. "Maybe they are. I can't fucking remember."

"I'd remember if a dick had been shoved in my gob." She grimaced. "Sorry."

"If I were to see him, his mother will make those images public. There goes my teaching degree." I thought of Crisp's threats, and suddenly my body felt like concrete had been poured over it.

"You're hardly a celebrity." Lucy smiled sympathetically.

"Hello. Facebook. Employers check Facebook. Or Instagram. She'll put them on social media. Who'll employ me then?"

She nodded slowly. "He looked broken, lovie."

A sad smile grew on my face. "Did he?"

Selfish as that made me, I liked hearing that Declan missed me.

I didn't call him.
I couldn't.

CHAPTER 36

Declan

THE BOOT CAMP WAS due to open in two days. Cameras, media, the whole shebang, and I couldn't think straight.

My mother refused to give me a reason for dismissing Thea. She'd even offered a deal.

"Shut down your playground for criminals and I'll explain," she offered.

I stormed out, which had become a habit of mine when dealing with the woman who gave me life.

Will was chatting with the groundsman, Shane, when he looked over at me.

"Can I have a word?" I asked.

We walked over to the labyrinth, which seemed symbolically fitting considering the secrets that hung over this family.

Will had always liked to stay in the background. When he did speak, it was often witty, but mostly, he would stand by my father and now by my mother wearing a mild, understated manner.

"Have you come up with a name for the boot camp?" he asked.

"Reboot."

He nodded pensively. "Sounds apt."

"With you being close to Mother and everything, I need you to tell me what went down with Theadora."

"You haven't spoken to Theadora?" He looked surprised for some reason.

"No. Not for lack of trying." I puffed out a breath of frustration. "You've been with this family longer than you've been with my mother. Can you at least put me out of my misery and tell me what happened with Theadora?"

He scratched his shadowed jaw and took a moment to respond. "There are photos of Theadora that came into your mother's possession. Your mother offered her some money, and the girl wisely took it and left."

My brows drew in tightly. "Photos?"

Despite knowing how impoverished Theadora was, it hit hard hearing that she'd accepted an inducement to leave me. I would have given her anything.

"Have you seen them?"

He nodded.

"Are they that bad?"

He stared at me for a moment before nodding.

"I need to see them."

I never thought a woman could penetrate my emotions so profoundly. Each morning I woke up thinking about her. Each night I dreamt of touching and tasting her. I missed her warm body next to mine, and my nightmares had returned.

"Let me see what I can do," he said.

"I need to see them, Will." We locked eyes. I wasn't budging. Stonewalling was something I did well when pushed.

Two hours later, I was staring at Theadora with a cock in her fucking mouth.

Carson called me. "Hey, mate, where are you?"

I exhaled a jagged breath. "I'm on my way."

Ten minutes later, I was there at the newly fabricated camp.

We went through the course with a documentary maker, answering questions about Reboot.

After he left us, I turned to Carson. "I need to talk to you about something. And it's not about Reboot."

"Sure."

"Let's go into the hall, and I'll fix us a drink. We can talk there."

When we arrived at the hall, we ran into my sister, much to my frustration. She always loved to stop and chat whenever Carson was around.

With those tight torn jeans and a T-shirt that molded into his big shoulders, he was muscle upon muscle and a chick magnet.

"Hey." She was all smiles, and her eyes glued on him. "How's the boot camp going? I'd love to come over and watch sometime."

"It's not there for entertainment, you know," I said.

Carson turned to me. "She can come to the opening tomorrow night, though."

She nodded with a keen twinkle in her eyes.

"Why not? The more the merrier."

"Hey, don't sound so fucking enthusiastic," she said. "Ethan wants in too. You've sent him an invite, haven't you?"

"I thought he was off to New York," I said.

"Nuh. He's got some project on the boil. He plans to develop his parcel of land."

"Around the duck pond?" I loved that pond.

"Yep." She returned her attention to Carson. "More family drama. Can't wait."

"Mm... you thrive on it," I muttered, gesturing to Carson, who seemed too engrossed in my maneater sister, for us to keep moving.

He saluted her and followed me out to the garden, clutching his drink.

"What's up with you, man?" he asked, as we settled down on the marble bench by the fountain of the winged god Mercury. The same bench where I'd kissed Theadora's innocent lips. The same lips sucking some wanker's dick in those trashy photos.

I told him about the images that had turned my day into a shitstorm.

"She wanted you to remember her as that innocent girl you'd fallen for."

The muscle in my jaw flexed. "I nearly chucked up when I saw them."

He nodded sympathetically. "Are you sure it's her?"

The same thought had occurred to me as I wrestled with all kinds of demons, seeing her tits in some fucking greasy worm's face. "Great question. It's a profile shot. And I can't see her face."

"Maybe the photos are doctored?"

"She was a virgin, Carson. A fucking virgin. What virgin sucks dicks?"

His lips curled into a half-grin. "I believe they did in the olden days when virginity was a necessity for marriage." He shrugged. "Practicing Catholics still do."

I let out a breath. "Anyway, she's not a Catholic, and she's living in the now."

"Are you sure she was a virgin?"

"Have you ever been with one?" I asked.

He shook his head. "Nope. I've always gone for older women. I like the experienced ones, myself."

"Then, I'm telling you, there's no way she faked that. There was fucking blood and well..." How could I tell him she was so tight that my dick had yet to recover from that rare sensation?

"Forgive her. I mean, we've had more blow jobs than Christmas roasts."

My mouth curved for the first time in weeks. "Speak for yourself. But sure, I've had a few."

None as fucking good as Theadora's lips.

"It's also that she took the money. That preys on me. It shouldn't, seeing that she needs it and she's had a rough life."

"She left because she didn't want you to see the photos. That makes sense. That, in my opinion, is a dignified response."

"But what about the money?"

He shrugged. "I would have taken it. Are you in love with her?"

I raked through my hair, which kept falling over my forehead, and nodded. "I can't sleep. I can't stop thinking about her. I was her fucking first."

He nodded slowly with a sad smile. "That's a big thing for you. You swore black and blue you wouldn't have a relationship until you'd gotten your life together."

"Yeah, well, I didn't expect to meet Theadora, did I?"

"I'd find out if that's her in the photos. And if it is, I'd get over it. It's a double standard, man. You fucked around. It was before she met you too."

He was right. But it still felt like our relationship had been desecrated.

I hugged him and left for London.

CLUB PURR LOOKED DIFFERENT in the harsh light of day. After trying a few different routes, it took me some time to find the place where I'd rescued Theadora. I found myself walking up and down different routes until I finally spotted the club tucked away in a dead-end alley.

I rang a buzzer on the metal door, and after a few minutes a "Can I help you?" responded in a heavy Eastern European accent.

I lied about wanting to buy a virgin, and she let me in.

"Normally, this is done by invite only." She eyed my Rolex, a birthday gift from my grandfather.

"I was passing by, and I recalled hearing about it from Reynard Crisp," I bullshitted.

Her plucked eyebrow moved up slightly. She'd obviously recognized the name. "Won't you come in." She let me pass, and I followed her to a bar that smelt of stale cigars, alcohol, and aftershave.

"Can I offer you a drink?"

"Just a shot of whisky," I said.

She passed me a glass and then sat next to me on a bar stool.

"As you can see, we have a stage here where the girls parade." She pointed.

I felt sick, knowing that Theadora had been part of this sleazy establishment. I remembered her story well, about her accepting the job as a waitress out of desperation.

"Look, I'm not going to beat around the bush. I'm not here to buy a virgin, I'm here about these." I took the envelope out of my pocket and showed her the pictures.

Her face hardened. "I think you should go." She grabbed her phone.

I had a feeling she'd respond like that and came prepared. I took out a wad of notes and placed them on the bar.

"There's ten thousand pounds. Count it if you like. It's yours. I just want to know what happened that night and whether that's the same girl." I pointed from the face-on shot of Theadora to the pornographic image.

She glanced at the photo, then me, then the cash. It took her a moment. "Why do you need to know? How do I know you won't involve the cops?"

"I haven't so far. I was the one that saved her, while she was drugged to the eyeballs and trying to escape being raped by Reynard Crisp."

Her eyes widened slightly.

"All the girls sign consent forms."

"Oh, really? And what about drugging the non-consenting ones? That sounds like a crime to me."

She remained silent.

"I just need to know about these photos."

"I'm going to need more than that." Her head cocked towards the cash.

I pulled out another wad of notes and placed it on the bar.

"Who took the photo of Theadora in the mirror?"

"That was me." She took the cash, flicked through both piles, rose, grabbed her bag, and tucked them away.

"So you met her on the night?"

She nodded. "She was waitressing for us in costume. It's my job to help the new girls get fitted, and that's a photo of her in the dressing room. We normally take photos of all our girls for the board."

"For the board? You have this image on public display?"

Her mouth turned up at one end, making her appear sly. "I haven't checked, but maybe."

I could see she wanted more cash. I removed another wad of cash from my pocket. "Show me. Remove it and then I want the file on your phone and computer. And it's worth twenty thousand pounds."

Her eyebrows rose. "This girl must mean a lot to you."

"Show me."

I was taken to the board featuring images of scantily clad waitresses.

Unsurprisingly, Theadora's image stood out. She was by far the most beautiful creature there, with her voluptuous figure provocatively on display in that tiny corset.

She removed the photo and handed it to me. After she deleted the images from her computer and phone, I handed her the cash.

"Where are the others?" I asked.

"They don't exist. I don't have those ones."

"Are they of her?" I asked.

I removed another wad of notes and slapped it down on the bar. "Now speak."

She ran her tongue over her pumped lips. "They're not of her."

"How?"

"I don't know. This is the first time I'm seeing those. She didn't blow any client. She wouldn't have. We could barely get her to smile at clients that night, let alone sit on their laps and rub her tits in their faces. Not for the lack of trying. That's why we kept giving her drinks."

"You drugged her you mean?"

"Not me. It could have been any of the men there that night. I don't know."

"But if you didn't drug her, why were you confident she'd allow herself to be auctioned?"

"I wasn't. But she was drunk, and sure I tried to convince her, but she then tried to do a runner. Reynard, who'd seen her when she served him, said he wanted to buy her and to give her another drink."

"So he drugged her, then?"

She shrugged. "Look, I don't know. I had nothing to do with it."

"You still plied her with alcohol."

"She didn't need to take the drinks, did she?" She concocted a smile. "The new girls like to drink. It helps them relax. She was no different."

"Okay. So these photos are not Theadora?" I needed to be certain.

"As I said, she just served. She wasn't doing tricks. We leave that kind of thing between the girls and the clients."

"So who created these shots?" I asked. "You must have given them that image of her in the mirror. It was Crisp, wasn't it?"

She shrugged. "You got what you came for. I had nothing to do with those other images. They're not of her. That's all you need to know."

I stepped outside into daylight, feeling like a weight had been lifted. More for Theadora. Those photos must have put her through hell. That thought alone strengthened my resolve to bring that prick Crisp down to his knees, begging for mercy.

CHAPTER 37

Thea

I LOUNGED BACK, FEELING listless. I should have been working on a project for my final semester, and my hair needed washing badly. Depression had pounced on me again. Every time I hit pause that dark cloud swallowed me up.

The door opened and glad to have someone to talk to, I turned to greet Lucy when my spine stiffened.

"Look what the cat dragged in," she said with a chuckle, despite her apologetic grimace.

Just my luck, Declan had to see me wearing my shoddiest joggers, a stained, torn T-shirt, and a greasy ponytail. I looked like hell.

My mouth opened and "Oh" dropped out.

Seconds of strained silence seemed to drag on. I'm not sure who was more nervous, me or him.

"I'm sorry to barge in like this," he said rubbing his neck and wearing a faltering smile.

Lucy bit her lip and said, "He insisted. I..."

"It's okay, Luce." My mouth trembled into a tense smile.

She headed off into her bedroom. "I'll give you some space."

I turned to Declan. "Just give me a minute. I'll change into something, and we can go over to the park if you like."

"Sure. You look fine, though." He smiled sweetly.

"No, I don't." I held up a finger. "One minute."

I went into my bedroom. My heart thumped, and I had a sudden bout of brain fog when Lucy entered. "I'm sorry, but he followed me. I didn't know."

I sniffed a long sleeve T-shirt and popped it over my head and then wiggled into my nicest jeans. "Don't worry. I don't know what he wants, though."

"Hey, sound him out, will you?" She touched my arm.

"I look a fucking fright. My hair's filthy."

"You look gorgeous as always. Like you've just gotten out of bed."

I rolled my eyes. "And that's meant to make me feel better?"

She smiled. "Go on. You'll be okay."

I hugged my friend, drawing the strength I needed to face the man who'd stolen my heart.

As we crossed the road to the park, I could barely walk, and reading me well as always, Declan took me by the hand. Casting me a timid glance to see if I didn't mind.

As if?

I was too busy dealing with the tingles soaring through me to protest. Sure, I could do it myself, but it was nice to feel that large warm hand again.

We came to a park bench and sat down.

"I needed to see you." He faced me. "To talk to you."

"I thought you'd be busy with the boot camp."

"I am. But since you left, I haven't been able to do anything." His gaze intensified. "Why didn't you speak to me?"

I froze. What was I to tell him?

"I know about the photos," he said.

My mouth dropped open. "You do? But your mother promised. We had a deal."

"She didn't show me. Will did after I pressed him." He splayed his hands. "Why didn't you speak to me?"

"Your mother threatened to publish those photos if I continued to see you. My career would have been destroyed." My mouth trembled as I fought back sobs.

He took my hand. "Listen, those photos aren't of you."

My eyebrows gathered. "But how would you know that? I know they're not me. That is, except for the one in the mirror."

"I visited the club and spoke to a tall blonde Eastern European woman."

"You met Tania? She's the one that drugged me."

"She denies it. She doesn't know who did, but I wouldn't put it past that snake, Crisp."

I sighed. "No, I wouldn't either. He's turning into a fucking pest."

His frown deepened. "Has he been stalking you?"

"You could say that." I thought of what he'd just told me and looked into his eyes. "Thank you."

"You can press charges, you know? Against Reynard. I'll pay for a good lawyer."

I shook my head. "No. I want it over."

"I got her to remove your image from her files."

"How?" she asked.

"With cash."

"Oh, god. I've cost you so much, haven't I? I guess your mother told you about the money?"

"She did." He ran his thumb along his bottom lip. "At first, it upset me. But I've never wanted for anything, so I'm not in a position to make any harsh judgment."

"I still feel like shit about it." I took a breath. "It's been plaguing me for weeks. I was planning on repaying it. Bit by bit. I've got a part-time job, and I should graduate in a year, and after that—"

He leaned in and kissed me gently on the lips. A chaste kiss. But the warmth and softness made me forget everything.

"No need to pay it back. And if it will make you feel better, I will draw up a check and give it to my mother, on your behalf."

Floating on a high after that sweet-tasting kiss, I took a moment to respond. "Can you afford that? I would prefer to owe you than your mother."

He opened out his arm, and I leaned into his firm body. "I'm a billionaire in my own right, Theadora. There's no need to fret. It's yours. Do as you wish with it."

"That doesn't feel right. I want to pay you back. I wasn't with you for money."

He looked into my eyes, and tears splashed over my cheeks.

"There is something you could do," he said, wiping my tears with his T-shirt, revealing that six-pack of coiled muscle that released a silent sigh from my chest.

"What's that?" I gazed up at him.

"I want you to move in with me."

My neck cracked from the sudden head turn. "But that would make us a couple."

Taking my hand, he kissed my cheek. "I want you in my life, Theadora."

A lump took up residence in my throat, threatening to rob me of speech.

"At first, I thought it was just an arrangement." He continued to play with my fingers. "I've really missed you. Nothing feels the same without you close."

"I've missed you too." I fell into his arms and wept. The more I tried to stifle my sobs the louder they sounded. All the anguish of those photos, of missing him like I would my soul, and then being accused by his mother, poured out of me and drenched his T-shirt.

He crushed me with warmth. Holding me as I trembled in his arms.

Terrifying passion poured out of me like a psychic rupture. A confused mixture of elation and fear made my heart bleed tears.

I struggled to regain my breath as emotion poured out of me.

He continued to hold me close, comforting me. Almost encouraging my outpouring as a way to clear the passage so that we could be together, clean of dark, ugly secrets and memories.

We remained like that on the park bench for ages. Holding each other. His hard strong body against mine.

All it took was him uttering those caressing words "I want you in my life" to set me free.

With every softly placed kiss, he made my fears about living with him disappear till there was only bright hope and sweet desire.

I couldn't even remember returning to my apartment. It was an out-of-body experience. Declan virtually carried me, taking my weight against his body.

Lucy, bless her soul, had gone out to give us some space.

We fell onto the sofa, and he stared deeply into my eyes. His ocean-blue eyes darkened with lust.

Like attracting magnets, our bodies were clasped together. He ravished my lips as though we'd been lusting over each other for ages, and this was our first kiss.

From there I surrendered to a frenzy of burning desire. Impatient and needy for him to ravage me.

I ripped at his shirt and rubbed myself against those mounds of muscles, all smooth and hard.

His warm mouth explored mine, soft, then hungry, as his tongue parted my lips.

Trailing kisses down my neck, he sucked my nipples and breathed heavily as he handled my breasts.

I unzipped his pants, and his throbbing hard dick sat on my hand, dripping and hungry.

He ate my pussy like it was a delicious dessert. His moans matched mine as I came so many times my body overdosed on ecstasy.

When he entered me, the intense and fierce stretch made my eyes water. His hand gripped my hips and anchored me to his thrusts. His slow, deliberate penetration sent shivers of burning heat through my body. From slow and provocative to a piston pounding into me.

A cacophony of groans and breathy moans echoed, as we came together. Declan breathed "Theadora" followed by a drunken groan as he exploded.

My nails dug into his curvy biceps, and my nose buried in his damp salty neck, inhaling his masculine scent. I could feel the rise and fall of his muscular chest on mine.

I sighed and snuggled into his cradling arms.

He stroked my hair, and for several minutes we lay in comfortable silence. His warm body wrapped around mine, pressing us together, skin to skin. I couldn't imagine a safer place.

I looked up at him, and his smile was like a ray of sunshine on a dreary day. I finally felt whole again—a lost piece of my spirit restored.

Drenched with his affection, I curled into his strong body. Our hearts, beating as one, seemed glued together.

Gently, I reached out and traced his features with my fingertips. He smiled softly and kissed my hand as it brushed across his cheek.

CHAPTER 38

Declan

LAYING ON MY SIDE, I gazed at her. Like a man who'd found heaven, I couldn't stop smiling.

"What?" Theadora asked.

She hated me staring at her for some reason. Something to do with low self-esteem. I planned to remind her every day of our life together how beautiful she was.

"I was just admiring your ugly face."

She slapped me playfully. "I'm no uglier than you."

We looked at each other and laughed.

"No really, you're fucking exquisite, Theadora. And I love you best like this."

"Naked you mean?"

"Mm... that too. But your face without makeup."

Her brow flinched. "So, does that mean you don't like me glammed up?"

"I love you any way. But it's nice to see you the way nature intended."

"I'm sorry about this mess." She pointed at her bedroom which looked like it had been raided by thieves. "My life's rather hectic."

"Don't worry about anything. I've got you."

She frowned. "What do you mean?"

"I'm dragging you back with me, and then you can have and do whatever your pretty heart desires."

She sat up. Gloriously naked. Her tits hanging in that way that made men pay thousands just to perv. My dick sprung back to action. Hard as a rock, as though we hadn't spent the past hour fucking like randy teenagers.

"What about your mother?"

I traced her lips with my finger and then kissed her softly. "Darling, just come back."

Her brow smoothed out, and she smiled. "I have missed Bridesmere, I must admit."

"Is that all you've missed?" I inclined my head.

"Well, no... I mean there's this guy there. A tall, ex-army guy, who keeps pinching my arse and perving on my tits. And well, he's cute."

"Cute?" I pushed my head back.

"Okay. Not cute. Sexy, then."

We looked at each other and laughed.

She got up and dressed in a loose T-shirt and touched her stomach. "I'm starving."

"So am I. I have to go soon, though. Carson's expecting me."

"Then let me make you a toasted cheese sandwich and a cup of tea."

I sprung up off the bed. "You've convinced me."

She left me to dress and headed off into the kitchen, which was an extension of the living room.

I went to sit down when Theadora raced out of the tiny kitchen and cleared away the mess on the sofa.

"I am so sorry." She looked embarrassed. "I'm not the tidiest person."

I shrugged. "That's why maids were invented. And thank god for that."

"But you asked me to clean to get into my panties."

I stretched back on the lumpy sofa. "Guilty as charged." I chuckled. "I wanted you badly after watching you bend over in those tight blouses."

That steamy admission shot arousal down to my dick.

Not helped by seeing her move about in that T-shirt. Knowing that she was naked beneath, I begged the porno gods to make her bend over.

She poured water into cups. "You speak as though I seduced you on purpose."

I studied her face for signs of resentment. Instead, her eyes teased. "You don't have to do much for my dick to thicken."

She carried out a plate with a toasted sandwich and a cup of tea, and placed it on the table, clearing away sheet music, coursebooks, and notepads.

"How are your studies going?"

"They're going well enough." She went back into the kitchen and returned with another plate and cup of tea as she settled on the chair in front of me, propping her lean, toned legs on the coffee table.

I copped a view of her pussy as she repositioned herself, and the plate on my lap nearly flew off.

Hadn't we just fucked?

I pointed. "Um... I can see everything, Theadora, and I'm finding it hard to eat."

Giggling, she adjusted her T-shirt. "Sorry. We can't put you off your meal."

"Oh, you're not putting me off. If anything, I'm fucking ravenous again."

She laughed. "You're a sex maniac."

"Around you I am." I took a bite of the sandwich, and cheese oozed onto my tongue, and my taste buds jumped for joy.

"How is it?" she asked.

"Delicious. I'm starved. Great call."

"Is that enough? I can make more." She went to rise.

I gestured. "No. Please. Finish yours. This will be fine." I took a sip of the warm tea, made to perfection. Theadora had remembered how I liked my tea. Something I was fussy about.

"I hope you don't think I'm a slob living like this," she said.

"I'm not here to judge. I'm just loving every moment of being here with you. That's all. In my mind this is nirvana."

She giggled. "Hardly. You're used to opulence and everything around you is expensive and choice. But at least we're safe here."

I stopped eating and studied her. "By that, you mean you and Lucy?"

She nodded. Chewing away, she swallowed and then added, "That's why I took the money from your mother. I couldn't stand the idea of sharing with strangers again."

I shook my head. For the first time, I realized just what doing without might look like. "You're right about my life being filled with comforts and not having to face the grim prospect of homelessness. But I did do it rough in Afghanistan. We'd set up camp in caves sometimes. It was freezing and we didn't exactly have pretty vases and great art to gawk at."

She wore a sad smile. "That sounds terrifying. I know so little about your time as a soldier. Will you tell me about it someday?"

"Sure. The odd anecdote here and there. Like just now. It's not the sunniest conversation to share." I sniffed.

"I don't mind. You can talk to me about anything."

I wiped my lips with a tissue and rose to carry my plate to the kitchen. She pounced at it. "No. Leave it. The kitchen's feral."

I ignored her pleas and lifted her plate. "I don't give a shit, Theadora. You've been working hard at your course. I get it."

She followed me to the kitchen, removed orange juice from the fridge, and filled two glasses, passing one to me.

As she turned away, I grabbed her and rubbed myself against her.

"Mm... you feel fucking hot," I said, running my hands up her thigh to her naked butt and giving it a squeeze. My fingers continued up and fondled her heavy tits. "You've grown."

"I'm expecting my period, and my breasts tend to get bigger."

"Mm... you're perfect." I moaned as I rubbed myself against her. My finger rubbed her clit as it became drenched in her arousal. "I like this going about naked with only a T-shirt on."

I unzipped my jeans to release the ache and kept fingering her. She rubbed her arse against my dick, encouraging me to enter.

Her head fell back on my chest as I fluttered over her clit until my finger became soaked in her release.

Her soft body writhed against mine as I pumped into her. "Can I fuck you hard?"

"Please," she begged.

I pounded against her voluptuous arse. My balls rubbed against her soft curves and my heart throbbed like my cock.

"You're so wet and snug."

I had to bite into her neck to stop myself yelling.

I puffed out a breath as I held onto her. My chin rested on her shoulder, and my body became heavy. All I wanted to do was sleep and spend the day and night with this woman who'd stolen my heart, but I had to race back home.

Theadora stepped away from me just as Lucy walked through the door.

We must have looked guilty because she said, "Oh. Sorry. I should have called first."

"No. It's all good." I slapped Theadora gently on her arse.

After I'd visited the bathroom, I asked Lucy, "How would you like to join us in Bridesmere?"

Lucy looked at Theadora first before answering. "Like for a holiday?"

I smiled at how surprised she looked like I'd offered her a trip to an exotic location. "If you like. Or you could just move there. We're looking for an administrator at Reboot."

Her eyes grew wide.

"What a great idea." Theadora smiled.

"It is..." Lucy sounded hesitant. "Where would I live?"

"That's a small detail. We'll work that out, won't we?" I turned to the love of my life and to see that bright beaming smile alone I would have given my wealth away.

Theadora followed me to the door. "Thank you for that kind offer, Declan." She cuddled me.

"For what, sweetheart?" I stroked her hair.

"For asking Lucy to join me in Bridesmere."

"I just want you to be happy. And I can see she's an important part of your life. I've got Carson and Ethan and army mates." I hugged and kissed her. "Anything for you, Theadora. I just want you to be with me. Yes?"

I lowered my head, and our foreheads touched.

Her lips curled divinely. "You might have to give your mother some Xanax before breaking the news."

I laughed before turning serious again. "It's my life. And I want you in it."

CHAPTER 39

Thea

DECLAN WANTED TO DRAG me back with him. I had to keep promising him that I'd make it to the Reboot opening. After more kisses, I waved him goodbye and watched him jump in his SUV.

When I returned to our apartment, I found Lucy pacing about and intermittently shaking her head. Just like me, she questioned whether this was a dream.

"Please say yes," I said. "It will be fun. We can go to the beach."

"The beach?" I could see her trying to contain herself.

Eating at a restaurant and shopping at Marks and Spencer on that one occasion that I bought her lunch there, was as swish as things got for a girl who'd lived on scraps and worn nothing but hand-me-downs.

"I don't know what to pack," she said. "I'm all over the shop, to be honest."

I laughed. "Don't worry. Just bring enough for a week and then we can return and move properly. Yes?"

She nodded with stars in her eyes. I knew exactly how she felt. It was like we'd entered a parallel universe where only hunky lovers and the promise of endless sunshine existed.

"Before we leave, we're going shopping, and I'm paying for your makeover. Starting with your hair."

Her eyes bulged. "Are you for real?" She looked worried suddenly. "But what if this doesn't work?"

"What do you mean?"

She shrugged. "If you run away from Declan again. What will happen to me? There in a strange village all alone?"

"That's pessimistic," I said.

"I'm sorry." Her mouth turned down. "I shouldn't be so negative, but I'm nervous. I've got a job here."

"Listen, Luce, I'm keeping that man." I placed my hands on my hips, not allowing my insecurities to gatecrash my bliss. "Do you hear?" I put my arm around her shoulder. "Bridesmere is like something out of *Agatha Raisin* but by the sea. You'll love it there. I promise."

A big smile filled her face. Her excitement was mine, as we laughed and swung each other around.

After that, we went shopping. There was much to do, given that I'd promised to be in Bridesmere the next day.

I got the feeling Declan was scared I'd change my mind.

After spending that afternoon with him buried deep inside of me while peering into each other's eyes, falling deeper and deeper in, the likelihood of not going was like me, a serious acrophobe, jumping out of a plane.

NORMALLY, WINDOW SHOPPING WAS as good as it got for us in Oxford Street, but not today. We were to buy whatever we desired, and Lucy's wide-eyed stupor proved contagious. Like visitors from another galaxy, we stared with wonder at the many windows filled with the latest fashions.

In possession of a credit card that Declan placed in my hand, I'd been instructed to buy whatever we wanted. While I processed that insanely generous gesture, he mentioned something about buying a ballgown.

"Or I can arrange the family stylist if you like," he said as casually as someone asking if I wanted jam with my scones.

It was all too difficult to process, as though I'd slithered through a wormhole that ferried me to a universe promising endless pleasure.

I refused to take the card, but he wouldn't let up. Declan kept reminding me that he was loaded. Without bragging, of course. That wasn't his style, and one of the innumerable reasons why I liked him. Okay more than liked him.

It took a bit for me to swallow my pride, after reminding him of the money his mother had given me.

"Small change," he responded with that husky bedroom voice.

In the end, I relented and took it.

Lucy linked her arm with mine, and we virtually danced along that colorful strip of shops.

"This is so fucking exciting. A ball gown?" she asked.

"And one for you too. Declan insisted I spend up big. And not to forget you. He likes you, and he knows that you're my sister."

Her mouth trembled as she hugged me. I thought she was going to cry.

"Let's have a quick coffee and work out what we're going to buy. You've got that appointment for your hair later."

After that, we went shopping, and I bought myself jeans, shirts, a couple of dresses, and shoes. The same for Lucy, who just couldn't stop smiling.

"I'm exhausted." I leaned against a wall as people bustled by. "I don't get the allure of shopping."

Lucy shook her head. "I'm in heaven. I could do this forever. I've never had so much fun."

"The ball gown will have to wait," I said, considering Declan's offer of a stylist, who would probably have a better idea of how to kit me out for one of their posh events.

As much as I loved clothes like any young woman might, I'd never invested time and effort into thinking about them, so now that I found myself in this novel situation, I needed help and guidance.

I texted Declan. "When is this ball?"

He answered straight away. "In a week."

"I've got shopping exhaustion. I might take you up on that stylist."

"Anything for you, angel. Just get your pretty bottom back to Bridesmere. I'm determined never to spend another night without you."

"My arse doesn't want to spend another night without you either."

"You've made me hard again. Today was only a taste."

My mouth stretched the width of my face. "Then tomorrow I'll make sure to whip up a nice sauce to go with the main meal."

"We are talking about fucking?" he asked.

"Yeah. What else?" I laughed.

"I love you Theadora Hart."

"And I love you, Declan Lovechilde."

On that closing note, a tear trickled down my cheek again.

I'd never told anyone before in my life, other than Lucy, that I loved them.

This was big. This was real. This was scary.

CHAPTER 40

Declan

ETHAN AMBLED OVER TO join me among the huddle of media, friends, and curious onlookers. "This is quite a show," he said.

Reboot was finally up and running. Waiters roved and champagne flowed.

Looking like a goddess in a floral dress swishing over boots, Theadora took my breath away.

She'd only just arrived that morning.

I felt good. Relaxed. I couldn't give a shit about my mother and her silly antiquated views of who I should be with. There was no doubt that her rigid attitude would make for a bumpy ride, but with Theadora by my side, I could conquer anything, even a mother living in some glossy magazine version of family dynasties.

Although Lucy hadn't arrived as yet, I'd rented a cottage for her with a one-year lease, which brought tears to Theadora's eyes. I knew that they'd had it tough, and my making a difference to both their lives felt sweet.

Carson gave a tour of the facility, while I mingled.

Carrying a glass of champagne, Theadora joined me, and I put my arm around her waist, drawing her close and pressing my lips onto her silky hair. She looked around us before returning a hesitant crooked smile.

"You're going public, I see," Ethan said, raising his eyebrows. He knew about the photos and the potential for this relationship to cause a huge stir between me and our mother.

I kissed Theadora's cheek. "Yep. We sure are."

Savanah came over to join us. "Where are the mud patches and half-naked hunks crawling under wire?"

I laughed. "You have to go to an army training camp for that."

"That's what I thought this would be," she complained. "A demonstration of how it's done by *real* men."

"This is one notch above gym training with a trainer who sounds like he means it."

"Mm... I could use one of those," she said. "My thighs are starting to get a bit flabby."

My sister, and this obsession with body image, was one of many in our scene. I lost count of how many times I'd reassured her and Cleo and other women that they looked great just as they were. As a teenager, Savanah had succumbed to bulimic tendencies, and despite her promising to stop that frightful practice, I made sure I kept an eye on her. Especially if she'd lost weight.

At least, Theadora didn't seem to mind what she put in her mouth. My dick included.

An instructor stepped onto the field along with some former SAS soldiers who'd agreed to put on a show.

"Ah. That's more like it." Savanah looked at Theadora and bounced her eyebrows.

Ethan rolled his eyes. "How predictable."

"Don't you start," Savanah returned. "I bet if there were a bunch of bikini girls wrestling in the mud you'd be pretty chuffed."

"Oh, yeah." Ethan turned to me. "Is there a girly version of this?"

"Hey, I'll have you know that some of the female SAS are just as, if not, tougher than the blokes."

"I'm not disputing that," Ethan said. "I meant girls going a bit feral."

I shook my head and laughed. My brother and his silly adolescent fantasies. I could only put it down to a privileged upbringing. His toughest challenge was having to choose between the latest Aston Martin or Jaguar.

"Shh..." Savanah said. "I'm trying to concentrate. Wow. Did you see that?" She pointed. "He's pretty fucking strong. Is there a meet and greet afterward?"

I laughed. "Just hang out at the beer keg over there, and I'm sure you'll meet a few."

Like Savanah, the females seemed equally enthralled, going on the whistles, giggles, and moans in the audience as a bunch of beefy men did one-armed press-ups.

Carson instructed and then demonstrated, and I'm sure I could hear my sister moaning. I narrowed my eyes at her.

"What?" she asked. "Can't a girl drool?"

I chuckled. "I'm sure you can do more than that. Just go easy on him. He's a sensitive guy."

"Carson? Really?" She squinted in the sunlight.

"Alpha on the outside, beta on the inside," I said.

"Mm... I'll bear that in mind. I'm not interested, though."

"Hey, you should make this a regular event. Like a live performance. Can you get them to fight? Or wrestle?" Ethan asked.

I rolled my eyes and turned to Theadora, who giggled at my brother's silly suggestion.

"Why not?" Savanah interjected. "It's so entertaining seeing these strong men. I mean, look at those fucking muscles, will you?"

"Doesn't having all those muscles shrink your dick?" Ethan asked.

"Has it shrunk yours?" I had to ask, as ridiculous as this conversation was getting. But that was my siblings. It always descended into the juvenile.

"I'm not that stacked."

"I'm not sure about that. You're looking rather buff these days," I said.

"I've been a little more disciplined, I suppose. Thanks for noticing, bro." He tapped my arm. "Coming from you, looking like a fucking superhero, it means a lot."

I left my brother and sister and, with Theadora's hand in mine, we did the rounds, chatting to people and answering questions about Reboot's aims.

It was a great afternoon. I knew I'd made the right decisions about everything. With Theadora close and Reboot in full swing, I had plenty to smile about.

THE ANNUAL BALL WAS a calendar event, and despite relations being a little strained between me and my mother, I'd decided that I was going to take my place in that family as I'd always done. Tradition was everything to me. She'd just have to learn to accept Theadora. I would see to that.

Theadora stood before the mirror, looking like a goddess in a red gown. I stood behind her as she played with her hair in the mirror.

I breathed in her rose fragrance. "You'll be the envy of every woman there. The most beautiful girl at the ball."

She pulled a face. Theadora didn't have a vain bone in her body. If anything, she tended towards self-deprecation.

"You don't think this is too much?" She pointed at her hair. "The stylist suggested I wear it half up and down. It's a little old-fashioned, don't you think?"

I played with a tendril curving onto her chest and then ran my finger down that long soft cleavage, noticing her nipples spike through the silk.

"You look beautiful."

She kept tilting her head from side to side, as though trying to find something in the mirror. "You don't think this is over the top? I've never dressed like this before."

I shook my head. "This is how women dress for these events. And you look like a painting that I would pay a fortune to own."

She smiled sweetly. "You say such nice things."

I lifted a finger. "There's one thing missing. Just wait a minute." I went to a drawer and removed a velvet jewelry box and handed it to her. "A gift."

Her eyebrows drew apart. "Another one? You're spoiling me."

"Open it."

She lifted the diamond earrings from the box. "Oh my god. These are too much. Are they real?"

"Darling, I would never give you fakes."

"No, of course. But Declan, these are too much."

The sparkling earrings dangling against her long neck looked so perfect she could have made an advertisement for diamonds.

I stood back and nodded. "Stunning."

"Thank you, Declan. I'm frightened of losing them."

"They're insured. Don't worry."

Her eyes grew wide. "Are they that expensive?"

"Let's not talk money." I glanced down at my watch. "We should be going."

Theadora's fingers slid down the silk lapel of my tuxedo. "You look so handsome. I love your hair styled back."

Our eyes locked, and we fell into each other's gaze, which happened every time I visited her spellbinding dark eyes.

I placed my arm around her and drew her in close. "You're so much taller," I said.

She raised her dress to show me her high heels. "I'm sure I'll fall over. These are the highest shoes known to womankind."

I laughed. "I prefer you in flats myself. I love how I can tuck you under my chin. You're a perfect fit. In every sense." My eyebrow raised, and she giggled.

"That's nice. Only I'd dwarf all those supermodel exes of yours."

I stroked her cheek. "That's more Ethan's scene than mine."

Twenty minutes later, with Theadora on my arm, we walked through the filigree gates into Merivale.

Lanterns dispersed through the grounds making the trees and shrubs appear theatrical. Particularly the light show of changing colors splashing over the Mercury fountain capturing sprays of water.

"The grounds look stunning," Theadora said, wobbling slightly as I helped her along. "I don't know how I'd manage to walk without you here for balance."

"I've got you. Remember that." I stopped walking and turned to look at her. In the moonlight, she looked even more beautiful.

"You've got nothing to worry about, darling. No one's a patch on you. Money doesn't buy elegance," I said. "Remember that. Even in your uniform you display more grace than all those women in their expensive designer gowns combined."

"You're so nice." A frown pushed away her smile. "Does your mother know about us? Does she know that I'm coming?"

Sucking back a sharp breath, I nodded. My mother's disapproving frown flashed across my mind after I revealed that Theadora had moved in with me. Knowing how sensitive this subject was, I hadn't discussed my mother's displeasure with Theadora.

I took her hand, and together we climbed the stairs to the entrance of that imperial building I'd called home all my life.

When we entered, the guests stopped talking and watched us as though we were famous. I'm sure I heard a collective sigh and someone saying, "Declan's seeing that maid."

I couldn't care less.

Through the crowd of guests, I spied my mother chatting to Cleo.

"Please don't leave me," Theadora whispered, squeezing the life out of my hand. "Not until I've had a few champagnes at least."

"Don't worry, sweetheart. I'll be glued to your side."

Savanah and a couple of her girlfriends were the first to greet us. She seemed to treat Theadora well enough, which I appreciated. If anyone was a snob in that family, it was normally my sister. But she'd started to treat Theadora respectfully after hearing her perform with Mirabel Storm.

"Hey there," she said, reaching up and pecking my cheek.

She regarded Theadora. "This is nice." She touched the silky layer of Theadora's cascading gown, which unlike most of the younger women present, was modest in design. Only a hint of cleavage, but with a girl as voluptuous as Theadora, only a turtleneck would hide that.

Theadora smiled and pointed at my sister's purple fitted gown. "You look gorgeous."

"This old thing. It's an eighties Givenchy. Belonged to my aunt. A hand-me-down of sorts." She chuckled.

"It's stunning," Theadora said. "Beauty never dates."

Savanah nodded slowly with an appreciative frown. "No, it doesn't. Well said. I'm rather fond of classic lines, and vintage is so in." My sister turned to me. "All the usual bores are here. Including..."

I looked over her shoulder and muttered, "Fuck."

"Yep, Rey's here. Is that who you mean?" She turned to see who was making me grimace.

"Don't look," I said.

"We're seeing a lot of him lately."

"Yeah, well, I hate the prick," I muttered.

Savanah smirked. "I wonder what he's got going with Mother?"

"Great question. You're good at finding things out. When you do, be sure to tell me."

"He's got a thing for Theadora, too, hasn't he?" she asked, looking over my shoulder at the man I planned to ignore.

"Who told you?" I asked.

"Ethan, of course."

I shook my head. I should have known spilling my heart to my brother would travel.

"Did he tell you how he drugged her at that sleazy club?"

I turned to Theadora. "You don't mind me talking about this?"

She bit into a nail. "No. But I wish he wasn't here."

Savanah looked sympathetic. "Don't worry about Rey. He's just a sleaze. He tried it on me once. You should have laid charges, though."

"I've got no proof. And to be honest, I just want it over," Theadora said.

I couldn't let my sister's comment slide. "What do you mean he tried it on you?"

My normally unflappable sister grew serious. "Hey, no one knows. Okay."

"Why didn't you tell me?"

"You were having your own meltdown with that Jasmine affair."

I noticed Theadora's eyes narrow slightly.

Unwilling to go down that dysfunctional rabbit hole, I swung the topic back to Crisp. "Did he touch you?"

"He tried. I just kneed him in the balls. Told him if he tried that again, I'd report him. He just laughed it off. He's a fucking dick. I don't know what Mother sees in him."

"Did you tell her?" I asked.

"She just shrugged it off and told me that he's harmless enough."

My mother neglecting to protect her children from bastards like Crisp left a foul taste in my mouth.

"He's a fucking snake. I want him out of our lives."

"Good luck. He's in thick with Mother."

"Were they together before Dad?"

"I think they were. Ethan heard something from one of our long-lost relatives that Reynard broke Mummy's heart. He's not the committing kind. He likes them young." Her eyebrow arched.

Why was this shady character sewn at my mother's hip?

CHAPTER 41

Thea

THE NAME "JASMINE" MADE my ears burn. What had happened between her and Declan?

When I brought up this topic with Lucy, she sensibly reminded me that given Declan was thirty-two, he probably had a long romantic history. I understood that well enough, but Jasmine kept coming up in conversations.

Thanks to the excellent champagne, anxiety soon dissolved with each mouthful. I walked, or I should say, crept along as gracefully as those ridiculous shoes would allow and bumped into Amy, who was working that night.

"Holy shit, it's you," she said.

"Yep, it's me, the former maid. I'm not a figment of your imagination." I chuckled, feeling tipsy after just one drink.

She played with the fabric of my princess gown, which had cost the equivalent of Amy's annual wage. Forty thousand pounds to be exact.

Of course, I'd gone for the most expensive, which was a tendency of mine. Perhaps an instinct from growing up with a mother who wouldn't be seen dead in a shopping mall, opting for Bond Street boutiques instead.

I felt sick using Declan's credit card, despite his insistence I spend up big. An afternoon that had seen me buying Lucy enough new clothes to fill a wardrobe as we giggled like a pair of kids high on sugar at a free-for-all candy store.

Amy touched my earrings and shook her head in disbelief. "Are those real?"

I smiled. "It's surreal for me too."

"You look so beautiful. And all those rumors about you in those porno shots. Wow. Like lots of celebrities who get caught, they did you a favor."

How the fuck did she know about those? I took a deep breath. Amy had supersonic ears when it came to anything to do with that family.

"They weren't of me." I kept my tone cool and unaffected. "I guess that vital detail hasn't quite made the rounds yet."

Ignoring that comment, she leaned in and whispered, "Hey, I heard Reynard talking to Mrs. Lovechilde the other day."

I was about to walk off. But I couldn't resist. "What did you hear?"

"They're planning to develop the land, and she told him he'd get what she'd promised."

I nodded. "That's interesting. Hey, if you hear anything else, be sure to tell me. I'm at Declan's. I'll make it worth your while."

Was I turning Amy into my own personal spy?

"Are you really living together?"

"We are."

"Are you going to get married?"

I shrugged. "Let's see. One day at a time." I was about to walk off, when I asked, "Hey, what do you know about Declan and a girl named Jasmine."

Her hazel eyes held mine, and I saw that same cagey expression I'd seen before. She wanted something. "I might do."

"How much?" I asked.

"Mm... I don't know. Maybe we can catch up for coffee sometime. I could use a friend."

That took me aback. I studied her face for a hint of a smile or her characteristic cheeky smirk. Instead, I noticed a fragile glint in her eyes. After a lifetime of also feeling like an outsider, I felt for her, despite Amy's wagging tongue.

"Sure. Let's do that," I replied before leaving her to join the party.

I found Declan with his mother and Cleo, and on my approach, the women's attention diverted to me, frowning at me like I'd arrived to stir trouble.

Declan welcomed me by placing his arm around my shoulder.

His mother turned her back to me, and Cleo pulled a look of surprise like he was dating a freak. "Oh, so you're now an item, I see."

"We'll speak later," Mrs. Lovechilde said.

"No, Mother. You've heard all I've got to say." He took my hand. "Come and dance with me."

We floated off to the ballroom where a band fronted by a female singer played famous dance tunes.

He held me close, and we glided around.

"Your mother hates me," I said.

"Don't worry about her."

His erection rubbed against my stomach. "Is something arousing you at the moment?"

"Yes. I'm wondering what's beneath that pretty gown."

I giggled.

"Well, are you going to tell me?" He smirked, which was a welcome relief after his mother's icy treatment.

"A hint. It's uncomfortable."

"A corset?" A groan rumbling from his ribcage spoke volumes of his fetish for those uncomfortable undergarments.

We'd had one moment, a few days back, which had threatened to cloud our moment in the sun.

His laptop was opened, and when I went to close it, I noticed a thumbnail of a girl in a corset.

Unable to resist, I clicked on it and found a woman with long dark hair and big tits with a corset and nothing else. I felt a kick of jealousy.

Declan with those ocean eyes soaked in guilt admitted this fetish started after I'd crashed on his sofa.

He told me that he couldn't stop thinking about me. That lust had gotten the better of him, and he'd scoured the net for a woman who reminded him of me.

It was like a backhanded compliment of sorts.

Declan deleted it, and after that, I headed for a day trip to London and bought myself a collection of new corsets.

Despite scratching into my skin, lacy lingerie and underwear made me feel sexy.

He hissed. "Why did you have to tell me that? I want to go home now."

I laughed. "Maybe later you can show me your old bedroom."

"We can stay here if you like."

"Your mother's likely to poison my coffee."

He sniffed. "She'll come around. She'll have to."

"What do you mean?"

"What I mean is that I wish to marry you. That's if you'll have me."

Luckily, he held me because I nearly fainted. *What?*

"You're serious?" My brows contracted.

He nodded. "I've never been more serious. When you left, I missed you like crazy. And it wasn't just our amazing lovemaking. I also missed our chats. That's when I knew."

"You knew what?" I had to milk this moment. I'd become a glutton for Declan's encouraging words and warm, loving affection.

"I knew that our connection meant more to me than just lust. Even though you're incredibly sexy." His eyes grew hot. "I just want you around all of the time."

All of the time?

I was speechless as we continued to glide on the dance floor. My cheek on his warm neck, I breathed in his maleness, while my heart fluttered about like a butterfly on a sun-drenched flower.

When the song ended, we left the dance floor. I don't think I could feel my legs. I seemed to float, holding the hand of a handsome prince while all eyes were on us, as though we were that special couple they'd been reading about in glossy magazines. I imagined their interest was more to do with how gorgeous Declan looked in his black tuxedo.

Me married? To Declan Lovechilde?

He held my hand as we walked through the guests. All smiling and nodding at Declan, while looking me up and down.

"Are you okay?" he asked.

"I think so. It does feel a little weird seeing people whom I served at the dinner parties."

"Don't worry about that. They'll soon get used to seeing you around in designer dresses and forget you even worked here."

I turned to face him. "Designer dresses? Will I have to go through a whole makeover? Like cut my hair and end up looking like everyone here?"

He laughed. "Hell, no. I'd hate you to do that." He played with a lock of my hair. "I love your hair. I'm not a fan of clones. That's one thing I've often detested about this upper-class scene: everyone dressing, talking, and looking alike. That's why I love you."

Love? Someone pinch me.

His soft tender lips pressed gently against mine, leaving behind the promise of an endless summer.

"I thought you liked me for my body?" I asked, needing to lighten the conversation.

I'd become an emotional mess since meeting Declan. My eyes welled up over almost anything vaguely moving. Even movies and silly shows that normally I'd roll my eyes at for being too soppy. I'd never been like this before. If anything, I'd always identified as stoical.

But then, I'd never been in love.

"I need the bathroom," I said. "Back in a minute."

Our eyes locked, and I returned a tight, quivery smile. I needed to be alone to process what had just happened.

I walked off, lost to my thoughts, when I nearly bumped into Reynard of all people talking to Mrs. Lovechilde and Cleo.

"*Fucking marvelous,*" I muttered under my breath, sensing an ambush.

Reynard wore his usual supercilious smirk, which I was convinced was sculptured onto his face, while Mrs. Lovechilde remained cool. Her face barely moved, which I speculated was due to Botox combined with a cold heart.

Cleo turned to me and said, "Oh, it's the maid."

"I'm no longer that," I said with some ice in my tone.

"I can see that." Her eyes traveled up and down my dress.

"Excuse me." I pushed past her and headed to the bathroom when much to my horror, she entered.

"You're a couple now?"

I turned to face her square and nodded.

"You'll have to learn about our ways, I suppose."

"Your ways?" I frowned.

"Well, we like things a certain way. Declan included." Her eyes lingered over me as though looking for a loose thread or a stain. "He's broken a lot of hearts in this scene."

"I'm sure he has." I kept my tone neutral.

"Then there was Jasmine. He fucked up there."

There she was again. I needed to know about this Jasmine. So against my better judgment, I asked, "What do you mean?"

"He hasn't told you?" Her pout lifted at one end. "Mm... he spoke to me about her from the get-go. He used to talk to me about lots of things. Like how he felt about life. That's why I fell hard for him." She sighed as though saying these things to herself. For a moment, I felt sympathy. One didn't get over a man like Declan easily.

"Declan comes on strong. Like really strong at first and then after a while he loses interest and goes off to his next conquest."

"That doesn't sound like him." I leaned against the sink and played with my hair, determined to remain cool.

"You'll find out in good time. He's not the marrying kind."

She gave me a smug half-grin, and I wanted to slap her for trying to sabotage my moment of happiness.

"He's asked me to marry him," came flying out of my mouth before I could edit it.

Why was I sharing this life-changing announcement with a woman I barely knew?

Her eyebrows hit her scalp. "Really?"

"Yes. Now if you'll excuse me." I turned away and entered a cubicle, hoping she'd leave so I could call Lucy.

Instead, I sat on the toilet and held my chin, and took a deep breath in a bid to find sanity.

When I heard her leave, I went back to the mirror to fix my makeup and recompose myself.

Taking a deep breath, I left the bathroom, and just as I was about to join Declan again, who I could see chatting with a group of older men, Mrs. Lovechilde approached me.

"A word." She spoke with authority, as though I was still her maid and not her son's partner.

I sucked back some air and followed her into her office. Dressed in a silky green gown with her dark hair up, Mrs. Lovechilde looked even more beautiful than women half her age.

Her partner, Will, entered. "Oh, sorry. I didn't realize you were in a conference."

Her face softened. He gave me a faint smile. Will struck me as gentle-spirited in that I didn't get a bad feeling about him, but then, he could have been one of those silent two-faced types—amiable on the outside, scheming on the inside.

"Stay." She nodded and he pulled a hardback book from the tall bookshelf.

"I hear that you're going around saying that my son's going to marry you."

"He asked me earlier." Nerves tangled in my stomach. I regretted telling Cleo.

With alarming intensity, she scrutinized my face. "I can see what my son sees in you. You're a stunner. And you present well in designer. Maid, I could just bear, but not someone selling herself. That's slander on the Lovechilde name. He's always gone for the unwashed." She looked at Will, and his mouth twitched into a tight smile.

"Excuse me? I don't have to take these insults. I could have had Reynard Crisp charged for spiking my drink. He was recently stalking me in London."

"You could do worse. Men like Reynard are rare."

"You don't know your son well, do you?"

Just as I uttered that retort, Declan entered.

"No, she doesn't." He stared daggers at his mother.

CHAPTER 42

Declan

I TURNED TO WILL, who as usual appeared detached from the events taking place around him. "I need a word alone with my mother."

She shook her head. "He stays. We have no secrets."

Theadora stood up. "I'll go then."

I took her hand. "No. Stay." I turned to my mother. "Theadora is a part of my life."

"But marriage?" She stood at her large desk, acting more like the CEO of the family.

Turning my attention to Theadora, I frowned. "You told her?"

She shook her head. "Cleo was giving me a hard time in the bathroom. She mentioned something about Jasmine and how you'd let me down and that you aren't the marrying kind."

A sharp claw squeezed my shoulders.

For once my mother remained quiet. A slight curve tugged at her mouth. She seemed to extract some delight from this sudden tension between me and Theadora.

"Why did you tell her?" I asked. "I wanted to make that announcement formally. Not through some bathroom gossip."

"I can't do this. Excuse me." Theadora rushed off before I could stop her.

I was about to follow her when my mother held up her palm. "Wait. We haven't finished."

Taking a deep breath, I remained.

"You can do better than her, darling."

I leaned over the desk. My face was close to hers. Unruffled, she gazed back without blinking.

"I love her. She *will* be my wife. That's if she'll take me after the bullshit you're spinning here. Why can't you just accept that?"

"Because I want you to marry into a peerage. You're the eldest. I want my grandchildren to be lords and ladies."

"Oh, spare me," I said. "I'm sure Crisp can buy you one."

"He didn't spike her drink. She threw herself at him."

"Believe what you want. I was there. She was drugged and trying to escape." I puffed a breath. "Get over it. She doesn't want to be with him. He's a fucking worm."

She winced. "He's a very close friend of this family."

I turned to Will, who continued to stare down at a book, making me question whether blood ran through his veins.

"Will, tell me, what do you think of Reynard Crisp?"

He shrugged. "He's a big player. He brings contacts and wisdom into the mix. I respect him."

Of course, he'd side with my mother. She had him eating out of her well-manicured hand.

"Why haven't you told her about Jasmine?" she asked.

I rubbed my neck. "It's not a pleasant subject to discuss with anyone. It's in the past."

She shook her head. "Why do you keep disappointing me? Look at you. Film star looks. Clever. Nice. Too nice. And always attracting these down-and-out girls. Go to Europe for a while. Meet other girls and then see how you feel."

I shook my head. "You just don't get it. I love Theadora. I want to be with her. Forever." I puffed. "Why are you like this? Don't you wish me happiness?"

Her eyes softened just a little. "Of course, I do. But you need to think of the future of the name."

"Then focus on Ethan or Savvie."

"Your sister's just as bad as you. She goes for the gutter types, and Ethan isn't with a girl long enough to remember her name."

"I'm marrying Theadora. That's if she'll take me."

"She hasn't answered you yet?" Her eyebrows raised. "Maybe once she learns how you walked away from Jasmine, she might change her mind."

"I offered to bring up the child, Mother. I just refused to marry her. And why the fuck are you going on about this?"

I thought about that distressingly sad moment in my life. And the look of relief on my mother's face after learning the heart-shattering news of Jasmine's suicide.

While my father hugged me and expressed heartfelt sadness, my mother sat back coolly, looking at her nails and shrugging, muttering something like "It's for the best."

I'd had enough of trying to convince my mother and left in search of Theadora.

I found her in the courtyard by the Mercury fountain. Against the watery splashes of changing color, in that flowing red gown, she reminded me of a model in a *Vogue* magazine fashion shoot.

Her beauty made my breath hitch. The fact that she was unaware of her seductive powers only added to my attraction. Her pale skin looked luminous in the moonlight, and her red lips begged to be kissed.

"Here you are," I said, putting my arm around her.

She shivered. "I'm hiding from that fucking dickhead."

I let go and faced her. "Crisp?"

She nodded and bit her lip. "There are so many other girls here. Why won't he leave me alone?"

A sudden burst of adrenaline mixed with anger pounded through my veins. I'd had enough. He needed to be taught a fucking lesson.

"Let's go back inside," I said, through gritted teeth.

Her eyebrows drew in. "What are you going to do?"

"I'm going to do something I should have done ages ago." I sucked back a sharp breath.

She stopped walking. "Declan, please. Don't stir trouble on my behalf. God knows I'm already in the shit around here."

I tilted my head in sympathy, feeling a sudden wave of guilt for dragging her into my mother's prejudiced world.

I kissed her cheek. "Don't worry, angel. I can look after myself. And you're not despised. My mother's just got unrealistic expectations where I'm involved."

We walked back into the party, where women draped in slinky gowns talked loudly and screamed with laughter at jokes told by men in bespoke suits. The older guests flirted with other people's wives or husbands, just like every other ball at Merivale.

I caught sight of Crisp, who was chatting to a much younger woman. *How fucking predictable.*

On our approach, he caught my gaze before he shifted his eyes to Theadora. His gaze lingered over her as though to spite me.

"I'll be right back, okay?"

Her eyes glistened with suspicious concern. "Declan, what are you going to do?"

"I'm going to talk to him. That's all. Don't worry."

She grabbed my arm to stop me, but I gently released her hand. My lips strained into a reassuring smile.

I stood between him and the girl he was probably propositioning. "A word."

He glanced at the young woman who didn't even look twenty. Wearing a low-cut dress, the brunette was his latest project. By the looks of the stars in her eyes, he'd conquered her interest.

"Can't it wait?" He inclined his head towards his pretty fan.

"No. Now." I pointed at the exit. "Outside."

"Ooh... do I need my bodyguard?" He regarded his young victim and grinned.

I cocked my head. "Outside. Now."

Just as he turned his back, I whispered to the girl, "Watch your drink. He's known for spiking them."

I left her standing there with a shocked frown planted on her heavily made-up face.

Ethan, who was chatting to a couple of girls, watched on as I followed Crisp outside.

As I joined him outside, Crisp went to light a cigar, and I knocked it out of his mouth.

"Hey." His smirk faded, revealing the ugly man behind that mask of cool charm.

I grabbed him by the collar. My nose was close to rubbing his as I stared into his cold, indifferent eyes.

"Stop hitting on Theadora, you sleazy piece of shit."

"Let go of me, or I'll have you up for assault."

I mocked his threat with an untroubled grunt. "I don't fucking think so. I've got enough on you to take you down. The only reason I haven't done so is because, for some twisted reason, my mother is protecting you. You're a fucking grimy scumbag. A criminal."

"That's bullshit. I only go with consenting girls."

"By drugging them?"

He struggled out from my clutch, and I pushed him, causing him to stumble.

He got up and ironed out his shirt with his hands. "She wanted it. She opened her legs for all to see." His mouth turned up at one end. He was either a glutton for punishment or just plain stupid because that made me see red.

My knuckles crunched loudly, and he fell back onto the grass, where he writhed in pain, holding his face.

Ethan and some guests arrived just as I was picking him up like a sack of potatoes about to pummel him.

"Declan, no," Ethan implored. "It's not worth it."

I took a stilling breath. He was right.

In any case, Crisp had been clobbered, going on his bloodied nose.

I rubbed my fist, which throbbed in pain, and then straightened my jacket, smoothed down my hair, and re-entered the party, leaving Crisp with blood streaming down his face.

Ethan followed me back in. "That was one hell of a punch. You've missed your calling."

"It felt fucking good," I responded, as I headed back to my girl.

I found her chatting with her past colleagues.

She came and joined me, looking worried. "Are you okay? I wasn't sure what to do."

"It's all good, angel. I think he's got the message." Although not a fan of violence, that punch felt good, like an unsightly boil had finally burst.

I took her by the hand and led her into the sitting room, where a couple canoodled on the chaise lounge.

"Let's give them privacy, shall we?" She smiled back, and I led her up the stairs. "Let's go to my room."

I opened the door for her to pass.

She looked about. "It's different to how I imagined."

"Oh, really? What were you expecting?"

"I guess pictures of girls and cars. Sports stars." She scanned the blue walls, on which hung original landscapes. She picked up a framed picture of my former dog. "He's cute."

"I still miss him."

"Why not get another?" she asked.

"I hate it when they die. My heart broke when I lost him."

She cuddled me. "You're just a giant softy."

I ran my hands over her curves, and my night lightened. I went to lift her dress when she wiggled out of my arms.

"No. We need to talk."

Talk about a speedy comedown. I gulped. "Okay."

She stood at the window that opened into a balcony. "What happened with Jasmine?"

CHAPTER 43

Thea

DECLAN LOOKED AWAY, AND when his gaze returned, I read painful resignation. Fighting that inner child screaming at me to fall into his arms and take him any which way, I listened instead to my adult voice.

"If we're to marry, I need to know who you are. So far, it's been endless sex and you spoiling me." I stroked the diamonds dangling from my ears.

Lounging back in an antique silk-covered armchair, he reminded me of the muscular, gorgeous heartthrobs that women drooled over in magazines.

He stroked his bottom lip. "That's not something I can answer because I'm not sure who I really am."

"You're a hero," I returned. "My hero. And the hero of those mothers and children you saved in Afghanistan."

"That's just natural instinct. I'm talking about relationships."

"You doubt you can make me happy?" I stared him in the eyes.

"I'd do everything to make you happy. But beyond showering you with compliments, keeping you safe, and buying you everything your heart desires, I don't know what else I can offer."

"I don't need all of that. Just you by my side is enough." I chose my words carefully. "Being with you has made me the happiest I've ever been, but also the most anxious."

"The most anxious? Really?" A line formed between his brows. "Even with all that's happened in your past?"

"That's different. My stepfather terrified me, whereas with you I'm scared you'll break my heart."

He rose and joined me at the window.

Drawing me close, he kissed the top of my head.

"I've never felt this way about any woman. From the moment I saw you on my couch asleep, I couldn't stop thinking about you. And I was your first." He shook his head as though I'd handed him an unimaginable gift. "You're mine, Theadora. I want to possess you. I'd kill anyone if they tried to harm you."

Instead of anger at his words, I felt liberated by them. I wanted this man to possess me.

"But that only works if you let me possess you."

He lifted his palms in surrender. "You've got all of me. You can choose the colors of the walls. You can choose where we holiday. You can choose our children's names. You can tell me not to go out and play poker with my army mates. You can call the shots for all I care. I just want you with me forever."

"Forever?" That word floated out of my mouth like a spray of gossamer.

Snapping out of my dream and refusing to allow my swelling heart to hijack the moment, I looked away from his beautiful face. "Please tell me about Jasmine."

He puffed out a breath and rubbed his sharp jaw. "We went out for a month. She was nineteen, and I was twenty-one."

"Was she a virgin?" Although irrelevant, that small detail mattered to me.

"Are you kidding? She'd fucked half the village by the time I met her." He sniffed.

"And you fell for her?" I asked, surprised that a man like Declan would go out with the village floozy.

"Well, let's put it this way: she was very experienced." His raised eyebrow reminded me of Declan's high sex drive.

"So that's what appealed to you?"

"I was twenty-one, Theadora. I hadn't thought it out. And the girls who moved in our circles tended to be less…"

"Adventurous?" I asked.

He nodded with a guilty look. "She lived on one of the local farms. I'd known Jasmine since we were children. We met one night at the Mariner. She was playing the flute with Mirabel on guitar, and I fell for her."

Jealousy poked its spiky finger into my chest.

"My mother hated her of course."

"Did you love her?"

He shook his head. "I wasn't looking for a relationship. She knew that. I was still at college, trying to figure out what I wanted to do. And she was all over the place. She'd go into these dark places, which I couldn't navigate." He took a breath. "Anyway, when she fell pregnant, she insisted it was mine, despite her fucking other guys."

"Really? You weren't exclusive?" I asked, surprised that anyone would need other lovers with a man like Declan.

"No. I mean, I didn't fuck around, but she did. My request for a paternity test after the baby arrived, seriously pissed her off. She wanted me to marry her."

"Did your mother know?"

He nodded. "Jasmine saw to that. She went around telling everyone that I was going to turn her into a single mother. I hated how pressured that made me feel. My mother even offered her money to go away." He shook his head. "Unsurprisingly, my mother hated her."

"Yeah, unsurprisingly," I muttered.

He gave me an apologetic smile. "Yeah, well, my mother's another story."

"So what happened to Jasmine?"

"She killed herself. Slit her veins." The tremor in his voice was justified by that shocking detail.

I touched my mouth. "You're kidding."

He shook his head. "That's why I don't talk about it. I ran away after that and joined the army."

"Did she leave a note?"

"One was found. But it in illegible scrawl. Something vague like 'life wasn't worth living.'"

His voice cracked, and I studied his face. The shadow of night accentuated the depth of pain in his eyes.

I couldn't leave it there. I needed to know every tragic detail.

"Would you have married her had the child been yours?"

He turned sharply and held my stare. "I wasn't in love with her."

"But it isn't just love but responsibility, isn't it?"

"Well, yes, I would have provided for them. They wouldn't have wanted for anything. She knew that."

I nodded pensively.

"In any case, the child wasn't mine." His voice trailed off.

"Oh?" My eyebrows knitted. "They discovered that at the autopsy?"

"Yep." He looked like he'd seen a ghost with that pale face and remote expression. I felt guilty for dredging it up, but I needed to know everything. "My mother arranged it."

"The autopsy?"

"No, she insisted on a paternity test."

"They can do that?"

"I guess so. She was six months pregnant at the time."

"Shit." I grit my teeth. This story was getting uglier by the minute.

He rubbed his neck. "It was a horrible time. And being a tight-knit community, everyone talked about it. It was fucking awful, to be honest."

"I bet." I released a tight breath. "Did you feel responsible for her suicide?"

He shrugged. "Perhaps I should have given her more reassurance. But I wasn't ready to marry her or anyone. I don't know. Her mother also killed herself. Mental illness ran in the family. I'd seen it first-hand with Jasmine."

"You shouldn't blame yourself."

He exhaled. "There was little I could've done, to be honest, other than reassure her that she would be well provided for."

"Is that why you want to help troubled youth?"

He stared out into space. "On a subconscious level, perhaps." He took a deep breath and turned to look at me. "While we're on this subject of our pasts. My mother tells me that she got a call from your mother, requesting your phone number."

I winced at this jarring switch from him to me. With so much going on, I'd buried that recent gut-wrenching experience.

"Your mother doesn't know your number?" His shocked tone made me jittery. A reminder of how bad my relationship with her was.

"When I changed it, I never told her." I looked down at my feet. "She called me out of the blue. It was the first time since I left home."

"But you left home years ago." The furrows in his brow deepened.

"Yeah, well..." I clasped my hands and scratched my thumbnail. "She never called me for my birthday or Christmas. Ever. She completely ignored me."

He splayed his hands. "So why now?"

"That's what I asked her." I sniffed. "Apparently, she'd seen an image of us together, looking all loved up at the boot camp opening. It was all over the media. And you being wealthy piqued her curiosity, I suppose."

"So did you just talk over the phone?"

"Nope. I caught up with her in London."

I pictured that afternoon, meeting at a café close to Harrods, her favorite shopping destination. While sipping tea, like distant acquaintances, not mother and daughter, we exchanged courteous pleasantries as I struggled to maintain a façade of civility. My instincts were to go all feral and heap abuse at her. However painful, I resisted that urge and continued the charade.

As I kissed her cool cheek, I told myself I would never contact this woman again.

I gave her a chance. All I needed was an apology or some acknowledgment of how she regretted neglecting me as a child, but she seemed more caught up in talking about the Lovechildes and their impressive wealth.

"Something else came up in that discussion." I bit my lip, as I recalled my mother's unblinking glare while conveying how Declan had threatened my stepfather. "Why didn't you tell me you met him?" I frowned.

He shrugged. "To protect you. I met up with him and warned him to stay away or else."

"Or else?" My jaw dropped. "But why not tell me?"

"Because this was before we'd even started seeing each other. I know I overstepped the mark, but I couldn't get it out of my head. I saw the distress on your face. I wish you'd press charges."

I remained frozen. The thought of that horrible man talking to the love of my life made my skin crawl. "I can't go through that. I can't even face seeing him." My voice cracked.

He walked over to me and embraced me. His warmth helped remove the horror I felt at the mention of that ugly man.

After a few minutes, my body calmed, and I stepped away from him.

"So have you made up with your mother? I'd like to meet her," he said, his eyes softening and my heart melting in response.

"It's not going to happen." I knitted my fingers to ease the tremor. "I can't stand her."

"You need to resolve that, sweetheart. Spiteful anger can be corrosive. She *is* your mother."

"A mother would have protected me from that bastard, whereas mine blamed me for what had happened. I couldn't go near a man without breaking out into a fucking sweat."

Tears spurted from my eyes. I was unable to control them; the more I tried, the more my body shook.

He stood behind me and cradled me in his arms until my pain subsided. It was like a warm, cozy blanket had been placed over my shivering soul.

With his strong arms holding me, I felt more protected than I'd ever felt in my entire life.

He kissed my head. "She's not a good woman. You're right. And you gave her another chance."

I turned to face him. "They say we can't choose our families, but we can choose our friends. And I've chosen Lucy and now you as my family."

A smile shaped his lips. "Careful. That might make us incestuous."

He squeezed my butt, which was timely because all this heavy talk had to end now. My upbringing had hijacked my sanity for way too long.

Our eyes locked in a soul-searching gaze.

I broke away from him and opened my bag for a tissue. I gazed into the large gilt mirror and thanked the gods for waterproof makeup. I wiped my nose and took a deep breath.

"Won't your mother hate you if I agree to us marrying?" I asked.

He raked through his thick hair, which always managed to fall over his forehead, even when slicked back.

"I couldn't give a shit what she thinks, to be honest. I would like you, however, to meet my father." He inclined his head. "Would you mind coming to dinner with us?"

I smiled. Sunshine poured over me, melting away angst. "Of course. I'd love to meet him."

He looked into my eyes. "Then, we're good?"

"I think so." My mouth trembled.

He wiped the stray tear on my cheek with his finger, and his eyes filled with love and understanding.

"What about Reynard?" I asked.

He shrugged. "I don't give a fuck about him, and neither should you."

"Can't we just move somewhere else?"

"I love this place. I'd like to run organic farms."

"Like Prince Charles?" I grinned.

"A market would be nice."

I fell into his arms, and his lips landed on mine. From sweet and heartfelt it descended into a decadent, deep-tonguing kiss.

He unzipped my dress, and I stepped out of it as it pooled at my feet.

I stood before him in my white corset, lace stockings, and nothing else.

He hissed loudly and unzipped his slacks.

My gaze settled on that delicious bulge tenting his briefs.

He pointed at the bed with the embossed satin cover, reminding me of an image in *Home Beautiful*. "Just lie down and let me look at you."

Knowing what he wanted, I spread my legs.

I'd come prepared. No panties. It had been rather draughty going commando, but worth it if only to witness the lust in those dark-blue eyes and his big dick all engorged and hungry.

He got on his knees and placed his head between my legs. He licked up my thighs.

When the tip of his tongue settled on my bud, a warm shower of prickling heat blanketed me. I flinched as my muscles tensed and then surrendered and tensed again.

Lapping, sucking, and nibbling my clit, he gripped my naked butt and swallowed my orgasms one after another.

Grasping clumps of his hair, I writhed about and became a whimpering mess.

CHAPTER 44

Declan

THEADORA'S WHITE LACE STOCKINGS scratched teasingly against my cheeks, and her throaty moans sent a rush of testosterone to my balls just as she squirted a creamy release onto my tongue.

My heart pounded with urgency seeing her in that white lace corset with her raven hair snaking seductively over her breasts. Especially with that invitingly open slit, ripe red, and dripping in cum.

Wiping my lips, I stepped away for a better look. I loved that heavy-lidded gaze and parted lips that seemed to beg for my dick.

I undid the lace to her corset and her tits spilled out, sending a rush of blood down to my throbbing dick.

Turning her over, I said, "On all fours."

I grabbed her hips and buried my dick deep inside. My hands cupped her tits while watching us in the mirror.

Seeing her in that white corset, her tits bouncing in my hands and her curvy bum rubbing against my balls, drove me wild and my thrusts harder and faster.

Indulging in the delicious burn of friction, I pounded into her. Her pussy walls squeezed tightly around my dick.

"I need you to come." I breathed into her ear and tongued her.

Her moans grew more desperate, in tandem with the heat engulfing my body.

Her pussy convulsed around my shaft and, unable to hold back the explosion, a fiery climax gushed out of me.

I fell on my back and placed my arm around Theadora, drawing her into my chest while breathing her in.

I waited until my breath returned to normal before speaking. "Every time we make love, it gets better."

"For me too," she murmured.

I stroked her silky hair. "No one will ever hurt you again, my love. I'll see to that. You're a part of me. Your safety and happiness mean everything to me."

As we lay there, I visited that meeting with her scumbag stepfather.

His eyes darting about and unable to look me in the face. A sure sign of someone with something to hide.

I pointed at his weathered face. "You're being watched, and I've also got someone probing police complaints into child abuse. If there's even just a whisper of your name, you'll be pissing through a plastic bag all your fucking life."

"You can't make these threats. I'll report you," he said with a thin, wavering voice.

I knew his type. Gutless men who went around picking on weaker, smaller people.

I laughed in his face. "You're just lucky that Theadora's reluctant to take this further. Mainly because she doesn't want to see your greasy, ugly head again."

Pointing at his face, I finished that meeting with "You're a fucking piece of scum." I had to use all my inner control to stop myself from knocking his yellowing teeth out. And the only reason why I didn't kill him was because I wanted to spend my life with Theadora and not behind bars.

MY MOTHER WAITED A few days after the ball before asking to see me. I met her in the garden courtyard with the best ocean view. It was a sunny morning, and after a night of slow, heartfelt lovemaking, nothing could mess with my mood. Not even my mother's outrageous demands.

I sat down at the table and was served by Amy, carrying a tray with fresh scones and tea.

Amy went to pour the tea when I stopped her. "It's okay. I can do it. Thanks."

The maid nodded and turned away.

"Your new girlfriend's already influencing you, I see." Her eyes rested on my hand gripping the teapot.

"I don't need people to wipe my ass."

She scowled. "Don't be vulgar."

I smiled at her and poured our tea.

"Your behavior at the ball was abhorrent. Luckily, you didn't break his nose, and he's not laying charges."

I buttered my scone and took a bite. I waited until I'd swallowed before answering. "He's an immoral slug. He spiked Theodora's drink so that he could rape her."

"That's unsubstantiated and besides, she's a teaser."

My brows crashed. "What? Are you subscribing to that tired, if not deplorable, theory that women encourage rape?"

"You don't know what took place. Who's to say that our former maid isn't canoodling with whoever's the highest bidder."

"You cannot be serious." I stared into my mother's dark eyes, looking for a hint of goodness. "What's he got over you?"

"He's a business partner. One that we need right now."

"Right now? Are you telling me the family, who are worth twenty billion, are in financial straits?" I tried not to laugh at that ridiculous statement.

"Wealth in property and land, but there's a lack of cash flow. The tourist industry has been deeply impacted by this virus. The hotels, which were our cash cow, have been running at a loss."

"And you want to open up a fucking resort?" I asked.

"Language. You're educated. Swearing is for imbeciles with a low IQ."

I rolled my eyes at her patronizing tone.

"This virus can't impact our lives forever." She sipped her tea. "At least your brother's seen sense and has an architect draughting up plans for a spa by the duck pond. He understands, unlike you, that to maintain his extravagant lifestyle one needs cash."

"I've got plenty of my own cash. I invested in Bitcoin and Tesla before joining the army. I can cash those in and live a very comfortable life. There's no need to rip this land from the hearts of those families that have made this the food bowl of the region."

"In answer to your earlier question, Rey's my benefactor."

"In what way?"

"We're working on projects together."

"So he's investing in the destruction of the lands?"

"Darling, I wish you wouldn't be so negative about this. It's a marvelous opportunity to expand Lovechilde's reach. We're not even talking about every farm here. Only a mere three acres."

"It's lucky that Theadora's refused to press charges on Crisp for stalking her."

"Then she's brighter than I thought. Rey has promised to stop flirting with her, even though that's pretty harmless."

I sucked in a breath to placate a sudden burst of anger. The china cup in my hand clanged unsteadily on its saucer. "Harmless? Do you think unwanted advances, or, in gutter speak since he's gutter, trying to sleaze onto someone, is harmless? Not taking no for an answer, harmless?"

"Men will be men." She wiped her lips with a cloth napkin.

"I don't behave like that. Never have. Ethan's not like that."

She opened her palms. "You're both stunning boys with equally stunning bank accounts."

Disturbed by her earlier simplistic comment, I couldn't believe how she'd shrugged off deplorable males hitting on non-consenting women.

I couldn't help but wonder what had happened to my mother growing up. She never spoke about her past.

"I was humiliated by that violent display at the ball." She tapped her long fingernails on the table, giving me the same admonishing look she gave me when, as a child, I'd embarrass her in front of her friends by arriving muddied after kicking a football with the local kids.

Frustrated by her evasiveness, I shook my head. My mother and Reynard Crisp were thick. That's all I'd learned these past few months. Had it not been for Theadora begging me to let it go, I would have brought in the lawyers.

"You should choose less crooked friends." I rose.

"And you should stop seeing low-class girls."

"She's from wealth, Mother. You know that. I'm going." I'd had enough.

I headed off to meet Carson at Reboot.

The camp was in full swing. Forty youth. Most of whom acted up the first week, but I'd heard that they were taking to the many activities, which provided them with bonus points. If they finished the training course and activities, they were promised video games, weekend pizza, and all those regular treats that they'd been denied in prison.

I entered the activities' room—a large space with ceiling-to-floor windows that looked out to nothing but trees, rolling hills, and sky.

I remained at the entrance, watching on. There were around forty boys lost to their computers. One boy, the only one without his eyes on a screen, was drawing. He piqued my interest.

"They've had a big day," Carson said from behind.

I turned and greeted him.

"After their workout, they went on a three-mile run."

Impressed, I nodded. "Any trouble?"

"This week's been better. I had to pull Billy into line. He's an Irish lad." He inclined his head towards a tall, red-haired boy pressing down furiously on his gaming pad.

"They're playing games?" I asked.

"Some. Others are working on a project I've given them."

My face lit up. "What's that?"

"I've asked them to design a veggie garden."

"You're kidding. And they're interested?" My day just got better.

"Some are interested." He shrugged. "Look, there are a few trouble-makers, but they're good kids, I think." He lifted his chin towards a muscular, dark-haired, tattooed boy who looked more like a man to me. "He's the ringleader. They seem to follow him. Dylan Black."

"How so?" I asked, watching him draw.

"The first week he was pretty hard going, but he's so fucking strong and seems to get off on the training. A natural in many ways, but fuck-ing insubordinate. A talented troublemaker." He smirked.

I watched the boy with his head bowed, lost in what he was doing. "He doesn't strike me as unhinged."

Carson scratched his eyebrow. "That's the thing. Give him paper and pens and he's off in his own world. A brilliant artist. Heavy shit, though. You know, blood and guts, guns, naked girls. All the exciting stuff." He chuckled. "But it keeps him quiet. He's had it tough. Like most of the boys here." His eyes shone with sympathy. If anyone knew what that meant, it was Carson. "Grew up in a council estate with a single mother who drank too much, and changed her boyfriends as often she changed her underwear."

"Abused?" I had to ask.

"Probably. Punched out the shrink. No one knows."

I thought of Theadora and her heavy upbringing, and my stomach tightened at how these arseholes ruined innocent lives with their filth.

Somewhere in the back of my mind, I knew that once the dust had settled, and with Theadora by my side, I would do what I could to make a difference in these boys' lives.

DRESSED IN A FUR-TRIMMED collared coat and wearing her dark glossy hair in a ponytail, Theadora radiated that rare blend of class and individu-ality that turned a pretty flower into a prized bloom.

"You look lovely." I kissed her cheek touched by the crisp air.

"You look pretty good yourself." She ran her hands over my jacket. "I love you dressed up."

"I'll bear that in mind and get fitted for more designer jackets." I smiled.

"I like you in anything, Declan. My favorite being shirtless and..." A half-grin made her pretty eyes sparkle with cheek. "Without your pants. Okay, then, let's just say naked."

I played with her fingers and looking into her pretty eyes, I chuckled. "I'll bear that in mind and be sure to walk around home naked. Only if you do."

We giggled while entering the restaurant to meet my father.

I paused and turned towards her. "You haven't given me an answer yet."

"I will. Soon." She stared up at me, and I read that same perplexed uncertainty that I'd grown accustomed to.

Photos of Southern Italian villages covered the walls, and with its check tablecloths and animated waiters speaking in Italian, we could have just stepped into a Neapolitan trattoria.

The aroma of cooked tomatoes, garlic, and herbs fired up my appetite.

I spotted my father, who waved at us, and we joined him and his partner at their table.

My father rose and hugged me and then kissed Theadora on the cheek.

"Lovely to see you again," he told her.

Unlike my mother, my father put her at ease with his relaxed, inviting manner.

After we ordered and loosened up with a bit of small talk, I launched straight into it.

"Tell me about Reynard Crisp and Mother." I gave Luke an apologetic smile. "Family politics."

"I don't mind. Colorful families interest me. I wouldn't be a lawyer otherwise."

"Luke has moved into family law," my father added.

"Oh, I thought you were in entertainment law." I hadn't spoken that much to him, and was still unsure what to make of Luke. He seemed to make my father happy, which was all that mattered.

"I got bored with pop princesses and princes' hissy fits. And their 'do it now or I'll find another lawyer' taunts." He chuckled.

A waiter delivered another bottle of wine, and Luke gave him a lingering stare, which I found a little inappropriate. But that was me, old-fashioned and surprisingly possessive, something I'd only just discovered thanks to my obsession with Theadora.

The waiter placed the wine down and walked off with Luke's attention directed at the young man and his slight wiggle. I found myself questioning whether my father and Luke were exclusive.

I turned to my Dad. "Tell me what you know about Crisp and Mothers' relationship."

"They had a romance of sorts before I came along, and from what I gather, Rey broke her heart."

My eyebrows raised. I'd seen my mother's stolen glances directed at Crisp. Hearing how he'd hurt my unshakable mother, however, took me aback.

He ran his fingers up the stem of his wine glass. "Reynard broke a lot of women's hearts back then. Good looking. Filthy rich and brimming in playboy charm."

"I know he's not the marrying kind." A pang of sympathy swept through me. I might have resented her arrogance, but it pained me to know my mother had been hurt.

"He liked them young." My father looked at Theadora.

"I've noticed." I shook my head in disgust. "But Mother was young. She married you at twenty-two."

"She was eighteen when she was with Crisp. They were together for a year or so. But your mother wanted marriage. To marry wealth." He sniffed.

"I don't understand this obsession she has for money. Weren't her parents rich?" All we knew about them was that her mother and father died in a car accident when I was young. Even the photos she had were sketchy at best.

"Nope."

My eyes widened slightly. "But I thought she went to public school and had a wealthy upbringing."

"She got a scholarship to study history at Oxford. Your mother is a very intelligent woman, one of her few virtues." His mouth twitched into a smile. "She got as far as her masters but got caught up in society. She wanted to climb that ladder to wealth. That's why she married me."

"You weren't in love?" My brows gathered. Perhaps I was being over-romantic and unrealistic, but I liked to think that I'd been conceived by love.

"We were a little, I believe, but us marrying was also expedient. She wanted to marry into money, and I was experiencing emotional turmoil and needed rescuing." He took a deep breath before continuing. "I'd lost Alice, the love of my life and my fiancée, the year before. We met at college. She was my soulmate, and she died." He looked at Luke almost apologetically.

I figured Luke was only into men. I imagined that might have made for a confusing arrangement being with a bisexual man. It sure as hell confused me. I had nothing against homosexuals. I had a few good friends who were gay, but my father struck me as lost.

Theadora asked gently, "Do you mind me asking how she passed away?"

He puffed out a breath. "She disappeared without a trace. It was in the news. There's a million-pound reward. She's never been found." His eyes misted over.

I touched his hand. "I'm so sorry, Dad. Why have you never spoken about this?"

He shrugged. "I had to move on. I married your mother. Caroline was pregnant with you at the time."

That almost jarred. I was still processing the death of my father's soulmate. "A shotgun marriage?"

"Not as such. I wanted to marry her."

"And Crisp?"

"He's always been in the picture. Has invested in some of our ventures. Us rich hang together, as you know."

I nodded pensively. "He's a rake, Dad."

"I know that." He sipped his wine solemnly. "There's even talk of rape."

Theadora looked at me and rolled her eyes. "That doesn't surprise me."

I sat up. "Have you heard of any cases and names?"

My father studied me for a moment. "Declan, don't go there. It's a black hole. You might as well buy some lawyer a lavish lifestyle. Like a modern-day Jarndyce vs Jarndyce."

On noticing Theadora's frown, he added, "It's an endless and fruitless legal trial in Dicken's *Bleak House*."

"I must read it," Luke said. "I might get some useful insight on how to cream the wealthy." His dark chuckle sent me cold.

As much as I tried, I couldn't warm to Luke. There was something slippery about him. I couldn't understand my father's attraction. It must have just been physical. I could only assume.

"So why are Mother and Crisp still thick as thieves?" I asked.

"I can't say what Crisp has got over her. Maybe he's offering to finance part of the development and go into partnership."

"Wouldn't she tell you?" I asked.

He shrugged. "We're separated. And as you know, from our last board meeting, I am not budging. I'm applying for a heritage overlay as we speak. It's easier said than done, however." He looked at Luke.

"Mother cites cash flow issues. And you know Mother. When she jumps onto an idea, she doesn't budge."

The waiter arrived with menus.

After we ordered, we resumed our discussion about the family business. I gave Theadora an apologetic smile, and she nodded faintly. She understood the complex nature of my family life and how important the farmlands were to me.

"Weren't you thinking of expanding into New York?" I asked.

He nodded. "I'm just looking for an investor over there. I'm probably flying out at the end of the week."

"Everything's back to the way it was. In no time, the tourists will be back," I said.

"For sure. Look I've got a few billion in pharma shares that last time I looked have doubled."

Luke's eyes widened.

"I could easily draw a few billion out, but I want to keep it there for my children." His eyes glowed with sincerity.

I returned his warm smile. "I'm doing exceptionally well."

"I'm not worried about you. You've always been a hard worker. You've made me proud. No prouder than when you received that Medal of Valour. A first for a Lovechilde."

A lump grew in my throat, and Theadora, who could read me well, squeezed my hand.

"I worry about Ethan and Savvie. They've both been indulged all their lives. They've never worked."

"Ethan's got a project on the go. He's building a spa by the duck pond."

My father nodded. "So he tells me."

After dessert and some light chatter, helping to clear the air of family issues, we hugged and left for Mayfair.

CHAPTER 45

Thea

WE WOKE TO A fine sunny morning. After breakfast, Declan said, "How about a trip to Italy?"

My eyebrows flung up.

Although unexpected, I soon warmed to that exciting idea.

We'd been living in our own little bubble in Bridesmere, and I welcomed a break from all the issues percolating around us.

"When were you thinking?" I asked.

"How's next week sound?"

"I have my exam at the end of the week. I guess that could work."

"Why don't you bring Lucy?" He buttoned up his shirt.

"Really?" I thought about Lucy's infectious delight over her new administrative role at Reboot. She couldn't stop hugging me for dropping her into this dream world.

"I'm taking a fellow pilot, Matt, an old army mate."

"A fellow pilot?"

He nodded. "I've just purchased a jet."

He said it like he'd just bought a car. "Are you serious?"

"I am an experienced pilot," he said, combing back his hair in the mirror and looking dashingly handsome with that chiseled jaw and sculptured lips.

I shook my head in surprise. "I know so little about you."

He held me. "We have all our lives to get to know each other, haven't we?"

My heart expanded. "I still haven't given you an answer."

"I can live in hope, can't I?" He smiled so sweetly that all I wanted to do was marry him on the spot and then lay naked with him forever.

MY BREATH HITCHED WHEN I saw my handsome fiancé. Yes, I'd agreed to marry him. A decision I made within a second of him asking, but I felt I needed to give us time, and perhaps on a subconscious level, give him time to think it through. My inner pessimist found it difficult to process that this stunningly beautiful man would want to be with me forever.

Wearing a pilot's uniform, cap included, Declan, with that purposeful stride, left me speechless. I melted before him. That tall, well-built man, who, with that debonair accent, and classic good looks, could have played James Bond. He chatted with his friend as they came towards us.

"Bloody hell, Thea, they're in uniform," Lucy gushed.

"I know. Declan looks hot."

"So does the other one." Running her hands down her brown hair.

Declan hugged me, drenching me in his masculine scent, and while my hormones had broken into a sweat dancing up a storm, he introduced us to Matt.

A stewardess welcomed us onboard the shiny aircraft that Declan and Matt had just been circling and admiring as boys would with a new shiny toy.

"Hello, I'm Margot, and I'll be your host during this flight. Can I offer you some champagne?"

I sank into the red leather seats as Lucy answered a decisive "Yes."

Declan entered. "Do you want to see the cockpit?"

This is how lust-drugged I was around this man because at first, I thought he'd asked, "Do you want to see my cock?"

As Lucy sprung up with a "You bet" I snapped my dropped jaw shut, realizing what he'd actually said.

Mind you, I was always keen to see his cock.

Unlike Lucy, who was as excitable as a girl being fitted for a Cinderella gown, I experienced a flurry of nerves.

Declan touched my cheek. "Are you okay?"

"I'm fine. This is so unreal, and I've never been on a plane before."

He gave me one of his trademark sweet smiles. "Don't worry. We'll be sure to make it as smooth as possible. The conditions are great for flying. No major storms ahead."

"Show the way then, Captain." I giggled.

Lucy had beaten me to it and was engrossed in Matt's explanation of the flight instruments.

"I can't believe you can operate all of this," I said, regarding the panoply of monitors and dials.

"Yep. That's why we joined the SAS." Declan glanced at his friend who nodded.

He kissed me. "Enjoy the experience. I am honored to be your first time."

My eyebrow lifted. I leaned in close and whispered. "Another first to add to the list."

His eyes smiled back at me.

We returned to our seats and strapped ourselves in.

Lucy held my hand as we took off, and champagne helped quell my shakes.

She pointed out the window, chatting and laughing, which took my mind off all the possible disasters my overactive imagination cooked up.

After we were in the sky, I finally found a steady breath.

"Matt's cute," Lucy said.

"He's lovely."

"This is going to be amazing. Have you been studying up on your Italian?" She picked at a plate of cheese, olives, ham, and salami.

"Not really. I haven't had time. Between shopping with you and studying for my exams, it's been a crazy week."

"Do you think you passed?" She munched on a cracker.

I nodded. "The practical, I'm sure I did. For the rest, I'm not sure. Next semester I have to go and do some classroom teaching."

"Oh? In London?"

"No. I've requested somewhere close to the village."

Lucy didn't know of my decision to marry. I hadn't even told her that Declan had proposed. A secret that had twisted me in knots. I just wanted to make sure he meant it before sharing such mind-blowing news.

"You're going to keep living there, then?"

I nodded with a coy smile.

Her eyebrows moved together. "Hey, what aren't you telling me?"

I took a deep breath. "We're going to be married."

Her mouth parted. "You're kidding. When did this happen?"

"He asked me a while back. I've only just answered him."

"My god, Thea. That's insane." Her eyes lit up. "So is there going to be a big wedding?"

"I'm not sure. We haven't discussed it. I don't care. I'd marry him at the beach or the town hall."

Her mouth turned down. "Oh, you can't. You need a big, disgustingly rich wedding so that I can flirt with the best man."

I laughed. "Matt?"

She pulled an excitable smile. "He is cute."

"He's a tall, solid guy. I'm not sure if cute's the right description."

"No. Ex-army. Mm... hot."

She had that right. I thought of Declan and all those muscles on muscles, and heat traveled through my body thinking of how he felt inside of me while I gripped onto those powerful biceps.

I sighed silently. Yep, I was in the thrall of lust, but I was also in love.

Declan was there for me. I knew that he would protect me. And after the kind of life I'd had, protection meant more than pleasure. Although multiple orgasms had steadily become addictive too.

CHAPTER 46

Declan

THE PLANE HIT THE tarmac, and Matt yelled, "Woo-hoo! Textbook landing. Well done."

Drunk on adrenaline and endorphins, I grinned. "After Afghanistan and those impromptu landings, that was a breeze."

"Feels good, though, doesn't it?" He grinned.

"Oh, yeah. I've missed it."

He unstrapped himself. "Whenever you want to go anywhere, count me in. I've enjoyed this."

"I'm glad you're on board. I needed this." I rose from my seat and stretched my arms.

He looked outside the window. "It looks hot. Lucky I packed my board shorts."

"I'm hoping to get in some snorkeling. There are meant to be some amazing underwater caves."

His face lit up. "That sounds fucking amazing."

When we joined the girls, I noticed Theadora looking a little pale.

I put my arm around her. "Are you okay?"

"I'm good now."

Lucy chuckled. "You should have seen her during the landing. She was a mess."

She gently slapped her friend's arm. "I wasn't that bad."

"You were in great hands. That was one hell of a smooth landing," Matt said.

Holding onto the love of my life, we made our way out of the plane. Theadora giggled. "I'm okay to do this myself."

"You don't like me holding onto you?" I asked.

"I do," she whispered. "Especially when we're naked."

I smiled. "Mm... I think I'll need a siesta before we take in the sights."

Our eyes held, and my heart sang. Every time I studied that beautiful face, I saw a woman coming into her own. Like a rose blossoming into a breathtaking specimen of beauty.

Lucy brought out her phone. "Photos, please. In your uniforms. So that I'll know I haven't dreamt this up."

I laughed. I liked Lucy and appreciated their sisterly bond.

Unknown to both of them, I'd paid for Lucy's village apartment. I'd instructed the landlord to charge her a tiny rent so that she didn't get suspicious.

I stood next to Matt and smiled as Lucy took photos on her phone. "Can you take one of Theadora and me?" I asked her.

I placed my arm around my wife-to-be. Wearing a white summery dress with a red cardigan and her long, lustrous dark hair hanging freely. She reminded me of a local Italian girl.

"I'm only wearing my flats. I resemble a midget compared to you." She giggled.

Her head reached just below my shoulder. "You're a perfect fit." I went to take off my cap.

"No, with the cap on, please," she said with that coaxing smile that could have talked me into eating haggis.

We walked around Positano, a picture-perfect cliffside village that Theadora described as a fairy tale. It certainly resembled something out of the ordinary with its pastel buildings clinging miraculously onto a steep hillside surrounded by an aquamarine ocean.

The sea glistened under the late-afternoon sun, and tourists ambled along. After we settled at a café in the bustling piazza, we ordered a limoncello—a tangy local liqueur.

Feeling refreshed after a siesta and some hot sex with my fiancée, I must have been the happiest man alive.

From a distance, I saw Matt walking alongside Lucy, chatting and laughing.

I slanted my head in their direction. "They look happy."

"Lucy's a bit of a flirt, I'm afraid. She's got a thing for men in uniforms."

"I'm glad. Matt's single, and he seems to like her."

"Did he say something?" Theadora wore a hopeful gleam in her eyes. I could see her friend's happiness meant everything to her.

"We don't talk about things like that. And he's only just met her." A waiter arrived with the pizza we'd ordered as a snack. The aroma made my stomach leap with joy. "That smells delicious." I glanced up at the waiter. "*Grazie.*"

"*Prego.*" He nodded. "Can I get you another drink?"

I shook my head. "Not for me."

Theadora looked up at him. "Just some water, please."

We ate in hungry silence and welcomed Lucy and Matt.

"I'm overwhelmed by how beautiful this place is," Lucy said, standing at our table.

"Why don't you join us? Have some pizza," I said.

They sat down. "Only if there's enough."

"This is just a snack. I've booked a table for eight. You got my text to join us?" I asked Matt.

He nodded.

"Do you like where you're staying?" Theadora asked Lucy.

"You bet. There are so many amazing views of mountain villages and the sea. I'm taking so many photos."

AFTER TREKKING THROUGH COASTAL trails and discovering ancient villages with their olive groves and exquisite fragrant gardens, we sat in a small square in a mountainside garden of lemon trees. The air was redolent of citrus.

Theadora and I were alone. Lucy and Matt had not been spotted that day. We suspected they'd fallen into their own romantic bubble. After our first night, they'd hooked up, according to Theadora, and since then I'd only seen Matt once. We met up for a snorkel, visiting underwater caves that just blew my adventurous mind. I tried dragging Theadora along, but crossing her arms, she admitted to being scared of water. Something I planned to address by teaching her how to swim.

Selfish reasons, of course. I wanted to see her in a wet bikini.

I played with Theadora's fingers as I stared out to sea at sailing boats drifting along in the gentle breeze and gliding seabirds. The warm afternoon sun caressed my bare arms and face, and I'd never felt healthier.

An elderly woman, wearing a scarf around her hair and carrying a basket, trundled over and offered us flowers. *"Per la tua bella ragazza."*

I bought a few bunches and gave her extra. She returned a toothless smile. My heart went out to the woman who looked like the craggy hills around her. I read hard toil in her time-worn face and was reminded of the farmers back home who also resembled their land.

When she saw the five-hundred-Euro note, she kissed my hand. *"Dio vi benedica."*

Her old eyes glistened with depth and sincerity.

She left us singing to herself.

"Do you know what she said?" Theadora asked.

"God bless us."

"That was so nice of you. You made her day."

I smiled. "That's the joy of money. Giving it to people who need it."

Theadora's gaze shone with curiosity. "Are you really this good?"

I shrugged. "I've got a lot of money. So why not?"

She shook her head.

"What?"

"This all seems so unreal to me. I have to keep asking myself if I'm really here."

"Thank god you are." I turned to face her. "Why don't we get married now?"

Her brows knitted. "Like, this minute?"

"Well, later today. I've spoken to a priest in the village. In that lovely little chapel that we visited the other day. He's happy to do it."

"Today?" Her eyes widened.

"That's unless you want a big wedding back home. I'm good with that too. I'll do anything you want, Theadora. From now on, you call the shots."

She laughed. "Then we won't get much done. I'm shit at making decisions."

"Does that include now?"

"No. I want this. I like that idea." Her face brightened. "Let's do this. Only…"

"Only what?"

"What will I wear? And I've got to tell Lucy. God knows if those two have even left their room."

"I saw them earlier heading for the beach," I said. "Why don't we go down to the village? You can go shopping for something. Or wear whatever you like." I touched her floral dress. "This is very pretty."

"I can't get married in this," she protested. "We'll want photos, won't we?"

"We sure will. I guess I'll have to get dressed up too."

"I'd love you in white linen, like that man we saw the other day."

She was referring to the Italian tycoons getting around in their linen pants, cravats, and bright jackets.

"Then I better get shopping myself." I rose. "Are you sure?"

"We leave tomorrow, so I guess so."

Our eyes locked and then we both giggled. Something we often did for no real reason.

Life had that light breezy feel.

CHAPTER 47

Thea

LUCY AND I WANDERED through the serpentine streets. There were so many pretty boutiques that I needn't have worried about finding a dress.

"Tell me about you and Matt," I said.

Her face lit up. "Matty's gorgeous. Don't you think?"

I nodded. "He's a lovely man."

"Oh, look at us." She linked her arm with mine. "And now a wedding today."

I glanced down at my watch. "We better hurry. I need to decide."

"I think that white silk dress with red roses. It's so beautiful."

I had to agree. "It's a little low-cut, though."

"Yeah. Great. Very appropriate. This is Sophia Loren's country after all."

"She's from Naples," I said.

"Which isn't very far away."

I laughed at Lucy's obsession with the Hollywood classics.

I settled for the fitted, knee-length silk dress with a flattering, cross-over bodice. I found a pair of red strappy heels that set it off perfectly and a red rose for my hair.

We shopped for Lucy after I insisted on buying her a dress. She looked beautiful in green with her hazel eyes, which were wide and pretty. There was something about being in love. It made one prettier, I'd quickly discovered.

"I've never owned anything this expensive before," she said, whirling around in front of the mirror as we got ready for the big event.

I applied red lipstick and pinned the rose behind my ear. I wore my hair loose. One side tucked behind my ear, where the diamond earrings that Declan had gifted me glistened in the afternoon sunlight.

After being satisfied with how we looked, we made our way to the domed cathedral.

I had to watch my step and not get my heel caught in the cracks of the cobbled laneway. I held onto Lucy's arm, and a couple of waiters whistled as we walked past.

"How thrilling," she said. "And they're all so fucking hot around here."

I laughed. "I'm so glad you're here."

She stopped walking and hugged me. "Me too. It's been the best time of my life. And Matt likes me, I think."

Her face showed that same sign of insecurity I recognized in myself. I smiled sadly. "He's crazy about you."

"Has Declan said something?" Her eyes lit up with need.

"He just said that Matt looked the happiest he'd seen him."

Lucy's mouth opened wide as a big smile formed. "Oh, that's nice."

"Come on. We better get there. These shoes are so uncomfortable."

"They look great, and you look beautiful," Lucy said, her lips trembling slightly, making my eyes moisten.

"Don't you make me cry."

She put her arm around me, and we continued up a hill. With the sun beating on my face, sweat trickled down my arms. I prayed my makeup wouldn't slide off.

Stepping on an ancient Roman marine-themed mosaic, we walked up the steps to the cathedral.

Wearing linen pants and a pale blue jacket that accented his eyes, Declan looked like he belonged in a Vogue spread.

Matt in linen pants and a dark-blue blazer had Lucy frothing at the mouth as she tried to scream in a whisper.

"Pinch me," she said.

My husband-to-be trapped me with his spellbinding gaze and smiled, as a priest in gold and white waited for us.

"I'm not even Catholic," I whispered to Lucy, who had her arm linked in mine. "You're giving me away, you realize."

"I know. It's such an honor. You're my bestie." Her voice cracked, making tears burn at the back of my eyes.

The church with its white-and-gold dome seemed to sparkle in the afternoon light beaming through circular windows.

Colors intensified. I think I was drugged on bliss. The saints and angels on the walls seemed to follow me with beaming smiles. I almost expected a director to come out and say "cut" because this could have been a scene in a romance movie.

As I stepped next to Declan, our shoulders touched and warmth flushed through me.

His blue eyes turned turquoise in the soft light, and I had to take a deep, calming breath. I could never tire of staring at that face that boasted so many shades of handsome.

He leaned over. His cologne sent a shiver of desire through me. "You look beautiful." His lingering gaze, full of love, brought a lump to my throat.

We turned to the priest, who nodded his head and then recited something in Latin.

Despite having no idea of what he said, I thought I was listening to an exotic poem—like some profound and magical incantation binding our souls.

He did the sign of the cross and in broken English said, "Will you Declan Lovechilde take Theadora Hart to be your wife? To love and protect and cherish in sickness and in health for the rest of your life?"

Declan's deep "I do" resonated through my heart.

The priest turned to me and spoke the same words, and I answered with a quivery "I do."

Declan turned to Matt who passed him a gold ring. I'd picked up a carved gold wedding band that I'd sized from Declan's sapphire ring, which made the jeweler's eyes widen with appreciation.

He slid the ring onto my trembling finger, and I followed suit. As our hands touched, a shot of energy acted as a visceral reminder that we were now one.

We looked at each other as though that was the final important detail to seal our love.

He took me into his arms and kissed me tenderly and chastely.

Burying his nose into my hair he whispered, "I love you with all my heart."

The emotional volcano that had been bubbling away finally erupted within me, and tears poured down my face.

It was useless for me to try to maintain a cool façade. I'd been doing that for way too long. Perhaps the overly expressive Italians who seemed to switch from laughter to tears within the blink of an eye had rubbed off on me.

Lucy passed me tissues and then took my hand and virtually jumped up and down on the spot.

I laughed and cried at the same time. We stepped onto the portico overlooking the deep blue sea through a white arched wall draped in hot-pink flowers.

As the sun kissed my skin, it was a moment I would never forget.

I'd married my soulmate and had my whole life ahead of me with this kind-hearted, gorgeous man.

Declan came and joined me after, I sensed, donating a nice healthy sum to the church.

"Did you understand what he said?" I had to ask.

"Nope. I flunked Latin." Declan smirked. "Much to my mother's chagrin."

I shook my head. I hadn't even thought of my new mother-in-law. A cold wind rushed through me.

"Have you told her?"

Declan shook his head.

"Are you going to wait until we're back to break the news?"

He smiled at my grim tone. "That's the idea." He drew me close to his strong body. "Let's not worry about her. We are our own little universe, you and I. I can't wait to spend my life with you, Theadora Lovechilde."

I swallowed back another lump.

We stood at the top of that sun-drenched village. High up in the world. What a perfect setting for a wedding.

IT WAS EARLY EVENING when we ambled to our favorite piazza. All four of us, laughing and clowning around. Declan virtually carried me, as my feet were killing me due to my new, sexy, but very uncomfortable shoes.

The waiter, who by now knew us, bounced over and seemed to jump out of his skin. He gushed over how pretty us *signorinas* looked.

"We just got married," Declan said.

The waiter's eyes lit up. "Oh, then, we celebrate. Here. Yes?"

Declan smiled at me. The evening was warm and perfect. I couldn't have wanted a better place to sit, eat, drink, and stare into my beautiful husband's eyes accented by the sparkling blue sea.

I nodded.

Lucy, who was off in her own little romance, nodded enthusiastically at that suggestion. We loved this place. It was where we'd eaten most nights and the views had us as engrossed as any binge-worthy show might.

It was better because this was real.

CHAPTER 48

Declan

UNDER THE STARS, WE drank, ate, and an impromptu party was in full swing around us.

All the diners had joined in the celebration. Even a band had turned up. Giacomo, our waiter, on hearing of our nuptials, had designed it so that the piazza came alive.

"This is so much fun." Theadora's eyes widened as Giacomo brought out a detailed chocolate cake. "Wow. Will you look at that? You just whipped that up?"

"*Complimenti.*" The waiter smiled. "*Per il sposi.*"

I nodded in gratitude and let him know he'd be rewarded when all this was over.

He bowed his head.

It couldn't have been a better evening. The balmy air. The stars. The piazza alive with music, people, and laughter.

The band played classic Italian Neapolitan tunes. I turned to my wife. "Dance?"

We weren't the only ones. People were already waltzing, and much to my delight, Lucy had filmed everything on her phone. She even borrowed Matt's phone once hers flattened. This moment needed capturing because I couldn't have wished for a better wedding.

Theadora held onto my arm, giggling. "I'm a little drunk, and I can barely walk in these shoes."

"Don't worry. I'll hold you up." I faced her. "I'll always hold you up. No matter what."

Her eyes watered again. Theadora was an emotional girl. I loved that about her. Everything affected her. An old dog lumbering around made her cry.

The music floated through the air. The crooner poured his heart and soul into the song.

"This is so beautiful," she said. "And everyone, people we don't know, are all having such a great time too. We couldn't have designed it better. Even the cake. Yum."

I agreed. The cake with its complex creamy chocolate and liquor flavors would remain etched in my memory. As would seeing Theadora under the moonlight in that shimmering silk dress that hugged her curves in the most delectable way. Men's eyes were addicted. Despite that prickling at my jealousy, I understood. And at the end of the night, it was me who'd slide that dress off her and feel her breathy moans against my cheeks while she trembled through one orgasm after another.

We sat down and ate more cake and drank champagne and laughed at Matt's silly impersonations and jokes.

Then the band dropped the ballads and went all upbeat with a rendition of *Tu Vuo Fa l'Americano*.

Lucy screamed. "Oh my god, that's the song that Sophia Loren sang. I love this song."

She grabbed Theadora's hand. "Come on. We've got to dance to this."

The crowd was just as enthusiastic, and suddenly the piazza filled with people dancing like no one was watching.

I sat this one out so I could indulge on Theadora, barefooted, prancing up and down, swishing her hips, lifting her hair, and acting out the vixen, with Lucy following suit.

Matt laughed. "The girls are having a ball."

"I'm glad. It's such a great night."

WE ARRIVED HOME AFTER what had been one amazing experience. I'd flown again. My new jet was more than perfect, and I'd already made plans with a very enthusiastic Matt for more trips.

We'd only been back an hour when a knock came at the door.

Ethan stood at my door, looking ruffled. The serious frown stamped on his forehead was very uncharacteristic for my normally cheery, not-a-care-in-the-world brother.

No one knew about our marriage. I planned to arrange a dinner at Merivale to make an announcement.

He stepped inside. "I've been trying to call you all day." He glanced over at Theadora and nodded a greeting with a hint of a smile that quickly faded.

"What's happened?" I asked.

"Father's dead."

My eyes widened in shock. My heart squeezed into a ball, and the sheer force of shock pushed me down onto the sofa.

Theadora grabbed my hand.

"What happened?" My throat was constricted by a flood of emotion. I could barely speak.

"He was found unconscious in his apartment." Ethan headed straight for the whisky and poured us a shot. He gulped his down and then handed me a glass.

"Like a heart attack?" Theadora asked.

"They're not sure." Ethan turned to me. "We only just found out this morning. That's when Luke found Dad's body." He bit his lip, and tears streamed down his face.

"I better go to Merivale at once." I rose, combing through my hair. I wasn't sure what to do. I held back tears. Unlike my brother, I was stoical when called for. The army trained that into me. My heart, however, shattered into tiny pieces.

"What do you mean Luke found him this morning? Weren't they together?" I asked.

"Apparently not, according to Luke."

"But doesn't Luke live there?"

I released a tight breath, and Theadora came and hugged me. "It's okay, Declan. I'm sure you'll learn more soon. I'm so sorry, darling."

I remained in her arms, and tears finally burst through.

Ethan went and poured himself another drink. "I'm going back now. You should come. Savvie's freaking out."

"I bet she is." Although Savanah looked up to our mother as a role model, she adored our father. "What about Mother?"

"You know her. She doesn't show much in the way of emotion. A sign of weakness, she says." He shook his head as he stared down at the floor. His mouth trembled. "Then I'm piss weak because I'm fucking crushed."

I went to my brother, and we held each other. Sobbing.

We stepped away and took the tissues that Theadora handed us. She took my hand.

"I'm so sorry."

I held her tight. There was so much going on inside of me that I could barely breathe. But I held on tight to my soulmate because if she hadn't been there to steady and support me, I would have crumbled, just like Ethan, who held his head in his hands.

"Come on then. Let's go to Merivale," I said, placing my arm around my brother's shoulder.

I held out my hand to Theadora. "Coming?"

Ethan looked at me and Theadora, mystified. I think he expected this to be a family affair. He then noticed my hand and pointed to my finger.

"Is that what I think it is?"

Theadora nodded. "We're married."

Ethan's bloodshot eyes opened slightly. "Oh. Well…"

"Meet your new sister-in-law," I said.

He went to Theadora and kissed her on the cheek. "Welcome to the family."

He regarded me with a tight smile. I read my brother well. He knew the shitstorm that awaited me at Merivale and how my mother would react.

It didn't matter. Only two things mattered—my deep love for my wife and that I get to the bottom of my father's death. My heart pulled me in two directions: heart-swelling bliss and earth-shattering sadness.

EPILOGUE

Ethan

THE SUNNY ROOM AT the back of Merivale, where we normally hung out as a family, contrasted sharply with the gloom in the air.

Savanah huddled between me and Declan for support. She'd gone through a whole box of tissues, while my mother, as cool as a cucumber, sat at the table tenting her fingers, as her long red fingernails tapped together.

Where are her fucking tears?

Theadora entered the room, and my mother's cold and unwelcoming eyes followed her. This was going to be intense.

But more intense than my father dying?

Nothing sat well with me.

Normally I was the joker of the bunch. The one that brightened the room with silly pranks and childish gestures. I'd been hiding behind that clownish act since my balls dropped.

That was no longer me. Especially now with my father dead.

As I searched deep inside, I found an empty hole where my heart used to beat.

My new sister-in-law sat by Declan and took his hand. That warm, loving gesture sent a slither of envy. He'd always been the sensible one. Not that I resented my brother. Far from it. I respected him.

"Why is she here? This is a private family affair," my mother said, casting daggers at Theadora.

"Will's here," Declan said with matching coldness. He placed his hand on the table, and my mother's eyes zeroed in on his glistening gold wedding band.

A deep line formed between her normally smooth brow as she pointed at his finger.

"Yes, we're married." He turned to Theadora and pressed his lips into her hair. "I wish I could make this announcement at better times."

"We'll discuss this later." My mother glanced over at Will, who sat close by her side.

"Nothing to discuss. We're married. Theadora is part of this family, and you, like everyone else, will respect and treat her as such, in the same way we've welcomed Will," Declan said.

"Mm..." She picked up her cup and took a sip.

"What about Dad?" Savanah demanded. "What about Daddy?" Her voice cracked, and she lost it again, which made me want to lose it too.

I'd never experienced this type of crushing grief like I'd been buried under a heavy, wet blanket.

Will opened a folder and looked at my mother, who gave him a nod to proceed.

"It's believed that Harry choked to death."

"On food?" Declan asked.

Will shook his head. "Nope. Strangled."

At that gruesome detail, my body recoiled as though I'd witnessed it happening.

"Like someone killed him?" Savanah asked, her eyes wide and horrified, looking like I felt.

"It might have been suicide," Will said.

"What?" rang from all of us siblings at once.

"That's impossible," Savanah said. "Daddy wasn't depressed."

Will looked at my mother and shrugged. "Investigations are going on as we speak. It's inconclusive."

"Well, I want every forensic team in on this, because I'm as sure as fucking certain that Dad did not kill himself," I said.

Declan nodded. "I'm with Ethan. Who's leading the investigation?"

"There's not one specific detective," my mother said.

"Where was he found?" Declan asked.

"In his apartment," Will said.

"You've known him for years. You can't accept that he'd do such a thing," I said.

Will glanced at my mother. Although he always took his cues from her, that action still played on my curiosity.

"It's uncharacteristic, yes. But he's been a little down lately. His relationship with Luke was on the rails."

Declan rose with Theadora. "We'll appoint our own detective and lawyers to deal with this. Dad would not have killed himself."

"I need a word," my mother said to Declan.

Her favorite son had just got hitched to the wrong girl. There was no bitterness on my part, but it meant that now she would pressure me to marry someone with a peerage.

I wasn't going to marry anyone. Especially now. I couldn't even be with myself. So why put someone else through that hell? Besides, I'd gone through all types of women, and none had captured my heart. By now, I would have married if I'd been so inclined.

Despite my disinterest in marriage, I was pleased for my brother and gave Theadora a sympathetic smile to show her my support.

They were loved up, and if there was ever any excuse to marry, then that was it.

It was just me and my sister as I stared down at the floor. Savanah whimpered by my side, making me sadder than ever, when our mother joined us again.

"Well, your brother has brought a commoner into the family."

"I think that's hardly an issue compared to Daddy's death," Savanah snapped.

"It's an issue because we have a reputation and name to uphold."

"Bullshit. We're hardly the fucking royal family," I said.

"That's right." Savanah nodded. "In any case, look at what Kate Middleton has done for the royals."

Like Savanah, I was peeved that my mother seemed more stressed by our brother's new wife than our father's death.

THERE WAS ONLY ONE way to clear my head of this dark cloud, and that was copious alcohol at the Thirsty Mariner. Blending into a crowd of semi-sozzled strangers seemed more appropriate for my grief-stricken state than rubbing shoulders with a designer jacket at some glitzy London bar with my former college pals—all entitled prats looking for pussy and the odd scrape. Public school bullying had followed them into their privileged little banal lives. I just went along with it to be part of a scene, but deep down it disgusted me. I hated violence and that my-lawyer-will-clean-up-my-mess attitude prevalent in that scene.

The pub was in full swing. People were everywhere, all chatting and laughing. For a small village, Bridesmere attracted a crowd. I didn't hang out there often, only when I stayed at Merivale and needed a drink away from the family.

I leaned against the bar and ordered a stout and a shot of whisky. I didn't recognize anyone there. Most of my former close friends had married and, apart from being invited to all their major milestones like christenings and birthday parties, we rarely caught up for drinks. That suited me. Conversations about Ariel or Jasper's eating and sleeping habits bored me to tears. Their constant whinging about not having had a shag since the baby was born and that they felt guilty for staring at the nanny's tits seriously put me off marrying.

There was one person I recognized as I sipped stout, and that was Mirabel Storm. Balancing a guitar on her lap, she was about to perform.

Dressed in a green velvet dress with that long red hair and green eyes, she was a stunner. The older she got, the more beautiful she became. I once had a crush on her, but she hated me. According to Mirabel, I was a shallow, entitled, rich bastard who treated women like toys. Instead of hurting me, her insults gave me a fucking erection.

At least we had a nice moment as eight-year-olds playing with the horses on her father's farm. The same farm that any minute now was about to turn into my spa destination.

My jaw clenched. That was not a topic for this night. I needed to get drunk, ogle Mirabel, admire those fiery green eyes, and sexy curves, and then harness that heartless developer. That thought alone made me want to puke.

I'd had it too easy up to now.

I had to make my own way into the world, and along with expanding Lovechilde hotels, a luxury spa was a good start.

The spotlight over the small makeshift stage made her hair look like it was on fire.

The soothing harp-like sound of her guitar strums massaged the tension away from my spine. Bewitching and siren-like, her voice reminded me of Kate Bush's haunting strains. In one of her rare moments of civility, Mirabel spoke of how that witchy chanteuse was her role model.

I leaned against the bar and let her song take me on a journey across the sea. The wind in her voice spoke of ebbs and flows and meetings and separations. Of how the trees talk to her soul and how the wind dances through her veins. Lost in meditation, I found myself on that ship and landing in a foreign land, searching for that person who spoke to my spirit.

Yes, she was deep. Terrifyingly so at times. That's why as a teenager, I gave up on trying to fuck her. She could read my bullshit a mile away.

The trouble was that when I visited her face, I found it hard to leave. Her deep green eyes held me captive. And despite, or because, of this mindfucking, I always ended up with a throbbing hard-on.

So I did what I do best. I acted like the shallow pillock she often called me.

Her voice hit a high note, and the words "He's the father of my soul. His wisdom my home" pulled on a heartstring.

It became difficult to swallow, and everything became blurry. I wasn't having a stroke. I was having an emotional breakdown.

My father was dead. Dead.

I wasn't ready for that to happen yet.

I tried to block my ears. I even thought of leaving. Her song hit a raw nerve that traveled to my soul. Even from a distance, this woman had found her way into me again.

Mirabel Storm was making me fucking cry.

In public.

I grabbed a tissue from my pocket and wiped my nose, glad that the place was dimly lit.

This was a first. I'd never cried over a song in public before. Maybe alone to Radiohead. Who hadn't? But not in a village pub with a local greenie singing about the wise old forest soothing her pain.

For half an hour or so, I remained transfixed. Sipping instead of guzzling as I'd intended. I fell into a spell, and it wasn't until the applause that I snapped out of it. That was strange, but helpful in that I'd forgotten to think.

That one meditation class I'd attended, only because I wanted to get into the instructor's yoga pants, never did that.

Possessing a regal bearing, Mirabel walked with her head held high and shoulders back.

Her subtle sway of hips reminded me that beneath that crushed velvet lived a voluptuous vixen. Growing up, she'd broken many of the local farmhands' hearts.

A mingling of admiration and determination took grip after learning of her man-eating ways. At the time, I wanted in. Only she just laughed at my purported shallowness and had me hobbling home with my dick in my hand instead of hers.

She joined me at the bar, and when her eyes caught mine, she nodded a greeting.

"You do your name justice. You sang up a storm," I said.

She chuckled dryly. "You're not the first person to say that. It is my real name, you know."

"I know. And it suits you." I fell into those big green eyes again and found myself in a forest with a sexy witch leading me to her private lair.

"Can I buy you a drink? That was sensational, by the way. Very moving. Almost too much."

"Too much?" Her brow furrowed.

"You made me want to cry."

Her eyebrows lifted in surprise like I'd confessed to becoming a militant environmentalist. "That's unexpected."

"I'm not always that shallow pillock you so eloquently described me as." I pulled a tight half-smile. "As a token of my appreciation for your hauntingly mesmerizing songs can I buy you a drink?"

A slow smile grew on her face. Without blinking, her bullshit-radar gaze penetrated deep, and my dick stirred. "Charming as always."

"It's no bullshit." I dropped the grin. "Your songs moved me. I was transfixed."

I'd flummoxed her because her face tilted slightly like she was trying to find another angle to who I was. "A G&T, then. Why not? I can abuse you later."

I laughed for the first time in two days. "Okay. I'll be sure to make it a double. I'm in the mood for a whipping."

Her luscious lips lifted slightly. "I'll bear that in mind."

My dick thickened. What was it about this girl? The more she hated me, the harder I got.

I passed her a drink, and our fingers touched, and tingles raced up my arm. Maybe it was the hard-to-get factor.

"Thanks. I'm just stepping out for a cigarette," she said.

"Mind if I join you? I could use some nicotine. I've had a hell of a day."

Her eyes searched mine like she was trying to read me. After a longish pause, she shrugged. "As long as you don't act like a tosser, I guess so."

"I'll try not to." I smirked.

My eyes headed straight for that sexy arse, which was bigger than my usual girl. But then, most of the women I associated with seemed addicted to gyms and dieting. Something told me Mirabel did nothing of the sort, which also turned me on.

MIRABEL

Yes, he was a shallow, rich boy who thought he could have anything at the click of his fingers, but right now he was confusing me. Either he was a brilliant actor, or he meant it. As he described my music, I could swear his eyes teared up.

He watched me rolling a cigarette which made me jittery for some reason.

"Do you mind making one for me? I don't know how to do that." With those big dark doleful eyes, he reminded me of a lost soul. A seriously gorgeous one.

Why the hell did he have to be so fucking good-looking?

In many ways, those Hollywood looks made it easier to hate him. Perfection annoyed the crap out of me. And hot men, with 'heartbreak-er' chiseled into those genetically perfect faces made me run in the opposite direction.

Ethan and I, however, went back to childhood. We used to play with horses. And being a tomboy, I'd often climb trees and play the kind of games that boys liked. He even gave me a football he'd received for Christmas once after I'd complained about only getting useless girly presents.

But then hormones kicked in, and he grew and grew and grew into a stunner, and suddenly every girl in the village jostled for his attention, tossing their trainer bras at him.

I just acted like I didn't notice him. Only I did.

One night, he caught me off guard. We were at Jasmine's party, where I'd drunk two Coronas and turned all giggly and silly, just like all the girls that I typically rolled my eyes at. I let him kiss me, and my body burned in a way I'd never experienced. Due to confused emotions, given that I was meant to hate him, I refused to let him remove my bra. The next minute, he was off with Mariah. No surprise there. She was the village floozy. I'd dodged a bullet because Ethan Lovechilde had turned into a heartbreaker.

However, as I grew older, the bullets kept coming, and instead of dodging them, I wore them. By this stage, masochism had set in, resulting in lots of scars to show for all the bad choices I'd made in men. Only Ethan Lovechilde was not one of them.

I rolled a cigarette and handed it to Ethan.

Under the dim lamp, he looked older. Or was that pain?

Although he normally swaggered through life, tonight he ambled with stooped shoulders.

I lit his cigarette and then mine.

Taking a puff, he coughed. "I haven't smoked for a while. I kicked the habit a while back."

"Oh, really? I feel bad for giving it to you."

"Don't be." He puffed out smoke.

"I only smoke when I drink," I said. "I'm planning to give up when I turn thirty."

"Oh? Then you've got another ten years to go," he said with a smirk, showing a hint of his old self.

"Ha ha ha. I turn thirty in November."

"Like me," he said. "We're the same age."

"You make that sound like it's a shock. I guess you're used to hanging out with girls half your age," I said.

He held my stare for a moment. "My head's spinning. Nicotine rush. Umm... half my age? Like fifteen? I don't fucking think so. I'm not that kind of criminal."

"What kind of criminal are you then?"

"The only illegal thing I've ever done is snort coke and the odd spliff. Oh, and I tend to drive fast." He smiled apologetically. "I like my racy cars."

"Fuel guzzlers. You're more of a criminal than you think," I said.

"How so?" The corner of his shapely mouth quirked up, and a puff of smoke twisted out into the air.

"Your family's plans to develop the farms. That will destroy the environment. While not punishable by the law, it's still criminal behavior."

He puffed on his cigarette, lost in thought. Or so it seemed. "My father was..." His face darkened, and he dropped his cigarette and stubbed it out.

"Your father?" I had to ask. "Has something happened?"

"He died. Yesterday." He bit his lip, and his face puckered slightly.

Was he about to cry? I tried not to stare as he struggled to keep a straight face. I sensed he was gathering strength to remain stoical.

"Oh. I'm so sorry." I hugged him, and his body melted into mine. At first tight but then he softened into my arms. I felt his heart beating against mine as he sobbed.

Time stretched as I held his quivering body, giving him space to grieve. In response, a lump rose in my throat. His pain summoned memories of my own experience with loss, and I had to fight back tears myself.

He extricated himself from my arms and wiped his eyes. "I'm sorry. I... don't normally... but then I've never experienced this kind of fucking grief. And even in there. When I heard your song about the forest being your father, I went to fucking pieces."

My eyes steamed up. This was the highest form of praise for an artist—to pluck at people's heartstrings. Moving people was why I created music. My total motivation as a songwriter.

This was not the shallow, hot dickhead up the road, but a deep soul in pain.

"It's natural to cry, Ethan. I was a total mess when I lost my father."

His watery dark eyes looked into mine, almost pleading, as though I'd just offered a cure for some rare disease. "How did you cope with it?"

"With time you learn to deal with it, I suppose. I mean, I miss him for sure. But now it's nice memories, you know?"

He nodded slowly. "Yeah. It's still very raw for me. He was a good man. He was actually against the development."

"I didn't know him that well, but my father always spoke well of him. Maybe not so much of your mother." I pulled a face. "Sorry."

"No need. Mother's a different person. She's nothing like my father... was." He let out a long, jagged breath. "I probably shouldn't have come out, but I was desperate for a change of scenery. I hated being on my own. All fucking maudlin. And my brother, who I normally would hang out with when I need a shoulder to cry on, just got married, so I felt he needed the space to grieve with his wife."

I nodded slowly, listening to a man who was showing a side of himself that made me feel like shit for all the abuse I'd dished out to him over the years. That was me, quick to judge. An ugly habit.

"And here I am listening to your hauntingly soulful tunes that clawed at this." He tapped his heart. "And I'm a fucking mess again. I should just go home and hang out with a bottle of whisky, I think."

He was about to leave.

"No. Wait. You shouldn't be alone," I said. "I've finished for the night. Why don't you come back to mine for a few drinks? I'll be happy to listen or whatever."

Whatever?

It took him a moment to respond. "I'd like that." He smiled faintly and followed me back into the pub.

As Ethan helped me pack up my equipment, I said, "You don't need to do this."

He continued winding up the leads anyway. I sensed he appreciated having something to do.

I collected my pay, which consisted of a damp note, thanked Jim, the bar owner, and left.

"Is that all you get?" Ethan carried my guitar, even though I'd tried to stop him. My feminist instincts stayed out of it. He seemed insistent, and I wasn't about to argue with a broken man.

I shrugged. "Fifty pounds goes far for me, and I get to sell CDs."

"That reminds me. I want to buy one, please."

I smiled. "Hey, that's not me trying to sell you anything."

"I didn't think you were. I love your stuff. It's deep." He stopped walking. "Like you. And you've got a stunning voice."

Now who didn't like a compliment? I was human after all. Especially when it came to my music.

MY MESSY FLAT SMELT of stale incense, and I felt a little uneasy having a visitor. Particularly a billionaire who was probably used to all the fineries of life. Although, at that moment, it was hard to think of him as anything but a kindred spirit seeking company.

"Make yourself at home," I said. "I'll make us a drink if you like. I've got beer or vodka."

"Vodka then." He placed down the guitar and then made himself at home on the sloppy sofa with his long legs stretched out.

In his ripped designer jeans and dark green cardigan, Ethan looked incongruous in that cluttered room.

I put some music on.

"Nick Drake," he said, sitting up.

"Oh, you know of him?" I asked, placing the vodka down on the coffee table strewn with everything from my tarot cards to crystals, sheet music, and scrawled notes.

"I do." Staring in the distance again, he looked lost in himself.

I sat down on the sofa, only because it was either that or the floor. There we drank in silence listening to *River Man.*

He buried his head in his hands, and I stroked his arm.

"Sorry," he said. "This song is so fucking sad."

I rose. "I shouldn't have put it on."

"No. Keep it. It's beautiful. It's sad but soothing too."

"I know. His music is like that for me. Melancholia has this way of talking to our souls."

He turned to look at me. Really look at me. His eyes trapped my eyes. "Thank you for inviting me here. I needed this. You're real and strong."

A tinge of disappointment touched me. Unreasonable because those qualities I aspired to. However, the woman in me wanted to hear something else.

His eyes burned into mine, which kind of answered that. "You're also beautiful. When you perform, you become a goddess."

Now that made me melt.

I gazed into those dark, almost-black eyes, searching for the charmer I remembered. Instead, I found a man who had grown older, more serious, and as a result, more beautiful.

I moved closer, and like magnets drawn together, our lips touched.

His mouth on mine felt soft, warm, and tender. His tongue swept around the outline of my lips and found its way onto my tongue, and off we went into a world of sensual reds, and my core became moist and swollen.

He pressed himself against me, and I felt his penis swelling on my belly. I hadn't fucked for a long time. And feeling his big dick pressing hungrily against me made my nipples ache.

His hands traveled to my waist and explored the indentation. A groan entered my mouth as he caressed my breasts.

By this stage, I'd turned to putty.

"Do you want to go to bed?" I asked.

Heavy-lidded, he nodded. "I'd love that. We don't have to do anything. Just let me hold you."

We rose and, as though in a dream, I led him into my bedroom.

TAMED BY A BILLIONAIRE is book 2 of Lovechilde Saga.

jjsorel.com

ALSO BY J. J. SOREL

THORNHILL TRILOGY
   Book One Entrance
   Book Two Enlighten
   Book Three Enfold
   SIZZLING STEAMY NIGHTS SERIES
   A Taste of Peace
   Devoured
by Peace
   It Started in Venice
   LOVECHILDE SAGA
   Awakened by a Billionaire
   Tamed by a Billionaire
   Chased by a Billionaire
   Corrupted by a Billionaire
   The Importance of Being Wild
   The Importance of Being Bella
   In League with Ivy
   Take My Heart
   Dark Descent into Desire
   Uncovering Love
   BEAUTIFUL BUT STRANGE SERIES
   Flooded
   Flirted
   Flourished

jjsorel.com

Printed in Great Britain
by Amazon

27924223R00185